SOMEBODY'S LOVER

SOMEBODY'S LOVER

Jan Henley

Hodder & Stoughton

First published in Great Britain in 1997
by Hodder and Stoughton Ltd.
A division of Hodder Headline PLC

10 9 8 7 6 5 4 3 2 1

British Library Cataloguing in Publication Data

Henley, Jan
Somebody's lover
1. English fiction - 20th century
I. Title
823.9'14 [F]

ISBN 0 340 67243 9

Typeset by Avon Dataset Ltd, Bidford-on-Avon, Warks

Printed and bound in Great Britain by
Mackays of Chatham PLC, Chatham, Kent

Hodder and Stoughton
A division of Hodder Headline PLC
338 Euston Road
London NW1 3BH

For Wendy

Thanks are due to my friends and family for their time and continuing support, especially my husband Keith and my parents Daphne and Bert Squires. My thanks also go to Wendy Tomlins, Elizabeth Roy, Carolyn Caughey at Hodder, and to Morwenna.

Then come home my children, the sun is gone down
And the dews of night arise
Your spring and your day are wasted in play
And your winter and night in disguise.

William Blake

from Nurse's Song,
Songs Of Innocence and Of Experience.

Prologue

Rowan Brunswick awoke with a start, conscious of unexplained fear, disturbed to find her bedroom dark and desolate. Her night-light had not been switched on, and the door was firmly closed, not ajar as her mother or Zita always left it. During this hot summer, the night-breeze through her open window had been a cool balm on her skin. But not tonight. Tonight the air was still, and only silence wafted in to greet her.

Something was wrong.

She stared through the cloudy filtered moonlight at her tightly clamped bedroom door. And the unfamiliarity – no night-light, a closed door – made her shiver. She was in a cold sweat. Because her mother and Zita, the two women who cared for her, never forgot these things. In Rowan's seven-year-old mind they were as vital and life-giving as basic food and shelter. They never forgot. So what had happened to her mother and Zita?

She sat up in bed. Tomorrow's dress on a cushioned hanger loomed above her.

'How can I stop waking up in the night?' She often asked her mother that. It was a subject that bothered her.

'Simply roll over and go back to sleep, of course.' Audrey Brunswick – tall, elegant and always slightly distant – half-frowned, hardly listening.

'But what if I can't? Mummy, what if I can't?'

'You can at least try.' Audrey rose to her feet, her taupe cardigan swinging around her shoulders. And she had that look in her eyes, so Rowan knew her attention was wandering. Her mother's attention often wandered. And Zita seemed to understand that.

1

Zita said, 'She can't be doing with you all the time. Don't mean she doesn't love you.'

Rowan hadn't thought that. It had never crossed her mind until Zita mentioned it, although now it had been brought into her world, she saw its possibilities. And felt the need to pull her mother back from wherever it was she wanted to go without her.

'But if it's a bad dream . . .' Rowan tugged the taupe sleeve.

Her mother frowned again, deeply this time. She made to speak, looked down at her daughter, her eyes softened into a different kind of grey – dense, like the soft lead pencil Zita had given Rowan to draw with – and then she bent until their faces were less than a whisper away. 'If it's a bad dream, come and tell me, my darling. We'll make it go away together.'

'And if I'm . . .'

'If you're scared to get out of bed, then call me. Loudly.' She held up a slim white hand to stop Rowan's next question, which was a pity since she had it all ready. Rowan stared at the hand, faintly blue-veined, adorned with a dark red ring Mummy called her carnelian treasure. 'And if I don't hear you, then shout for Zita. Or Father,' she added by way of an afterthought.

'Father.' Rowan considered this. It seemed, after all, most unlikely that *he* would come.

Her mother moved away 'But you're a big girl now, darling,' she reminded her. 'Don't you think you're getting too old for bad dreams?'

Rowan stared at her. Should she be glad that bad dreams, apparently, disappeared with age? Or did that make her some sort of freak, since her own nightmares were getting worse rather than better

Not in the least reassured about night-time terrors, she watched her mother wander off towards the room where she kept her watercolours – for her mother wandered rather than walked. Mummy wandered, Zita swished and Father always strode. A bloke with a purpose, Zita called him, although she didn't say it in an admiring way. No, not at all.

Now, Rowan lay in her narrow bed watching the clamped-shut door and the darkling night-light, and wondered what kind of night-time it was. It could be the kind when adults were still up, just down the stairs, watching TV under bright lights, reading the paper, or

2

making tea, as Zita did constantly. She hoped it was this kind of night-time, although when she squinted into the darkness it seemed to have the same quality of shadow as the night-time she dreaded. The middle of the night, silent, dead kind of night-time, when Mummy and Zita weren't poised to protect her from burglars or bogey men or bad dreams. But instead, uncaring, oblivious, in their own bedrooms asleep. More separate than they ever were in daytime. Unreachable – except perhaps by a scream.

She couldn't, at any rate, roll over and go to sleep – not amid such unfamiliarity – so instead she stared at the door and wondered if she should open it. She gnawed her lip. Should she open it and discover which night-time lay beyond? Or should she – could she – stay in bed and wait for someone to come, switch on her night-light, leave her door ajar once more? It could take ages, all night, forever even. They might never come.

In one bound she was up and out, shivering uncontrollably, thin arms hunched around her chest, bare feet on the rug, dark hair framing her wild scared face with a brand of night madness. Tentatively she took a step forward, then another, slowly, slowly, her eyes fixed on the door handle, as if expecting to see it judder and come to life.

She reached to open it, even slower now, one finger at a time, waiting for the landing light. But no. More darkness outside. And then . . . Glorious sight! She collapsed against the wall with relief. A bright bulb glaring in the hall downstairs. People. People were here. A sense of security flooded her. She felt weak. She needed a wee.

Stumbling, but no longer afraid, she flicked the landing light switch and used the loo – as usual neglecting to shut the door, although Father kept telling her that it was vulgar to leave it open. On the loo she allowed herself another memory, one lost in the terror of waking. Her mother had gone out. It solved everything. The jumble of a jigsaw slotted into sanity. Of course. Mummy was out, and it was Zita's London weekend. Once a month she went back to the 'bright lights' as she called it, although Mummy said Hammersmith hardly qualified as that . . .

She went to stay with her sister Nell who ran a pie and mash shop there.

3

'One of the last ones left,' Zita said with pride. 'There's still a demand. You'd be surprised.'

'I'd be surprised if you didn't always come back smelling of mashed potato and parsley sauce,' her mother responded, pretending to flick bits of it out of Zita's dark-red hair. It was the kind of teasing that made Rowan feel safe, gave her a glow of contentment in her belly that she didn't often have.

That was why her night-light wasn't on. That was why the door had been clamped shut on the adult world she trusted, creating a prison for dreams.

She remembered her mother's distracted explanation. There was something she had promised to do. Something about the art gallery that might be opening soon in Padstow. 'I have to go out. I promised I'd help. Will you be able to look after her, Philip?'

'Don't be ridiculous.' Funny, her father often did that. Threw accusations, where only an answer was called for.

'I shouldn't have arranged it on Zita's London weekend.' Her mother was murmuring, half to herself, but in a way that told Rowan she would still go, whatever. That it was important to her.

'When will Zita be back?' Rowan asked. Zita was her mainstay, a solid, dependable anchor in a sea of confusion she might otherwise find hard to stay afloat in. Zita didn't always explain fully, but she made things easier to understand.

'Sunday night, same as usual.' Audrey Brunswick was surveying her with an uncertain look in her eye. 'I'll put her to bed before I go,' she declared in a rush to Rowan's father.

'Can I still have a story?'

'One.' She glanced at her watch. 'A short one.'

'How long will you be out?'

'For as long as it takes.' Audrey looked anxiously across at her husband, who rustled his newspaper and disappeared behind self-important folds.

'What kind of a mother . . .' Rowan thought she heard.

'It's only one evening.' Rowan saw her mother put her hand to her fair hair, and recognised the frustration, although she could never have put it into the right words. Her father and her mother were at odds with each other, she knew that much. Father ruled the house,

Mummy fought back with words. What more did she need to know?

Rowan decided not to flush the loo, creeping reluctantly back to her bedroom, scared once more, because if neither Zita nor her mother were here, then who would come to save her if she were to need saving?

Outside her parents' bedroom door, she stopped, hearing a sound, unfamiliar and yet uniting with the rest of the alien night. A rustle, then a giggle. Mummy *must* be home. But this bedroom door was also shut. What was happening tonight? Why so many closed doors?

Ever so quietly, ever so slowly, she turned the handle, aware that all was different now that she stood on the other side of the dark unknown.

A band of light streamed from the lamp above her mother's side of the bed which she often used for reading, sitting up against the pillows in her pink satin robe. But tonight the band of light illuminated a spectacle unlike any Rowan had ever seen.

The arms and legs of two people were wrapped around each other, all mixed up, white skin against tan, hairy next to smooth. The straight upright body of her father was barely recognisable – it twisted and turned, humped and heaved. There was shouting and sweating and . . . What was going on here?

The woman – a woman in her mother's place, a woman Rowan had never seen before – was writhing amongst tangled white sheets. A faceless woman with dark hair on her head, a matted triangle between her legs and patches under her arms, which she raised as she laughed. She cackled, her flesh wobbled, and Rowan's head spun.

As she watched, the faceless woman with the spreading flesh and hairy armpits, climbed on top of him. 'Yes, Philip,' she said. 'Yes, Philip. Yes. Yes!'

'Beautiful bitch,' he muttered. 'Beautiful, sexy, gorgeous piece of . . .'

'Yes, Philip,' the woman groaned.

Rowan watched with horror and incomprehension. Was this some kind of a battle? And yet fragments of memories rapped on her mind. Of a couple kissing in the village park, then racing, hand in hand, to the deserted pavilion. Kids laughing – kids who knew more than she did – laughing and smoking. A hand up someone's dress, someone finding a limp balloon-like thing under the hydrangeas. The way she felt sometimes when she was hot and sweaty in bed, a funny feeling that bothered her, one she couldn't always shake off, didn't always want to shake off, insistent as a bad dream. The look in her father's eye when he watched Zita and didn't know he was being watched himself. A book she'd seen in the library at school with pictures of African women, half-naked, with heavy pendulous breasts. Rowan found herself unable to leave the room. A scream rose and broke silently in her throat.

'Give it to me, Philip.'

'I know how much you want it, sugar.'

'Yes, oh yes, Philip!' Bulbous breasts swung above his face.

Rowan thought she might be sick. They hadn't seen her. They were oblivious, utterly absorbed in each other, in this act.

Her father's big fingers reached out for the woman's flesh. He took her breast in his mouth and with his hands, adjusted her on his hips, grinding her body closer to his. 'Is this what you want?' he took breath to say. 'And this? And this?'

Rowan took a step back towards the door. The goosebumps were hard on her skin and her feet refused to move in coordination. His words rained on her head. And the look of him. The look of *her*.

She opened the door, snatching one last glimpse over her shoulder of the half-lit scene being enacted on her parents' bed. The woman's dark head was thrown back in rapture or agony, her features contorted so that Rowan wondered if she would recognise her again.

Father was still driving into her, harder and harder, he must be hurting her, killing her maybe. He was still speaking through half-closed lips, muttering words she couldn't understand. But his dark eyes were wide open, and he was staring straight at Rowan. Unblinking, unseeing, staring straight at Rowan. 'Give it to me, sugar,' he said, his thin mouth twisted.

Rowan froze, part of the tableau herself.

'Yes, Philip,' the woman screamed, shuddering to a halt.

Rowan grabbed the door handle and flew out of the room, not stopping, not breathing until she was back in her own room, back in the comforting well of darkness that was her own darkness. She needed this now, for herself. She slammed the door shut behind her, clamped now into her own space, the prison becoming the womb.

She was seven years old. At seven, she had learned a lesson about adult space, and she had claimed her own. Never again would she want the door left ajar, never again would she need the comforting sound of adult conversation to lull her into sleep. Even her worst nightmare, her worst imaginings, could never be as bad as this.

Part One

Chapter 1

—•◦•—

Six years later

Philip Brunswick was in his study dealing with correspondence. He had been fascinated by the world of finance since an early age – even now he recalled the sweet security of his first safe complete with lock and key that his father had given him one Christmas.

Some might laugh. But *Money is power,* his father had told him. *Money is control.*

Having money had not prevented Philip's father losing his wife, neither had it prevented a slow-growing dissatisfaction, which Henry Brunswick had passed down to his son. But yes, over the years Philip had conceded that his father – although emotionally cold – was rationally correct. Money gave freedom and it gave choice. And when you could take money – preferably money that belonged to other people – and make it multiply as if by magic, that was the biggest thrill of all.

For this reason Philip Brunswick, financial consultant, had remained with Corbets of London for only as long as it took him to learn everything they knew. He then turned to freelance work. He became independent, nurtured a select clientele which had grown, developed, blossomed under his guidance. Money had been made, before the recession, large sums of money that had enabled him and his family to live well in London. The 80s had thrown up problems for sure, especially since their move to Cornwall which had removed Philip from the pulse of things. But the word was that the recession would soon be a thing of the past – and Philip was sure of it. This was the start of a new decade, a new period of prosperity.

If he wanted to, even now, he could sit back in relative security, perhaps never work again. But that didn't satisfy Philip. He wanted to dip his fingers again and again into the financial market – into the complex web of stocks, shares, unit trusts and bonds. He simply couldn't resist it, couldn't live without the sense of power it conferred.

But on this particular day, his mind was, uncharacteristically, not on money. Ostensibly he was working, but in reality he was thinking of his mistress.

It had been a while . . . In some ways he would rather it had been even longer – he made it a matter of self-discipline to hold out for as long as he possibly could without her – each unsuccumbed week becoming a triumph. But by now the memory of her swivelling hips was playing too much havoc with his working day. It was clearly time to pay her a visit. His thin lips compressed into a smile. She was always available and that was one of the things he liked most about her.

He had never intended to be unfaithful to his wife – let alone allow this to continue for so long. It was fifteen years since their affair had begun. But she wasn't any old tart who provided sex and nothing else. Oh no. He had virtually invented her, certainly he had made her what she was, and for that reason she gave him so much more than a quick screw whenever he felt the urge.

Philip's lip curled. That alone would never have interested him for so long. But this – this renewal of his very identity as a man with power – this was something else.

He had first met her through his secretary – her sister – back in the days when he'd worked and lived in London, the days before North Cornwall. Stolid, grey kind of days most of them, but he'd still been learning then. Still climbing the ladder, and if you were doing that, you had to stay pretty close to all the other rungs or you'd be overlooked.

'This is my boss.' His secretary Esme was speaking to an attractive dark girl by her side.

Then Esme turned to him. 'My sister's here – come for the weekend, she has.'

They were Cornish girls, and there was something sexy about that broad accent of theirs – something peasanty that appealed to Philip. He'd never taken much notice of Esme – she was a prim little thing, pretty perhaps in a small-featured way, but not inviting. He hadn't felt the slightest urge to abuse his position as her employer, which was probably a good thing. But the sister was different, he saw that straight off. She had a red pouting mouth turned into a sly smile, sleepy and slanty come-to-bed eyes – liquid sex appeal they were – and masses of curves squeezed into a black dress at least two sizes too small for her.

He'd felt the urge then, all right. Lust, and power too. It kind of streaked through him as if he were about seven feet tall with limbs and organs to match. Whoa-hey . . .

He held out his hand to her, and felt the charge as the soft flesh sank into his palm. 'Good to meet you. I hope you'll let me buy you a drink later. You can tell me all about Cornwall.'

'What do you need to know?' Her eyes said more.

'Everything.' He stared at her. 'My wife and I are planning to go there in the summer. Rent a little cottage, perhaps.' His mention of Audrey was intentional, and he saw immediately that this girl could cope.

Audrey knew everything about art and etiquette – the right things to do, say and look at – but his wife had never been a sexual woman. Not primitive enough or sensual enough – not, he licked his lips, *basic* enough. Whereas this girl . . .

He hadn't found it in the least difficult to impress – that was another of the things he liked about her. That she appreciated the cut of his suit, the colour of his tie, the way his dark hair had been swept back into a style that he considered both up to the minute and distinguished, though Audrey said it was too young for him. And then there was money. She was impressed by money all right, and what it could buy. Money meant nothing to Audrey – she'd had more than enough of it all her life, never had to work for it, never had to think of it – whereas this was a girl whose eyes gleamed when she saw a twenty pound note.

'Philip! Oh Philip . . .' He recalled the sweet gasp that gave the hit of glory.

And so, after that, Philip made sure she saw plenty.

He took her to bed on the first night, always knowing it wouldn't be a struggle. There wouldn't be any tedious games, pointless role-playing, or pretence that this wasn't what they were both here for. Sex.

Still, he knew how to do the right thing. He took her out to dinner first – to a place that wasn't exclusive (she'd never have fitted in, he was being kind really) but wasn't cheap either. Pretentious, Audrey would have called it, with her nose for effortless class stuck high in the air. But this girl – now she thought it was simply wonderful. And the marvel of the restaurant became Philip himself, he could wallow in it up to his armpits.

In bed he hadn't been disappointed. She was only twenty-one. Not a virgin; in fact she was married to a man in Cornwall, so Esme had told him. But that was all to the good since he'd hardly want her hanging round his neck the whole time, that wouldn't do at all.

And when he asked her – quite matter-of-factly, for in this day and age you couldn't be too careful – she confided that her husband was only her second lover. This seemed comparatively safe, although he couldn't help wondering who had taken her virginity, wishing it had been him. But it seemed an adequate precaution. She was a country girl, good and wholesome. And Philip loathed using condoms. It was undignified – scrabbling around to get them out of those ridiculous foil wrappers – and worse, he was likely to wilt during all that rolling on. Now that wouldn't impress one bit.

So she wasn't completely inexperienced, but neither was she a slag. In short, he could do what he liked with her.

'I shall buy you something special,' he said. 'Something to make you think of me when you're back in Cornwall. Something to draw you back here one day soon.'

'Do what?' She sounded suspicious.

'Something expensive.' He laughed. She would understand that all right. They were in the flat above the office where he stayed overnight sometimes, and which he also used during the day for assignations and entertaining clients. On the bedside table were some late summer roses that the little sister, the innocent Esme, had thoughtfully placed there when he'd asked her to clean the place up this morning.

He plucked one from the water, and placed it between the full

14

breasts. 'Mmm.' He tweaked a nipple playfully.

She giggled, clearly delighted. He'd like to bet that no-one had ever put a flower in that delicious cleavage before.

'What will you buy me then?' She was coy.

His tongue darted forwards to the hardening nipple. 'What would you like?' His voice grew thick. Already, did he want her again already? He felt the power rise, it was awesome. 'A pretty new dress?'

As he drew back he recognised the disappointment in her eyes. 'Some creamy white pearls?' He rolled the suggestion along his tongue.

'Mmm. Lovely.' She was mollified. Excited again too. Good-oh, that was what he liked to see.

'Pearls. They look cool but they're so sexy.' He grinned. 'Like saliva. Like love juice. I'll give you a pearl necklace, I will.'

She giggled too. 'You're a one, you are. What will my husband say, I'd like to know?'

'Ssh. Don't mention him, sugar. We've got something special, we have. I'll buy you some pretty pearls and you keep them hidden away. Keep me hidden away. And then when I call you . . .'

She arched closer towards him. Her nipples brushed his arm. 'And when you call me?'

'You'll come,' he whispered, putting his fingers inside her. 'And there'll be more pretty things, more white silent secrets . . .'

'But . . .'

He put a finger to her lips. 'You'll find an excuse to get away.' He laughed. 'There's always Esme.'

She sucked at his finger and he entered her abruptly, unable to wait. He didn't go on for long, but what would she expect, even though it was second time around?

Afterwards he wanted to get back to work – and quickly. Her lipstick was smudged. He must buy her a better quality one. And some scent. He sniffed cautiously. 'What are you wearing?'

'Not a lot.' She giggled again. 'Only a rose.'

'What perfume?' He found himself hoping she wasn't too stupid. He wanted her to be sharp, but not clever, malleable but not refined, primitive but not lowly. Ah . . . He wanted a perfect prostitute, that's what he wanted.

'Lavender mist.'

He grimaced. He would replace that. Not with one of Audrey's Saint-Laurents or Kleins. Something less designer-flashy, but acceptable. Musky perhaps.

'Don't you like it?' She was coy again, fishing for compliments.

'I like you.' Briefly, he nuzzled her again, into the faint curve of her stomach, down into the wet dark warmth that seemed like some sort of primal beginning. Philip wanted that beginning.

Sexy underwear, he would buy that too. It would make it still better. Black silk, stockings and suspenders. Mmm, nice. He desired her again, just thinking about it. And he could have her again, couldn't he? Not now, but perhaps later before she went back home to some dreary little house in some equally dreary backwater somewhere. But he could have her again, as often or infrequently as he chose. That was the beauty of it.

And when he tired of her? Because surely he would tire of her? Well then, she would simply slip away into the shadows, and a blue-eyed girl with loose black curls and sloping shoulders would remain – married, in Cornwall, having lost nothing but gained a few tastes of the luxury she would never know for real.

Philip shuffled the papers on his desk with some irritation, scrawled a flourish of a signature, and rose from his seat to stare out of the window. But he hadn't tired of her, had he?

She had returned to Cornwall and he had wanted her. He had paid for her to come back again and again, he had showered her with presents, and eventually he had even moved here himself. Not because of her, he told himself quickly, opening a window to let in some of the warm June sunshine. He'd made her what she was, hadn't he? He was her lover, he was still in control. But he'd moved here because of the child, and Audrey, and . . . well, he wouldn't think of that now. He mustn't think of that now. He straightened his already stiff back. Self-discipline, that was the way.

He had moved here and he had continued to see her because she was his and she gave him exactly what he needed – no more, no less. She had never been a demanding woman, and although her figure had broadened over the years, she had kept herself in good shape. For him.

From time to time he lifted her out of the mundane existence she loathed, by taking her away for clandestine week-ends. He knew she enjoyed the subterfuge if she were honest, relished telling all and sundry she was staying with her sister Esme. Esme was a loyal girl, they had nothing to fear there. She'd never dare give them away, though she probably wished she were in her sister's shoes. He chuckled.

As for the husband – he had remained as anonymous as Philip would have liked, but, honestly, he must be dense as they come. How did she explain the flowers Philip was always sending? And did the man never catch sight of the jewellery she hardly ever used, or wonder why she visited her sister so often?

But he didn't think too much about her husband – whoever he was, he couldn't give her what she wanted, that was what mattered. Whereas Philip could help her pretend to be what she'd never be. It was easy, gratifying even, like playing God.

And in return she gave him . . . excitement. Because she had surprised Philip, not merely by confirming what he'd recognised in her from the beginning, but by providing so much more. She was his, she made him feel such a man, and he loved that. And then she was naughty – naughty in bed – and he loved that too. Perhaps, in some strange way, he even loved her . . .

A flash of red across his vision made Philip blink. His daughter was racing across the lawn fifty yards away, her long legs eating up the distance between her and the far gate, her dark hair flying out behind her. Rowan.

Quickly, he pushed thoughts of his mistress from his mind, and replaced them with thoughts – still worse – of a terrible night, when he thought he'd seen Rowan in his bedroom. No, he *knew* he'd seen her. She'd been there all right . . . Maybe Rowan didn't remember – she was only a child then – but he should never have succumbed to that temptation, should never have brought his mistress here to the house. Never have screwed her in the bed he shared with Audrey . . .

Determinedly he pushed her image away once more. Yes, yes, he would see her soon. Philip cleared his throat, re-adjusted his grey pin-striped trousers.

'Rowan!' He called out of the window, thought he sensed her hesitation, but she ran on as if she hadn't heard. Blast her. The relationship between Philip and his daughter was ambivalent. Naturally, he loved her, wanted the best for her. But he also sensed that he was being pushed out of her life – that the women he lived with merely tolerated him. And he wasn't sure what to do about that. He liked, after all, to have the final say.

'Rowan!' But she was almost out of sight.

The girl had too much freedom. It hadn't been as beneficial for her as he'd hoped, moving from London to Cornwall. She was turning into a wild thing.

Philip reluctantly returned to the correspondence on his desk. He had spoken to Audrey on many occasions, he'd even tried to have it out with *that woman*, as he always referred to Zita, sensing that it was actually she who ran the house virtually single-handed. But neither of them took the blindest bit of notice. They simply nodded and ummed and aahed and got on with whatever they did without him. Got on with their living, he supposed. Audrey was so vague these days, he hardly knew what to make of her. She'd always been rather an enigma to him, and now sometimes he wondered if she were actually losing her mind here in Cornwall.

Perhaps he shouldn't have made it so difficult for her to find other interests. Her heart had been set on that art gallery project six years ago. But at the time . . . He was unsure enough of her as it was, and he did think home was a wife's place and all that. It might not be the fashion but Philip was hot on traditional values. And how would he ever have got rid of the Zita woman with Audrey working all hours?

But, as he'd told her then, there were plenty of other things she could have done. Voluntary work, committees . . . She didn't have to be – well – so *ambitious*.

'But I want to do *this,* Philip,' she had complained, her grey eyes for once extremely determined.

'And I'm not stopping you.' He'd spread his hands, all innocence.

But of course he had stopped her. There were ways, better ways, more subtle ways, than simply saying no.

Still, how could the way she was be all his fault? What could he do when he spent hours, sometimes days in the City?

He shook his head and frowned. As for Rowan, it simply wasn't right for a thirteen year-old girl to be racing round the countryside in this day and age, doing God knows what. He'd paid for her to go to a decent school, she had riding lessons, piano tuition, her own computer and a generous clothes allowance. What more could a girl want, for heaven's sake? What more did they expect from him?

Philip signed the last letter, blotted it neatly, replaced the cap on his gold fountain pen, leaned back in his chair, and reached for the phone. He pressed each digit with a mixture of wariness and sweet anticipation.

'Is that you, sugar?' he whispered. 'Are you all alone?'

Three rooms away, through a window similarly facing west over the great sweep of lawn leading to the gate, Audrey Brunswick was also watching her daughter. Her beautiful, flying Rowan. A small smile tugged at her lips, yet she couldn't quite give way to it. If asked, she would have said she had no ambivalent feelings towards Rowan. She simply loved her, and wanted her to escape the worst of life. The best she could do for her was to give the girl some freedom.

Until she had looked up, distracted by the figure in red, Audrey had been what she called doodling, which was actually painting tiny intricate water colours, usually of the garden. She painted them either outdoors, sitting in a cane chair wearing a huge wide-bimmed hat that protected her eyes, or from the French windows of her green room, a kind of working room, but more perhaps a thinking room, since that was what Audrey did most of. Once, she had thought she might do more than doodle. Once, she'd had different hopes for herself . . .

The walls were painted deep jade.

'You can't possibly be serious,' Philip had said, when she told him what she wanted.

But of course she'd got her way as she generally did in matters of taste. Philip had no vision. Magnolia and pastels were safe enough, but Audrey relished the risk factor. She enjoyed visualising themes, and this room, the room she spent more and more time in, as Zita took over the care of the house and its occupants, had always been destined to be green.

In one corner a bamboo table was half hidden by variegated ivy and ficus plants trailing up, down and around, in another was her old dresser piled with books and paintings, and in front of the window were her rocking chair, her high stool and her easel. Here too was the only light that spread down on to her work from an Anglepoise. The rest was up-lighting, the shades ranging from delicate lime to the deepest forest, casting pools of light on to the high ceiling painted in the palest of leaf greens. She had compromised with the floor.

'Not a green carpet, surely?' Philip had begged.

'Much too much,' she agreed. 'We'll have the floorboards scrubbed and varnished. Mats – Indian, Chinese. Or hessian.'

Philip shrugged and left her to it. And why not? It was only one room in the house. She didn't object to the stately rosewood and mahogany that she suspected made him feel rather important and successful, and she hardly wrinkled her nose at the tasteful prints he hung, of a Renaissance art Philip was far from appreciating. All right in Florence. But in an – albeit large – cottage in North Cornwall? In her room it was Cézanne or nothing. He'd had rather a way with green himself.

There was a light knock at the door.

'Come in, Zita.'

She watched her enter, armed as usual with the canary-yellow feather duster she seemed to need to carry to justify her entrance into any room. And Zita couldn't fail to make an entrance. She always moved quickly, suggesting a string of jobs to be done and goals to be reached. At forty-one, Zita was a striking looking woman. Only three years older than Audrey herself, she was big-boned and well-rounded. She had dark eyes that were always fierce or friendly with no half-measures, and a mass of red-brown hair, usually controlled by a lurid bandana. Today it was lime green and turquoise, conflicting dangerously with dangling parrot ear-rings of scarlet and jade, and baggy blue dungarees.

Audrey was used to Zita's eccentric appearance – it seemed part of her charm, she even quite liked the fact that for Philip it was a threat. Conventions, she supposed, were safe enough.

'Where's that girl shooting off to this time?' Zita flicked at imaginary cobwebs on the Anglepoise.

'Who knows?' Audrey returned to her watercolour. She loved Zita – she had been with them for so long that she was neither cook nor housekeeper nor nanny. She was Audrey's best friend, although not precisely that because there was still that slight tension between them that preserved Audrey's status. Audrey paid her. Lived with her, loved her, relied on her, and paid her. And it was pretty much a satisfactory bargain. But however much Audrey cared for Zita, she wasn't sure that even Zita could save her this time.

'Dinner in an hour – if I get around to cooking it.'

Audrey caught the look in her eye. Zita rarely complained though she took on so much.

She wet her brush. 'You know he'd pay for someone to come in and help you.' Audrey, who rarely referred to her husband by name, had said this many times.

'Who wants strangers cluttering up the place?' Zita sniffed.

'Well, then.'

'And you should watch out for that girl.' Now they were getting to it, Zita's real reason for coming into the green room with her feather duster, when she'd done the same thing only this morning.

'Why's that?' Audrey didn't betray her irritation.

'There's a lot of scum around, that's why.'

'You lived in London too long, Zita.'

'What makes you think nothing rotten grows here?'

'This is the country.' Audrey put down her brush. It was the best thing they'd ever done, moving to Cornwall – she had to believe that. Painting grey streets and neon lighting had never been to her taste. Here she could paint trees, grass and flowers. And Rowan could discover life in her own way, on her own terms. Freedom. That was the gift she wanted for her daughter. 'If she can't run off to be alone from time to time in a place like this, then where can she?'

Zita looked doubtful. 'Maybe she can't. Maybe at her age she should be having mates round to listen to records, watch telly or play on that computer thingy.'

'Hmmm.' Audrey had never been one for 'mates' and she could see nothing enriching in zapping little computer men from a screen.

'It's a big bad world out there.' Zita was getting into her stride. She folded her arms across her chest, a bad sign. 'Rapists, murderers, all kinds of maniacs. They hang about the lonely woods, lurk around the beaches, crawl along the deserted lanes in their cars . . .'

'Shut up, Zita.' Audrey tried to smile but suddenly she was scared. Was she doing the right thing for her daughter? Shouldn't she rather be wrapping her round with maternal love, even if it meant stifling her? Shouldn't she be protecting her from the world, not shooing her out into it?

No. Audrey swung her head round as an unpleasant thought occurred to her. 'Has he been going on at you again?' Her eyes blazed. Very few things made Audrey Brunswick angry, but Philip's attitude to Zita was one of them. If he couldn't get what he wanted through Audrey, then he turned on Zita, coming between them without a qualm.

Zita looked down, fiddled with a strand of red-brown hair that had escaped from the confines of the bandana. 'Never stops, does he?' She hesitated. 'He's got a point, though.'

Audrey sighed. 'He always thinks he's got a point. He's like my father.' Her voice changed, slowing into reminiscence. Daddy was long gone now, and she'd not shed one tear at his funeral although she'd worshipped the ground he walked on.

'Kept on at you all the time, did he?'

Audrey shook her head. It was so easy to talk to Zita. 'It wasn't that.' He hadn't kept on at her, he had treasured her. Treasured her all for himself. 'He never allowed me out. He wanted me at home all the time.' Home too easily became synonymous with prison. Perhaps that was why she'd never had a group of friends, or mates, as Zita put it. 'If someone was having a party or a crowd were going swimming, I'd ask him – can I go Daddy, just this once?'

'And he never let you?'

'He certainly did not. "You've got all you want here, my darling," he used to say. "Everything you'll ever need." '

'And did you?' Zita's kind dark eyes were on her. 'Have everything you needed?'

Audrey frowned, remembering the things that had always been meaningless compared with what other girls had. 'Nothing worth having,' she whispered. 'Nothing that he hadn't bought and paid for. Nothing that came for free.'

Zita shook her head but Audrey could see that she understood. That she was on Audrey's side, as always. 'She'll be fine, that girl of yours will. Don't give it a thought. I'll tell her not to stray too far.'

'Thanks, Zita.' Audrey reached out for the comforting hands that never failed to soothe her. She could feel the world beginning to swim away from her as it so often did. It worried her more for Rowan than for herself. She'd suffered from depression for as long as she could remember – it came and went and none of the specialists she'd ever seen could do a damn thing about it. There were always drugs, but drugs took you even further away . . .

But Zita was here. She could feel the world still there, through Zita's hands. She squeezed them gratefully. This woman would always look after her daughter.

Zita Porter swayed from one side to the other, crooning gently. 'You should take better care of yourself, you should.'

Audrey smiled. She had Zita for that, didn't she? 'Don't ever leave us. For God's sake, don't ever let Philip . . .'

'You just get yourself some rest now,' Zita cut in, her dark eyes glazing over. 'That's what you need. Dinner can wait a bit longer. And in the meantime, I'll make us both a nice cup of tea.'

Rowan Brunswick ran like the wind across the lawn. She heard her father's voice dimly, as if he were in another time or place, but she ran on. No-one could stop her now. Zita had kept her practising at the piano for an hour whilst outside the sun glinted its invitation and a breeze beckoned with delicious fingers. Purgatory. Pure purgatory to be stuck inside. So now she had to run.

She vaulted the gate in a way that always made Zita scream with horror, although she'd never tripped, not once. And after only the tiniest hesitation, she headed up the hill rather than down into Folyforth village. It was only a hundred yards up the lane, she could do it easily at a jog without stopping to catch breath, and if she hopped once every five paces without losing count or balance the whole way, then there'd be something especially good for dinner.

At the top, by the disused tin mine – the wheal – she paused. Her socks were by her ankles, her new whiter than white trainers nicely scuffed and grass-stained, almost ready to take to school. To her left, sheep grazed placidly in the field, and to the right the path that led to Folyforth House and the cliff wound out of sight. The top was a dead end. A wood, to be strictly accurate, but a wood that had been fenced

23

high with barbed wire, was strictly out of bounds and apparently led nowhere. She wasn't even sure if it was part of the grounds of Folyforth House, but she did know that she wasn't supposed to go in there.

Rowan took the path to the right, passing close by the granite walls of the house her father had always wanted to buy, and sat down on the worn wooden bench placed beyond it by some thoughtful person long ago. From here, there was a stupendous view of the path that sloped, parallel with the lush green valley, winding through gorse and heather to the cliff edge. On the other side of the valley the cliff of layered granite cut into the skyline, and ahead the sea shimmered in the late afternoon sun. It was the view from Folyforth House, the view from the top of the hill, that her father had wanted so desperately. As if you could own a view. Rowan snorted with derision.

Every time they ventured into Folyforth . . . 'If anyone knows how I can get hold of that place, it'll be that little outfit in the village,' Father always said, as he dragged them into the estate agent's. He had done exactly that last week.

'It's still not on the market then?' Father obviously didn't need to specify which house he was on about. He'd been pestering the poor man for ages.

'And not likely to be as far as I can tell.' The estate agent tried his best, but Rowan sensed that he disliked her father, disliked them all perhaps with their London ways and brisk manner of doing business without so much as passing the time of day. She yawned, wishing she'd been born here.

Father leaned forwards, his thin body all right angles and hair-pin corners. 'And how far, exactly, *can* you tell?'

The young man blushed. 'Now, Mr Brunswick . . .' He attempted a teasing voice that Rowan could have told him would be wasted on her father. 'I've told you before that I'm simply not at liberty to disclose . . .'

'Who owns it, why they won't sell it, why it's left empty, why the best house in the whole damn village is going to rot away.' Philip Brunswick brushed back his dark hair in an irritated gesture. 'Yes, yes I know all that. You don't have to use estate-agent-speak on me.'

Rowan heard her mother's almost silent groan, as she folded her gloves together. Any moment now she'd disown Father completely.

He reached into his inside jacket pocket. 'But couldn't I persuade you to . . . point me in the right direction, so to speak?'

Audrey Brunswick raised her eyes to the ceiling and clicked her tongue with disapproval. The young estate agent leaped from his chair like a scalded cat, and even Rowan had to giggle.

'Mr Brunswick!' Outrage made him almost incoherent as he struggled for the right lines. 'It's more than my . . .'

'Job's worth. Yes, yes, I know that too.' Rowan's father shook his head in despair, his dark liquid eyes showing his loss, his frustration at being thwarted. 'You wouldn't have this trouble in London,' he muttered half-under his breath.

'Perhaps one *should* have this trouble in London,' Audrey said. 'Perhaps it's not such a bad thing.' She smiled sweetly at the estate agent.

Philip turned on her. 'You said you loved the place.'

'That's irrelevant.' She turned away, sweeping out of the shop, re-buttoning her fawn raincoat, which instantly assumed the lines of style.

Rowan smiled. Sometimes she couldn't quite understand her mother, but she knew she loved her, and she also trusted her judgement. Her father, she was aware, was more difficult and yet more straightforward at the same time. Rowan was convinced that he didn't understand her mother either, and she certainly wasn't sure if she loved him.

'Everything has a price.' Philip strode along the narrow pavement, his words almost lost in the buffeting wind.

Rowan ran to keep up, at the same time peering into shop door-ways, sniffing the mouthwatering fragrance of freshly baked bread and pasties, grabbing glimpses of seductive shells and gemstones hanging from leather thongs – tourist tat her parents would both have called it, agreeing for once about something. She caught sight of weathered, interesting looking people that she would dearly have loved to stop and talk to.

They all did that in the village – those that lived at the bottom of the hill – they passed the time of day in their slow soft voices, exchanged items of news and confidences, stood and watched the world go by. They hardly belonged to the 1990s. Rowan had seen them and envied them. They were outdoor people, she thought. They only disappeared back into the slate-roofed houses of the little grey village when the emmets filled the streets – the tourists – who were both bane and salvation for the Cornish folk, according to Miss Trevis who taught Geography at school, and who favoured the regional focus. That woman could favour the regional focus for hours, and Rowan lapped it up.

'No.' Audrey slowed, almost to a halt, until her husband looked rather silly striding forth on his own.

'No, what?' He waited for her, foot tapping on the pavement.

'Not everything has a price. Some things can't be bought. It's not just a question of money.'

'Don't tell me.' His thin mouth became a sneer. 'Like love and friendship and honesty.'

'I wouldn't dream of telling you if you don't already know.' Audrey caught her daughter's arm. '*Some* people are slow in that department. But I'm sure whoever owns that house has a good reason for keeping it empty. And you should respect their right to privacy.'

'I'll tell you what I should do.' His face twisted as he fell in beside them, on the other side of Rowan, sandwiching her between two tall forms and two angry faces.

She leaned closer to her mother, their sleeves brushing together in silent harmony.

'I should find out. And I will. It's so easy, it's a joke. Any little fool in a council office or water board could tell me who pays the rates. I'll make it my business to find out.'

'Really?' Rowan adored the manner in which her mother could pour scorn and yet cut a conversation stone dead at the same time.

'Yes, really,' he mocked.

Rowan's mother laughed back at him. 'And what good will that do you if they're not interested in selling?'

He moved his face close to hers. 'You just watch me. I'll prove to you that everyone has their price.'

Looking over at Folyforth House, Rowan wondered exactly what it was that made her father so obsessive about the place. Yes, there was a wonderful view; yes, he would be lording it over the rest of the village. And she supposed it was a pretty house with its square leaded windows, granite walls and chimneys like miniature church spires. But really she hoped he never got his way. She knew instinctively that it would spoil this place if the house were to be inhabited. She preferred it empty, desolate, open to her imaginings.

Some days Rowan would take the path to the cliff, climb down to the bay and, if it were low tide, walk along the beach to the village where the fishing boats clustered, their nets stretched out to dry across the rocks and sand. From there she could walk up the lane and back home, though she would always lie if her father asked her where she had been. He didn't approve of the village people; sometimes she wondered why he bothered to live here at all. Did he just like the feeling of superiority it seemed to give him?

If it were summer and there were tourists around then she could walk back in relative obscurity, although she missed the air of isolation that hung over the small fishing village in winter after they'd all gone home, or in early spring before the invasion began. In winter, Folyforth was real, the place was itself and the people too, although some of the kids poked their tongues out at her or whispered behind their fingers. Worse sometimes.

A few weeks ago, some teenager from the village, a boy with a big face, an ugly face, had confronted her. Rowan shivered as she remembered the raw redness of him, the smell of the fish and salt that clung to his hands. He'd been gutting fish from the last catch while the fishermen grabbed mugs of tea from the café on the waterfront.

'What d'*you* want then, Miss Snooty Pants?' he'd yelled, marching towards her.

Rowan measured the shortest distance to the road with her eyes. He could cut her off very easily. She stuck her hands in her pockets. 'Nothing.'

'Don't want no fish, then?'

'Not today.' She tried to smile, but her mouth was stiff.

He glared at her. Pale eyes. 'You think you're so bloody wonderful. Well cool. Miss know-it-all, you are.'

Dumbly she shook her head. What did he want from her? She

walked faster but he was right in front of her now, to her left was the sea wall.

'Oh yes, you do. I've seen you.' He nodded. 'I've seen you loads of times. I've seen you heading off to that snotty school you go to in Padstow, in that bloody stupid hat and blazer. Look pathetic in that, you do.'

'Oh.' Privately Rowan agreed about her hated school uniform, but now wasn't the time to compare notes.

'Too good for the village school, an't you?'

'Well, actually . . .' Rowan decided not to tell him that she'd much rather have gone to the village school but her father wouldn't hear of it. 'We haven't moved to Cornwall so that you can go to some no-hoper village school,' he'd said, rather obscurely.

'*Well, actually* . . .' he jeered. 'Will you listen to her? Miss snotty superior cow with a mad dyke mother.'

Fear hit her then. She moved, so close to the wall she could feel the hard slate cutting into her spine. 'You leave my mother out of this.'

'*Leave my mother out of this*,' he mimicked her yet again. 'Too bloody right, I will. Old dyke like her. What about you then? D'you like boys?'

Before Rowan could protest, scream or move away, he thrust his hand up her skirt.

She saw red. Livid, manic red. 'Get off me!' Fury lent her strength. 'Get off me, you little . . . *turd*!' She pushed, hard, and had the dubious pleasure of seeing her attacker lying in an undignified position on the sand at her feet.

'Bitch . . .' he muttered through clenched teeth.

'How dare you!' She stood there, hands on hips, eyes blazing, with no intention of running now she'd got the better of him. 'Take it back. What you said about my mother.'

'Push me, wouldya?' Panting, breath coming thick and fast, he lunged and caught her ankle.

Rowan half-screamed as he brought her down and then he was on top of her, cheering, pinning her by the shoulders with rough, gritty hands. She turned her face away, tearing her arms free, pummelling his chest.

'I'll teach you, you little rich cow.' His hand closed over her face.

Rowan bit, hard. She felt her teeth sinking into his foul tasting wrist, and then she shoved him away with all her strength while he was at a disadvantage. But he yelled, recovered, slapped her. Once, twice . . .

Rowan felt her eyes rolling, her stomach heaving. And then he wasn't there any more. He had been pulled off, she realised, and there was another voice – a different, gentle voice, the accent just as broad Cornish but with a lilt to it that calmed her.

'Are you all right, then?'

She managed to nod, but her neck felt stiff.

Her rescuer – a boy of about her own age – turned on her attacker. 'What the hell did you think you were up to, Jory Jago, you bloody idiot, you?'

'Oh, gerroff me. I were just teasing.'

'Didn't look like teasing.'

'Shouldn't have tried to fight me, then, should she?'

'You'd better piss off and hope her Dad don't come looking for you.'

Rowan sat up gingerly as her attacker slunk away. 'Thanks.'

The dark-skinned boy – who had a mass of black curls and the greenest eyes Rowan had ever seen – just shrugged. 'You should stay out of here,' he said. 'Go back where you belong.'

Rowan felt a renewed gust of anger. 'I live here.'

He shook his head. 'You live up the hill.' His meaning was plain.

She winced. 'Friend of yours, is he?'

He looked away. 'He's all right.'

'He didn't look all right from where I was.' She got to her feet, and dusted herself down. 'But I'm grateful to you anyway.'

He grinned, and the grin transformed his face. He looked, Rowan thought, a bit gypsyish – rather exciting and terribly romantic.

'Keep it to yourself, eh?' He loped off, and she stood watching him.

What a strange lot they were in the village. And just what did they have to be so bitter about?

She didn't belong. She lived here, but she didn't belong.

29

Today, Rowan knew she had no time to go to the village, and reluctantly she turned back towards the lane and the dead-end wood. But as she reached it she heard voices coming up the hill. Loud teenage voices. Rowan instinctively shrank back against the barbed wire fence. She knew one of those voices, and the thought of meeting Jory Jago again in this deserted place filled her with terror – she couldn't face another confrontation now, she really couldn't. But they'd be in sight any second, and there was nowhere to hide.

She skirted the wheal at a run, took the fence to the field in one leap, edged along the barbed wire of the wood, and to her relief spotted a way in. Only a few inches, but she was skinny as a rake and if she wriggled through on her stomach . . .

She did this, her nostrils filling with the sweet scent of bark, damp grass and earth, pulled forwards on her elbows, squeezed through and hid behind a huge oak seconds before they came into sight. She inched out to see. Four of them. Two unknown to her, one was her rescuer – whose name she didn't know, but whose face had remained lodged in her mind – and the other was Jory Jago.

'How about the wood? We could do it in the wood,' Jory said.

'It belongs to Folyforth House, that wood does.' The boy with the tangled dark curls and gypsy eyes spoke – a flat statement. 'And it's haunted.'

Rowan shivered and glanced over her shoulder. Nothing there but darkness, trees and undergrowth. She could quite believe the wood was haunted though, and she couldn't wait to get out of it.

'That's an old wives' tale.' Jory paused. 'An't it?' Rowan held her breath.

'I used to reckon so, meself.' He drew them into a circle, this strange boy who fascinated her. 'Until I went in there one day. And what d'you think happened?' His voice dropped to a whisper, and despite straining every nerve to hear his words, Rowan missed it all. But she didn't miss the gasps of horror that came in response.

'Naw!'

'You're kidding?'

He shook his head. 'They was never seen again.'

'Christ Almighty!' Jory led the way towards the path of Folyforth House. 'You won't catch me going in there. Here'll do. C'mon.'

They turned away, but as Rowan watched, the dark-haired boy looked over towards the wood, almost as if he could see her crouched in her hiding place, almost as if he knew. His sudden grin lit up the dark features, and then he was gone, after them. With them, but very much a soul apart.

Rowan turned to go back the way she'd come. Thank God for ghost stories . . . Thank God for the boy with the gypsy eyes.

But as she picked her way round a rotting tree stump covered in ivy and fungus, she imagined she saw a flash of green in the distance. A kind of glade. She hesitated. She loved to explore. Since they'd moved here she'd covered every inch of the surrounding countryside.

Everything but this wood, a voice told her. She paused, thinking of the soft words spoken down there by the wheal. It belonged to Folyforth House, but no-one lived in the house, did they? So who would know? And as for the ghosts – did she really believe in them?

She was scared. There was no denying it was creepy in this wood, the silence broken only by the occasional rustle of rabbit or bird or . . . A ghost perhaps? But she was here now, wasn't she? It seemed a shame to go back so soon. There were no such things as ghosts. And as for that tantalising patch of green . . .

The memory of his grin persuaded her. It was no good – she couldn't leave this place until she'd at least gone in a bit further. And most of those stories were probably local superstition – according to Miss Trevis there was enough local superstition around here to fill a classroom full of history books.

She took a deep breath, one tentative step and then another. As she moved from the outskirts of the wood – still wet from last night's downpour – it became darker and denser, the going more tough and the odd haunting atmosphere more discernible. Then the trees began to thin, and she spotted a muddy path – a faint path to be sure, but certainly one that had been used, and maybe not so long ago either.

Only a few more steps and she would . . . She rounded the last tree, almost stumbled over a rock and blinked. In front of her was a small grassy glade. And beyond it a dip. Built into the dip . . . half-buried in earth, undergrowth, ivy and rock, was a ghostly grey ruin of a building looming out of the wet wood.

Chapter 2

Audrey Brunswick lay in her own bed between comforting linen sheets and listened to the night noises. She couldn't remember exactly when she and Philip had changed their sleeping arrangements, although she thought it was more than five years ago, and she also imagined that it had been Philip's suggestion, although she really wasn't sure. But she certainly hadn't objected . . .

Outside, she could hear the soft rush of breeze through leaves, the occasional shuffle of a nocturnal animal – she liked to think of them scurrying outside when the people were in bed – and the hoot of an owl about to go hunting.

Inside the house the slap-slap of Zita's slippered footsteps had ground to a halt. She had made hot chocolate an hour ago and by now would be in bed, reading the problem page or horoscopes of some women's magazine or other.

Philip however, was still up. Audrey could hear the TV downstairs, only an indistinct vibration from this distance. But she recognised the moment when he rose from his armchair, cleared his throat, and pressed the remote control.

She heard him march up the stairs towards his own room – please God, to his own room – and heard the dismal routine of teeth and toilet, the flush of lavatory, timed with a precision that made her want to hold her head in her hands and scream.

This was the moment when . . . She held her breath, crossed her fingers, and curled foetus-like in the bed she didn't share with him for sleeping but sometimes shared for sex.

He came out of the bathroom and she seemed to hear his hesitation as it rested between their two rooms, their two lives, for a moment. It

33

rested on the dim landing with the small hope left for their marriage, and then the footsteps came closer and the dread slowly picked a hole in her stomach. Oh, God. Please, no.

He knocked softly on the door. 'Audrey?'

She ignored him, crawling down further into the double bed.

'Audrey, are you awake?' A touch of irritation.

She groaned, believing it to be silent, but perhaps he had heard it because he opened the door.

'You're not asleep already, are you?' He came closer. She could smell him, the spearmint toothpaste he used that reminded her of chewing gum, the lemon grass soap she'd bought for him last Christmas along with his favourite aftershave – the sort of present you might buy an employee, an acquaintance, someone for whom you could think of no other present at all . . .

'Audrey?'

'What?' She rolled over and switched on the bedside lamp which she knew he hated. His hair was newly brushed, standing with static away from his head like a small baby's, his eyes small in the leanness of his face. 'What is it?' As if she didn't know . . .

'Move up a bit, darling.' He only called her *darling* when he wanted sex.

As he took off his dressing-gown, she distracted herself by remembering the other things he did when he wanted sex. He didn't argue with her, he stared out of the window a lot, he drank more whisky, smiled more, became almost playful. He also came to bed early. Audrey wasn't sure she liked him very much when he wanted sex.

And afterwards? The *darlings* lasted until their first disagreement. Oh, to have *darlings* that might last for ever . . . He was better-tempered, even whistled sometimes, and teased Rowan until she giggled. Did it make him feel amusing? Sad, she thought, to be a man, so easily transformed by such a silly thing.

'How are you feeling tonight?' Still wearing his striped cotton pyjamas with the white cord, ordered specially from London, Philip climbed in beside her.

Audrey inched over to the other side, almost slipping over the edge. She almost laughed at this thought – for of course this was indeed the direction in which she seemed to be heading. Her nightdress was done up to her chin, half-strangling her in fact, but she could hardly pretend she didn't know what he was here for, when entering her was the only reason for him entering her bed. They didn't have any other physical closeness remaining, only that which kept them even further apart.

'All right.' She submitted to his fumblings with the buttons.

'Why do you wear this damn thing?' His breath quickened.

'Would you believe me if I said it was to make you excited?' she drawled into his ear.

'Shut up, Audrey.' The *darlings* had disappeared quickly this time. She mustn't be Audrey at all if she were to keep his *darlings*.

He yanked the fabric up, not bothering to touch or undress her with any care, and Audrey closed her eyes, hearing the click of the light switch moving them into darkness, seeing the black behind her eyelids as another kind of night-time, cave, oblivion.

She hardly bothered to move, feeling the weight of him but shrugging it off in her mind, waiting for him to be finished, which he was, quickly, without a caress.

She rolled over, trying not to feel a savage hatred, a sense of violation. He was her husband.

Philip left the room without another *darling* or even a backward glance. But it was a long while before Audrey could sleep.

Zita brought her tea at seven-thirty.

'Will you help me move the bed this morning?'

'Hmm?' Audrey saw from Zita's expression that she looked a sight. Hardly surprising. She'd had only a couple of hours' undisturbed sleep; her eyes were heavy, her head aching.

'The bed. I want to move it.' She sat up with difficulty.

'Nearer to the window?'

'Downstairs.'

Zita arched one eyebrow in that way she had and stuck her hands on her hips. 'To the green room?'

Audrey nodded. She knew what she was saying, what this meant, and Philip would know it too. He never entered the green room – it was an unspoken agreement between them. It was her sanctuary, the

35

place she could be alone if she so desired. And now, she desired exactly that – to be left alone, in peace. He wouldn't enter her if she slept in the green room. No more. 'As soon as you like.' She slipped out of bed and pulled her robe over the creased, stained nightdress.

'Before breakfast?' Zita watched her. She knew.

'Before breakfast.'

A grin twitched at Zita's mouth. 'We won't manage it on our own.'

Audrey pulled off the sheets in one fierce movement. This linen wouldn't be comforting her any longer until it had been in the wash. 'Then we'd better get Rowan to give us a hand,' she said.

After breakfast, or maybe before lunch – Audrey wasn't sure because the day was swimming away from her in the manner that days sometimes did – she came to the conclusion that she should go out. Not that she wanted to – there was nothing easier than staying in the green room painting and thinking – but she was aware that it would be difficult to go out, and that she had to fight it, this sense of not belonging to the world any more.

So she pulled on rubber boots – it was misty and drizzling this morning – an old wet-weather coat and a bush hat she found at the bottom of her wardrobe, and went out. Unlike Rowan, she headed straight down the hill without hesitation, plodding along the muddy lane, pleased that the rain half-hid her from the world and that she could see it none too clearly with the drizzle-blind in front of her tired face.

At last she reached the sea. Wild and stormy like her daughter's eyes, but too far away. There were few people around, and the boats were out. Maybe a storm had been forecast; Audrey knew it was a good time to fish during or just after a storm. Best time for anything. She hugged her coat closer. Just what she needed – a storm to whip up and clear the air.

But for now the tide was out, so she set off round the headland, picking her way over boulders of granite and tiny rock pools, pausing every now and then to poke at a scuttling crab as it disappeared under a crown of weed. Most of the rocks were covered with tiny mussels clinging like blue-black bruises to the rock face, small islands in the sand. This was where Audrey could be alone.

She wouldn't leave Philip. The thought came to her from the distant horizon, as she turned to stride towards the sea. She wouldn't leave Philip, but not because she loved him. She had never loved him, that had never been a factor. But she wouldn't leave him because he wasn't cruel enough. In fact he wasn't cruel at all, and besides, there was Rowan. Her reward for a loveless marriage. Her beautiful daughter Rowan.

She paused, her footprints cutting into the wet sand. She traced her own name with the toe of her boot as if to persuade herself that she was who she thought she was, then scrubbed it out with her heel. Soon the sea would wipe it from sight.

The odd thing was, she couldn't remember meeting Philip at all. She couldn't recall the moment when she had first seen his face.

Of course, in those days there were always people coming and going at the house. Father was sociable, Mummy too had been sociable when she'd been alive, God bless her, and Father was sought after by people – usually middle-aged men in whom Audrey had not the slightest interest.

She was very young when Philip Brunswick first turned up at the house – less than twenty – and had hardly lived although she was old enough to recognise the ambition in Philip's dark eyes. It was hard to do much in the way of living, when Father held the apron strings, the purse strings and even the emotional ones too.

Philip was just one of many visitors to the house, but he stuck in her mind because he was the only one who consistently beat her at chess. Father had taught her to play to win. She knew she was good, and it gave her a shaft of satisfaction way down in her belly to beat those middle-aged men who were politicians or chairmen of rich companies.

Unlike most of the others, Philip hardly watched her while they played, and unlike them he had never expected her to lose. He was an attractive man, with dark hair and very pale skin, and she enjoyed the way his brow furrowed in concentration. She didn't even mind that he took so long over his moves, although when he came to the house she took to using a small hour glass and insisting they move within an allotted time-limit. She could beat him then, she found. Sometimes. Philip needed a long while to make his moves.

Time after time she played him, and apart from that they rarely talked, although more and more she looked up to find him watching her in that appraising, thoughtful way he had. One time he was playing badly, and she seemed to catch his mood, feeling jumpy and on edge. Outside it was raining, she was hemmed in, stuck in this house for another winter.

He began making crazy moves, leaving first his bishop then his rook wide open, and she found herself emulating him, playing wildly, heedless of the consequences. She lost her queen, something she almost always avoided. They played, unlike before, with abandon, until they were both out of position. She was trapped and exposed.

He grabbed her hand. 'Will you marry me, Audrey?'

She stared at him. A gust of turbulent laughter rose in her throat, but she couldn't let it go. He was serious, for heaven's sake. But what did she know of him?

Her father was coming down the hall, she could hear his voice. 'Audrey will take care of it. Let me have a word,' he was saying to his companion.

'She's a treasure.'

'Better than that.' Her father's voice was low. 'I'd be lost without her, you know. She's my right hand man, make no mistake.'

Audrey tensed. *Make no mistake.* She looked down at the chessboard. There were no more moves open to her. She felt Philip squeeze her hand.

'I expect you think this is ridiculously sudden.' He laughed, shame-faced, a gesture that instantly endeared him to her.

'No, I'm flattered.' She extracted her hand.

'But you'd like some time to think it over,' he pressed.

Audrey watched the sand sifting through the glass. He had made his moves very quickly tonight. 'I haven't even met your parents,' she hedged. *I hardly know you*, she meant.

His expression changed. 'My mother died when I was small,' he said. 'I barely remember her.'

Audrey stared at him. 'Mine too . . .' It seemed like a sign.

'And my father doesn't get out the way he used to. I could take you to see him . . .'

'Audrey!' Her father was calling her. She rose quickly to her feet.

'Audrey!' There was something in his voice that she hated. She'd always loved him and yet . . . she couldn't be free of him, could she?

'I accept,' she told Philip.

His eyes darkened. 'Really? You mean it? I . . .'

'But you should speak to Father,' she advised. 'Play it by ear, but I should pretend you haven't asked me yet.'

She knew how it would be. Father would say she was too young, Philip would plead his case, and Father would realise that the decision would greatly simplify his life. This way she could still be his untainted treasure. Philip Brunswick – his protégé – would not be a threat to him. This way he wouldn't lose her – or so he would imagine.

She was proved right. The engagement was a short one and Audrey was closeted in the hurricane eye of it as it spun around her, the centre of it all, without touching her. It didn't seem possible that Philip Brunswick was about to be her marriage partner, let alone her partner for life. She hadn't chosen him, had she? He had been her opponent at chess, that was all, and he had offered her an option. What was the matter with her? Was she quite mad?

Several times she tried to talk to Philip, but although older and much more worldly than she, he seemed equally helpless. Or perhaps he wanted it this way. Other people took over – her own father, Philip's invalid father and elderly aunt, the caterers, the florist, the dressmaker, the cake designer. She and Philip were thrown from one to the other like confetti themselves – weightless, insubstantial to the touch, their views irrelevant. And before Audrey could catch breath, it was her wedding day, and her father was about to take her to the church.

'Are you sure, honey bunch?' he asked her. 'You really want to go through with this? You'd leave your old Father, would you?' He laughed.

Something stirred within her. 'No.'

'Hmm?' He straightened his cravat.

'No.' She looked out at him from under her veil. 'I'm not sure. Not sure at all.'

He laughed again, more forced this time. 'Now, Audrey. Every-one has doubts. It's just last minute nerves, you know that. But now isn't the time to give in to them.'

'Then when is the time?' She felt the panic rising. During the service with everyone hanging on to your every word? After the service perhaps, when you were man and wife? She shuddered. Desperately she wished her mother were still alive. Never had she missed her more.

He turned round to face her. 'The time is long gone. It's much too late for second thoughts.' He looked out of the window. 'And the car is here.' The relief showed plainly on his face.

It's too late because the car is here, Audrey thought. The car is here and so we must get into it and go to the church. 'I don't want to marry Philip Brunswick,' she said clearly. 'I never really did.' She had only wanted to get away from this man she adored.

Anger flared in her father's eyes. 'Don't be ridiculous,' he hissed. 'He's a fine young man. And he's got a great future ahead of him.'

'But . . .'

'Get into the car.'

Silently she followed him, the tears not coming to the surface, not spoiling the beauty make-over that had taken an hour of her time this morning. But they drenched her inside, those tears.

'Come on, Audrey.' He opened the door.

'Daddy . . .' she began, as the limousine glided away.

'Stop it.' He grasped her hand in much the same way as Philip Brunswick had done when he asked her to marry him. 'He will make you happy.'

Audrey stared out of the window. It was an order. He will make you happy. Father has spoken. It was, perhaps, the only time since her mother's death that she had asked something of him. And his betrayal of any sort of love he might have felt for her sank deep into her heart.

Audrey trudged back to the village what seemed like hours later. She had walked around the headland, beyond the next two rocky bays – both of them deserted – and sat on a huge flat boulder to do her thinking. She had watched the sea, thick and green as it rolled closer, waited whilst the storm passed by several miles away with only a half-hearted bellow of thunder. Her mind drifted and the tide drew in, threatening to cut off her return.

Coming to her senses, she just made it, wind and sea-battered, back to the beach where fishermen in oilskins were bringing in their catches, drinking mugs of steaming tea or gutting fish ready for sale on the waterfront.

She made her way to the café – more like a village meeting-place really – and was pleased to note, as she bought tea and sat down at an empty table, that no-one spared her a second glance, windswept as she was in her bush hat and wet-weather gear, the sand and salt still on her rubber boots and burning on her face as the mug of tea clutched between red hands warmed her from the inside out.

The conversation of the women on the table behind her lulled Audrey, bringing her a sense of peacefulness. They lived in the real world, these women. They weren't closeted in some ivory tower not even knowing what day it was. They cooked, cleaned and held random displaced conversations like the one she was half-hearing now about someone from the village who was having an affair with some man. Neither of the women had time for this man they talked of. He was above himself, they said. He looked down on them. He looked down on them all. But he was ready enough to take one of them to his bed.

Audrey smiled. A world apart . . . Slowly she stirred her tea.

Rowan raced past Folyforth House with uncharacteristic speed, barely acknowledging the shadowy form she imagined – just for a moment – that she saw behind the stained glass window of the front door, beyond the wrought iron gates. She had other, more pressing concerns on her mind.

And in minutes she was standing once more in front of the granite building in the green glade in the dead-end wood, for the second time in two days. On this occasion, however, she allowed it to seep into her senses.

It was such an odd place, she'd certainly seen nothing like it before. Yesterday, the sight of it looming in front of her so unexpectedly had sent her bolting back towards the lane and then home. And in her thoughts, later, the stone building had intertwined with the strange dark-haired boy's tales of ghostly goings on. Whatever those tales were, it had certainly looked the part, this bizarre monument in the glade, even at first sight, when all she'd seen was the round tower spiralled with ivy and clothed with moss, the battlements that made it look like part of a castle plucked and transported to an illogical resting place, and the rusty octagonal clock.

Once home, she'd regretted her hasty departure. It was unlike her to be scared off so easily, and so she'd been champing at the bit all day today to get back there, to the glade. To find out about the place – to explore the inside of it if she could.

So she grabbed her first opportunity after school when for once Zita wasn't chuntering on about homework, but instead was looking distracted, hardly noticing whether Rowan were there or not. She changed into jeans and a sweatshirt and raced there without further delay.

Rowan felt some trepidation as she entered the dark wood, a shiver of fear as she picked her way through to the path, and now a frisson of excitement as she tasted the chill in the air. This weird building looked so utterly out of place . . . Like her, it hardly belonged here.

Gingerly she stepped closer. The weeds grew high around the granite – bindweed, dandelions and thistles, right up to . . . yes, an arrow slit window. She almost laughed out loud. And above the clock – which had lost its hour hand – on the tower, was a Gothic shaped doorway leading through to some sort of look-out post. It was crazy though . . . Rowan stared in confusion. The building was only about forty feet high, no taller than many of the pines surrounding it, so what could possibly be seen from such a viewing position? She reached out to touch the stone, dank and cold against her fingers. Was there a way in?

Walking around the tower she found a small doorway almost obscured by grass and weed. Would it be locked, or stiff with rust and age? She pushed hard, and was surprised to feel it yielding. Harder, she pushed with all her weight until slowly it creaked open to reveal a tiny spiral stone staircase. Rowan paused and put a hand to her head. Heaven help her . . . Was she dreaming this? It didn't seem real at all.

Slowly she ascended the treacherously steep stairs, passing the arrow-slit in the granite. Had someone fired arrows from here? She giggled with nerves, peered round the turn of the spiral where a gap in the stone wall led through to the battlements. Cautiously, Rowan climbed through. It was dusty, dirty, threaded with ivy and bindweed, but she sensed someone had been here and recently. She leaned against the castellated stone, listening carefully and watching the dark wet wood. But it was as silent as a grave. With a shiver she returned to the spiral staircase. She must go on.

Three more steps up and she came to the entrance of the look-out that she'd spotted from below. She eased herself out there. This *was* crazy. From here she could see next to nothing – only trees and a bit of sky. Some look-out . . . She sank back against the cold stone. The staircase led nowhere. This place was a joke.

She returned to the battlements, explored a couple of stone cellars that sank deep into the bowels of the building, settled herself down into a comfortable hollow of stone, against the battlements, and closed her eyes, soaking up the atmosphere.

There wasn't just a thrill of fear running through the building. There was also, unmistakeably, a thrill of romance. She shivered. Was it her imagination – over-active at the best of times, Zita said – or did this mock castle simply reek of some age-old love affair?

It might be a joke but this was a wonderful place. A place where you could come to be alone. A special place . . .

'Well, well. You certainly get around, don't you?'

Rowan's eyes snapped open. Instantly she was on her feet, alert, scared. But it wasn't her tormenter from the village standing in front of her as she had feared. It was the dark-haired boy with the gypsy eyes who had rescued her.

He must have crept up that stone staircase as silent as a cat. He must . . . This must be his place, she thought. Where he came to be alone.

'Is this . . . ? Am I . . . ?' She was angry with herself, feeling an intruder. 'Is this private property?'

'I reckon so,' he drawled. 'Though some might call it open to anyone who finds it.' He was taller than she, but only by about an inch, narrow-shouldered, lean and tightly sprung. Close up, she was conscious once again of the piratical look of him – accentuated by a small gold hoop in his left ear lobe that she hadn't noticed before. His hair was just as tangled though, and she found herself wondering if he ever brushed it.

'You said it was haunted,' she accused.

'Did I?' His dark eyebrows almost joined together as he frowned, looking around them, as if a poltergeist were about to leap from the stone. 'Now when did I say the folly was haunted?' He scrutinised her thoughtfully.

The folly. She smiled. Of course, that's what it was. A folly. She'd seen them occasionally before – there was a small white tower up from Boscastle harbour, and she'd heard Miss Trevis and others speak of them – buildings with no purpose, built according to a whim, a fancy, for decoration and amusement alone.

She drew her hands slowly over the cold granite. But that didn't seem quite right. There seemed to be more to this folly, something she couldn't quite put her finger on, some alternative use for it perhaps. 'Who built it?'

'I haven't the foggiest.' He was still watching her carefully, she realised. He didn't trust her, and she guessed that whatever he knew, it would be more than he'd ever tell her. 'And when did I say it was haunted?' he repeated.

'You were talking about the wood, not the folly.' To escape from his scrutiny, Rowan leaned over the battlements to stare into the wood. A mixture of oaks and pines – probably planted here by man, not nature.

From this vantage point it was just as mysterious as it was when ploughing through the wet undergrowth itself. The wood could indeed quite easily be haunted. But how had it got here in the first place? Why build a place like this in a wood where no-one could even see it?

'You were listening to us.' He cocked his head to one side like a bird. 'Yesterday. I thought I saw something move by one of the old oaks. Something red.' His eyes narrowed but she felt no threat. She was sure that he meant her no harm, after all, he'd stuck his neck out for her safety once before, hadn't he?

'I wasn't listening on purpose,' she told him.

His lean body was poised and waiting. 'What else did you hear?'

'Not much.' She shrugged. She hadn't heard as much as she would have liked. 'Just that the wood was haunted.'

'And you still came here exploring?' He laughed. 'Not very easily put off, are you?'

She shook her head.

'I reckon I should have spoken up a bit, let you hear the whole thing.'

Rowan didn't want him to laugh at her. 'I'm not easily *scared*, if that's what you mean.'

'Oh no?' He moved closer.

If she stretched out her hand she could touch his shoulder or the dark curly hair. 'No.' She turned away. 'And you were making it all up, weren't you?'

'Maybe.'

'So why did you say it? If it's not true?'

'Don't you ever lie to people?' His voice was a whisper that seemed to reach into her soul. That was ridiculous, wasn't it? *You're going to grow up a soppy old romantic,* Zita always told her whenever she caught Rowan crying, as she often did over a sad story or some black and white matinée showing on the television.

But the truth was that nothing seemed ridiculous today. Nothing seemed too far-fetched as they stood in this miniature granite castle in the middle of a wood that was supposed to lead nowhere. Everything leads somewhere, Rowan found herself thinking.

'Don't you?' he repeated. 'Ever lie?'

'Only if I have to.'

'I had to.'

She turned to face him. 'Why?'

'To stop them coming into the wood, of course. To stop them finding this place.'

She thought of the high barbed wire. That wouldn't be enough to deter a gang of boys intent on exploring. Neither would the fact that the wood was part of Folyforth House, if the house were empty. But the ghost stories must have done it, she supposed. 'They *are* your friends.' He was a strange person, all right. She would have thought he'd be proud to show off what he'd discovered. And yet there was a kind of privacy about him too. She hazarded a guess that there would be an awful lot his friends didn't know about him. A lot that nobody knew.

'I didn't say they weren't mates.' He scuffed a dirty trainer against the granite. 'But that don't mean I want them knowing about all this.' His green eyes flashed.

'Because it's your private place,' she supplied. She knew all about that sort of thing. Everyone needed to get away.

'Right.' He grinned again, forging a bond between them, his wariness apparently forgotten.

Reluctantly Rowan got to her feet, not wanting to leave the folly now that she too had discovered it, not wanting to leave this dark-eyed boy either, with his proud way with words and appealing grin. She dusted her jeans down. 'I'll leave you to it, then.'

'What?' He seemed surprised.

'I don't want to intrude. The last thing you need is someone butting in when you've found . . .'

'You could share it with me.' He wouldn't look at her. He was staring out into the wood, a glassy expression on the dark face. 'If you want.'

'Why?' She was sure that if their positions were reversed she'd be thinking . . . why doesn't he go? Didn't I find it first? Or would she? Wasn't she drawn to him in a way she couldn't explain?

'Room for both of us, I reckon.' He swung a small rucksack from his shoulder. 'Hungry?'

Rowan shook her head, but the instant he pulled the food out of the bag – lemonade, chocolate, bread and a thick wedge of cheese, she felt starving. 'Actually, I am a bit.'

He took a small square of blanket from the rucksack, spread it on the stone, and Rowan sat down, hugging her knees.

'What's your name?' She bit hungrily into the cheese he offered her. It was the longest she'd ever talked to anyone without even knowing their name.

'Glyn Penbray.'

She smiled. 'That sounds like a nice old Cornish name.'

'I come from a nice old Cornish family,' he teased.

'Where do you live?'

'Down by the waterfront.'

'What does your father do?' These were her stock questions – the kind of questions the girls at school asked each other when they first met. Questions that helped them set up a background in relation to themselves and their position in the world.

But he laughed and Rowan realised that these questions were all wrong for Glyn Penbray, the world he lived in and their place here among the grey battlements of the folly. He had no relation to her world, and she was glad.

'You do have a father?' she pressed.

'He's a fisherman.'

Rowan nodded. One of the grizzly Cornish men she'd seen down at the waterfront many a time in ribbed jumpers falling apart at the seams and yellow oilskin trousers. 'D'you go out there with him?' She'd always fancied that – escaping into the vast ocean, away from towns and people and the mess they made.

'Sometimes.' Glyn was not very forthcoming. 'Most of the blokes round here are fishermen,' he reminded her gently.

She leaned forwards with a sly grin. 'Those that aren't concerned with the tourist trade, you mean. That's what you think I am, deep down, isn't it? One of your emmets?'

'They're not mine.' His lilting voice remained soft, the tone the old Cornish dialect that many of the older villagers still used, and that Rowan found so appealing. 'And you're no tourist either.'

She sighed. 'I might live here. But I don't belong. You said as much.'

'You're envied, that's what you are.' He laughed. 'Down in the village they talk about you and others like you . . .'

'I'm not just some little rich girl who lives up on the hill.' Rowan jumped to her feet, eyes blazing. She didn't want to be different, or talked about, and certainly she didn't want to be envied. She wanted to be part of this place.

'I bet you're not.' His slow grin, as he looked her up and down, made her sit back down again with a thump. She winced as the hard stone bruised her. 'You're much more'n that.' He bit into the chocolate, his eyes holding her gaze.

Rowan hunched her knees closer to her chest as a hot uncomfortable sensation bristled at her skin. 'And what about your mother?' she asked politely.

'What about her?' Glyn Penbray stretched out long legs in torn denim jeans, apparently perfectly at home and at ease. Rowan wondered how many other picnics he'd enjoyed here. Had he always been alone or had he ever brought anyone to share his cheese and chocolate?

'What does she do?' Rowan stared at the places on his knees where the blue denim was torn and mud-stained, his dark flesh a shadow behind the fabric.

'What does any woman do?' He took a swig from the bottle of lemonade. 'Keeps house, cooks, nags, gossips.' His eyes gleamed with humour. 'Oh, and she works in the Bull and Packet.'

'Bull and . . . ?'

'The pub.' He laughed. 'Jesus wept, you are a little innocent.'

She stiffened. 'I'm not a kid.'

'How old are you, then?' She would swear he was staring at the rise of her breasts under her sweatshirt. He had some nerve.

'Almost fourteen.'

'Almost grown-up,' he mocked.

'And you?' She tried to subject him to a similar stare, but it rolled off him like water on oil, barely skimming his surface.

'About the same.' He grinned. 'But I've been going in the pub since I were seven.'

'I've been in there too.' She recalled the time. It was a few months back, when they'd been in the village and her mother had felt faint. Father had wanted to get her back home but Mum had insisted on a medicinal brandy. Rowan remembered the red and gold interior . . .

'Like a brothel,' Mum had said with a sigh.

She remembered the dry smoky atmosphere that had made her cough, the smelly beer-stained carpet, and most of all the curious looks of the people supping at the bar.

'I know.' He laughed again. 'The whole village were talking about it for weeks.'

'Don't exaggerate.' She blushed. 'We're not any different, not really. And we're not snobs, you know . . .' Although whether that were true in her father's case she wasn't entirely sure.

'Course you're not.' To her surprise, Glyn leaned forwards, brushing a strand of dark hair from her eyes. 'We're all the same under the old surface gloss, I reckon. Hmm?' His hands were gentle, not as she expected at all, his fingers long and tapered, his skin warm, not rough to the touch despite the callouses on his hands. A soft shiver ran through her body, a shiver that made her blush still more furiously. She didn't want any of *that*.

48

'People always talk.' Glyn's hand returned to his side. He was perfectly casual, as if he hadn't touched her at all, as if he hadn't felt the tension between them, skin to skin. 'There'll always be stories.'

Rowan looked around her. 'And you don't know any of the stories about this place?' She heard the little-girl disappointment in her own voice.

'Oh, there's plenty of *stories*.' Glyn leaned back against the battlements and closed his eyes. 'But I thought you weren't interested in those.'

'It depends.'

He opened one eye. 'On what?'

'On whether they're true, of course.'

Glyn shrugged. 'Athwenna Trelawney would tell you there's a fine line between legend and history, between what's just some old myth and . . .' he paused. 'Well, and what's the truth.'

She stared at him. 'Athwenna . . . ?'

'Trelawney.' His mouth tightened, as if he were already regretting the admission.

Rowan leaned closer towards him. 'Who is she?'

'She's close to being a legend herself.' He watched her. 'The oldest woman in Folyforth, is Athwenna. She knows a thing or two.'

'Where can I find her?' Rowan felt the excitement return. She sensed instinctively that if anyone knew the story of the folly, the secrets it held, it would be this woman he spoke of.

'You can't.' Glyn looked away. 'If she ever wants you to find her, she'll do it herself. You'd do better looking for your own shadow, I reckon.'

Her shoulders drooped. 'Because I don't belong.'

He was silent, not contradicting her.

It's not fair, she thought. But she too was silent, before it struck her that she'd been here for ages, that it was getting late, and Zita would be frantic. She glanced at her watch, jumped to her feet. 'I must go . . .'

'Yeah?'

'Yes, of course. They'll be worried . . .' Suddenly she didn't want to be part of a family who worried, who lived up the hill, who had Zita and who didn't belong. She wanted – suddenly and desperately

– to be part of a family with a mother who did what all women did. Who spent her time cooking, cleaning, gossiping and nagging. Who pulled pints in the Bull and Packet, instead of spending whole days painting and staring into space.

'Where does Athwenna Trelawney live?' she asked him with renewed determination. If she could find out the secrets of the folly, she might find out how to belong.

He leaned on one elbow. 'I don't reckon I should tell you.'

'Why on earth not?' Rowan folded her arms. Really, this boy could be so exasperating.

''Cause maybe she wouldn't thank me for it.'

'Please?' she begged.

But he only laughed. 'Maybe you should have patience, little girl. Maybe if you thought about it you could work it out for yourself.'

Rowan made for the staircase. 'I'm *not* a little girl.'

In a moment he was up beside her, his hand catching her wrist, his expression changing. 'Will you come here again?'

She looked into solemn eyes. If you don't tease me, she wanted to say. If you don't make me feel different, and if you tell me where I can find this woman, the one who knows all the stories. But she said none of this. 'I'd like to.' At last she looked away, and his fingers touched her hair, just once. She could almost have imagined it.

'Good.'

'Shall I meet you?' She hesitated.

'I'll find you.' He watched her. 'Are you scared to go back through the wood alone?'

The light was fading but it wasn't yet dark. Rowan shivered. 'Course not.'

He grinned. 'See you then.'

She guessed that he was watching her from the battlements as she sped across the glade and plunged into the dark wood, which seemed even more creepy than ever. Maybe she should have admitted her fear, maybe she should have admitted that what she wanted was to run into the wood, fast, wind through their hair, Glyn Penbray by her side. But all she could think of was his broad grin, and all that she could feel was the warmth inside her from the touch of his hand.

Getting no joy from Philip Brunswick, and not knowing what else to do, Zita Porter at last put on her red quilted jacket and black shoes and stomped down the lane to the village. No taxi had come to the house and Audrey no longer drove. Where could she have got to? She had taken her green wellies as if going for a walk in the country, but that was hours ago and no-one walked all day in the country, not someone like Audrey Brunswick anyhow. Zita sighed. She was getting worried. Very worried.

The waterfront was almost deserted and the shops closed up for the night. Daylight was dimming and rooms were being lit up inside grey cottages. She could see women bustling about clearing kitchens, children going to bed, men settling in armchairs. Where the heck was Audrey?

Zita was concerned for her safety, she'd been concerned for some time, in a general way. Audrey was getting worse – no doubt of that. This depression, her marriage . . . All that business of humping the blasted bed downstairs this morning – and she'd refused to let Philip help. What a fool she was – they'd damn near broken their backs, the three of them.

Zita couldn't understand her. If her marriage was so awful why the heck didn't she just leave the man and be done with it? No-one would blame her, would they, and Zita wasn't about to let her struggle on alone. She'd be there for her, Audrey must know that. But it wasn't her place to say too much. She knew her boundaries. Zita was still an employee, Audrey the boss.

There was no sign of her at the waterfront and the tide was too high to consider going round the headland. A sudden thought occurred to Zita, jarring her with fear. Supposing Audrey had got cut off by the tide? Supposing she was scrabbling now along the rocks trying to find a way through? Supposing she had drowned? Supposing – God forbid – she'd done herself in?

A man approached her, a weathered and beaten looking fisherman who might have been in his forties or fifties – it was impossible to tell – with a red face and a salt and pepper beard.

'Yeah?' Zita glared at him.

'Think I know who you're after.' He scratched at his beard.

It was his eyes that held her – the bluest eyes she'd ever seen.

Honest eyes, she'd call them. 'Where is she?' she whispered.

He nodded towards the café on the waterfront. 'In there.'

'Thanks.' Zita strode towards the building, apprehension clutching at her heart. She shoved her hands into the pockets of the red coat. At least she was all right. But Zita hadn't liked the way he'd spoken. As if Audrey . . .

'Take it easy now.' His voice, soft behind her.

She nodded, not looking around.

The café was quiet, apart from the woman serving tea, two other women huddled in one corner whispering, and Audrey sitting at a table alone. A bush hat was slightly askew on her fair head, her wet weather jacket was pulled up to her neck. Her chin was cupped in her hands, she was gazing in front of her with sightless blank eyes, and crying noiselessly.

'Audrey?' Zita was almost scared to disturb her.

'Not right in the head,' she heard someone say. Zita shot a glance of contempt over her shoulder.

'What's wrong with her?' came a voice from the doorway.

And, 'How was I to know who she was? It weren't my fault.'

Zita fixed this last speaker with a challenging stare as if to cement her in memory.

'Audrey?' She moved closer and knelt beside her. 'Time to go home, Audrey,' she said. 'Come on now.'

Audrey barely acknowledged her existence, though the tears continued to fall, not passionate but whispering tears channelling the lines of her face.

She was saying something, but Zita couldn't hear. She leaned closer.

Behind her she was conscious of the grizzled fisherman.

'I'll give you a hand back up the lane, shall I?'

She nodded gratefully. 'Please.'

Audrey put a hand on her arm and sighed the words. 'You know, Zita . . . I have been such a fool.'

Chapter 3

Just a quick glance over her shoulder, and he was helping her – this grizzled man from the beach with the honest blue eyes.

They got Audrey to her feet – although she was slim and seemed insubstantial, she was a tall woman – and supporting her weight between them, half-carried her out of the café, both of them ignoring the stares of the silent women watching. Zita paused and braced herself for confrontation, but a warning glance from the man beside her made her repress the impulse to give them a piece of her mind. What was the point? They wouldn't understand – and could she blame them?

'Thanks . . . er?'

'Harry.' He was shouldering far more of Audrey's weight than she.

'We live about half a mile up the lane,' she said dubiously. 'Maybe we should call a cab.' Or phone Philip, she added in silence to herself. But she was loth to do that – he would assume Audrey had finally lost her marbles. Who wouldn't? And Audrey would go doolally if Philip were brought into this . . . whatever this was all about.

Harry laughed, as if the suggestion were plain ridiculous. 'I reckon we can manage her between us.' He shot her another look from those penetrating eyes. 'If it suits you.'

She shrugged. 'It suits me.' The drizzle had eased off now, though the lane was still wet from the last downpour; it had grown dark, and an after-rain scent hung in the night air.

For a while they trudged in silence, concentrating on the load supported between them. The load that was Audrey . . .

She was barely awake, limp as if heavily drugged. Something had knocked the stuffing out of her all right, and the stuffing was flimsy enough in the first place. Zita wondered what could have happened.

Surely she hadn't been sitting there in the café all day?

Every now and then she glanced at the man walking on the other side of Audrey, aware of his heavy even breathing, the slap-thud of his shoes on the wet lane, and his dark silhouette moving with purpose beside her.

Was he used to manual labour? 'I suppose this is a bit like hauling a fishing boat up the sand.' She smiled at her own choice of words, despite her concerns.

Harry chuckled. 'You could say that. Although I don't know that Madam here would welcome the likeness.'

Zita grimaced with effort. 'Madam here is in no position to complain.' There might be boundaries, but her relationship with Audrey had long ago moved away from careful politeness. Zita could, at least, be honest. And now that she was no longer so concerned for Audrey's welfare, she was starting to get angry – she had, after all, been sitting around worrying for the past three hours.

'Don't see you in the village too much,' Harry said after a long pause. 'Don't see you walking round the countryside neither.'

'I got my hands full.' Truth was she saw no call for wandering around this countryside, or any other countryside. It was all right in its way, but . . . 'I miss London,' she confessed. 'That's why I go back so often. To re-charge me batteries.'

'Ah.' He paused. And was it her imagination, or was he looking with curiosity at the red jacket, damp from the rain, and at the bright bandana she wore to keep her hair in check? 'Why did you come here, then?'

That was a question and a half. Zita had often wondered herself. 'It's more than a job,' she said obliquely.

'Ah.'

'I've been with the family since Rowan was born. With Mrs Brunswick, that is,' she corrected.

'Rowan, eh? She's a right little adventurer, that girl.'

So he knew Rowan. Knew them all, perhaps. She felt ashamed that to her he had been merely another of those ageless Folyforth fishermen.

'Zita . . .' Audrey groaned.

'It's all right, love. We're just getting you home.' Zita squeezed

54

her hand, which felt limp and frail to the touch.

'An unusual name, that one,' he observed, shifting his weight so that Zita had even less to support. 'Zita . . .'

'I had an unusual mother.' She laughed. 'Me Dad chose my older sister's name – he called her Nell. Far too ordinary for me Mum. When I was born with red hair and dark eyes – so the story goes – Mum came over all melodramatic. It was Zita or nothing.'

'Pretty, I reckon.'

Zita smiled to herself in the dark as the silence stretched once more between them. He wasn't the most talkative of blokes, but what he did say, she liked.

'Will she be all right, d'you think?' He nodded towards Audrey.

'I'm no doctor.' Although privately she didn't consider that a doctor was what Audrey needed at all. Audrey insisted on seeing that specialist of hers regularly, and although Zita had all the sympathy in the world for Audrey, she couldn't help wondering if she needed what her Mum would have called a hefty kick up the arse, more than she needed those fancy tablets. What she did know was that Audrey was drifting farther and farther away from her, and all Zita could do now was to care for her and the girl as best she could.

'If you want, I could get hold of one. She seems kind of dozy.'

Audrey groaned once more. 'Will you two stop talking about me as if I weren't here?'

Harry jumped, loosening his hold, and she nearly fell.

'You're not here, are you?' Zita peered into her eyes. 'Not in mind anyway.'

'Don't be ridiculous.' Audrey straightened her hat. 'There's absolutely nothing the matter with me.'

'Apart from not being able to walk, that is.' Zita winked at Harry.

'I can manage perfectly.' Audrey leaned on Zita's arm with remarkable poise and took two wobbly steps forward. 'You see?'

Zita turned to Harry with some reluctance. His presence had been comforting somehow. 'I think we'll be all right from here. But thanks for your help. I couldn't have managed on me own . . .'

Audrey fumbled in her pockets. 'Please allow me to . . .'

Zita glimpsed the light dimming in his eyes as Harry turned away. 'No, Audrey.' Her voice was firm.

Audrey shot a look from one to the other. 'No, of course not. Ridiculous of me.' She smiled warily. 'Then, thanks.'

'No trouble, ma'am.' Harry touched his forelock – like a chauffeur from the old days, Zita observed – and stepped away and off into the night, the soft slap-thud of his footsteps receding down the lane.

'Nice man, mmm, Zita?' Audrey sighed.

Zita squeezed her arm. Odd, but she seemed almost back to normal. A remarkable recovery, or what? 'He's a nice man, all right,' she agreed.

Harry Penbray trudged back down to the village, and walked into the comforting arms of the Bull and Packet.

His wife raised dark and perfectly plucked eyebrows. 'You're late today.'

'Gettin' worried, were you?' He watched her pull his pint. A good looking woman was his wife – still in her prime and she knew it. She had all the blokes in this pub eating out of her hand. Sometimes he didn't mind sitting and supping and watching. But sometimes it made him sick.

'Don't kid yourself.' She slapped the tankard on the counter in front of him. 'I was thinking about our Glyn alone in the house.'

'He's all right.' Harry had no similar qualms about his son – he reckoned Glyn had the world worked out in a way Harry himself had never quite managed. But he was still Lynette's baby, Harry supposed.

'What would you know when you're not even there?' Her voice, scissor-sharp, changed abruptly. 'Yes, Dewy? What can I do for you?'

Dewy Jago – who lived with his family in the cottage next to the Penbrays, and ran a successful gift shop in the village – leered approvingly, sparing hardly a glance for Harry. Everyone knew who wore the trousers in the Penbray household, and that Lynette could do whatever she pleased. Living next door, Dewy probably knew more than most. 'That would be telling.' He grinned at Harry. 'Or as your old man's here, maybe I'll just have me a pint of best.'

How come she didn't tire of hearing the same old chat night after night?

'Been trying to get rid of him,' Lynette laughed. 'But he will keep hanging around. Anyone would think he didn't trust me.' She leaned over the bar and both men were treated to a glimpse of her impressive cleavage. 'What do you think, Dewy? You look after your family, you do. It's all right for some that can drink away and fill their stomachs on the money I earn, don't you reckon?'

'Have one yourself, my little darlin'.' Dewy grasped her hand and pressed a five pound note into it. 'You deserve it. You're a sight for sore eyes, you are. Have whatever you want.'

'It'll be a pleasure, you old charmer, you. I don't half envy that Tamsyn of yours. Some men know how to treat a lady . . .' Giggling, Lynette held his hand for a fair bit longer than necessary.

Harry got to his feet, his pint not even finished. His conversation with a decent woman walking up the hill was still hot on his mind, and this was another of those nights when his wife's behaviour made him sick.

'No sense of humour,' he heard her say as he walked out of the door. 'I don't know what I'm to do with him.'

But Harry knew Lynette wouldn't be worrying that he'd be angry. She knew him better than that. Maybe he didn't care enough to be angry any more.

He took a detour to check on the boat and nets. She never used to be like that, needing so much male attention, needing to believe she was wanted. He'd wed Lynette when she was only eighteen, just moved from South Cornwall. Crammed full of life that girl had been, and so good-looking that she'd plain knocked him out. He was ten years older, but he'd never really noticed it, not at first.

He wondered – many times he'd wondered – if it were his fault. If he'd tried to give her too much or not given her enough in those early days. If he'd treated her too much like his little girl. Even if this was her way of showing that he'd not fulfilled all her hopes, like. Had the young Lynette believed that her Harry would be a success? Had she expected him to give up fishing when it stopped being lucrative, hoped he'd open a gift shop like Dewy Jago perhaps, thought he'd be happy fleecing tourists in summer and taking it easy in the winter?

Harry would never know for sure, because on the rare occasions he brought the subject up – Harry wasn't one for talking himself – she wouldn't give him the time of day. Called him a crazy old fisherman to waste her time when she had dinner to get and a house to clean.

He knew that those men in the pub meant nothing to her – she was scathing enough about them once she got home. He knew that to Lynette being a barmaid was just a job, a job that allowed her to show herself off, get a bit of attention, and that she meant no harm. But still it saddened him, that she had to do that, saddened him that their marriage meant so little, that sometimes when he was out at sea he thought of her and couldn't imagine her any longer as being connected with him, only as separate. They had separate lives now.

Harry opened the door of the cottage but the place was silent and clearly unoccupied. 'Glyn!' he shouted anyway, just in case.

No answer.

He checked the boy's room. It was strangely bare of his character and interests – not as he would expect a teenage boy's room to be. But Glyn was like that, closed into himself, secretive, a loner. Harry loved his son, but he didn't know what made him tick. Glyn would make sure that no-one knew that.

Harry put on the kettle and wandered out into the yard. From here he could see the dark jagged coastline against the night sky as it folded out away from his sight, and the mass of black beyond that was the sea he loved.

He thought of Zita in her bright red coat, like some bird of paradise – so she missed London, did she? Harry shook his head. He'd never been there, couldn't imagine it somehow and certainly he wouldn't want it.

What was it like for her stuck up at that fancy house? Maid of all work most likely, for he couldn't imagine Madam Hoity-Toity lifting a finger. Was it any worse than his own life? Out at sea all hours, all weathers, lucky to catch enough to keep them in food and clothes? But out at sea he wasn't answerable to anyone – he was free, wasn't he? That was the difference. Whereas Zita – it sounded to him like she was there out of pity – or guilt.

A night-bird screeched in the distance and he squinted his eyes to see. Over on the far cliff, maybe half a mile away as the crow flies, a figure was silhouetted against the night sky, just visible from the light of a crescent moon as a cloud slipped away. It was Glyn. He knew that it was Glyn.

Harry went inside to fetch his pipe. 'What you doing up there, boy?' he said softly. Of course there was no answer, but as he watched, the figure turned and raced into the night, bound for home, no doubt. Harry shook his head and went back inside to make his tea. No need for Lynette to worry about that boy. He knew what he was about, no mistake.

A week before Rowan's fourteenth birthday, her father cornered her in the conservatory just as she was pulling on her trainers, about to race off to meet Glyn at the folly.

'Where are you off to, young lady?'

Rowan hated it when he called her that. 'Just going for a walk.' She felt herself prickly and defensive, unable to meet his gaze.

'I never see you these days,' he complained.

These days. She'd never seen much of him, had she? Why on earth should he pretend otherwise? And yet she knew what he meant. Once, there had been something more between them than this. But now he was entirely outside everything that mattered, outside her life. Now, there were sides in this family and Rowan had to take her place on one or the other. Her loyalty was to her mother and Zita – those who had cared for her. It was no contest as far as Rowan was concerned.

'I've been busy,' she told him.

'Busy!' He laughed.

Was it so very unlikely? Rowan didn't flinch. Yes, she'd been busy in the past month. Busy meeting Glyn Penbray in the dead-end wood that defied its very name in leading to the folly. Their folly, as she had come to think of it, for she was convinced no-one else knew of its existence, apart from Athwenna Trelawney. Still, the place only came alive when Glyn was there.

Sometimes Rowan dashed there straight from school, waited and waited, only to see no sign of him. On those days there was a chill in the very air she breathed. There was something undeniably creepy about the folly, in both the past and present of it, in the romance mingled with danger that still seemed to reside there.

On one of those days she was leaving the wood, squeezing under the barbed wire without checking that the lane was deserted as usual – disappointment that Glyn had not appeared making her careless – when she straightened and simultaneously became aware of an old woman standing by the gates of Folyforth House. Rowan stared at her.

The old woman, bent and dressed in black with a brown face as wrinkled as a walnut, held her gaze for several moments before turning to hobble down the driveway to Folyforth House. Astounded, Rowan came closer to watch her. But the house was empty . . . Surely the house was empty?

The old woman scrabbled in a purse for a key, fitted it in the lock and slipped inside. The curtains remained drawn, the house dark and silent. It seemed as empty as it ever had. Rowan frowned. Who was she?

Athwenna Trelawney? She asked herself as she ran home. Could it be? Glyn had implied that the wood was private property, he had also said that she should be able to work out for herself where Athwenna might live. And yet . . .

Rowan thought of her father's efforts to buy Folyforth House. She didn't know if he had bothered to find out who owned it – and what he had done about it if he had. The estate agent had not actually *said* that the house was empty. It was simply the assumption they had all made because they never saw anyone there, because the curtains were always drawn, the garden overgrown and the house itself in general disrepair. She smiled. She liked the idea of some old woman from the village living there, denying her father his desire to own the house, own the view, be the superior Lord of the Manor she was convinced he wanted to be.

And how much did Glyn know of all this? He had told her that the folly had been built in the eighteenth century. But the stories that Athwenna Trelawney would have to tell! To Rowan, the old woman seemed to be representative of Cornwall itself.

On the other days when Glyn came, soft and silent as a cat, the atmosphere lifted into something strange, new and exciting. They argued often. He teased her and made her mad with frustration and anger. Sometimes she would race away from him out of the wood and go home, furious tears stinging her eyes, bitter words on her lips. But always, she would regret it. Always she would count the hours until she could see him again.

And when it was good between them, it was revelation. He told her stories of Cornwall – a lot more interesting than Miss Trevis's – tales of treachery, smuggling and romance. He took her walking in the woods and taught her ways to use the plants and vegetation to survive. How to build a shelter, make a rope out of nettles without getting stung, and which plants, roots and fungi were edible.

'But how do you know all this?' she asked him.

'Instinct for survival.' He grinned.

'Oh, yeah?'

'My old man taught me.'

'Your father?' Rowan had tried to ask him about his parents, but Glyn was strangely reticent. Strangely reticent about all areas of his life apart from the one she shared with him here in the folly and the wood. She knew nothing of his friends or family, other than the existence of Jory Jago. But Jory, she guessed, meant little to him.

'Yes, my father,' he mocked, mimicking her tones. 'He's Cornish born and bred. A fisherman, like I told you before.'

'I'd like to meet him.'

His face darkened, the eyebrows drawing together as he frowned. 'That, you'll never do.'

She was hurt, but determined not to show it. 'Why not?'

He took her by the shoulders. 'Because, Rowan, you live in another world, don't you realise that?'

'I live *here*.' She stamped her foot, aware how childish it must seem. And she didn't want to appear childish to Glyn Penbray. 'We're living in the twentieth century, Glyn. The class system is a thing of the past. I know it is. Our teacher told us . . .'

She stopped talking as, very gently, he smoothed the dark hair from her face in the way he had done on the day they'd first met in the folly. As then, she wanted to fold under his touch like an animal might, the sensation bringing a perfect comfort.

'You live here, Rowan, because your father has earned enough money to buy a big house and he wants to escape from the big city where he earned all his big money in the first place.'

'You must despise us.' She hung her head, ashamed of her father. Why couldn't he have stayed where he was? Why was he trying to pretend to be what he wasn't? Why couldn't he be ordinary, why did he have to be different? Only then . . . Only then, she realised, if he'd stayed in London, she would never have met Glyn.

He drew her down to sit on a tree stump nearby. 'Of course I don't despise you.' He laughed. 'I think you're wonderful.'

'Don't tease me, Glyn.'

'I think you're beautiful.'

'Shut up.' But something in his voice made her look at him and just as quickly she looked away. She didn't understand what she was feeling – this sweet rush that came from deep inside, that streaked through her, that couldn't be dismissed. She felt it often when she was with Glyn and yet she'd never felt it in her life before. Could it be love?

'It's true. You are beautiful.' He leaned back, lazily, watching her.

'But I'm still different.' She knew he enjoyed disconcerting her, and she hated that. She never knew when he meant what he said. She jumped to her feet to create a distance between them.

'We can still be friends.' He got up, came closer.

'Friends?' she whispered.

'Hmmm.'

'But only here in the wood?' She wanted to get this straight, needed to get it straight. Knowing their limitations might give her some security.

'Isn't that enough for you?' He turned her to face him, held her face between his hands. Warm, warm hands.

Rowan closed her eyes. 'I don't know,' she said with honesty.

'Isn't it special?' His voice whispered deep into her. 'Isn't it something special, what we have here, in this wood, in the folly? Our private place.'

'But it isn't, is it?' She opened her eyes and stared at him.

'How do you mean?' His expression changed, and she was glad, feeling that at last she knew something that he wasn't aware of. He didn't know that she'd seen Athwenna Trelawney. For she was sure it was her. She had turned the strange meeting over in her head until she was sure. Who else could it be?

'I've seen her,' she whispered. 'She lives in the house, doesn't she? She knows about the folly, she must do.'

'Oh, that.' He grinned. 'Oh yeah, old Athwenna knows about the place – course she does. She knows more than anyone.'

'So . . .'

'She can't *get* here, can she? She don't even go down to the village any more. Someone brings up her groceries. Folk know she's here, but mostly they keep away. They think she's a witch.'

Rowan's eyes grew round. 'And is she?'

He snorted with derision. 'Don't talk daft. You're a little dreamer, you are.'

'But would she mind – me coming here, I mean?' Rowan didn't want to incur her displeasure, witch or not.

'What did she say to you?' He eyed her curiously.

'Nothing. She just looked at me.'

He nodded with satisfaction. 'Then she don't mind.'

'Simple as that?'

'Simple as that.'

'You're sure?'

'I'm sure.' He chuckled, stroked her cheek. 'But apart from Athwenna . . . No-one knows about the folly, about us?' His fingers tensed. 'You haven't told anyone, have you Rowan?'

She glared at him. 'No! No, of course I haven't. We agreed . . .'

'Good girl.'

She stared at him. His eyes weren't just green as she'd once thought. They were flecked with greys and browns, the lashes were long, slightly curling – some girls would die for those eyes.

He spoke, and the words didn't reach her brain, she was too busy staring at him. He was beautiful, that was the truth. 'What did you say?'

He grinned. 'I said – I bet you've never been kissed. Such a dreamer . . . Little innocent Rowan.'

The sweet rush came again, low, long, hot and scary. 'Of course I have.'

'Oh yeah?' He leaned closer.

'Yeah.' He'd know she was lying. She ducked under his arm and ran, through the trees, swift and sure, hearing herself snap twigs and bracken, hearing his laughter and his footsteps as he ploughed after her. Faster and faster she ran, oblivious to the trees and brambles scratching her bare arms and legs, as if she were running for her life. And sometimes it seemed like that – the only way to get rid of the sweet rush was to run, and run for your life.

63

'I'm coming after you . . .' he called. 'I'm gonna catch you, Rowan Brunswick.'

'No chance!' She ducked under branches, swerved and twisted. Her legs were as long as his, but this was his world – he'd as good as grown up in this habitat – and she knew he was gaining on her.

She came upon the path, her chance for escape. If she went to the right it would lead her out of the wood, and he wouldn't follow her because she'd be out of their shared territory. If she went to the left she would come to the glade and the folly and he would catch her for sure. She paused for a split second.

There was another option. Another fork to the path, overgrown and disused but still there nevertheless, a way she hadn't taken before, not leading to the folly but staying in the wood. She took it.

'Rowan!' She heard him yell. 'Rowan, not that way!'

Hah, she had him now! She would go a bit further and then swerve round and circle back. She plunged on, the path getting more and more difficult, with brambles and tall clumps of thistles spreading thick in front of her and slowing her down.

'Rowan!' He shouted something that she didn't quite catch. This should be slowing him down too, but he was still gaining on her and faster than before. Rowan was tiring. She wasn't quite sure why she was doing this – what was she trying to run away from?

There was a moment when the trees changed in character – a fact that nudged at her brain but got no further. A moment when the pathway cleared before her, but she was going so fast that she couldn't stop. And then he was on her, grabbing her waist from behind, pulling her backwards towards him, on top of him with a force that amazed her. Digging his heels into the soft grass that had appeared so abruptly along with the kind of wind-crippled trees that she'd often seen before – at the cliff edge.

Rowan sat up, looked down at the drop not six feet away. 'Jesus Christ.' She crawled closer on her hands and knees until she could see the deserted bay maybe four hundred feet below – shingle, sand and clumps of granite, and the sea creeping closer in neat crimped curls. 'Bloody hellfire.'

'Not nice language for a lady,' he drawled. 'Especially not a little innocent like you.'

She crawled back to him. He was still panting from the exertion of catching her, his pupils dilated, his hair stuck with bramble pins and briars, and a scratch livid across his face. Rowan traced the line of it with her fingertip. He winced.

'Does it hurt?'

He shook his head.

'Brave boy.' Laughter was in her eyes. Laughter and relief. She looked at him. And love. She became solemn. 'You saved my life.'

He shrugged. 'Do I get a reward?'

She edged closer, not sure if she'd been shocked into it, or just got tired of running. 'Course you do.'

The kiss – when it came – was quite different from what she'd dreamed of. The rush began when his lips touched hers, swept through her as if her insides were being washed right out, and then exploded as he pulled her closer, as his tongue edged into her mouth, as his body hardened against hers.

When at last he released her, Rowan was lost for breath, for words, for the strength to move. They stayed there, the two of them, lying side by side but not touching and not moving, the late afternoon sun beating down on their bodies, the tension a minefield – too delicate even to approach – between them.

Eventually Rowan dragged herself to her feet. 'I've got to go.'

He nodded, watching her. 'Don't worry. You can trust me.'

She knew what he meant. 'Walk with me back to the path?'

It was the first time she had asked him for this. He smiled, jumped up and took her hand, as if this perhaps, was his very first triumph.

Rowan blinked up at her father, realising that he was still talking. Since that day there had been other kisses – but never any more than kisses. She was frightened, sometimes, at what she was feeling. Because what she was feeling was that she wanted more. Sometimes a kiss didn't seem enough now that she was used to them. Sometimes she wanted him to touch her, wanted to touch him. It shocked her. She shocked herself. She worried that she was a tart. Girls at school talked about other girls, called them tarts among other things. They seemed to know so much, they made Rowan feel such an idiot. She pretended to know it all, but sensed she knew nothing at all.

There was also pleasure, but the fear wouldn't go. Sometimes it seemed there was only fear, white, cold, slicing through her. What was she doing? Could she cope with whatever it was?

It was the first time she'd had no-one to turn to. Her friends from school were only companions to pass the time of day with – there was no-one she could trust. Her mother was acting crazy half the time, and Zita – well, Zita was a possibility, but Zita's loyalty was to her mother. Zita would tell Mum, Mum might tell Father . . . Then she would be stopped from going to the folly, from seeing Glyn, for sure.

Besides, she had promised him, hadn't she? Our secret, he had said. She couldn't betray that, betray him. So she must keep his existence from everyone, and the existence of her own opening sexuality as well. Even though it was a secret that seemed too vast and confusing to comprehend.

'So I wondered about a horse?'

Rowan stared at her father, quite baffled. 'What?'

'For your birthday.' Irritation. She noted it in the gesture of hand to hair.

'Oh.' She felt cold towards him. He seemed to have nothing to do with her. Almost as if her mother had . . . well, of course that was impossible . . . But how could this stiff and upright man who spent his time fiddling figures, playing with money as if life were Monopoly, as if everyone wanted to buy and sell and build at the right moment for profit alone, how could he be her father? It seemed extremely unlikely.

'*Oh*?' He laughed, but it was unconvincing. 'Is that all you can say to your old Dad?' He attempted to ruffle her hair, but she shrank from his touch, shrank from his pretence, his playing the jovial family man. She preferred it when he went to London and left them alone. At least then he was being himself.

'I don't really want one. Thank you,' she added politely, remembering her manners just in time. A horse would be part of the other world, the part that she didn't want. The part that had nothing to do with Glyn, that made her different – the little rich girl up on the hill.

'I see.' His eyes darkened, she recognised his anger. 'Do I take it you no longer want riding lessons then, if you don't want a horse of your own?' He paused, then – clearly unable to resist the temptation, 'Which most girls would do *anything* to have, let me tell you, young lady.'

'I don't have riding lessons any more.' She'd told Mum over a month ago that she didn't want to bother. It was taking too much precious time away from Glyn and the folly, for a start. And Glyn had laughed at her when she told him she went riding.

'Of course you do,' he'd mocked. 'In your little black hat and boots. All the best little rich girls go riding, don't they?'

'Since when?' her father spluttered.

She told him. 'Mum knows.' There was so much, she realised with a faint stab of pleasure, that her father was not aware of. He didn't know about the folly or Glyn, for starters. And he didn't seem to know about Athwenna Trelawney living in Folyforth House – the house he wanted to own more than he wanted any other thing, she suspected. A slow smile crept on to her face. She sensed that Athwenna would never let it go – a house so much a part of Folyforth's history.

'What your mother knows . . .' he began, then clearly thought better of it. He took a deep breath. 'Then what do you want for your birthday?'

'I don't know. I don't care.' What she wanted was to be free of this conversation, to be free to race off to the folly where Glyn would surely be waiting for her.

He turned to stare out into the garden. Rowan thought she heard him say, 'Ungrateful little cow', but she couldn't be sure.

'Can I go now?'

He spun around. 'Just where do you go to when you go off out every day?'

Her guard went up, panic rising. Despite what he didn't know, her father had the power to curtail her visits to the folly, the power to destroy her happiness. She shrugged with a casualness she was far from feeling, 'Oh, just around. I like walking in the country.' Pause. 'Sometimes Miss Trevis sets us nature trails for botany, you know. We have to collect specimens and stuff . . .' She eyed him warily.

He looked sceptical. 'Really?'

She nodded.

'And does it help you with mathematics?'

Rowan shook her head. 'Not my strong subject, I'm afraid.'

'Then you should practice.' He took a step closer and Rowan shrank against the wall. Even the smell of him she disliked these days, the pine-spice aftershave or whatever it was he splashed all over himself. But at least he hadn't started drinking yet today. That was the smell she hated most – the stench of whisky on his breath. And lately it had been there more often.

'Yes, Father.' It was a time for meekness. 'I will, I promise.'

'You should stay home more, study more, take more time over your homework, practise your maths.'

'Yes, Father.'

His eyes drifted through the window to the dining room, seemed to come to rest on the bottle of whisky sitting in the open cabinet. 'All right. Off you go.'

'Thanks, Father.' She flew. Out of the alien house where she didn't belong any more.

Glyn was wrong when he said that she wasn't part of the world he lived in. It was this world she no longer lived in, this world of her parents and money and horses for birthday presents, that she didn't relate to. It was different for Glyn. He only gave a part of himself to the wood, the folly, to Rowan. But as for Rowan, she wanted to give it all.

Chapter 4

———— ·•◆•· ————

'I can't help but notice . . .' Audrey sucked her paintbrush thoughtfully, 'that you've been going out a bit more than usual in the last week or so, Zita, hmm?'

These days she didn't so much paint, as contemplate. Looking at the pigments, the paper, or even the scene itself, did nothing to bring painting closer. It had only ever been, she supposed, a hobby. Still, she had enjoyed it, and without it she wasn't sure what was left.

'Nothing wrong with going out.' She heard Zita respond, faintly, as if she weren't in the same room.

No, there was nothing wrong in it. People went out, didn't they? It was a part of their lives to do so. But since overhearing that conversation in the café on the waterfront, that part of life seemed impossible for Audrey too. How could she go out? Probably the entire village knew that her husband was having an affair. He had made her a laughing stock. She had never asked much of him, but apparently this *thing* – as she referred to it in her mind – had been going on for years. Years! And she'd only moved her bed into her own green room a few weeks ago. It was quite insupportable.

'I didn't say there was anything *wrong* in it,' she murmured. Really, that powder yellow was very bright on the eyes . . .

'I've not let anything slide.' Zita was immediately on the defensive. She pushed a strand of loose red-brown hair back under the lime-green bandana.

But Audrey had noticed that Zita sometimes discarded the bandana when she went on these jaunts of hers. Sometimes she allowed her thick hair to cascade freely around her face and over her shoulders. 'Heavens, I'm not accusing you of anything.' How could Zita misinterpret her so? 'I know how hard you work.'

Zita made a snorting noise of disbelief.

'Zita . . .' Audrey surveyed her. She was looking different, too. A brightness in her eyes, a ruddiness in her cheeks, her hair windblown. She was looking almost . . . Audrey blinked. Almost sexy.

'Well?'

'I'm only interested,' she chided. 'Who wouldn't be? You spend years hardly leaving the house except to go back to London, then you go out three times in one week.'

'Who's counting?' Zita switched the vacuum cleaner back on.

Audrey waited patiently until she'd finished. 'I'm counting. And I'm curious too.' She watched her, this woman who had become friend, but never quite confidante. She had not, after all, told Zita about her husband's affair with that woman from the village. She wondered vaguely why not – perhaps, unlike other women, she had no need of a confidante, and it wasn't as if she loved him. But it wasn't just that, was it? If she didn't admit it out loud, it might remain only tittle-tattle. She had to do anything possible to prevent it becoming the kind of reality one had to actually deal with.

She dismissed it from her mind. 'I'm only curious,' she repeated.

Zita snorted once more. 'You know what curiosity did?'

'Zita, I am not a cat.' Audrey put down her brush and got to her feet. 'Is it a secret?'

'Not really.'

'Then . . . ?'

Stubborn silence.

Audrey sighed, aware that she was being unfair, ridiculous even. Why should Zita tell her a thing? Well, why should she? When all was said and done Zita was still her employee. Zita's life was her own. Or it should have been her own. It would have been if she had ever chosen to so take it.

Was that what she was doing now? Claiming a life of her own? Zita wasn't paid to reveal her private affairs, was she? But the injustice of her own behaviour made Audrey all the more determined to find out. 'So you refuse to tell me?'

Zita stood the vacuum cleaner upright and waited, hands on hips. 'Are you ordering me to, or what?'

'Of course not.' Disgruntled, Audrey looked away. Zita was not playing the game. Then she had a flash of inspiration. 'It's that man!'

'What man?' Zita spun on her heels to attack the dresser with her feather duster, but not before a deep and sudden flush had stained her cheeks and forehead. It made her look quite beautiful.

'So, it is!' Audrey felt almost well again, almost back to her old self for a minute. 'You've been seeing that man, haven't you? I know you have.'

They'd thought she was nothing but a zombie, the two of them, when they had brought her back from the café on the waterfront. And it had suited Audrey not to have to think, not to have to concentrate on even putting one foot in front of another. After what she'd heard . . . But of course she hadn't gone deaf. She listened to the conversation between Zita and the fisherman, and what's more she was aware of the barely discernible tension between the two of them. They had been attracted to each other. Sexually attracted. Fancy. Zita and some fisherman from Folyforth. Philip would have a fit. She smiled.

'No call to ask then, is there? If you already know.' Zita stomped across to the bookcase to refill it with the volumes of poetry that Audrey had left littered at different places round the room. Why was she reading so much poetry all of a sudden? Why was she so damned untidy?

And so what if Zita had been seeing Harry Penbray?

Zita had told herself that she'd only gone down to the waterfront for fresh fish. Admittedly there was fish in the freezer, and most days she would have made do – she doubted Audrey could tell the difference anyway, and she didn't give a monkey's what Philip thought. But the sun was shining, there was a sweetness in the air that drew her into the back garden where she grew her herbs and lavender, and Audrey had definitely said that she fancied some nice fish for dinner. From the back garden it was a short distance to the lane.

It's good to get out once in a while, she said to herself as she walked down the lane. It was very different in the daytime – quite pretty, with wild roses rambling over high hedges, and all manner of flowers covering the grassy banks at her feet. She really should do this more often . . .

She nodded good morning to a couple of villagers, walked briskly down to the waterfront and squinted into the sun. Not that she was looking for him. He probably wouldn't even be here. Maybe it was the wrong time of day . . .

Then she spotted him. His nets were still steaming in the warm sun – he'd obviously only just got in, and he was unloading fish into a big white tub. There you go. She grinned. You couldn't get much fresher than that. She fingered the tiny purse in her pocket, suddenly nervous.

Several others had obviously had the same idea because by the time she reached him there were two women in front, passing the time of day with Harry in lazy drawling Cornish dialect. Zita hung back. It wasn't just a matter of fresh fish. She wanted to thank him properly and all.

He saw her almost immediately, craning his neck round, such a great grin stretching across his face that the other two women stared round at her too, probably wondering who the heck she was.

It took an age for it to be her turn. As Harry served her, gutting the fish at high speed and with expert precision, the customer in front of Zita still hadn't moved off.

'It's good to see you.' He smelled of the sea, a salty tang clinging to his skin and hair, the blue of it in his eyes. He was wearing sea-stained baggy old jeans and a faded tee-shirt this morning. She stared at the hair on his arms – speckled fair, white and brown like his beard – smooth and fine on the dark weathered skin.

'And you.' Why was she so nervous?

'How's . . . ?' He grunted. 'Mrs Thingummy? How's she been keeping? All right?'

The other woman's eyes flicked back to them.

Nosey cow. Zita stared at her pointedly. 'Not so bad. She's picked up.'

'Glad to hear it.' He paused, seemed about to say something else, then turned round. 'Was there something else you wanted, Tamsyn?'

'Just looking.' She snapped her bag shut with a decisive click. 'No law against looking.'

'Depends what you're looking at.' He spoke under his breath, and they both giggled. Like a couple of kids, Zita thought.

'I wanted to thank you for your help,' she said when the woman called Tamsyn – now wearing a victimised expression – had moved out of earshot.

'You already did.' He handed her the packet of fish. 'Not that I'm complaining about being thanked twice, mind.'

'I hope you weren't offended by . . . well, you know.' Zita transferred the damp package to her other hand. 'When Audrey tried to give you something for your trouble.'

He shrugged. 'It's what she's used to.'

'She didn't mean . . .'

'I know that.'

'Good.' Fumbling with her purse, Zita paid him. What else could she say? She turned to go.

'You know . . .' He cleared his throat. 'It's not so bad, this little part of the Cornish coast. Some folk reckon it's real pretty.'

She smiled encouragingly. 'I'm sure.'

'And good walking. A lot to see.'

Zita put the fish in her string bag. The wind was gusting through her hair, and as she pushed it out of her eyes she saw someone else approaching Harry's stall from just across the bay. 'I wouldn't know about that. I've never been much of a walker.' She paused. 'Not that I didn't want to. Do some walking, I mean. Only I never got round to it somehow. I wouldn't know where to start.' God, what a load of waffle. Now why should he even bother with her?

He scratched his beard. 'Reckon I could show you a nice walk one of these days, if you ever had the time, like.'

The new customer was drawing closer.

Zita moved closer too. To Harry. 'When?'

'Whenever you like.'

They stared at each other for a moment.

'Got any cod, Harry?' Zita stood back while the woman was served, pretending an absorbing interest in the contents of Harry's white tub.

'Tomorrow lunchtime?' she suggested, when the woman had gone. Her heart seemed to be lurching through her rib cage. What on earth was the matter with her all of a sudden? He had only suggested a walk, she'd half talked him into it, and the man was certainly no Adonis. Neither was she anything to write home about, come to that.

'Tide'll be about right.'

'Oh. For fishing?'

'For walking round the headland.' He grinned.

She laughed in response. 'Shall I see you here?'

'Wagging tongues.' He frowned. 'I'll meet you up the lane by your house. I know a way through and down to the beach. We can bypass the village easy enough.'

She felt a thrill of excitement. 'And bypass the wagging tongues, as well.'

But she wasn't so sure of that when she walked past the shops and up the lane back home. Was it her imagination, or was she being watched already? Still, nothing could wipe the silly grin from her face. Maybe there was something to be said for living in the country, after all.

'I bet he's married.' Audrey began to hum softly.

'We only went for a bit of a walk – or a couple of walks, I should say.' Zita smiled at the memory. She'd had no idea walking could be so darned pleasant. Not just because of the store of interesting information she'd drawn from him about the countryside he'd grown up in, although that was an eye opener in itself, but also the feeling of companionship, of being side by side, in contact with a like human being, with Nature and with the elements. The elements had mainly been what prevented her from getting the washing out or made her draw the blinds, before.

'You can still get into trouble going out walking with a married man,' Audrey pointed out. 'If he *is* married.'

Damn and blast her. 'Walking never got anyone into trouble.'

It had come as a bit of a shock, mind. She hadn't expected him to be married. Silly, really. Why shouldn't he be? It was just that he'd seemed a loner. Lonely too. In need.

'His wife might cause you some trouble.' Audrey drew her cardigan closer around her thin shoulders. Her grey eyes were inscrutable. 'If he has one.'

Zita snapped. 'I know he's married, all right? And I don't give a damn about his wife. He's just a friend. That's all.'

* * *

It had been practically the first thing that Harry had told her . . .

'You'll maybe know already,' he had said. 'I've got a wife, in name.'

'I see.' She hadn't.

'I don't love her – haven't for years. But there's our boy. I reckon he keeps us together.'

'Don't you care about him being married?' Audrey asked. 'There's hardly much future in it.'

'Who said I was looking for a future?' Zita hated the streak of cruelty that she occasionally witnessed in Audrey. That supercilious way she had of looking down her nose sometimes, after you'd done all you could and yet she still wanted more. Zita knew, mind, what this was all about. Audrey was just scared she'd lose her. But why should she lose her? When he was married . . .

'Still, everyone needs something in the future to look forward to.' Audrey looked unsure of her ground. Did she feel that *she* had much of a future married to Philip Brunswick?

'Harry's isn't much of a marriage.' Zita knew she shouldn't be drawn further into this conversation. She hadn't wanted to discuss Harry in the first place. She had wanted, childishly perhaps, to hug the secret of him close to herself for a while.

Audrey looked up from her painting. 'Isn't that what they all say?'

'No, it bloody well isn't.' Wasn't she entitled to her own life for a change – without being lectured over the rights and wrongs?

Then she realised. Audrey was bitter about something else. This wasn't just to do with Zita and Harry. This was about Audrey as well. There was something . . . 'You're jealous.'

Hardly reacting, Audrey stooped to pour fresh tea. 'Perhaps I am.' Tears filled her eyes, the emotion coming so swiftly that Zita was shocked.

'Audrey . . .'

'Perhaps I am.' She grasped Zita's hand. 'Or perhaps I can't help seeing things from the other side.'

'The other side?' Zita frowned, but Audrey only shook her head.

'God knows you deserve some happiness. But a married man . . . Will he give you any?'

* * *

Meanwhile, the man to whom Audrey was married was lying fully dressed on a lumpy bed in a seedy hotel in a town a safe ten miles away, watching his mistress take off her clothes.

She never failed to excite him, even when she wasn't trying, like today. God, it had been a long time. Too long. 'I've missed you, sugar.' His voice was husky.

'Why d'you leave it so long before you phone me, then?' She slipped off her blouse to reveal breasts squeezed together and uplifted into seemingly perfect large globes of white flesh by an expensive, wired black lace bra he'd bought her six months ago. 'Why do you only phone me when you want what you think you're always going to get? What's always on offer . . . ?'

Philip smiled approvingly, and simultaneously his throat went dry. Jesus, how he wanted her. How he wanted those delicious tits to sink on top of him, to sway in front of him, to . . .

'You're not even listening,' she complained.

'I am.'

'You're not. You're leering.' As she undid the last button, her skirt fell to the floor and she stepped neatly out, scooping it up and draping it across the chair.

Despite himself, he caught his breath again, guessing his eyes were bulging, and by now his erection was too.

'Don't you think I know you well enough by now to be able to see when you're leering?'

Did she know him well? Philip liked to think that he remained a mystery to the women in his life, but he couldn't be sure. This woman certainly knew what he wanted before he even knew himself, and as for Audrey . . . Well, Audrey didn't seem to care much one way or another these days.

He was beginning to wonder if he understood women at all. It had seemed so simple at one time. He had followed his father's lead, learned to do without the kind of emotion he only vaguely recalled from his own mother.

He had married Audrey because she had both class and money, and because he'd recognised in her an untouched quality that he knew to be rare. He could have it all – he had still thought that when the woman with him now in this sleazy room first came into his life. Oh,

he'd excused himself by saying he'd never have needed a woman like
this if Audrey had possessed an ounce of the sensuality he craved . . .
But still, Philip was left with the feeling that something had passed
him by.

'Come here.' He held out his hand beseechingly, but she stayed
where she was. Why was she giving him such a hard time today?
Why all these questions? He only had an hour. Shouldn't she be in
his arms by now?

'Don't know if I should, when I'm not appreciated.'

His spirits fell. 'What's the matter?' Why did they have to talk so
much before sex? Why couldn't they just get on with it? She was
wearing black lacy knickers and suspenders to match. God bless this
woman for never wearing tights. Where was the pleasure in tights?

'I hate this place.' Walking over to the fireplace, still in her high
heels, she helped herself to some of Philip's whisky. He didn't like to
see her drinking it, it didn't seem quite right, he saw her as more
suited to sipping something sweet, light and frothy. Dressed like that
too. And frothy conversation with plenty of giggles in between. That's
what he wanted from her.

But Philip chose to say nothing. Because he wanted to get her into
bed even more.

'Jesus . . .' She looked around her.

'What's wrong with this place?' He sighed. It seemed perfectly
convenient to him – and he always gave her the taxi fare, didn't he?

'Need you ask?' There was bitterness in her voice, and he hated it
when she whined. 'It's seedy, it's grubby, it's a tacky little hole. The
bed's uncomfortable, the wash-basin's chipped and there's never any
hot water.'

'Is that all?' He hoped to make her laugh, but clearly she wasn't in
a laughing mood.

'No, it is not.' She poured more whisky. 'The woman on the desk
always looks me up and down like I'm a prostitute.' She glared at
him as if challenging him to deny this.

'We'll go somewhere different next time,' he soothed. He didn't
bloody care where they went, so long as it had a bed, privacy and
didn't cost a fortune. Even the bed wasn't strictly necessary. But
now . . .

'Come here, sugar, for Christ's sake.' He had an ache, such an ache. He had let it build for weeks, but now he needed release.

She held back. Her breasts seemed to be straining against the lace of her bra. 'You said that last time. And the time before. You said we wouldn't be coming here any more.'

Had he? He couldn't even remember. He was liable to make any promise in the heat of the moment, not always so likely to keep it. 'I'm sorry. This time I mean it.'

She looked doubtful.

'I do.' This time . . . He groaned. 'Come here, will you?'

'And we haven't been away for a week-end in ages. I can't even remember the last one.' She kicked off her shoes just as he'd been imagining her walking across his back in them. Though perhaps she was a bit on the weighty side for that, these days. He'd read stories . . . But did people really do that kind of thing? In his briefcase Philip had some natural yoghurt. Once, she'd let him . . . He shifted his position. Mustn't think of that. She wasn't always so willing these days, although a couple of times she'd been tempted by strawberries and cream.

'I will take you away for the week-end,' he sighed. 'Anything. Anywhere. Any time.' He must go to London, couldn't keep putting it off. There was no denying that something funny was happening on the market – he had a nose for these things, although this time he'd been a bit slow on the uptake. Too many other worries, he supposed. Audrey, Rowan, that bloody Folyforth House that he was determined to get his hands on. There had been some opposition, but as he'd told Audrey, it had been relatively easy to find out who paid the bills. Athwenna Trelawney – what kind of name was that, for God's sake? But more importantly for Philip's purposes she was a woman – probably old, most likely alone. She wouldn't stand a chance . . .

And he was equally determined to get his hands on this woman in front of him. 'Sugar . . .'

'When?' She downed the second whisky in one.

'Soon.'

'Next week-end?'

Philip groaned. It was almost as if she'd engineered this whole situation to create this choice for him. 'It's Rowan's birthday. I'll have to be around for that.'

'That girl . . .' She turned away. 'She makes me sick.'

'Sugar . . .'

'You owe me, Philip Brunswick.' She spun around, her eyes dark fury. 'And don't you forget it.'

Philip got to his feet, went to her and took her hand.

'Sugar, what is it? What's wrong?'

She shook her head.

Philip couldn't understand it. She never used to be like this. She used to be – for years – so compliant, so sweet. 'Is it your period?' he asked softly. No-one could accuse him of not being understanding.

She broke away. 'No, it is not my fucking period,' she yelled.

He was shocked and silenced. Sometimes he wondered if she was as surely his as he'd always imagined. Sometimes he even wondered if he knew her at all.

She sat on the bed and he sat beside her. It must be her hormones playing up. He just had to learn to handle her in a slightly different way, that was all. It wouldn't take long. 'Don't I give you enough?'

She wouldn't look at him.

'Don't I?'

'Not lately.'

He tilted her chin. So that was it. He'd been neglecting her. 'What would you like? A nice little present?'

'I've got no use for any of it, have I?' But she didn't protest as he undid the clasp of her bra and caught her breasts, cradled in his arms as they fell from their constraint. At last, at last. She'd just been playing hard to get, teasing him.

'Money then?' He leaned closer, took one in his mouth, slowly, lovingly. He'd make her feel better. He knew how to please her.

'How would I explain it?' Her voice sounded bleak, much bleaker than it should when Philip was sucking her breasts, his mouth swooping from one to the other, fondling them with eager fingers.

'You'll think of something, you clever girl.' His voice was muffled against the warmth of her. His mouth travelled up her neck and to her lips. To his surprise he still liked kissing her.

She pushed him away. 'You smell horrible today. You stink of whisky.'

Anger stabbed into his head. Anger and frustration too. She was being a right little charmer. And after all he'd done for her . . . 'I'm not the only one who's been drinking whisky. I'm surprised you can smell it at all.'

Her expression changed. 'I may have the odd glass. I may *need* the odd glass.' She stared at him pointedly. 'But I'm not a bloody alkie, Philip Brunswick.'

'I never said you were.' He watched, in both relief and despair as she got to her feet, and pulled off her knickers. At least she was going to come across. But she also knew quite well that he liked to take them off himself.

'Let's get it over with, then,' she said in a cool voice.

Philip was crushed. In that moment he almost wanted to strangle her. Once, she had given him something that was even better than sex. She had made him feel . . . Jesus, as if he were really important. And now . . . Now, she was beginning to remind him horribly of Audrey. And that wasn't all. Now she was making him wither inside. He snapped. 'What is it with you? What the hell do you want from me?' He knew he was shouting. He could feel the vein throbbing in his temple. He was shouting because she was pushing him too far. His right eye was twitching spasmodically – he'd hardly slept last night re-doing the figures and trying not to think of sex.

'Not to be shouted at, that's for sure,' she yelled back, grabbing her knickers and pulling them on again. 'I can get that just about anywhere.'

He tried to stop her, taking her hands, suddenly scared, realising too late what was happening. God, no. He had to have her and he had to have her now. 'Okay, next week-end, then. Whatever. We'll go somewhere nice. Only let me do that, sugar. Let me touch you . . .' God, he didn't want to even listen to himself. She was making him sound pathetic.

She pulled away from him. 'What about *Rowan*?' Her voice was bitter and sneering. He didn't like that, but right now it wasn't his first consideration.

'I'd rather be with you.' Well, that was what she wanted to hear, wasn't it? She hated Rowan, he knew that. It was a complicated situation, but he couldn't think of that now.

'And I've changed my mind.' Evading his groping hands, she pulled on her bra and clipped the beautiful globes back into place. 'I don't want to see you next week-end. I can't. I've got other things to do.'

Philip groaned. 'Paris. Amsterdam. Florence. Take your clothes back off, will you?' He lunged.

She squirmed away. 'No.'

'Where then?' He stood, hands outspread, feeling a fool. Who was he kidding? He had no control whatever over this woman. When he needed her, he'd offer her anything.

'Nowhere.' She pulled on her skirt. 'I'm making no bargain with you today, Philip Brunswick. I'm not providing sex in return for Paris. I'm no prostitute. And I want more than that.'

'Please, sugar . . .' Damn and blast her. He wanted to strike out at her. He wanted to force her to stay with him. He wanted to force himself on to her, for God's sake. But he didn't move. He felt suddenly lost and impotent. He watched her leave him and she left without a backward glance.

When she had gone, he went over to carry on watching her from the window.

She crossed the street, high heels clicking towards the taxi rank. Panic, frustration and anger cocktailed inside him, stirring and shifting until he felt sick. He didn't know what else to do so he slammed his fist against the wall.

'Damn!' It made him feel a bit better so he did it again. 'Damn, damn, damn!'

Chapter 5

———◆———

'You said you'd got me a present.' Rowan glanced at Glyn from under her eyelashes, feeling more confident of him today. Today put her on a level pegging with him. It was her fourteenth birthday.

'I did?'

'Uh huh.' She knew he was teasing her again. He'd whispered it yesterday, whispered into her hair, just before he waved her goodbye. 'Make sure you come tomorrow. I'll have a present for you.'

'What kind of present did you want from me?' He laughed, but there was a harshness in it. He held a broken twig in his hand, and was prodding it into gaps between the granite castellations, digging out bits of clay and dirt. She wanted him to stop that, wanted his attention for herself – at least for a while.

'Whatever you've got me, of course.' She cupped her chin in her hands, watching him. He was being sulky today, and he shouldn't be like that, not on her birthday.

'Maybe whatever I got isn't good enough for a girl like you.'

Rowan frowned, hating it when he made them different, when he tried to drive wedges of separateness between them. She lived in a world apart from him, he always said. But despite everything – maybe because of everything – she wanted them to be joined in some way that would close them off from the rest of civilisation. That would cement them together for good. 'I don't want anything in particular.'

He dropped the twig, grabbed her round the waist and hoisted her up on to the castellated edge of the folly's battlements. She supposed she should be scared – she was certainly a long way from the ground – but she only grinned and swung her legs like a little kid. She trusted him.

'You're the queen of the castle,' he murmured. His green eyes were unblinking.

She didn't understand Glyn Penbray at all, he was totally unlike anyone she'd ever known before. 'And what does that make you?'

It was a hot July day, but instead of wearing the cotton shorts Zita had left on the bed and which seemed too childish for a girl of her newly acquired years, Rowan had sneaked out of the house wearing a skirt that clung to her narrow hips and came half way up her thighs. And she was glad she'd done so when she saw the way Glyn looked her, rapidly, up and down with an intensity that burned into her, before turning his attention to the twig and the castellations of the folly.

He relaxed. 'I know what I am, don't you fret about that.' He rested his hands lightly, very lightly, one on each of her thighs, just above the knee. She looked at them, dark brown olive hands, loving the warmth of his skin, but scared too. Scared of the small spirals of white light spinning round in her belly. She was higher up than him. If he bent slightly, his dark head could rest on her legs and she'd feel the harsh tangled curls tickle her flesh.

'When will you trust me?' She addressed the air just above his head.

'Don't I trust you?' He moved away and she was immediately desolate.

'No, you don't.' She hung her head. 'And you haven't got any present to give me either. You forgot.'

'I didn't know what you wanted.' He shrugged.

'You could have guessed.'

'Yeah.' He picked up the twig again. 'I could have guessed, all right. A little present wrapped in gold paper. A little something that I bought from a little shop somewhere. That's what you'd have liked.'

She blushed furiously, jumped down from the parapet, grabbed his arm. 'No, it's not.' How could he think so little of her? After their times together – their walks, their talking, that kiss . . . and all the ones that had followed. Deep kissing that seemed to suck out her soul.

'What then?' He looked into her eyes.

'Whatever you want to give me.' She gazed back at him, eyes unblinking, sure he'd hear her heart pumping away like that of some mad creature.

'I'll give you something, birthday girl.' He touched her hair. 'But you're not dressed for it today.' He glanced down at the skirt and Rowan instantly regretted her choice. She should have worn jeans and sweltered.

'Oh, yes I am.' She couldn't bear not to see it now, whatever it was. 'I can do anything in this old thing that I can do in jeans.' Hands on hips, she watched him. 'If there really is something . . .' She let the words hang, knowing he wouldn't resist.

'You sure?' Glyn seemed to be making some mental calculation. Slowly, he dusted his hands on his blue denims.

'I'm sure.'

Still he hesitated. 'Well . . .'

She wrapped her arms around his neck, her lips close to the gypsy earring he wore in his ear lobe, sniffing the slightly animal scent of him that she loved. 'Glyn, please . . .'

He grinned, seeming to make up his mind. 'Come on, then. Follow me.'

They ran down the narrow spiral staircase, out into the warm glade and across to the wood. At the fork in the path he turned towards the cliff.

'Glyn?' She waited.

'You were the one talking about trust. Don't you trust *me?*' One flash of his eyes and he was gone. She could either wait here and be safe, or follow him and find out what the mysterious gift might be. She grinned. No contest.

Rowan ploughed through the brambles after him, thorns and prickles scraping and stinging her bare legs, furious that she was unable to take the big strides necessary to keep up with him. 'Damn this thing.' She felt like ripping the skirt right off.

At the cliff edge he was waiting for her. 'This way.'

'Glyn!' She thought for one horrible moment he was going to plunge over, but he took a sharp left – Rowan wouldn't have dared to put a foot there in case it was just fresh air – and disappeared from view behind a wind-crippled gorse bush.

'Glyn?' Tentatively she followed him. The breeze was strong up here, it shunted strands of dark hair into her eyes, billowing her white blouse from her body. Angrily she held back the hair with one hand, grabbing precarious handholds with the other.

As she rounded the gorse she almost fell over him sitting, waiting for her. 'Brave girl,' he teased, reminding her of how she had once teased him, when they sat near the cliff edge just before their first kiss.

'Where are we going?' She crouched down beside him.

'This is it.' He pointed ahead.

'It?'

'Your present.' He jumped to his feet.

She was confused. 'But what . . . ?'

'It's a path.' He turned around and inched his foot out behind him. 'A secret path. And I'll show you where it leads.'

Rowan stared at the sea beyond and below, shimmering into the distance like some great carpet billowing in the breeze. 'We're going down?' Was he mad?

'All the way.' He grinned. 'Hitch up your skirt.'

She hesitated for a moment, but there was no other way if she wanted to go further. She hitched it right up almost to her knickers. Freedom at last.

Glyn hardly blinked. 'Now take my hand.' He stretched it out and she did so. She realised belatedly that she would follow him anywhere. She did trust him. She knew he would keep her safe.

'It's a good path, but take the first bit slowly. Okay?'

She nodded. Her tongue was brackish inside her dry mouth, her limbs tense with the effort of keeping balance on the steep downhill slope. This wasn't how she'd envisaged passing her birthday at all. What on earth would they say at home? She shivered. But she knew where she'd rather be – wherever Glyn Penbray wanted to take her.

As he'd predicted, the going was treacherous at first, then the path became more easily passable, and she began to relax, even enjoy the descent. It had been cut into the granite a long time ago, she guessed, and was flanked by gorse bushes that probably made their progress invisible from both the cliff top and even from down below, since the path twisted and turned so many times.

She tried not to look down, tried to focus only on the patch of ground at her feet, but the sharp twists in the path and the breeze buffeting her bare legs made her dizzy. She shook her head angrily, but felt almost drunk with the movement, the height, and the smell of the hard dry granite and the gorse, and as they got closer, the damp rocks and sand down below.

At last they reached the bay, and she collapsed on the sand beside him. Of course she had been here before when walking along the beach from further up the coast, beyond Folyforth House. But then it had not been cut off by the tide, then it had not been a secret place.

'I'll never get up to the top again.' She looked back the way they'd come. There was absolutely no clue that the path existed – even the start of it was hidden behind some sea lavender and a huge lump of granite.

'Maybe you won't have to.' He lay down on the sand, staring up at the sky, shielding his eyes with his hand.

'Why not?'

He pointed. 'Tide's on its way out. We're only trapped here for the next hour. After that you could walk on round to the village if you don't fancy the climb.'

She turned on to her belly, raising herself up with her elbows. 'An hour!'

'Somewhere you had to be?' His arm looped out, he caught her by the shoulders and pulled her towards him. Their faces were only inches apart. Rowan felt every nerve tingling. Would he kiss her again? He didn't kiss her every time they were together, but when he did . . . When he did, she no longer trusted herself.

'They'll wonder where I am.' She forced herself to hold back. Didn't nice girls always hold back? But there was a cruel stiffness in the neck that she longed to relax, to allow to fall against him.

'Let 'em wonder.' His voice was a balm for her nervousness. Like the lulling roll of the waves behind them, it soothed her into a kind of unreality, a kind of peace. It swept conscience and concerns from her mind.

She let her head rest on his chest. It felt hard and yet strangely comforting, as if this were its proper place.

His hands were on her hair, caressing, sending small spindles of desire through her head, her limbs, her body. She relaxed, slowly, the tension ebbing from her as surely as the tide. The salt smell in her nostrils, the hot sun dripping down on their two bodies, surrounded them in a hazy intimate embrace, wrapped them with each other, separated them from the rest of the world. Exactly how she wanted to be . . .

And as she lay there with his hands playing with her hair, listening to the sea, Rowan realised that Glyn had given her a special present, one that she should treasure far more than a new piece of jewellery or a CD. He had given her a piece of himself, a private piece of the land with which he was so interlocked, and a piece of his own privacy.

'Who else knows about this place?' she whispered.

'Far as I know, only you and me.' His hand strayed to her neck. His chest was rising and falling in rhythm with his breathing. Her head too, rising with him, seemed connected to his heart.

'Thank you, Glyn.' She wondered who had carved the pathway. Who had known, in days gone by, about the cliff, the wood and the folly? Who had lived here, as she and Glyn lived here? Who had loved here as . . .

She was barely conscious of his fingers trailing across the back of her thighs. His dark probing fingers, running narrow channels of longing into her skin. Her skirt was still hitched up, of course. But surely he wouldn't . . . ?

And then – whilst she was still lost in that same dreamy state, of heat and touch and sensuality – she felt the same fingers up high, pushing apart the fabric of her skirt at the top of her thighs, his touch on the delicate rawness of her legs. Close, very close.

And she wanted to open for him. She wanted to shout for him, pull him close and open her legs to him in welcome. The channels of longing were getting wider, and the sweet rush was climbing up, up into her belly, into her womb it seemed. She could feel it turn into liquid warmth as he thrust his hand up her skirt just a little too hard, a little too quickly, and she was jerked back to reality with a judder of fear mixed with desire. 'Glyn!' She raised her head, pushed the invading hand away.

He laughed. 'You shouldn't have worn that skirt.' No apology, no thought for her.

Frantically she pulled it down, but of course it wasn't very long in the first place. 'Don't blame me. I *thought* I could trust you.' She rolled away from him, almost unable to bear the feel of the air now between them. She sat up. What happened next?

'You *can* trust me.' He sat up too, reached out his hand again, this time for her breast.

She watched fascinated, as he touched it through the white cotton of her blouse and bra, his thumb so gentle on her nipple. He smiled, cradling her small breast in his palm. The desire returned, with such unexpected force that she closed her eyes as if that way she could control it.

'You know you want to.' His voice, hypnotic, was cradling her mind as his hand cradled her breast.

'I've never done this before.' Scared, she looked into his eyes. What could she see there? A kind of timelessness that only drew her nearer to him. And a dark desire.

'So?' He undid the top two buttons of her blouse. Shouldn't he be saying something? Telling her that she was beautiful? That he wanted her, that he loved her, that he couldn't live without her?

'You haven't said that you . . .' she began.

'Words.' He slipped her blouse from her shoulders. 'We don't need them, Rowan. You *know.*'

Did she? She was used to words, even if they did state the obvious sometimes. With words at least you knew where you were. Or did you? After all, they were only as true as the person who spoke them. And this boy . . . This boy . . .

Glyn eased her skirt up to her waist.

Suddenly aware of her state of undress she darted a look behind her. 'Someone might come.'

'No-one can.' He un-clipped the skimpy lace bra that she was so proud of. It had been one of Zita's birthday presents – she at least was aware that Rowan was growing up. 'The tide's too far in.' He held her breasts again, this time skin to skin, his palms rubbing against her nipples.

She groaned. 'But Glyn . . .' A pure primeval terror streaked through her, cutting through her longing. What was she doing? What were they doing? 'I'm only fourteen,' was all she could think of to say. He must understand that she couldn't possibly go all the way.

He traced a pattern around her breast with his fingertip. 'How old do you want to be?' he teased.

'But . . .'

Zita's voice filled her head. She pulled away from him. Zita's talk about periods and pregnancy, boys, sex, drugs, Aids. It never stopped. The perils of the world according to Zita – and there sure were a lot of them.

But what about the need to live a little? The need to find out for yourself what it was all about?

This thing – this thing that was taking over all her senses, the most beautiful sweet rush in the world, was one of Zita's perils. Was that really fair? Did you have to pay for those pleasures? Or was there another way?

'Hush. I'll be careful,' he said.

She wanted to trust him. She looked into his eyes and she wanted to trust him more than she wanted anything. Even more than she wanted this. 'Not all the way, Glyn,' she whispered.

He smiled. Slowly he took off his shirt. His chest was half-boy's half-man's. There were the beginnings of dark chest hair, but there were narrow shoulders and hips, tight muscles, no redundant flesh, his dark skin stretched taut over a wiry frame. She put her hands on his shoulders, feeling the warmth, conscious of the answering warmth in her.

'You haven't even kissed me,' she said, her lips moving towards his. With her fingertips she touched the tiny cleft in his chin.

'I'll kiss you.' His eyes glazed over in a curious way. He seemed to Rowan, in that moment, to belong to another age, another time. Then his mouth was on hers, his tongue on her lips, in her mouth, his tongue on her tongue, coating her with honey. His hands were on her breasts, her belly. He swung her over on to her back, and she was under him, his fingers exploring once more, her legs, the sharp angles of her hips. Together they pulled off the last of her clothing, his clothing, until they were naked in the sand, rolling over, giggling, covered in each other's sweat, sand, saturated with each other's desire.

At last he pinned her down. His mouth hovered over her breast, his body over hers. 'I'll kiss you all over,' he said.

She closed her eyes because she couldn't hang on to the sight of him as well as to the touch. It was too much. That's when she knew she was lost to him. Any other voice she'd ever listened to faded into glorious insignificance. All the way was the only way to go. She belonged to him, body and soul.

Zita was sitting outside the back door, head in hands, thinking.

She'd never been one for that, she realised. When she was a kid – perhaps. But since she'd been with the Brunswicks . . . no, she only did the planning kind of thinking – what to cook for dinner, the next job on her list, when she'd have time to put her feet up and read the problem page in her favourite magazine. And she always planned whilst getting on with something else, because wasn't it a waste of time otherwise? While mixing a batter or vacuuming – that sort of thing.

But this kind of thinking . . . She'd never done it. It was more a kind of dreaming, she supposed.

She was here on the step because no-one but her ever came out this way, and because just now Audrey had caught her sitting on the stairs, feather duster conspicuously inactive.

'Zita! What in heaven's name are you doing?' she'd asked.

Well, it must have looked pretty strange, a woman of her age sitting dreaming on the stairs like some little kid. Although if anyone might understand, surely Audrey . . .

'Nothing.' She held her ground.

And Audrey merely turned and drifted back into the green room. 'You never used to do that,' Zita thought she heard her say.

No, she never used to do that.

So why was she doing it now?

Her thoughts drew her back to the time when she'd joined this family. At twenty-eight, she'd been disillusioned to say the least. 'Unlucky in love' as her Mum put it to all and sundry. Matter of fact she'd been engaged to a right bastard who took advantage and then dumped her. Might as well call a spade a spade.

'You need to get away, love,' Mum had said, clicking her tongue and providing an ample bosom to cry all those tears on. 'You've given him your best years, but it's not the end of the world. Why don't you look for another job? That shop'll never be enough for you.'

Mum was right. She always was. The department store had not

provided the quick promotion it had promised, and although she'd been there for years Zita had never fitted in – never found it easy to be polite to difficult customers, never really felt herself. But more than that, she wanted to escape from the cliquey mentality of the place. It was swamping her. They all knew about Reg, and they knew that he was now seeing Doreen from the accounts office as well. There would be sniggering and whispering. There already was, and the more she looked like she didn't care, the more it bruised her inside.

Then she saw Audrey's ad. That would be different all right.

The woman who answered the smartly painted front door in Kensington was cool but friendly. 'I need some help with the house,' she told Zita. 'Bits of ironing, cooking and cleaning. And a hand with the baby.'

'Baby?' Zita's spirits rose. She knew she had a way with young children.

'She's upstairs.' And Audrey had taken her up to a sugar-pink confetti-paradise of a nursery, where a baby was sleeping peacefully in a crib, long lashes resting on rose-coloured chubby cheeks.

'This is Rowan.'

The child awoke just at that moment, and it seemed to Zita that she looked straight at her and smiled.

'Could I hold her?'

Audrey nodded, and gingerly Zita took her out of the crib. 'Hello, Rowan,' she whispered. It was love at first sight.

'Do you have any experience?' Audrey asked her. But she'd smiled even as she spoke the words, and somehow it hadn't seemed to matter to either of them. They clicked.

Zita was offered the job and had been with the family ever since. She and Rowan had always got on like a house on fire. Closeness with Audrey had come more slowly, but now her loyalty was to them both. To them both . . .

When the family decided to move to Cornwall, Zita agreed to go along. But she missed the life in London. By contrast, Cornwall was dead as the dodo, as she told her sister Nell. But Audrey Brunswick wasn't stupid. She encouraged Zita to go back often, even paid her fares, and so retained her services against all odds.

After Zita's mother died it was harder. Nell wanted her back in town. She and her husband Ted had bought a pie and mash shop, of all things, with their share of the legacy – one heck of a surprise to both of them that money had been – and she suggested Zita joined them in the venture.

Zita had laughed at first. 'I thought those places were all closing down?' Although she had to admit to a nostalgia when she remembered going to the shop to collect their pie and mash every Thursday clutching the bowl her mother had given her to put it in.

'Don't you believe it,' Nell admonished. 'Traditions don't die that easy. Come any time. Just say the word and you're in with us. It's not a bad life. You'd be your own boss. And I miss you, you know.'

Zita missed her too. But it wasn't so simple. She ran the house in Cornwall these days. She was more than a nanny or a housekeeper. 'I'm used to them,' she said. 'They need me.'

'But what kind of life is it?' Nell knew her so well. 'Where's the fun in slaving away for other people? Do you want to be a drudge all your life?'

'I'm part of the family.' Zita only half-believed this. Maybe she was part of Audrey and Rowan's family, but she'd never be part of Philip's. Philip Brunswick was a snob of the worst kind – there was no getting away from it.

'Stuff and nonsense.' Nell looked her up and down. 'This is your family, girl. You'll never be more than a servant to that lot.'

Zita sighed. It would be so easy to up sticks and go back to London – she'd often been tempted. The Brunswicks had come to depend on her – yes, but Rowan was almost grown up now. Was she deluding herself, to imagine that Audrey couldn't cope without her? Maybe she only needed a bit of a jolt to get herself into gear again. Was Nell right? Was it high time she thought of herself for a change?

Zita smiled slowly. And now there was Harry.

The scent of the lavender, thyme and lemon balm rose in the breeze towards her as she lifted her head and thought of Harry Penbray. Whoever would have thought it?

They'd taken to meeting in the evenings – three or four times a week it was now – and she could no longer pretend that it was only friendship that drew them together.

Not that he'd touched her. Harry was a gentleman – she'd known that from the first – one of the old school, honest and upright in every way. Zita grinned. She liked that, although sometimes she was tempted to say something a bit naughty to the old devil. Somehow she knew he wouldn't mind.

It was the little things he did that showed her he cared. The way he held out his hand to help her along the more difficult pathways, his concern for her welfare – was she thirsty, did she need a coat, should they turn back? He brought her the best fresh fish from the catch, handing it to her as if it were gold dust. Oh yes, Harry Penbray cared all right.

'I reckon you and me have got some thinking to do,' he'd said to her last night as he walked her back to the house. He wouldn't leave her in the lane, he would walk her right up to the back door and then wait to see her in, his shadow silent and unmoving in the night-time air.

'What about, Harry?' Zita tasted the despair. She'd known it wouldn't last. He was far too honest to keep this up. In fact she was surprised he'd let it go as far as it had. Why had he? Had he, like her, reached a point in his life when he realised happiness had to be grabbed? That you couldn't sit back and let it happen, because sometimes it flounced on past and happened to some other lucky blighter just to spite you?

He stopped walking, took her hand. 'I'll be straight with you – I liked you from the moment I first laid eyes on you.'

Zita felt immensely flattered. 'I like you too, Harry.' She paused. 'But you're a married man.' Might as well help him say it.

'More fool me.'

'Your wife . . .'

'She'll not care.' It was the first time she'd heard bitterness. And it made her wonder. Why ever hadn't Harry's wife cherished him in the way he deserved? And what was he saying? Was he suggesting that they had a future after all?

Zita struggled with her conscience. 'I'm sure she would care.' Her voice was gentle, but she had to be the strong one now. 'We hardly know each other, you and me.'

'We know enough.' He tucked her arm in his and continued walking.

Blimey O'Reilly. He was so sure. How could he be so sure when Zita was racked with doubts, guilt and uncertainty? Harry Penbray seemed to know exactly what he wanted.

She heard the rumble of a car engine in the near distance. Harry stepped out in front of her as the headlights hit them, shielding her from the light, preventing her from being seen. Protecting her.

'You're going too fast,' she whispered. 'I need time.'

'You think on it.' They left the lane and walked through to the back of the house.

Like a couple of servants, Zita found herself thinking. Maybe Nell was right.

'But what would we do?' She turned to Harry and wailed. She could see him now more clearly in the light from the lamp outside the back door. He stood, sturdy, concern for her in his honest eyes. He looked as if he could weather any storm. 'You're married. What would we do?'

'You mustn't worry yourself.' He smiled, his hand reaching out to gently caress her cheek.

She grabbed hold of it, kissed the worn calloused fingers. 'But . . .' She wanted to be sure, but nothing seemed straightforward any longer.

'Like I said – we've got some thinking to do.' He nodded. 'We'll work it out.'

Was that what all this sitting and thinking was about, then? Was she doing what Harry had suggested? She sighed once more. If so, she didn't seem to be getting too far. She was getting too sentimental these days.

The sound of a movement nearby made her jump. She looked up to see a figure creeping stealthily around to the back of the house.

'Rowan?'

The girl started, seemed relieved to see it was Zita, and hastily brushed down the short skirt she was wearing, although from where Zita was standing it looked beyond repair.

'Oh, Zita, it's you. I've just been – um – out walking.'

'Walking?' She looked more like she'd been dragged through a hedge backwards. Zita smiled. She was a wild thing all right.

She got to her feet, waiting as the girl drew nearer. 'You'd better tidy yourself up before you see your father this evening, birthday or not. You'd better . . .' The words died on her lips.

Rowan's eyes were bright and dilated, her mouth swollen, her cheeks flushed. Her white blouse looked as if it had been pulled off in a hurry, and her dark hair was all over the place stuck with leaves and briars, and matted with sand.

Sand? Zita took a pace closer, grabbed Rowan's arm, saw the girl's eyes – grey and wild as the Cornish sea they were – widen into alarm. 'What've you been up to, young lady? Out with it!'

She knew though, without being told. She could see the passion still in the bloom of her face, the marks of it on her young body. Jesus wept. Fourteen. Zita shook her head in despair. She was still only a child.

'I told you . . .' Rowan's voice changed into fear. 'I went for a walk and I . . .'

Their eyes met. Her words tailed into nothing.

And why shouldn't she be scared? Zita had brought her up, hadn't she? Almost single handed. And she hadn't brought her up for this. She had Zita to answer to.

Zita was responsible for her welfare. Good God Almighty. What would her father say?

'Do you think I was born yesterday? You're going to tell me everything, my girl.' She tightened her hold on Rowan's arm as she led her inside. 'I want the truth. And I want it now.'

Chapter 6

———•◆•———

Glyn Penbray was whistling as he strolled home, hands thrust in the pockets of his jeans. Every so often he stopped to grin to himself. He couldn't help it. He just felt so bloody good.

He hadn't intended it to happen, that wasn't why he'd taken Rowan down to the bay – course it wasn't. It had been a bit of a laugh to start with; the path was pretty steep and he never thought she'd make it. He'd forgotten to get her a present for her birthday and then it had come to him. Why not show her the cliff path? Why not share it with someone after all this time? True, he'd sworn once that he'd never tell a soul. But did it really matter since he was the only one who went down there?

Athwenna Trelawney would have said something by now if she objected to Rowan Brunswick. Everyone who belonged in Folyforth knew the kind of power Athwenna had – a natural kind of authority, he supposed it was. The kind conferred by past traditions, by a long legacy of history. It was true that some thought her a witch. But it was also true that she had their respect.

Oh yeah, old Athwenna would have looked into him and through him with those penetrating blue eyes of hers and shaken her head. *No, boy,* she would have said. *Not that one.* But she hadn't. She'd as good as given her permission.

And he wanted to give Rowan something – he really wanted to share a part of himself with Rowan Brunswick. Maybe he was going soft, but she was something else. He was beginning to feel she was special. Special in a way that made him wonder if he was such a loner after all – if there might be, for all their differences, someone who understood. Someone who could move him.

But he hadn't intended to make love to her.

Glyn lost the note he was holding in a moment of self-doubt, but the moment was soon gone. Because who could blame him? When a girl looked at you that way, what were you supposed to do? And now that it had happened, now that he'd had her there on the sand, there was no going back.

He took the side gate in one leap. He was hungry. Starving hungry.

'What have you got to smirk about, then?'

Damn it. He stopped whistling. His mother was gathering a billowing sheet in her arms, bringing the washing in from the small square patch of garden outside the cottage.

'I'll give you a hand with that.' He moved towards her, grabbing two white cotton corners, avoiding her eyes.

She frowned. 'Being helpful too? Now that is a turn up.'

'Always a first time for everything.' Glyn felt the grin resurface.

His mother seemed to freeze for a second as she watched him. 'I asked you what you had to be smirking over like that?' Tight-lipped, she took the sheet from him, folded it over her arm, tossed it into the laundry basket.

'Don't know what you're on about, do I?'

'You're certainly happy about something.' She passed him the basket. 'Take this inside for me, will you?'

He lifted it, out of habit balancing it on one lean hip as his mother did. She was too sharp for her own good, his mother was. Never missed a trick. 'Maybe I was just looking forward to seeing you. Maybe I was looking forward to your smile.' He grinned once more.

'And maybe pigs will be flying over Folyforth this evening.'

His mother might enjoy flattery, but Glyn knew she was never fooled by it. Once inside, she moved to the stove and began stirring what he hoped was his dinner.

'Smells good.'

But he couldn't distract her. She pulled on her apron. 'And just *maybe* you've been up to no good, my lad.' At least she was half-smiling.

'What makes you say that?' He grabbed some milk from the fridge. Jesus, he was thirsty. Did sex make you thirsty? He'd only done it once before, with Melanie Fowler at the back of the school field behind a horse chestnut tree, when they'd skipped geography one time. Afterwards, he'd plunged his face into the drinking water fountain, but never been sure if it was thirst he was trying to rid himself of, or the smell of her stale perfume.

Rowan wasn't like that. Rowan Brunswick smelled sweet – whiffs of birch-bark mixed with wild roses and grass cuttings.

'I say it because I think it.' Lynette poked at a carrot and drew it tenderly towards her mouth. 'Look at the state of you. I reckon you've been up to something.'

'Huh?' Glyn replaced the empty bottle in the fridge, and peered into the broken mirror to the right of the sink. He couldn't see a thing. What was she on about? From his pocket he tugged out a comb and re-arranged the dark curls, which immediately sprang back to where they'd been before. Some grains of sand scattered on to the draining board.

'Not in here, you dirty bounder.' She was standing behind him, her eyes narrowed.

He turned and she pulled the comb from his hand. 'Come into the bedroom. I'll sort it out for you.'

'Jesus, Mum . . .' This was his mother's version of torture, and usually included interrogation into the bargain.

She stood waiting, hands on generous hips. 'Come on.'

Glyn knew better than to argue when she was in this mood. Sometimes she got like this after a heavy lunchtime session down the pub when she'd been bought too many G and T's by the likes of Dewy Jago, that prat next door with more money than sense, only to come home with a sore head to find Dad still out fishing. She had a tongue like a whiplash, his mother, but he could usually win her over in the end.

He followed her into the dingy room with the maroon velveteen curtains that she shared with his Dad, sighed, and allowed her to position him on the stool in front of the fake mahogany dressing-table, her hands clamped on his shoulders. 'Aw, Mum . . .'

She glared at his reflection. 'How long since you had it cut?'

'I dunno.'

'You should get it cut more often.'

'It grows quick.'

'Hmmph.' His mother hoisted herself into a sitting position on the high bed and started yanking at his hair with the silver-plated brush.

'Ouch!' Glyn was suffering. He couldn't remember a time when his mother hadn't taken her temper out on his tangled curls.

'Baby.' In the dressing-table mirror, he saw her thin lips narrow into a smile. She loved it, she did. The brush pounded against his head.

'You're bloody hurting me, you are.'

'Don't swear.'

'Well, give it a rest, then.'

'I'll finish when I'm ready to.'

'Jesus . . .' He stared at her pots of creams and potions. Creams to put on her face to change the colour of her skin, creams to take the colour off again. Tubes and pots and powders. Why did she bother?

Once more he thought of Rowan. She wore no make up. But how long would it be before she too thought she should dress up for show, add a few colours that she imagined the world wanted to see? It had started today, hadn't it? With that skirt . . .

The thought of the skirt hitched up to her white cotton panties made him sweat. Jesus . . . when she was coming down that cliff face behind him he only had to look up and . . . Well, no-one could blame him, could they? He wasn't made of stone, was he?

The brushing was getting harder, more insistent, as if his mother were scoring lines of revenge into his scalp. He peered at her tight face in the mirror once more and realised her expression had changed. She looked bloody angry. Jesus. She wasn't a mind reader, was she? He flushed.

'So where *have* you been?' Her lips were compressed into a slash of red lipstick. No smile now.

'When?'

The brush came down hard. 'You know when, my lad. Today, that's when. All afternoon, that's when.'

'Nowhere much.' He was getting nervous. If she carried on like this, she'd break his bloody skull.

'Where exactly?' Her eyes glittered. She stopped brushing and the hands rested once more on his shoulders. Pressure.

Silently, he absorbed the threat. 'Up the cliff.'

'Who with?' She turned him round by the shoulders and he had to shuffle his knees so that he was facing her, his eyes level with her breasts, looking up at her because she was still sitting on the high bed.

'No-one.' His breath was coming harder, laced up tight in his chest.

'Who with?' Her voice rose.

'What does it matter who with? What d'you want to know for, anyway?' He pulled himself away from her hands, got to his feet and sank on to the bed beside her. His head hurt. She'd given him a bloody headache, that's what she'd done.

'Why do you think I want to know, you dirty little sod.' She pointed the brush at him. 'I've told you before, I know what you're like. I know what you've been doing. And I want to know who you were doing it with.'

How could she be so sure? He gazed up at her. Was it written on his face, or something?

'Who was it?' Lynette knelt back on her heels. 'Tell me who it was.'

'Some slag,' he mumbled. Sorry, Rowan. Sorry, Rowan but it's for the best. She must never know. No-one must ever know.

'Who?'

She wouldn't rest, would she? Dad always said that. *Women, they'll not rest till they know it all.* 'Mum . . .'

'Who?'

'Melanie Fowler.' Like nothing on earth he prayed that the girl hadn't walked past the house an hour ago or something. If she had, if his mum so much as suspected he was lying, he'd be finished, he would. She could be a right cruel bitch if she wanted to.

He sensed her relax and he felt almost numb with the relief.

'Little tart. You should be careful of little tarts like that one.'

'I am careful.'

'You use something then?'

'Aw, Mum. Give it a rest, will you?' But he sensed this was all minor stuff now, that she wouldn't push it.

'And not fifteen yet.' She eyed him with what seemed like maternal pride.

'Can I go?' He got up, held out a hand to help his mother off the bed.

'Melanie Fowler, eh?' She grasped the hand tight. 'Nothing to do with that girl up on the hill, then?'

'What?' He stared at her, feeling her nails cutting into his palm. He'd been so careful. How the hell did she know about Rowan?

'The girl up on the hill.' She released his hand, replaced the brush with the silver-plated handle on her dressing-table, turned and touched his cheek, slow, like a caress. 'Don't pretend you don't know who I mean.'

'I know who you mean.' He took a deep breath, hardened his eyes. 'But why should I be with that snotty-nosed bitch?' Rowan, forgive me.

She laughed. 'I've seen the way you look at her, son.' Her voice was soft, too soft. It worried him.

'Nah. You're imagining things.' As he watched his mother, standing in front of him now, smaller than him in stature but stubborn as a donkey, he knew he must be more careful.

'Oh yes, I have. I've seen you.' She tousled the hair that she'd just been brushing, her fingers threading through the curls. 'You look at her as if you want what you see.'

He shook his head. 'Not likely.'

She laughed once more. 'You can fool your Dad but you can't pull the wool over my eyes, Glyn Penbray.'

'I wouldn't touch that one with a barge pole.' He took both her hands, squeezed them gently, bent his head close to hers and kissed her cheek. Her dark hair smelled of waxy hair spray, and she tasted of whatever she'd put on her face.

'I'm glad to hear it, son.' At last she smiled again. 'They don't belong in the village, that lot don't. You stay away from them.'

Five minutes later Glyn was sitting at the kitchen table watching her dish up his supper. 'We won't wait for your Dad,' she said. 'Heaven knows what time he'll be back.'

She sat down opposite him. He watched his mother forking vegetables, cutting meat, licking a drip of gravy from her lips. But it was the face of Rowan Brunswick that filled his mind. Forbidden fruit. She was as delicious as forbidden fruit. He remembered the feel of her hair – her thick dark hair hanging over his face, tickling his chest. It smelt of long summer grasses and a shampoo as sweet as honey. He saw her grey eyes, troubled one second, wild with fury the next. Dense with passion, open as the sea, open as love. He rubbed his hands along her sweet chestnut limbs, smooth skin, salty shoulders. His tongue was tasting her wide wide mouth, her white teeth, her breasts like strawberries. The smell of her was in his mouth, on his fingers. She was beautiful, oh yes. And all the nicer for being forbidden.

Not one of us. But he could taste her. *Not one of us.* But he could have her. *Not one of us.* But he could come into her, possess her. He could make her cry out, he could make her love him. She could be all his. His own, most precious forbidden and exotic fruit.

'I know what I'm doing, Zita.' Rowan stood, straight, uncompromising, and utterly believing. She just had to make Zita believe it too.

'You're only fourteen.' Zita flung herself into one of the kitchen chairs. 'How the heck can you know what you're doing?'

Rowan felt rather sorry for her. She was so fond of Zita. Zita had, in her childhood, always known the answers. And now she was, quite obviously, flummoxed, when the world was crystal clear and perfectly wonderful to Rowan. But how could she possibly explain this marvellous thing that had happened? 'Let me make you some tea.' She filled the kettle, fiddled with tea-bags. It would make Zita feel better – it had always calmed her before.

Zita stared at her. 'A cup of tea won't help us now.' She swept her fingers through her untidy auburn hair. 'I don't understand how you could have done it, Rowan. After all I've told you, after the talks we've had. I don't understand how you could have let anyone . . .' She sighed. 'A girl like you.'

'A girl like me?' Rowan frowned.

'Don't you see? You're only a child.'

'No.' Rowan had expected all this – that was why it had to be a secret. Adults would never understand how it was. 'I don't feel like a child.' Serenely she faced her. She was a woman now. Glyn Penbray had done that. He had given her a special birthday gift indeed.

'I can see that.' Zita drummed her fingernails on the table. 'But the fact remains that you *are* a child. Don't you know that intercourse is against the law if you're under age?'

103

For the first time since she'd left Glyn in the wood, the enormity of what they had done occurred to Rowan. She paled. 'You won't *tell* anyone, will you?' It had to be a secret. They had agreed. 'Oh, Zita, you won't get him into trouble?'

'Who?'

'I can't tell you.' She twisted away from her. Even Zita didn't have the least idea what was at stake. All she wanted was to know his name, so that she could tell the others . . .

'Don't you trust me, Rowan love?'

Rowan couldn't fathom out why Zita looked so sad. Her dark eyes were often dreaming these days, sometimes happy, but more often sad. 'It's not that.' In seconds, Rowan was beside her, penitent, on her knees, looking up to Zita as she always had. 'But I promised, you see.' And she couldn't break a promise made to Glyn. She'd rather die.

'He made you promise?' Zita took her hands.

'We *both* promised,' she corrected. 'We both wanted to promise.'

'How old is he?' Zita seemed to be scrutinising her so closely. Could she see all the differences that Rowan felt so keenly? The differences in her body, the changes in her emotions, in her mind?

'Old enough.' She wouldn't divulge anything. It was the only way. For the first time Zita smiled. 'That's pretty obvious, I'd say.'

'I love him, Zita.' Rowan laid her head on Zita's lap. 'I never meant to do it. I'm sure he didn't either. Really. I remembered everything that you'd told me, but in the end I couldn't help it. I just love him so much, you see. It took me over. I couldn't hear you any more.'

Slowly, Zita stroked the thick hair. She had watched this hair thicken and grow, seen it change from baby blonde to this deep bark-brown. She had raised Rowan as if she were her own, and yet now she was as helpless as a baby herself. Love. What could this child know of love?

'Will you tell them – Mum and Father?' Rowan lifted her head, her eyes beseeching. 'Please don't.'

How could she not, for heaven's sake? How could she take the responsibility of knowing their fourteen year-old daughter was having sex with some boy from the village – for it must be someone from the village, she felt sure – and not tell them? Audrey and Philip had entrusted her, so many times, with their daughter's safety. How could she dream of betraying that trust? How on God's earth could she be sitting here wondering how she could justify not telling them? Because that's what she was doing. She was – heaven help her – tempted to believe in this love of the young girl she cared for so deeply. Tempted to believe that it couldn't be so bad, that forcing her to part with it, with him, might damage her more severely still. What was the matter with her – to be thinking this way?

'Only if you promise not to do it again.' Even as she spoke, as she felt Rowan's slender body tense in her arms, she knew it was useless. Impossible. How could she even ask it?

'I can't.'

'You could wait.' She drew back, holding her at arm's length. This discussion wasn't going at all in the way she'd envisaged. Rowan the child seemed to have been transformed into someone with authority. A Brunswick in her own right. 'You should wait until you're sixteen, at least. If you cared for each other you'd wait. He would understand.'

Rowan shook her head. 'We couldn't wait.'

'Rowan. My God, your father would . . .'

'You mustn't tell him.' Her eyes became wild, the pupils dilated. 'He mustn't know. He'd kill me.'

'Don't be daft . . .' Zita's voice tailed off. But she didn't want to think about how Philip would react. And as for Audrey . . . She sighed. 'Are you at least taking precautions?'

Rowan got to her feet to make the tea, the curtain of hair hiding her face. 'Of course.'

She was lying.

'You must!'

'I will!' She swung round. 'Only don't tell my parents, Zita, please. If you've ever felt anything for me, don't tell them. Not yet.'

'Then I want to meet him.'

Rowan stared at her. 'Meet him?'

'Yes.' Zita folded her arms. 'I want to talk to him and see if . . .'

'His intentions are honourable?' Rowan laughed.

'Now look here, young lady.' Zita's mouth twitched. 'This is no laughing matter. I want to meet him, and if you can't trust me to make a decision then I'll tell your father right now.'

'I'll ask him.' She seemed doubtful. 'But I don't know if he would want . . .'

'I think he has what he wants.' Zita nodded, the decision made. She sipped her tea. If she could only see this boy, she was sure she could persuade him not to take advantage of Rowan again. If he didn't care for her he would run a mile. And if he did care . . . if he did care then he must be made to see sense. They must wait. They must at least be sensible, take precautions. In this day and age . . .

'Still,' Rowan demurred. 'It's supposed to be a secret.'

'Secret or no, I'm sure he'd rather meet me any day of the week than have your father on the warpath.'

'Maybe.' Rowan bit her lip.

'You tell him.' Zita decided a digestive biscuit would go down nicely. She would quite enjoy giving some whippersnapper a good talking to. Rowan had been a silly girl. But she wouldn't be the first, and surely not the last. With a bit of luck there'd be no harm done, and the Brunswicks wouldn't even have to know. Zita could sort it out. Didn't she sort everything out? Didn't she run this house single-handed? Love? Pah, Rowan didn't even know she was born.

Sitting in her green room that same evening, Audrey found herself thinking of the people who lived in this house. She had seen no-one for three hours, not since she'd found Zita mooning around on the stairs, and yet she knew they were all here. She could hear occasional voices, doors shutting, footsteps pacing; people noises. But they lived in the rest of the house, and she lived here. Alone. That was how it seemed.

Getting to her feet, she stared at the last watercolour she had completed this morning. It had taken her two weeks to finish, and she was certain she would do no more.

How good was it? She took it to the window, looked out at the neat lawn and borders, the expanse of cool green and the distant beeches. It was only as good as the view itself. It said nothing more. It was a cheap copy, that was all. She would rather have the view alone.

Audrey ripped the painting slowly in two.

When they'd first come to Cornwall, she had been glad. It seemed to offer not only a new landscape to paint, but more importantly a new background for the bringing up of her daughter, for her marriage

– which left a lot to be desired, if one had the energy, which most of the time Audrey did not.

Her new landscape had never lived up to her expectations, but she could blame no-one but herself. Not even Philip, not really, because she *could* have stood up to him. She should have stood up to him, claimed her rights.

But instead, she had allowed herself to sink into this landscape that had at least been bearable, perfectly bearable, until she walked to the waterfront that day. Until she had seen the great arm of the coastline cliff with its jagged cruel fingers stretching out and away from her. Until she had gone into that café and heard that her husband was having an affair with some woman from the village. With some woman called Lynette Penbray. It wasn't just tittle-tattle. She couldn't pretend that.

She was a bit of a tart, by all accounts, a barmaid in the Bull and Packet. But it seemed strange – so strange – that Audrey didn't even know what she looked like.

It wasn't just that he was having an affair either. She recalled the Cornish voices.

He buys her things you know . . .

She was flashing a diamond ring at all and sundry in the pub last night. The size of that stone. A whopper and no mistake . . .

She thinks she's it, that one does. As if her head weren't big enough already . . .

She's making a right monkey of him . . .

Making a right monkey of her old man and all . . .

And making a monkey of Audrey, too, that was the truth.

What did she have left now? And what hurt the most? She ripped the painting into still more pieces. What hurt the most was that Philip had not stuck to his own, had not considered his wife in the slightest. If he had *required a* mistress . . . Her lip curled. He could so easily have found one in London, an anonymous mistress who could remove his money and his frustrations in one clean sweep, leaving – who knows? – possibly a rather nicer man to be married to. In the city – if he chose to be discreet – who would ever know of the affair? Surely no-one who also knew Audrey.

But to choose a woman from Folyforth, a woman who worked in

the pub, a woman who got herself talked about . . . That was what hurt the most. And to know that he had followed her here.

By now the painting was in hundreds of tiny pieces and Audrey's fingers were sore. She opened her fists and watched the pieces of painted green and blue flutter down to the carpet.

It was unforgivable. Philip had tried to make himself Lord of the Manor, then he had made the potential Lady into nothing but a laughing-stock.

Zita would find these pieces of her tomorrow. She would call them litter or bits of old rubbish, and she would screw up her nose like this . . . Audrey contorted her face, moved the pieces of light card into a different pattern with her stockinged toe. Zita would find them and she would get out her vacuum cleaner and suck them all up out of sight. Out of sight, out of mind.

Audrey picked up another painting, not framed, one she had completed last month. It didn't please her. Slowly she ripped it in two.

Perhaps life had even been bearable when it was Audrey, Zita and Rowan against Philip. When she knew Zita would always be around, would always understand, would care for Rowan when Audrey could care no longer.

It was different now. She ripped the two pieces into two more. Zita was different now. Always sneaking off to meet some barnacle from the village, a man who stank of fish and stale seaweed. And when she was here she mooned around with cheap sentiment in her eyes not knowing what day it was, let alone caring for Rowan as she was paid to do. As she'd *promised* to do . . .

With vicious fingers, Audrey tore the painting into more pieces and let them fall to the ground. Maybe it was self-pity, but whatever it was, it was destructive and it had taken her over today. She grabbed another painting. How long would it be before Zita left them?

She ripped the painting in two.

Zita had usurped her daughter, her own role as a mother, her house, her life. And now she would leave. She would leave to be some Cornish fisherman's woman and she would vacuum his house, gut his fish and make wholesome stock out of the bones that were left behind.

Zita, don't go.

She touched her own breast, slowly, tentatively with exploratory fingers. What would become of Rowan?

Perhaps she should blame Philip. But she had never loved Philip enough to hate him.

Instead she blamed Zita. Blamed her with all her heart.

Philip Brunswick, trying to work in his study whilst figures with green haloes swam in front of his eyes, looked up at the knock on his door. 'Come.'

It was the Zita woman. Well, it wouldn't be Audrey, would it? She never came to this part of the house – his part of the house – any more.

'Are you eating in here tonight?' Zita looked as if she didn't give a damn.

'Where will Audrey be?' Why bother to ask? His wife might as well be renting a bed-sit. She already had a kettle and one of those hob things in that green room of hers. What would be next?

'In her room,' Zita confirmed.

Philip watched her as she half-leaned on the door frame. She'd lost weight recently, and it suited her. But there was something else very different about the Zita woman. Something that he couldn't quite put his finger on.

'Well, then. I'll be . . .'

'You'll be taking her a tray?' he asked as Zita made a move to leave.

She frowned. 'Audrey said at lunch-time she wouldn't be wanting dinner.'

'But you have checked with her since then?' He got to his feet, playing for time, took his glass over to the mahogany drinks cabinet for a refill. His third scotch before dinner, but it had been a bad day. Every day had been bad since that afternoon with Lynette. He'd phoned, tried to persuade her to come away for a week-end with him, he'd sent flowers, even a gold bracelet, for Christ's sake. And what had she told him on the phone? *Just you wait, Philip Brunswick. I'll let you know when I'm ready* . . . He sighed. Unfeeling bitch. Why was it that he couldn't seem to pull the strings any more?

No joy from the Trelawney character either. Three letters he'd sent, and received not a word of reply. Some crazy old woman who didn't recognise a gift horse when it looked her in the mouth. But he wasn't finished yet. He'd hardly even started.

Zita shrugged. 'Audrey's not eating much at the moment. She's lost her appetite.'

And that wasn't all she'd lost. Philip frowned. At least when he'd needed her before, Audrey had always been available. But now, she was acting like an invalid. What the hell was the matter with her anyway? He threw back his head and swallowed the scotch in one gulp.

'So do you want dinner in here, or what?' He thought he read contempt in the Zita woman's eyes. Philip blinked. Of course. That was what was different about her. Her eyes were kind of bright these days. She'd always looked him full in the face, but now there was something else there that made him want to respond to the challenge.

'Do you fancy a drink?' he asked her.

Zita shook her head. 'Dinner's about ready.'

'Oh, come on Zita, for Christ's sake.' Philip tore his fingers through his hair. What was wrong with the woman? 'Have a bloody sherry at least.'

Zita hesitated for a moment. 'All right.' She entered the room, leaving the door open behind her. 'I'll have a bloody sherry. It'll have to be a quick one though or you'll be getting burnt potatoes.'

Philip poured it, passed it to her. Her hair was different too, come to think of it. She wasn't wearing that scarf thing round her head, her hair was hanging loose over her shoulders and yet a bit of make-up had made her appearance more striking than ever. He wondered what she was wearing under the apron. 'Cheers,' he said.

'What's all this in aid of, then?' She sipped cautiously.

'How do you mean?' Actually, she was quite an attractive woman. She could probably carry off a low neckline as well as Lynette, and that was saying something.

'I mean that I've been working for you for fourteen years, and you've never offered me a sherry before.'

Philip grinned, beginning to enjoy himself. 'Then it's long overdue. Take off your apron, you're not a drudge. Sit yourself down.'

Zita stared at him as if he'd grown two heads.

'Go on. Please.'

He waited until she sat gingerly on the couch, then moved to the door and closed it quietly.

Zita jumped to her feet. 'What the . . . ?'

'I wanted to talk to you.' He put a finger to his lips, motioned her to sit down again.

She did so, warily. 'What about?'

'About Audrey.' He sat on the desk quite close to her and stared pointedly at her legs. Surely she never usually wore dresses this short? Legs that good shouldn't be hidden under a bloody apron.

'What about her?' He saw Zita bristle, wondered vaguely how Audrey had ever inspired such loyalty.

Philip got himself another scotch – his fourth, but who was counting? – and sat down beside her. 'I think she needs some professional help.' Almost casually he laid a hand on Zita's knee. Audrey was about the last thing on his mind. But didn't this woman know better than anyone how bloody difficult she was being right now. Mightn't Zita then feel a bit sorry for him? She wasn't Lynette Penbray. But she could be exciting in her own way.

'Take your bloody hands off me.' Zita spoke in even tones, and for a moment Philip thought he'd heard her wrong.

'Come on, Zita . . .' His hands moved swiftly up her dress.

'I said . . .'

But her words were lost in a flurry of bodies as Philip Brunswick's frustration – fired by the sensation of his fingers on female thighs – led him to launch himself on top of her, his mouth hungrily swallowing her words of refusal.

It was another few seconds before she reacted, taking a deep breath to push off the weight of him, struggling to her feet, half-aware that he was already unbuckling the belt of his trousers, and that somehow her dress had got torn at the front.

'For God's sake,' she began. 'What the hell do you think you're doing?'

There was sherry everywhere, though the glass had only bounced on the thick carpet. The rich sickly smell of sherry, the dark stain of it, and his horrible shamefaced grin as he began to do up the belt of his trousers – that was all she was aware of. Zita could hardly bring herself to look at him, she was so disgusted.

111

But she had no time to say anything else, no time to think, or even to cover her partly-bared breasts, before Audrey Brunswick opened the door of her husband's private sanctuary and stood there in perfect silence watching them both.

Chapter 7

Audrey said nothing. She only stared at them.

Zita looked down at the floor. How embarrassing . . . How soon could she decently edge out of the room and leave them to it? The bloody nerve of the man . . . But he'd done it now, hadn't he? Now he'd get his come-uppance. Audrey would realize straight off what had happened. Wasn't it obvious? She wouldn't like to be in Philip Brunswick's shoes now. . . .

But the moments passed and at last Zita looked up to see Audrey still staring. Zita didn't much like her expression either. As if Zita were a piece of dog dirt stuck to Audrey's shoe. What in God's name was she thinking? Surely she didn't imagine that Zita and Philip Brunswick were . . . would ever . . . ?

'Audrey?' she whispered.

'What's been going on here?' Audrey's voice at least was calm, but her pale hands were moving nervously, twitching at the fawn cardigan pulled around her shoulders.

'Nothing to worry about,' Zita soothed, taking a step towards her. She might as well underplay it. He'd been drinking, that was all. No need to create a song and dance, no call to make everyone's life a misery when they had to share the same house.

'Nothing to worry about?'

'Philip just lost his head for a minute,' she said, realising that her torn dress told at least half the story. She pulled her apron back on, hoping it would cover her up a bit.

What *had* he been thinking of, lunging at her like that? Had he gone mad? She glared at Philip as he cleared his throat to speak. About bloody time too.

113

'Well, *you* won't oblige, will you?' he snapped at Audrey. 'A man has his needs. A man's got to take it where he can get it.'

'What?' Zita couldn't believe he'd said that. She stared at him as he turned round, grabbed his half-empty glass from the desk where he'd left it and gulped the liquid down.

'What the hell does she expect?' he muttered into it. 'What do any of them expect?'

'I don't know why he tried it on like that, Audrey. I just don't know why . . .' Zita took another step towards her, but Audrey drew herself inwards and away from her. And there was an expression that seemed like a hatred in her eyes, that gave Zita the shivers. Surely Audrey didn't hate her? What had she ever done apart from care for her and Rowan?

Us and them – the thought spun in her brain. Suddenly, after all these years, she felt like a servant again.

Audrey poked at the thick dark stain on the carpet with the toe of her shoe. 'Did he give you *sherry*?'

'Yes, but . . .'

'And you took it?'

Zita braced herself. 'Why the hell shouldn't I take it?'

'For God's sake, Zita.' Open contempt was drawn on Audrey's narrow features. 'What were you thinking of?'

'What was I thinking of?' Zita looked from one to the other. Had she missed something here?

'And you took off your apron,' Audrey muttered.

'Well, yes, but . . .' Zita put a hand to her hair and realised how messed up it was. What on earth did she look like? 'You don't think I *encouraged* him?' How could Audrey know her so little? How could she suspect her of such a thing? How could she imagine her capable?

'I don't know what to think.' Audrey's eyes flickered from one to the other.

'Come on, Audrey . . .' Didn't she realise that Zita loathed Philip Brunswick even more than Audrey did?

'It takes two to tango.' Philip's voice slurred into his glass.

Zita wanted to slap him.

'As for you – you're drunk.' Audrey took a step towards him.

'I'd have to be drunk to look twice . . .' His voice tailed off. He sat heavily down on his desk.

Audrey clicked her tongue. Her foot was tapping, up and down as if with a life of its own. And she was wearing high-heeled black shoes as though she were about to go out. But Audrey hadn't gone out for days, weeks maybe. Her skin was pale, her hair dry and lifeless.

'Audrey, you must know that I would never do anything . . .' Zita was beginning to absorb her own helplessness. 'Anything to hurt you.' Us and them. She felt naked; she felt *guilty*, for heaven's sake.

'I know what I saw.' Audrey spun round in sudden attack. 'I know that you've been drinking sherry, the room stinks of it. The door was shut. You were both on the sofa.' Her mouth twisted with distaste. 'And I can see . . .' She looked pointedly at the torn dress still visible under Zita's apron, 'that drinking isn't all you've been doing with my husband.'

Zita felt the anger rise to the surface. 'He took a lunge at me, Audrey.' She turned to Philip. 'Tell her. Tell her how it was.'

But Philip remained silent. His shoulders were hunched, his clothes dishevelled, a drop of saliva clinging to his thin lower lip. He no longer looked like a man with his finger on the pulse of the City. He looked like a loser.

'How could you be so stupid?' Audrey's fragility seemed to have vanished. 'How could you imagine that I wouldn't find out what was going on, here in my own house? How could you . . . ?'

'Tell her,' Zita shrieked at Philip.

He shrugged. His eyes held no feeling, no warmth. 'I thought you wanted it.'

'What?' If she hadn't been so angry, Zita would have laughed. 'What did you say?' She took a step towards him. What a bastard. What a complete and utter bastard. 'Wanted it? From you? Are you crazy?'

Philip just looked away.

'And what about you?' She spun round to face Audrey. 'Are you crazy too? Do you really think I would have encouraged him? Don't you know what he's like, what he is? How can you even go on living with him? That's what I can't understand. He's no better than a common rapist.'

There was a stunned silence, and Zita wondered if she'd gone too far. Us and them . . .

'Who do you think you're talking to?' Audrey answered after an eternity. Her voice was soft, but she seemed totally in control.

Zita forced herself to remain equally calm. 'He tried to assault me, Audrey.'

'Vindictive cow.' Philip twisted round to face Audrey. 'You can't believe a word she says. She's jealous of you, that's all. Always has been. In fact I don't know why the hell you ever employed her.' His eyes gleamed in victory.

'Because . . .' Zita could see that Audrey was struggling. She was looking from one to the other of them in confusion. Audrey had first employed Zita because she had never wanted to be a full-time mother or housewife. She had employed her because she wanted to do something else with her life. Something she had never done. So? Did that mean Zita was redundant now? Please don't let him win, Zita thought. Please be strong.

'She thinks she's bloody Lady Muck these days,' Philip continued. 'All she does is give me the come-on and sit around dreaming all day.'

'That's not true . . .' Zita stared at him. Bloody liar.

'She seems to have forgotten that she works for us.' Philip grinned. 'She's only a servant, after all.'

'What did you say?' Zita sat abruptly on the couch She wasn't sure her legs would hold her any longer. She wasn't sure what was going on, but she knew she'd been a fool to accept that sherry. She hadn't had her wits about her, she'd been thinking of that trouble with Rowan and how she was going to deal with it. She hadn't dreamed for one minute that Philip Brunswick . . .

Audrey swayed closer. 'Why did you do it, Philip?'

Zita watched in fascination as the pale cardigan slipped from the thin shoulders. Audrey was shaking with rage.

'Do what?' Philip Brunswick's expression changed to one of fear. Belatedly Zita realised that Audrey was referring to something else and he knew it. Something that Zita knew nothing about, that didn't concern her, something that was making Audrey behave this way.

'You know what.'

He shook his head.

She took a step closer. 'Why do you have to screw them, Philip?' Her face was contorted. 'Why do you have to screw these common sluts that you've found in some gutter somewhere?'

Zita blinked.

'That's what makes me so bloody angry.' She put a hand to her temple. She was still swaying, slowly. 'Why couldn't you pick on someone from London?' She bit her lip. It seemed bloodless to Zita. Audrey herself seemed bloodless. 'Why couldn't you hide it from me?' she whispered.

'Audrey . . .' Zita moved to take her arm, but Audrey turned on her, shaking her off. 'And you?' Her grey eyes were devoid of emotion, of reason. 'How could you?'

'How could I what? I haven't done anything, I told you.'

Audrey ignored her. 'How could you let me down after all I've done for you? After I've taken you into my home, treated you as one of the family, trusted you with . . .' She caught her breath. 'With everything I hold dear.'

Zita stared at her. What about everything *she* had done for Audrey? What about giving up her own family, her own life, for the sake of the Brunswicks? What about loyalty, what about love? She had done much more than she'd ever been paid to do, for this family.

'Drinking his sherry . . .' Audrey said. 'Making eyes. Women like you . . .'

'Stop it, Audrey.' Zita's head was pounding.

'I'll stop it. Oh yes, I'll do that.' Audrey took a deep breath. 'Get out.' Her eyes looked right through Zita. 'Get out of my house.'

Zita rose to her feet. She'd had more than enough of this. 'It'll be a pleasure.' She spun on her heel.

'Audrey?' For the first time Philip seemed doubtful. 'Are you sure you know what you're doing?'

Funny. Zita felt the urge to laugh at them. If she didn't laugh, maybe she'd cry and she might never stop. Hadn't he been trying to get rid of her for years?

'Has she lost her marbles?' Rowan stared back at Zita. 'Has she finally lost it completely?'

Zita shrugged. 'She's not herself, that's for sure.' She wouldn't say too much to Rowan, but inside she was still seething with it all – the appalling manner in which she'd been treated, and worse, a friendship betrayed.

'But there must be some proper reason. Why would she suddenly tell you to go?'

'She misunderstood. She thought . . .' Zita flung another woollen cardigan into her case. 'I'm not really sure what she thought,' she whispered.

'What did Father say?' Rowan was still watching her, watching with baffled eyes and biting on her fingernails. Who would tell her to stop doing that now?'

Zita pulled a face. 'Your father and I have never got on. You know that.' She stopped her frenzied packing, held the girl's hands in hers for a moment. 'Maybe he won't mind so much.'

'He'll mind having no-one to look after the house.'

'Anyone can look after a house.'

'But you and Mum have always been so close.' Rowan was shaking her head in confusion. And it was hardly surprising.

'I know, love.' How could she tell her the whole truth? She might be old enough for a romp in the sand, but she certainly wasn't old enough to hear the truth about her father. And talking of romps in the sand . . .

'And what about you, Rowan? What are you going to do?'

'What about?' The grey eyes were vague.

'About this bloke of yours.' Zita smoothed the dark hair from Rowan's face. So young. Too young for love, much too young for sex.

'You said you wouldn't tell them.' Rowan pulled away from her grasp. 'You promised.'

'I did nothing of the kind. But . . .' She held up her arm as Rowan began to protest. 'But I won't tell them.'

'Oh Zita, I do love you . . .'

'But neither will I be able to meet him.' That was Zita's biggest regret. No, she couldn't go to Audrey or Philip with Rowan's story, especially if she were not going to be around to defend and support her. But that meant she would be leaving the fourteen-year-old girl she loved to . . . To what? Fate, and to the arms of a young man who clearly wasn't the most responsible young person in the world.

She sighed. Who would remind Rowan about the harsh realities of life? About pregnancy and disease, not to mention her reputation? North Cornwall wasn't London, and even in London girls were labelled as swiftly and unfairly as ever. Perhaps they always would be.

'But you're not really going to leave us, Zita. You can't.' Her expression remained troubled. Zita wanted to hug her and hug her and not let go. 'What will we do without you?'

'No doubt you'll manage.' She became brisk. 'People do. I expect your father will get someone in to help, your mother might . . . well, she might . . .'

'Get off her arse?' Rowan laughed.

'Cheeky.' But Zita laughed too. Maybe Audrey would get off her arse. Maybe this would do her a power of good. But still she couldn't forgive her, couldn't think of her without bitterness. Those things she had said still hurt, probably always would.

Rowan became serious once more. 'I'm not just thinking about housework, Zita. You know it's much more than that. Nothing will be the same without you.'

'No, it won't be the same.' Blast the girl, for pulling her emotions all over the shop. Zita was trying her best to be brave, when what she wanted was to bawl her eyes out at the thought of leaving this place. It was her home, for heaven's sake. It was her home as much as it had ever been the Brunswicks' home. But if Rowan carried on like this, she wouldn't be brave much longer.

'But change can be a good thing.' She looked into her face. She would be beautiful, would Rowan Brunswick. 'You're growing up. And I want you to promise me two things.'

'Only two?' Rowan was trying to hold back the tears too, she could see it. She had some courage, this girl. She was strong-minded too. There would be battles ahead but Zita wouldn't be around to referee.

'Write to me. Often.'

'If you'll write back.'

Zita nodded.

'And the other thing?'

'Think about what I said, Rowan.' Zita tried to cram all her worry

119

for the girl into these words of caution. 'Please be careful. Don't get yourself into trouble. Remember everything I told you. Take things slowly.' She sighed. 'Love . . .'

'Yes?' Rowan was such an eager spirit. What would happen to this careless bravery when she was hurt for the very first time? When some young lad picked her up and ripped her in two as casually as if she were worth nothing?

'Love's all very well. But don't let it sweep everything else out of sight.'

'Oh, Zita . . .'

Glyn Penbray woke up at six-thirty the next morning, pulled a sweatshirt and jeans over his nakedness and went to the window, drawing back the curtain, leaning on the sill. From his room he could see the waterfront. The first sight of the sun touching the water against the pale morning sky was always a treat, and today was no exception.

Depending on the tides, sometimes the waterfront was busy even this early in the day. Often the men had been out night fishing and were just returning, bringing in their catches. Sometimes Glyn was one of them but he didn't intend to be a fisherman all his life. He had other dreams; he was ambitious, was Glyn Penbray.

But he often ran down to the beach to help his dad sort out the catch, to take over for a bit to give him a chance to get himself some tea and breakfast, help gut and wash the fish, lay out the nets to dry.

They weren't back yet this morning. Maybe that meant bad news – that the catch was poor and his Mum would be scowling and moaning that she'd have to work more hours in the pub. He hoped not. He could see a few boats in the distance, but it didn't look as if they were on their way back. The waterfront was deserted except for . . .

He squinted. A woman was standing by the sea wall with a black bag at her feet. He recognised her at once – she had a shock of red-brown hair that was flying around in the mad morning breeze, and she was wearing a red quilted jacket pulled in at the neck – one hand on her jacket, the other trying to keep her hair out of her face. It was the woman from the house up on the hill. Not Rowan's mother – he'd never laid eyes on her, though she was weird by all accounts. No, this was the other woman. The woman they said was like a housekeeper.

She was in her early forties, he supposed, though he was no good at women's ages. He thought he'd seen her with Dad on the cliffs one day. Must have been dreaming though – Mum would go potty, Dad would never dare.

But what the heck was she up to? She looked kind of crazy-wild. As if she were waiting for something – or someone. As if she were waiting for someone to carry her off someplace. He frowned.

Zita looked and looked towards the sea but there were no fishing boats coming in, and even if there had been, she couldn't stay here and wait. She had to go.

If only she could have talked to him last night. What wouldn't she have given to lay her head against his warm chest, have him stroke her hair and tell her it was all going to be all right, in that comforting way he had?

But she couldn't contact him, could she? Because he was married, because she didn't even know his address, nor his phone number – or even if he had one. She knew so little about the man.

If it hadn't been so late, if it hadn't been for Rowan, she might well have left the house last night, she was that angry. But where could she have gone at that time? There were no trains to London till the morning. And where else could she go but London? She had to go back to London, where at least she knew she had Nell and some kind of sanity. *But what about Harry Penbray?* The thought kept plaguing her. What about Harry?

That was why she had come here, now, to the waterfront, hoping to see him before she left for good. Perhaps there was no future in it, maybe that had only ever been a bit of a dream. But she had to let him know. There was a taxi waiting fifty yards away by the cottages, time ticking away on the cabby's meter, as he waited to take her to the station. And from there the train would take her to London. But how could she contact Harry?

She stood like a madwoman, the wind in her hair, staring out to sea as if he might suddenly appear out of the waves. As if it were likely that he would be here, waiting for her. And if he did appear – what would she say? Goodbye. She had to say goodbye.

A movement behind, by the cottages, alerted her, gave her another idea. She ran back. In one of the houses a youngish woman – vaguely familiar to her – in a pink towelling bathrobe was bringing in milk.

Zita hurried towards her. A woman who lived in one of the terraced cottages. This, any of these, might be Harry's house. But what the heck, she had to do something.

'Excuse me.' Zita looked into the woman's sleepy blue eyes. Heavens . . . This could even be Harry's wife.

'Yes?' She looked Zita up and down as if she were indeed a lunatic. And there was something hostile in her expression too.

'Can you tell me . . . which is Harry Penbray's house?' she blurted. Well, at least she had to *try.*

The woman raised her eyebrows. 'And who might you be, then?'

'It doesn't matter who I am.' Zita turned her head. The taxi meter was still ticking away. She had a note that she'd written last night, clutched in her palm, but she didn't know where she could leave it.

'Doesn't it indeed?' The woman would have folded her arms and stuck out one hip if she hadn't been holding two pints of milk, Zita just knew she would.

She shook her head. 'Please . . .' She didn't care what any of them thought. She was past that now.

'Don't matter to you lot up the hill. But it might matter to Lynette Penbray, I reckon.'

Tamsyn Jago got some satisfaction from the look on her face. That'd teach her and Harry Penbray to laugh at her, down on the waterfront.

Who did he think he was? And who did this woman think she was, asking after other folk's husbands, stealing other folk's husbands, no doubt. Tamsyn had no time for women like her. She didn't have a lot of time for Lynette Penbray either, but at least she was one of them. And there'd be trouble and a half if Lynette got to hear that her husband and this woman . . . Well, something was going on, that was for sure. Tamsyn had a good mind to tell her. She would do too, only it struck her that Lynette Penbray was a whole lot safer married to Harry and having it off with the bloke from London who lived up the hill, than she'd be if she were free and single. After all, Tamsyn had seen the way Dewy looked at her sometimes.

'But . . .'

Tamsyn almost felt sorry for the windblown woman on the step, there was such a desperate look about her.

'Who's that then, Tamsyn?' She heard Dewy's voice.

Resolutely, she shook her head, tightened her lips, and closed the door.

Zita leaned on the granite wall of the cottage for a moment and groaned. What had she expected? They were a closed lot these villagers. Why should any of them help a stranger?

She surveyed the row of drab cottages. Which one? Up at a window two doors off she saw a boy – a lad of about Rowan's age, staring at her. Who could blame him? He must think she was off her rocker.

Slowly she looked back at the bleak sea, at the distant fishing boats, at the taxi waiting for her.

'You'll miss your train, love.' The cabby tapped his watch. 'Time to be off.'

'I'm just coming.' Slowly she trailed back to the taxi.

And after all – how long had she known Harry? Not five minutes when you came to think of it. He was married, wasn't he? She knew nothing about him, bar that.

We know enough, he had said. But it wasn't enough, was it? It wasn't enough because she had to stop being a stupid romantic fool. She had to stop being a fool, get in this taxicab and get back to where she belonged. Back to London, back to Nell.

Sod the Brunswicks – apart from Rowan, that is. And sod Cornwall. 'Goodbye Harry,' she whispered, as the taxi drove away. He'd never hear her. But maybe he knew enough to understand.

Chapter 8

Rowan Brunswick stood naked in her bedroom. She walked across to the wardrobe mirror and ran her hands slowly over her breasts, past her waist and across her hips. Her dark hair fell to just below her shoulders, her limbs were straight and slender. Glyn loved her, didn't he? He loved her, though in the past two years he had never – at least voluntarily – told her so.

But she sensed a turning point, because ahead of them were two whole days, two wonderful days when they would be alone together and away from their parents and Folyforth. What had once been a secret shared – the folly, the wood, their loving – had become a burden to Rowan. She wanted to shout about it.

For two whole days they would be free to show each other and the world how they felt. They wouldn't have to sneak around, pretend they hardly knew one another, meet in secret places, make illicit love. They could walk hand in hand, for they wouldn't see a soul they knew on the lonely moors of Bodmin in the middle of the week in June. They could walk together, talk together, kiss and . . .

Rowan touched the smooth roundness of her breasts. That was how it would be, their future. They would get a taste of how it would be during these two days away together, and then Glyn would be as sure as Rowan was. Then he would tell her how much he loved her without being asked twice.

Slowly, Rowan began to get dressed, pulling on a tee-shirt and jeans. Somehow she had manufactured this opportunity – it just showed what you could achieve if you put your mind to it. She had learned, in the past two years, how to get round her father. And as for her mother . . . well, she didn't want to think about her mother. She would never stop loving her, but there seemed so little left to love these days. She didn't know *how* to help her even while she sensed that she ought to. So instead, she avoided the pale lonely figure in the green room. Avoided her just as her father avoided her. As if then her mother and her guilt might, unnoticed, just slip away.

Rowan nipped into her father's bedroom to use his phone. He had gone down to the village pub for a drink – one of his more recent habits – so she knew she was safe for a while.

'Tania?' she whispered, without knowing why. 'Are you still on for tomorrow?'

Tania was her alibi – not a friend as such, Rowan had made no real friends at school, although she had plenty of acquaintances – and Tania was a girl who would do almost anything for a few Mars Bars. As far as her father was concerned, Rowan was going home from school with Tania tomorrow, working on a project with her, staying the night with her in Padstow, and going to school with her the next day. Which meant she could skip school and have two wonderful days alone with Glyn. Oh yes. She grinned, unable to stop, just full of it.

With the arrangements finalised – Tania must make sure she answered the phone tomorrow in case Rowan's father called to check up on her, and she also had the name and phone number of the B & B in Bodmin in case of emergencies – Rowan packed a small overnight bag.

Her new sexy underwear, a lacy bra, the black negligée she'd bought from a department store in Truro where her father had taken her last month – he'd kill her if he saw it. She couldn't wait for Glyn to see it though. Jeans, tee-shirt, sweater and boots. This was a holiday with Glyn after all, and they were going to Bodmin Moor.

It had been Rowan's idea to go away together. She was tired of not having enough of him, of subterfuge, of not being able to admit openly at school that, yes, she had a boyfriend, and yes, of course they had sex. Didn't everyone? She wasn't sure how much longer she could keep their secret. She wanted everyone to know that she was loved.

'We'll never get away with it,' Glyn had said

'And why not?' She stood, naked from the waist up, for she had been drowning in early summer sun and the feel of Glyn's magic fingers for the past hour. She stood, hands on hips, eyes flashing warning signals, challenging him.

'Who's your alibi?'

She told him.

'What if your old man checks up on it?'

'He won't.' Actually it was unlikely. Rowan's father seemed to trust her these days – or perhaps he just had too many other things on his mind .

He had told her they must pull in their belts because the stock market wasn't what it once was, and she knew he was worried they might even lose their home. 'There's no such thing as a safe investment,' he had told her once. 'And since Lloyds everyone's aware of that. We have to be.'

Rowan wasn't sure exactly what he meant. But it must be serious – he never so much as spoke of Folyforth House any longer, and if anyone else did, his face turned black as thunder.

It still amused Rowan that old Athwenna Trelawney had proved herself a formidable opponent for Philip Brunswick. She smiled. Even if her father *had* ever found out the name of the owner of Folyforth House, he knew nothing else about Athwenna, Rowan was sure of that. So she had one up on her father after all. And what's more, she had become much more a part of Cornwall than he would ever be.

She had seen Athwenna many a time, standing by the wrought iron gates, so insubstantial that it seemed she'd just materialised there without having to walk down the drive. Other times she thought she saw Athwenna's silhouette on the other side of the stained glass of the front door. And sometimes . . . Sometimes she imagined that Athwenna was about to speak to her. That if Rowan could summon the courage, she might welcome her into the secrets of Folyforth – the house and especially the folly – as she had welcomed Glyn. But Athwenna Trelawney never spoke, and Rowan never approached her. Perhaps she was still too conscious that she was on probation. That she still didn't really belong.

'Well, where would we stay?' Glyn seemed determined to raise objections. What had happened to devil-may-care?

'Don't you want to come away with me?'

'Course I do.' He pulled at his ear lobe and twisted the small gold ring in a nervous gesture. 'But where would we stay?'

'Anywhere.' She laughed. 'I'll find somewhere. I'll book it up.'

He frowned as if he didn't like this idea. 'I don't know, Rowan. When they see us . . .'

'They won't bat an eyelid.' She grinned. 'We look old for our age, both of us. And I'll wear make-up.'

He pulled a face.

'Only to look older. We'll be students. Travelling together.' With a giggle she pulled a wedding band out of her pocket. It was only brass, but no-one would know. She'd bought it from the gift shop in the village. 'Married students.'

She thought she saw a spark of fear in the green eyes before he pulled her towards him. 'Now I know you're crazy. No-one would believe we're married.'

The rough fabric of his shirt rubbed on her breasts. She kissed his nose, tangled her fingers through his dark curls. 'Why wouldn't they?' Sometimes she felt married, more than married, so irrevocably joined to him.

He let her go abruptly. 'They just wouldn't.'

Rowan replaced the ring in the pocket of her jeans. What was the matter with Glyn today? 'We could go to London,' she said to cheer him up. 'See the sights. We'd be totally anonymous in London.' Maybe they could even see Zita, although she wasn't sure that Glyn would go for that. He seemed paranoid about being seen together, getting caught, as he put it. What did he think anyone would do to them, for goodness sake? They hadn't committed a crime. She smiled. At least they wouldn't have, after her sixteenth birthday next month.

'We should stick closer to home.' He thrust his hands in his pockets.

Rowan glared at him. '*Why* should we?'

He didn't answer, merely looked out to sea, his expression inscrutable. As if he knew how much she hated that, since it excluded her so totally. 'Glyn?'

'It'd take too long to get to London.' He swung round to face her. 'Tide's coming in. We should get back.'

We should stick closer to home. We should get back. Caution, caution. But Rowan didn't want to be cautious. It wasn't in her nature to be cautious. It never *used* to be in Glyn's nature, she reflected gloomily.

She pulled on her sweatshirt. 'Where then?' If they couldn't even agree about where to go, what hope was there?

'Bodmin Moor.' He swung past the sea lavender and lump of granite that obscured their secret path, and started the uphill climb back to the wood. 'That's where I want to go.'

'Bodmin?' She was about to object. It was hardly any distance away, it wasn't like going any place at all. But something in his set expression as Glyn turned to give her a hand up the path, stopped her. Glyn wouldn't have the money to go very far, would he? For some reason it was important to him to stay in his own territory, and she should respect that. 'Okay, Bodmin it is,' she conceded. Better that than go nowhere at all. Better that than lose him.

'Will you be able to get away?' she asked.

'Don't you worry about me,' he called back over his shoulder, his strides taking him further away from her. 'You sort yourself out, that's all.'

Rowan smiled secretly to herself as she followed him up into the wood. She would go to the library, find a list of tourist information, choose a B & B, no problem. She knew what to do, and she could hardly wait.

Two whole days, Rowan thought to herself as she lay awake, waiting for the slow morning to arrive. Two whole days and one very glorious night.

'He's after you, that one.' Nell and Zita, in the pie and mash shop in Hammersmith, were waiting to close up after the lunch time session.

The pie and mash shop was more or less unique to London, having begun as a cheap source of nutrition, when the old market traders selling eels moved indoors. Its heyday was in the twenties and thirties, although it had remained popular in the fifties and sixties – especially with working-class London. But more and more of the shops had closed down over the last two decades, become take-aways, burger joints, wine-bars, restaurants specialising in foreign muck, as Nell called it. Everything was changing, and not always for the better, in Zita's opinion. Now, there were only a few other mash shops left –

all of them in East London – and Nell's place had become almost a curiosity. But Zita had come round to Nell's way of thinking. She could see the appeal. And it was good to feel that you were making a contribution to the old traditions, stopping them from disappearing altogether.

The layout of the shop was in the traditional style, but had been subtly up-dated. It was big, light and airy, and reminded her strangely of an old music hall. On the walls were deco-styled signs such as that proclaiming Fruit Pie and Custard, huge mirrors secured with clips in the form of intertwined eels, and walls tiled in blue, green and white that were both attractive and easy to clean. There was a long art-deco style counter, marble-topped tables, and seats like pews for the customers, of whom there were many, mostly older people, working-class, friendly and ready for a chat. Zita was astonished how many people frequented the place, for both take-aways and sit-ins, even for the traditionally limited menu of minced beef pies, mash and eels, all served positively dripping with the bright green parsley sauce they called liquor. For pudding, the mainstay was still rhubarb and custard, and whoever said this was a dying tradition, had never entered Nell's Pie and Mash shop.

No, it certainly hadn't taken Zita long to fit in.

The object of Nell's remark – an unremarkable looking man called Johnny Standish – was on his fourth round of bread and butter accompanying his pie, mash and liquor.

'Where does he put it all?' Zita glanced at him only briefly; it was no good encouraging Nell to get ideas. Johnny Standish certainly was skinny as a rake. Almost part of the furniture ever since the place had opened, Nell had told Zita. In here twice a week, and lately more often than that.

'I wish I knew.' Nell patted her own ample stomach and eyed Zita thoughtfully. 'What do you think of him?'

'He's all right.' To distract herself, Zita began cleaning the counter and clattering pans about. All she wanted from Johnny Standish was for him to get out of here so she and Nell could sit down with a nice cup of tea and put their feet up. It was hard work running this place, for she had come in on equal terms when Ted died a year ago. Not that Zita didn't enjoy the sensation of working for herself for a change, building up a business that she and hers would benefit from. But it was darned hard work, just the same.

'I think he's a real nice bloke,' Nell said. She sounded as casual as she ever did, but Zita knew she was still watching her out of the corner of her eye. Nell tried to match-make for her sister almost as often as she made hot dinners.

'Is that right, Nell?' she teased. 'If you like him so much, do you want me to put a good word in for you, or what?'

'Get off,' Nell sighed. 'I've been there, love. Ted was a good bloke, but he wasn't easy. I don't mind being on me own. I know when I'm well off, I do.'

Zita grinned. 'Maybe I do too.'

'You've still got more life left in you, you have. You're young enough. And you've not even tried the other way yet.' Nell filled the kettle. 'Let's have a cuppa.' She leaned forwards, dropping her voice still further. 'Has he asked you out yet?'

'Don't be daft.' But Zita could feel herself colouring as, once more, Johnny Standish glanced towards her, smiled his toothy grin. He wasn't a bad bloke. But she wasn't in the market for blokes – bad or otherwise.

'I saw him chatting to you earlier. He was talking about some film on at the Odeon, wasn't he?'

'If you know so much then why are you asking?' Zita loved Nell, she was happy living with Nell, and glad that she'd been around to help her through since Ted had died. Nell was her senior by ten years and had always looked out for Zita's best interests. But sometimes she interfered too much. The biggest-hearted woman in the world. But . . . And it was a big but.

'So he asked you?'

'Yes, he asked me,' she hissed.

'And?'

'And nothing.' Zita slammed the warming cupboard to with a bang.

A chair scraped across the tiled floor and they both looked up. 'See you later, then.' Johnny Standish waved, grinned and walked out of the door. His plate was clean, his knife and fork neatly together.

'About bloody time too.' Zita darted over to lock up behind him and draw the blinds, while Nell poured the tea.

They sat down at a marble-topped table.

'You never really told me what happened back in Cornwall.' Once more, Zita was aware of her sister's scrutiny.

'Yes, I did.' She had related the whole story of Philip Brunswick and his lunge, and Nell had been duly horrified, although thankfully she had refrained from telling Zita that she'd told her so.

'I don't mean all that.' Nell loaded sugar into her cup.

'What then?' Zita felt herself closing up inside.

'You know . . .' Nell stirred her tea. 'Why you came back with such sad eyes . . . Why you won't go to the pictures with a nice bloke who asks you . . . Why you work and work.'

Zita leaned her back wearily against the side of the bench-seat and put her feet up. She refused to even look at Nell. 'I'm used to work.'

'Was there someone special?' Nell's voice was soft.

What was she, a bloody mind reader? But Zita realised with a shock that she wanted to speak of it. She had told no-one about Harry Penbray, and now she needed to acknowledge to another human being that he had actually happened. 'There was a bloke . . .' she began. 'Harry, his name was.'

'Harry . . .' Nell seemed to twirl it around her tongue.

'He was a fisherman.'

Nell was waiting for her to go on. But what more could she say? That was it, wasn't it? Apart from . . . 'He was married.'

Nell made a kind of snorting noise in the back of her throat. 'Those are the ones to steer clear of.'

'D'you think I don't know that?' Zita jerked the white china cup to her lips and a few drops of tea spilled on to the marbled surface. Maybe this was why she hadn't told a soul. She didn't want or need their judgements.

'And what happened?' Nell asked.

'Nothing happened.' Well, that was the truth, sure enough. Although if she had stayed longer . . . who would ever know?

'You didn't keep in touch then?'

Zita traced a pattern with her finger in the spilt tea. 'No.' That was her regret. If you could change anything . . . what would it be?

'And tonight? Are you going to the pictures tonight.'

Zita got wearily to her feet to clear away. 'No.' A thought occurred to her. 'I'll be staying in. I'm planning on writing a letter tonight.'

132

*   *   *

Rowan had wanted to meet Glyn at the folly – pure sentimentality on her part she supposed – but he had decided it was too risky.

'We can't walk to the station *together*,' he'd said as if she were quite mad. 'We'll meet on the platform . . . but if there's anyone around we'll have to get on the train separately as well.'

Rowan was peeved. 'Are you sure you don't want me to make my own way to Bodmin? Maybe I could stay in a different B & B if you'd prefer.'

'Sarky, sarky. You wouldn't want someone to tell your old man, would you, eh?' He grinned and she forgave him instantly. He was right. Of course he was right.

Nevertheless, when she received Zita's letter, Rowan decided to go to the folly to open it – she had plenty of time before the train was due, and she wanted to be alone and in a special place when she read it. Zita had only written to her at birthdays and Christmas up to now. Rowan missed Zita. Without her there seemed to be no-one with a brand of practical common-sense whom Rowan could turn to. No-one who could be counted on for a smile, a hug, a sticking plaster. Zita was someone who always made it better – whatever it might be.

She left the house at her usual time with her overnight bag and satchel of school books, raced past Folyforth House, dumped her bags just inside the wood, and ran through to the folly. She settled herself in her favourite place tucked inside the battlements, on one of the cushions that she and Glyn kept there.

Dearest Rowan . . . she read.

The letter began with an account of a day of Zita's life, but the mundane descriptions and flashes of humour made Hammersmith, the pie and mash shop and Zita's sister Nell come alive for Rowan, made her miss Zita more than ever.

I want you to write and tell me about you and that young man of yours, she read. *If it's all still lovey dovey between you, that is.* Rowan smiled. What would Zita say if she knew they were heading for a romantic rendezvous on Bodmin Moor? Would she flip, or would she understand?

At least she would approve of the fact that since that first time in the bay, Glyn had withdrawn from her quickly when they made love, a sensation that Rowan hated more and more as their relationship progressed. She supposed he was right to take precautions, although she hated playing safe, loved to take risks once in a while. Life didn't seem worth living if you only played safe. He was right and Zita would approve. But she wanted all of him, needed all of him, just as she had that first time.

And as it's the holidays soon, I wondered if you'd like to come and stay with us for a bit. Here, Rowan sensed her hesitation. *With a friend if you prefer. Would you like to?*

'Oh, yes,' Rowan breathed. 'I'd love to.'

Do you think your mother and father would let you? Maybe you could ask them. And . . . Once again the writing seemed to falter, as if this had been difficult for Zita. *How is Audrey? Give her my love. I often think of you all.*

Not a word about her father, Rowan noticed. Would he let her go to visit Zita? She clutched the letter closer. She certainly hoped so. But she still wasn't sure what had happened between them.

There's one more thing.

Rowan raised her eyebrows as she read on. She would miss the train if she weren't careful, but she couldn't resist finishing the letter first.

This done, she shoved it in her pocket and ran like the wind, hair flying, almost forgetting to pick up her bags from where she'd dumped them at the edge of the wood. Zita and Harry Penbray. Well, well, well. Whoever would have thought it?

Glyn Penbray, waiting on the station platform, hunched himself closer into his jacket and wished that he were invisible. He hoped Rowan wouldn't be early – that she wouldn't rush over to him, make it obvious, even kiss him or something equally awful. He was even terrified of seeing anyone he knew – crazy really, because his mum actually knew he was catching this train.

Along with all his camping gear . . . He looked down at his feet. Rowan would scream with laughter when she saw all this stuff he'd had to bring along. *What about the B & B?* He could just imagine it. Oh God. He'd made a pig's ear out of this, no mistake.

And what was worse was that for the first time he didn't feel in control of the situation between himself and Rowan Brunswick. She had known how to go about all this, he hadn't had a clue. She had wanted to go to London, a journey that meant nothing to her; he'd never been there in his life, and with only a few quid in his pocket he wouldn't be going there now.

It hadn't been so easy to manufacture a mate as an alibi – in the village most people knew each other's business in any case, so Glyn had told his mother he wanted to go off camping alone for a couple of days.

'Camping?' He recalled the astonishment in her blue eyes. 'You?'

'I've got all the stuff.'

'Who with?' That was his mum – immediately suspicious. Immediately thinking he was taking some girl – which of course he was. Or she was taking him.

'Not with anyone.' Every muscle twitched with the effort as he lied to her. 'I want some time on my own.'

'On your own? Who do you think you're kidding, Glyn Penbray . . .'

She nagged him for days after, raising every objection under the sun:

'Who's going to help your Dad with the catch?'

'What about the school work you'll miss?'

'Why can't you go on a week-end?'

And, 'What exactly are you up to, anyway?'

She nagged and nagged, hadn't stopped since he'd first mentioned it, and in the end it was his Dad who saved his bacon.

'Leave the lad alone, woman,' he'd growled in that way he had. 'Give him some time and space. He'll be leaving school in a few weeks anyway – what difference does it make?'

For a moment Glyn glanced up and caught a certain look in his father's eyes, a certain kind of understanding. And then the moment was gone.

'All right,' she grumbled. 'All right. Go on with you, then.'

Funny, Glyn reflected, but no matter how much she nagged, no matter how totally she seemed to be the boss in every situation, when his Dad did speak up, it meant something to her. Dad still meant something to her.

Even so, Glyn had a lot of doubts about this mad scheme of Rowan's.

It worried him that they were pushing things too far, taking too many risks, that they'd be found out. It was a miracle they'd gone two years with no-one catching them out – especially his mother.

How much longer did they have? Every week he meant to end it, aware he'd taken on more than he could handle. But every week he looked into those eyes of hers – so like the wild Cornish sea he loved, and drawing him just as strongly – felt his blood rising, and knew that he couldn't do it. He was being pulled by Rowan Brunswick, and sometimes she was so wild, so bloody exciting, that he just didn't care where she was pulling him to.

He looked at his watch. All this time he'd been worrying that she'd be early, and now she was late, for God's sake. The train was due in any second. She wouldn't make it. After all this, she wouldn't make it.

Glyn's stomach dipped in panic, he rose to his feet to see if she was coming and at the same time heard the sound of the train approaching, before he actually saw it in the distance. Please, no. Rowan . . .

The train pulled in to the platform, there was still no sign of her, and Glyn's world swiftly became dark and heavy. What could he do? Where could he go without her?

The guard shot him a strange look, he lugged the camping gear across to the train, but his emotions seemed to be in little pieces at his feet. Rowan . . .

He opened the door. Shut it again. Turned away from the train and then he saw her – pelting on to the platform, face flushed, hair dishevelled, swinging two bags one on each shoulder. 'Glyn! Glyn!'

And suddenly he didn't care about being seen or discovered. He didn't care about her kissing him in public, in broad daylight. He didn't have any more worries, because Rowan Brunswick had cannoned into him, re-entered his world and made it light up again.

He half-pulled her on to the train, took her face between his hands, and kissed her, full on her soft and beautiful mouth.

Chapter 9

———◆———

'What is it about Bodmin Moor that you like so much?' Rowan asked Glyn. 'Why did we have to come here?'

They had spent the day exploring some of the wild expanse of bleak open country dotted with standing stones, hut circles and tors that lay beyond the moorland village in which they were staying the night. It had been a hot and dusty day; at times Rowan had wished Glyn wasn't so energetic, but he was an explorer at heart – he wouldn't be satisfied until he'd seen it all.

They walked and walked until her legs were aching and her throat was parched. But eventually even Glyn got tired and they headed back to the village, stopping to eat dinner in a local pub on the way. Now at last it was growing dark, and they were only half a mile from their B & B.

'Nature in the raw.' He took her hand. 'That's why I wanted to come here. Can't you feel it?'

'Yes, of course.' She squeezed his hand back, it was warm to the touch. 'But why here, with me?'

'Because we belong with nature.' He laughed, but she wasn't quite sure how serious he was being. 'You and me, Rowan, we belong in this wild kind of landscape. Don't you think?'

'Maybe . . .' But she was doubtful. She didn't want to think of them in only one landscape. She wanted to think of them as belonging everywhere together. 'Anywhere's wonderful with you,' she told him.

He slung his arm around her shoulders. 'Let's sit down for a minute.'

Rowan sank to the rocky ground beside him, secretly wanting to walk on, to get back to where they were staying. She didn't want to waste any of this precious night.

'The sky's clear.' Once more his attention seemed to move swiftly away from her. 'You can see all the stars, look.' He pointed. 'Those seven stars make up the Plough. It's always high over- head in the spring. That's part of the constellation called the Great Bear.'

'Hmm.' Rowan lay back on the hard mossy earth. The sky was beautiful, night-time velvet, but they were only stars, weren't they?

'And near to Orion is Gemini.'

'The twins?'

He nodded. 'Castor and Pollux are the two brightest stars in Gemini. In mythology they were twins. Pollux was immortal but when Castor died he begged to be allowed to join him. The gods answered his prayer and turned them both into stars, side by side in the heavens, so they'd never be parted.'

Rowan stared up at him. He was certainly full of surprises. 'How do you know all this?'

'From my Dad.' Glyn laughed. 'Most fishermen know a lot about the night sky – they use it to navigate.'

Rowan snuggled closer to him. 'I bet most fishermen don't know about the twins that wouldn't be parted.'

'Maybe they don't at that.' He leaned on one elbow, slipped his hand up her sweatshirt, slowly exploring.

She wriggled with pleasure. 'Not here, Glyn . . .'

'Why not?' His touch became more urgent. His lips were close to hers, his breath warm on her face.

'Because we've finally got somewhere to go to tonight.' Half-heartedly she pushed him away, but the truth was that she wanted him. His fingers were like fire to her; when she was with Glyn the sweet rush never quite left her.

'I like it under the stars.' His lips brushed against hers, teasing, his fingers easing her breasts free, his legs and lean hips pressing hard against her.

With a groan she pulled him closer, felt the familiar sensation of a cool breeze on her bare skin, denim being pulled from her thighs. It wasn't what she'd intended for tonight, but she couldn't resist him. Side by side in the heavens. Twin stars that wouldn't be parted.

She slept like a baby in the unfamiliar bed, but awoke early, before

Glyn, relishing the child-like look of him as he lay beside her, his dark hair on the white pillow slip, the brown skin becoming a man's skin, the faint stubble already on his jaw, his fist clenched in sleep. She smiled, and at that second he awoke.

'Jesus.' He rubbed his eyes, stared at her as if she were a stranger. 'This feels so weird.'

'Being here with me?' She kissed a lonely curl that had settled on his brow, and climbed out of bed to plug in the kettle. 'Being made tea in bed by a naked girl?' Goodness knows where her negligée had got to – she hadn't kept it on very long.

'This. The whole thing. Are we crazy, Rowan?'

She laughed delightedly. 'This is how it'll be. You and me. When we're together.'

'We are together.' He watched her as she plumped up pillows and crawled back in beside him. Wasn't this enough for her? He was here, wasn't he?

'No.' She laughed again. 'I mean really together. Living together.'

A sliver of fear seemed to grow in his belly, moving up and outwards. 'Living together?'

'Well, married then. Whatever.' She snuggled her head into his neck.

He felt stifled, suffocated. He tried to say something light and funny but no sound emerged. Why should the prospect of living with Rowan scare him half to death? He frowned. Was it the prospect of living with anyone that scared him? He stroked her thick dark hair, but found himself wishing she'd take the weight of her head from his shoulder. He was sixteen. She was talking commitment.

'I can't wait to escape from my parents,' she was saying. 'I'm trapped there. Sometimes I feel like I can't breathe.'

Glyn knew exactly how she felt. He was feeling the same thing right now.

'I don't want to bother with university or any of that stuff. School's a waste of time.'

'What *do* you want to do?' His voice came out as a croak.

'Be with you.' Her fingers were playing a tune across his chest, twisting through the dark hair. But somehow it didn't turn him on like it usually did.

'And?' He felt himself tense. 'What else?'

'Does there have to be anything else?' Rowan stretched out her legs like a cat. 'God, I slept well. And I can't imagine anything more blissful than being with you.' She turned to him. 'For always, Glyn.'

He smiled. Behind the smile was desperation. 'How about that tea?'

'Chauvinist.' But she swung herself out of the bed again, and busied herself with the tea tray.

'What do you think they'd say?' She brought the tray over to the bed.

'They?'

'Oh, you know.' She passed him his cup. 'Our parents, people in the village.'

Glyn felt so sick he had to put the cup straight down again. He recalled his mother's words about the people who lived in the house on the hill, and thought he knew pretty well what she'd say.

'It'll be funny when they find out.' She sipped her tea, looked at Glyn, and put it down next to his on the bedside table. 'Glyn, you do *love* me?'

'Course I do.' He couldn't look at her. Perhaps this had been a mistake after all. It was getting too serious.

'Really?'

'Really.'

'How much?'

He groaned and laughed at the same time. 'How much do you want? As much as the world? A hundred times more than the moon? A thousand times more than the stars?'

She nodded. 'At least.'

'But as for the rest . . .' He traced a pattern on her cheek with his fingertip.

'Yes?' She sounded too eager.

'I can't see that far ahead.' How could he tell her? He wanted to get away, he wanted adventure, he wanted . . . Yes, he wanted a woman, but he didn't want just one woman. Although if it had to be one woman, he realised, it would probably be this one.

'You're scared,' she informed him.

'Of what?'

'Of whom.' She lay back. 'I'll just go to my father and tell him we want to be together.'

He couldn't help laughing at her, she looked so sure of herself lying there, sometimes a girl and sometimes almost a woman. 'You think it's that simple, then?' he teased.

'Isn't it?' Her eyes were asking for confirmation but he knew he couldn't give it to her.

'It's not simple at all, you little dreamer, you,' he sighed. 'What would I do? How would we live? Where would we go?' Somehow, he must make her see.

'We could go to London.' Her face was flushed with excitement. 'We could elope, even before we're eighteen. Go to Gretna Green.' She turned towards him, passion in her voice, her face. 'You could do anything. You're wonderful.'

'No.' He pulled her closer. 'You're wonderful. And I don't deserve you.' And stop this talk of marriage, he thought. Please stop.

'Zita was wrong,' she murmured, as his mouth closed in on her once again, as she caught the sweet rush before it exploded.

'More.' She pulled him to her and wouldn't let him draw back when he wanted to, as he always did. Pulled him closer with a strength she hadn't even known she had, empowered by some primeval urge that had beaten her, beaten him.

'Rowan . . .' His voice was husky in her ear.

Zita was wrong, that's all she could think. Love was everything. It was all there was. Only love.

Lynette Penbray knew something was up. She was only surprised that her son thought she could be so easily fooled, that he knew her so little. She pulled the sheets off his bed and threw them into a crumpled heap in the corner. More washing – it was never ending.

Why would a young lad like Glyn suddenly decide to take himself off camping on Bodmin Moor in the middle of the week? It sounded pretty daft, and whatever else he was, her Glyn wasn't daft. And if there *was* an innocent explanation – though she was blowed if she could think of one – then why had the lad looked so darned sheepish when he first brought the subject up?

Lynette pulled fresh sheets out of the airing cupboard, and groaned as she reached over to tuck them in. Her back was playing up. Too many nights standing around serving beer in the Bull and Packet. Where was that taste of luxury in her life that she'd always longed for? That she had hoped might materialise through Philip Brunswick? Not the presents he gave her to keep her sweet, she didn't mean that. Her lip curled. She had never wanted just presents . . .

Where had she gone wrong? Was she destined to keep house, cook and work as a barmaid all her days?

She straightened, and found herself looking at a photo Glyn kept on his wall of the two of them. She looked young, carefree almost. Her arm was round his shoulders. Her boy . . .

Lynette sighed. She had to find out what this was all about, that was for sure. He had come back home from Bodmin late last night looking so moony-faced that she suspected a girl was involved.

Lynette thought – she'd often thought – that Glyn had a girlfriend. After all he was sixteen now and, though she said it herself, a real smasher to look at. But she wasn't sure who it was, and though he'd mentioned Melanie Fowler more than once, and the girl had a fancy for Glyn – anyone could see that – Lynette thought there was a lot more to it. Maybe it was a succession of girls, maybe Glyn wouldn't be a one woman man. Lynette smiled. She was all for that. She didn't want some silly girl to trap him into settling down when he was still young enough to be off having a good time and playing the field. Lynette didn't mind much what Glyn got up to. But the fact was, she wanted to know.

She heard the door go, and her son's footsteps.

'Mum?'

'In your room.' Lynette sat wearily on the newly made bed.

He came in, threw his rucksack on to the quilt.

'How was school?'

'Boring. Total waste of time.' She knew what he'd say before he even opened his mouth, had thought it herself when she was sixteen and couldn't wait to leave school. But what would he do once he'd left? What was there in the world for her son?

Lynette worried over this. On the one hand she didn't want him to end up in some dead end job – and please, not a fisherman. Anything but a fisherman like Harry with calluses on arthritic hands, cold all winter through, out in all weathers for next to nothing. He deserved better. But on the other hand, she wouldn't want him to leave Folyforth, to leave her. Sometimes she thought Glyn her very reason for existence.

'You should listen, maybe you might learn something.' She spoke automatically, not really meaning it.

Glyn walked to the window and stared out towards the sea. 'Maybe I might learn more at home. I might learn more from you, I reckon . . .' His voice tailed off.

'Oh, yes my lad. I could teach you a thing or two . . .' But Lynette realised he wasn't listening. He was staring out towards the waterfront and his face had turned chalk-white.

'Glyn? What is it?' She got to her feet, but he turned, recovering quickly.

'Nothing.' He laughed. 'Felt someone walking over my grave, that's all.' He stood in front of the window, casually blocking her view.

All right. Lynette smiled grimly. Two could play at that one. So he wanted to play games, did he? 'I'll take this stuff down for the washing tomorrow, then.'

She gathered the discarded bed-linen in her arms and left the room, half running down the stairs. She dropped it in the kitchen and slipped out of the back door, squinting towards the waterfront. But she couldn't see a damn thing, and if she went further out Glyn would see her, so she hitched up her dress and climbed on top of the coal bunker. She had to get a view of whatever it was Glyn had seen, whatever had made his face lose all its colour like that.

At first she couldn't make out what it could be. She could see Harry talking to someone by the fish stall, a few others wandering around the waterfront, even a couple of early emmets – they didn't get the main invasion until July. Then she looked again. The girl talking to Harry was Rowan Brunswick – no mistaking it, even from this distance.

Her mind went into overdrive. Was that what had made Glyn panic? Harry talking to the girl from the house up on the hill? But why? Unless . . .

'No.' She jumped down from the coal bunker. 'No.' She wouldn't have it.

Once, two years ago, she had seen Glyn looking at Rowan

Brunswick, and her blood had run cold. But he'd convinced her that she was wrong – or even if she were right, that nothing could possibly come of it. How could it?

And in the last two years it had never happened again. If the girl was ever around then Glyn would likely avert his eyes and ignore her rather than . . . But of course. She hit her head with the palm of her hand. It wasn't natural to *ignore* her, was it? In fact, it would be pretty strange to ignore someone who was an object of curiosity for other folk. Unless . . . unless . . . She couldn't get her head round it.

What girl in the village would have been able to take off for two days without the whole village knowing? No-one – apart from the Brunswick girl. Lynette racked her brains to remember if she'd seen her while Glyn was away. Nope. And, ye gods – Lynette hated to admit it – she was beautiful. What young lad wouldn't want her?

Somehow, she got herself into the kitchen, steadied herself for a moment, her hands resting on the drainer. She had to play this very carefully. Of course it had to be stopped – no question – but it had to be stopped in the right way. She didn't want to arouse the wrong kind of attention or lose Glyn. She *wouldn't* lose Glyn. There was only one way to do this, she realised.

Lynette called Glyn downstairs and sent him out to get milk from the shop in the village. 'I need extra for custard tonight,' she told him, glad, for once, that she had become so good at lying over the years.

He looked doubtful, scared almost, as she pressed the money into his hand. 'Get on with you, then.'

She watched him leave the house, waited a moment, then slowly picked up the phone.

'You are Harry Penbray?' Rowan felt strangely nervous talking to Glyn's father. Although, of course, her dark-eyed Glyn with his tangled wild hair and gypsy ear-ring looked nothing at all like the blue-eyed salt-and-pepper fisherman dressed in baggy jeans and braces that she was now confronting.

'Who's asking?' Harry looked up. Zita had been right – the girl had turned out pretty enough to turn heads a plenty. She was dressed in school uniform but she looked too old to be a schoolgirl, in his opinion.

'My name is Rowan Brunswick.' She held out her hand, and he took it, small in his worn red palm.

'And what can I do for you, Rowan Brunswick?' He grinned, for she looked ill at ease. 'Were you wanting some fish? 'Cause there's not much left; I was about to pack up.'

'Oh, no. No fish. At least . . .' She smiled. 'Not today, thank you.'

Polite too. Zita had brought the girl up well. But she had something on her mind, and he waited for her to spit it out.

'I wanted a word,' she said at last. 'Zita wrote to me . . .'

'And how is she?' He asked it quickly, too quickly. The truth was that he often thought of Zita Porter, and with regret. Maybe he'd rushed her, maybe he'd got it all wrong. No fool like an old fool, they say. It certainly hadn't taken her long to shoot off once he'd made his intentions plain. Think on't, he'd told her. Never dreamt she'd run away.

'She's fine.' Rowan seemed to relax, as if now she were on safe ground. 'She's living with her sister. In Hammersmith.'

'Hammersmith,' he echoed. Like another world. 'She always said she missed London.'

Rowan nodded. 'They've got a pie and mash shop there.'

He laughed, though he wasn't sure exactly what that might be. 'Good for her.' He hadn't forgotten Zita. And he hadn't forgotten the way she made him feel. Life in the old dog yet. Harry had surprised even himself.

'She wanted me to tell you,' Rowan blurted. 'She tried to say goodbye before she left.'

'Goodbye?' He was confused. 'Did she now?'

'Only it was all so sudden, you see.' The girl seemed embarrassed. 'There was this awful row between my parents, and Zita was somehow in the middle of it. They told her to leave.'

'Told her to leave?' Harry tried to take this in, but it had never crossed his mind before that she hadn't left entirely of her own free will. Why should it? She had gone more or less straight after that conversation they'd had about the future. What was he supposed to think?

'I'm afraid so.' Rowan looked down as if ashamed of her parents' behaviour. And well she might. Harry knew how much Zita had done for that family, knew half of it without even being told.

'I'm terribly sorry. I had no idea you were . . .' She hesitated. 'Friends. Otherwise of course I would have talked to you before.'

'And she's only just told you to mention it, like?' Harry could see now how it had been, but why on earth hadn't she sent a message sooner? She could have saved him all those empty wondering days out at sea. Why hadn't she written or . . . ?

'She didn't know where you lived.' Rowan pulled the letter out of her pocket, and ran her finger down the untidy looped hand. But Harry could hardly see it, let alone read it, and his reading was never good at the best of times.

'She says here, look . . .'

'Read it to me?' he whispered.

Rowan glanced at him, took a deep breath.

Tell him I came down to the waterfront that morning. I wanted to see him to say goodbye, but all the boats were out. Tell him I asked someone where Harry Penbray lived but they wouldn't tell me. Tell him I didn't want to cause any trouble. He'll understand . . .'

'Do you?' She folded the letter, looked at him with those searching grey eyes. They reminded Harry of the eyes of the woman in the café. Audrey Brunswick. And of the night he'd helped Zita take her home. But those eyes had been blank and lifeless. This girl's eyes had a whole lot of living ahead of them.

He nodded. 'Thanks for telling me.' He couldn't think straight, he hardly knew what to think.

'See you, then.' He watched the tall young girl walk away, swinging her black school bag as she went, flicking her dark hair from her shoulders. 'Nice talking to you, Harry.'

She wasn't a bit like they said, he thought. Not a bit snooty. She was a nice girl, that one. 'Rowan?' he called.

She turned. 'Yeah?'

Harry moved a few paces towards her, dropped his voice slightly. You never could tell with these busybodies that lived around here. He wondered who it had been that had snubbed Zita that morning on the waterfront? 'Could you give me her address? Write it down for me?' He didn't know what he was thinking of – how was he going to sit down and write to her when he'd never written a letter in his life? But he knew he had to try.

'Course I can.' She pulled a notebook and pen out of her satchel, squatted down by the rocks and wrote in large capitals, handing him the sheet of paper.

'Thanks.' He took it, frowning, as if by concentration he could make the letters stop dancing and become words.

Rowan hesitated. 'Can I give her a message?'

He nodded. 'Tell her I miss her, that's all. Tell her I think of her. Tell her . . .' He grinned. 'Tell her I might even be seeing her one of these days.'

Chapter 10

As soon as she'd left Harry Penbray, Rowan ran home to change into her jeans, and from there to the folly to see Glyn as arranged.

As always, when she entered the glade and saw the folly rising out of the rocks, undergrowth and ivy, she felt a sense of awe. The squat mossy tower and heavy castellations were a powerful combination, complemented by the rusty octagonal clock with only an hour hand, which was so out of proportion to the rest of the folly that Rowan wondered if someone had been given the clock and simply felt compelled to build somewhere to house it.

She and Glyn had made this their special retreat, but of course she knew that the folly didn't belong to them at all, and not just because of Athwenna Trelawney and Folyforth House. The folly remained aloof and inscrutable, with an air of mystery it was giving away to no-one. Surely it couldn't even have belonged to whoever had built it? Nor to any lovers of the past that she liked to imagine meeting here.

The more questions she asked him, the more Glyn laughed at her. Glyn often laughed at her; he told her that it wasn't love that had been made here, but money.

She picked her way through the nettles and thistles to the small Gothic doorway surrounded by ivy and bindweed. Pushing the door open, she felt a frisson of fear sweep over her, in response to the chill that seemed to live inside the granite folly. She ran up the treacherous stone spiral steps to the battlements.

As she'd half-expected, Glyn wasn't yet here, so she settled herself in what had become her own comfortable hollow of stone, with a cushion to prevent the cold seeping through to her skin, pulled her notebook out of her pocket, and began writing to Zita. Her pen flew over the paper as she poured it all out – her love for Glyn, their two days in Bodmin, and the difficulties at home.

I hardly see Mum, she admitted, aware of the usual guilt pang. But what could she have done differently? She wanted to live, didn't she? And Audrey appeared to have put living behind her.

She stays in that green room of hers most of the time. We have someone in to cook and clean – some old cow from the village who pinches up her face and looks down on us as if we're crazy. She paused, sucking the pen. *And perhaps since you left, we are a little crazy.*

She'd written three pages before she realised she hadn't mentioned Harry Penbray, so now she did so, faithfully relating the details of their conversation, adding only the love and wistfulness that she was sure she'd seen in his honest blue eyes.

Glyn would call her a romantic fool, and she wasn't altogether happy about aiding and abetting a relationship which could potentially divide Glyn's parents. But Glyn had told her something of his home background, and the one thing missing was love. Well, that was the one thing Rowan believed in – she would support love, wherever she found it, to the end. She liked Harry Penbray – he deserved to be loved. And so, of course, did Zita. She shouldn't be condemned to cooking, cleaning, working all her life. She should have fun; she should be somebody's lover, and have someone to love her back.

Rowan finished her letter and Glyn still hadn't come, so she lay back on the cushion, her hands tucked under her head, her legs curled in front of her, to wait for him.

Glyn . . . he filled every waking moment. She longed for the time when they could be together properly. She didn't care a fig what anyone thought or said. She loved Glyn. They were destined for each other – twin stars, side by side in the heavens, never to be parted . . .

But he wasn't with her now, was he? And as time went by it seemed less and less likely that he would come. Until at last it grew chilly, so chilly and late that she reluctantly rose to go home, knowing he wouldn't come now, conscious only of desolation. She stumbled down the stone stairs, almost tripping, saving herself only by flinging her hands against the damp granite walls. Where was he? Why hadn't he come?

She ran home, arriving dishevelled, out of breath and miserable, to find her father standing at the door waiting for her. His features were chiselled like stone, his expression an unexploded thundercloud.

'Father?' She tried to think of something to say. 'I'm sorry I'm late. I . . .' He had never stood at the door waiting for her before.

'Get inside.' It seemed an effort for him to speak.

Her throat constricted, a sudden cramp twisted in her stomach.

'In here.' He half pushed her into his study, and for the first time she was really scared. She looked at his face, at the thin sour mouth turned down with distaste and anger.

The pain in her stomach made her want to double up for relief. She thought she might be sick right there, on his expensive thick pile carpet.

'Now.' He stood, tall and straight in front of the door, arms folded, as if to bar her escape. His eyes were robotic, but his adam's apple was throbbing, working up and down in his throat.

She stared at it, transfixed.

'You can start by telling me where you've been. Where you go. Who you meet. What you've been doing.' He held up one hand to prevent her protest. 'And you're not leaving this room until you do.'

In the Penbray cottage on the waterfront, Glyn was still concerned about what he'd seen, half inclined to rush to the folly straight away to find out from Rowan what she'd been doing talking to his dad, and half inclined to teach her a lesson by not showing up. All that talk about marriage and being together for eternity had worried him – it wasn't in Glyn's nature to think as far ahead as forever. He loved Rowan Brunswick – no doubt of that. But he wanted to dictate the terms of that love. Loving a girl and living with her for ever were two entirely different things for Glyn.

In the end the matter was decided by his mother, who said she wanted to talk to him.

'What about?' He wondered if – despite his efforts – she'd seen his father talking to Rowan. He wouldn't put it past her – in fact he wouldn't put anything past her – but his mother seemed innocence personified this afternoon, standing there in a flowery apron offering him a huge slab of chocolate cake to have with his tea.

He sat down, watching her. She was still an attractive woman, his mother. Nice figure – if a little overweight – curly dark hair always neat. Never went out without smart clothes and lipstick. Too much lipstick in his opinion, but Glyn had seen men from the village giving her the eye, wondering perhaps if she were available. Not to mention the not so neighbourly visits of Dewy Jago . . .

'Now then. All this talk about going to Bodmin and needing some time on your own . . .' She paused and Glyn wriggled uncomfortably.

'What about it?' He was immediately on the defensive.

'It made me think, that's what. You're leaving school soon.' Lynette poured milk into two mugs. 'Seems to me you should be considering your future.'

'P'raps.' Glyn didn't want to commit himself to any kind of agreements until he knew where his mother was going.

She passed him some more cake. 'Seems to me you should think very carefully, my lad.'

He took the plate wondering why he felt so nervous when this was his own home, and his own mother. 'What about?'

'About what you want to do with the rest of your life.' She smiled. 'Me and your dad don't want you to rush into anything you might live to regret.'

Me and your dad? Glyn wondered if his dad had actually had any say in all this, but he nodded agreement because his mouth was full. He didn't want to rush into anything he might live to regret either. She had it exactly right there.

'Have you got any ideas?' Lynette sat almost primly, her knees together, waiting, looking like a different kind of mother from the one he'd always known. Glyn had the unwelcome impression that she was playing a part.

He stared back at her.

'Well, have you?' A flicker of impatience crossed her face.

Oh yes, he had ideas. Sure he had ideas, but they were all about travelling, adventure, seeing the world. He didn't have any ideas that involved Folyforth. Rowan was the one who had those. 'I dunno,' he said.

Lynette frowned. 'You don't want to take up fishing, then?'

He pulled a face.

'Good.' She passed him his tea. 'Well, how about going away for a bit?'

'Away?' Glyn stared at his mother. He'd never known her suggest he went away anywhere before – nowhere that she wasn't going anyhow. 'Where to?'

'I've got friends.' She pursed her mouth and glanced rather scathingly around the room, as if she were used to better things. 'In London,' she elaborated. 'You could go and stay with them for a bit, if you wanted.'

'What for?' Glyn struggled to make sense of this suggestion. He was all for adventure, but this was coming a bit sudden.

'It's a big city.' Lynette smiled, her blue eyes softening as if she were remembering something that had nothing to do with Glyn or his future. 'There are things to see and do. Opportunities. A chance to experience a way of life you've never even dreamed of, my lad.'

He grinned back at her. 'You trying to get rid of me, or what?' Did she know? Could she possibly know?

Lynette came and sat on the arm of his chair. Her fingers tangled lightly in his hair and he looked up at her. His mother. Once adored. And now? Now it was a bit more complicated and he didn't really want to think about it.

'I'm thinking of you, my lad,' she said softly. 'And it's time you were thinking of yourself and all.'

'What sort of opportunities?' He watched her mouth, painted with ruby-red, as it drew a picture for him of a different life, an exciting life. She was right, he supposed. London was the place to be.

'I know someone who would see you're looked after.' She put a hand on his shoulder. 'Who could help you get a job, who has contacts.'

'Who?' He laid his palm lightly on top of her hand. Their eyes met.

'Never you mind who.' She smiled. 'Are you interested?'

He thought of Rowan. First he thought of her face, and how it felt and looked when he held it between his hands. Her eyes – hardly ever still, always brimming with anger, torment, passion, wild as the Cornish sea itself. Her mouth, wide, soft and ready to kiss, always ready to kiss. He thought of her long supple body, her breasts, the delicious curve of her slender hips, and the mass of dark hair as it fell over his face, his chest, his legs. He tasted her skin, the sweet grass-cuttings scent of her, wild roses and birch bark.

Then he thought of Bodmin and the words she'd spoken. *For always, Glyn.* Her head heavy on his shoulder. Once more he felt the fear. Commitment. Those long grasping claws of commitment scared the hell out of him.

'How long for?' he asked his mother. 'How long would I go away for?'

'For as long as you want.' He thought he saw a shaft of victory light up her eyes. 'It's your decision, not mine. I want you to feel free to do whatever you like. I don't want you to be trapped.'

Freedom. It was a tantalising thought.

'Well?' She smiled, as if she knew she'd pressed the right buttons.

'Okay.' He grinned back at her. 'I'd like to get away for a bit.' But not yet. He needed some time to square it with Rowan. It wasn't fair, after all they'd meant to each other, to just dump her.

Lynette nodded with satisfaction. 'Good lad. I know you're making the right decision.' She got up from the chair. 'It'll do you good to get away for a while.'

'Will it?' Once more, Glyn thought of Rowan, already half regretting his decision. How would he manage without her loving, without the way she made him feel?

'It certainly will,' Lynette called over her shoulder. She seemed so sure of what would be good for him. 'And help yourself to some more cake. It won't taste so good tomorrow.'

'What have I done?' Rowan stared at her father. It wasn't just anger, she realised. It went deeper, and on top of it was an even scarier studied control.

'You tell me.' He looked her up and down as if she were dirt. 'I've talked with your friend Tania's mother. I know you didn't stay the night there. I know you've never been there. She didn't even know who the hell you were.' There was a pause. A long pause. 'So if you weren't with Tania in Padstow, then where were you, Rowan?'

'With a different friend.' It was worth a try. She thought and spoke quickly. 'Me and Tania had a row. I didn't want to do the project with her after all, so I . . .'

'Save it.' He took a step towards her. 'Save it for someone who might believe your pathetic lies.'

Something in his voice made her stand up straighter. He was right. She wouldn't lie any more. They – she and Glyn – were worth more. What they had was worth more. 'I was with a boy,' she said.

'Oh yes?' His brown eyes glinted. 'Now we're coming to it. And which boy might this be?'

She hesitated, desperately not wanting to get him into trouble. 'A boy from the village.'

'Name?' He rapped it out like a sergeant major.

She had no choice. 'Glyn Penbray.' The name – even in this situation – was sweet on her tongue.

Abruptly he twisted away from her. All she could see was his straight ramrod back and tense shoulders. He was a tall man, her father, and yet for the first time now, as his shoulders sagged, as he leaned heavily against the wall, he seemed to become smaller, weaker. Rowan gathered strength.

'We love each other, Father.' She had to make him see.

'Love!' He spat into the silent wall only inches from his face. 'What the hell do you think you know of love?'

Why did they always say that? She thought of Zita. How did your age make any difference? She knew what she felt, didn't she, when Glyn was close to her? She knew about the sweet rush that took her over, and the infinite tenderness she felt when she touched his skin. She cared for him, thought of him endlessly every day, she worried for him, wanted to protect him, cherish him. What was love, if it wasn't all that?

Her father turned to face her, and she was surprised to see his eyes, bloodshot, almost as if he'd been forcing back tears. 'You know nothing,' he repeated sadly.

'I know enough.' She stood her ground, still facing him. 'I know that I want to be with him, spend my life with him.'

He shook his head. 'Oh no, you don't . . .'

'I know that I want to marry him.'

Her father's jaw sagged. Then to her annoyance, he began to laugh, slowly at first, then louder, the hysteria rising.

'I do,' she shouted, as if it were a marriage vow itself.

'And what does this *boy* say?' he jeered.

For the first time, she hesitated. What did Glyn say? He hadn't exactly said no to marriage or to commitment, but he certainly hadn't said yes. He'd said that he couldn't see that far ahead, that he couldn't make those sort of plans. He had granted her insecurity, and yet if he could hear this conversation now, if he were here with her, he'd understand, wouldn't he? He would support her. 'He loves me,' she said staunchly. Surely that, at least, was true.

'Hah!' Her father clearly believed that this statement only confirmed his argument. 'No talk of marriage, then?'

'We haven't discussed it,' she lied. 'But he loves me.'

'Of course he *would* say that, wouldn't he?' He strode past her to the drinks cabinet, poured himself a whisky with trembling hands. 'Who wouldn't say it? Saying that gets him into your knickers, doesn't it?'

She turned away, knowing the disgust she felt must be etched on her face. How could he be so coarse? How could he degrade their love this way?

He came closer, the whisky tumbler in his hand. 'Can't you understand that, you silly girl?'

She shook her head. 'It's not like that.'

'Then how is it?' His voice was slurred as he turned away. She realised he'd probably been drinking for half the afternoon.

'You wouldn't understand.' How would someone like her father know the first thing about love?

'I understand that you've let him screw you. I understand that you're nothing but a little tramp.'

She stared at him.

'And I also understand that you're not even sixteen.' He swallowed half the tumbler-full in one gulp. 'You seem to have this *relationship* of yours worked out. You do know sex is illegal before you're sixteen?'

She nodded, trying not to look at him. 'But . . .'

'Yes, I know.' He held up one hand. 'You *love* him.' Slowly, carefully he put down his glass and approached her. Put his hands on her shoulders. Suddenly she wanted to cry. She wanted to see Zita and cry in her arms as she had done when she scraped her knee as a child.

'You must forget him.'

'I can't.' She tried to break away from his grip, but he was too strong. She could smell the whisky on his breath and it made her feel sick again as the cramp forked violently in her stomach once more.

'You must.' He looked into her eyes.

'Why? Give me one good reason.' But every reason in the world wouldn't be enough, she realised that. She was stuck to Glyn. Side by side in the heavens. Twin stars. Never to be parted.

He laughed thickly. 'I don't have to give you a reason. You're my daughter.'

She frowned. 'You don't own me.'

'But I can forbid you to see him.' His hands were pressing down on her. 'I can stop you from going out.'

She stared at him, unable to imagine her freedom curtailed, the freedom she'd always taken for granted.

'You've been allowed to run around all over the place for too long.' He loosened his grip on her shoulders. 'Like a bloody wild animal. Here there and everywhere.'

'But . . .'

'I told your mother.' His voice rose. 'I told both of them. And now look what's happened.'

'Nothing's happened.' She pulled away from him. Except that she'd fallen in love. 'What's so awful about being with Glyn, loving Glyn? We're not hurting anyone. What have you got against him? Why do you hate him? Why do you want to make me miserable for the rest of my life?' Her breathing was shallow, her chest heaving.

He laughed again. How she hated that sound. Why did he have to keep laughing?

'He's . . . He's not good enough for you.'

'You don't even know him.' She knew she was shouting but she couldn't help herself.

He hesitated once again. 'No boy from the village is good enough for you. No daughter of mine is going to shackle herself to some village yobbo for the rest of her life.'

'Then I won't *be* a daughter of yours!' Her voice was shaking, her body too. At that moment Rowan wanted to kill him. For his bloody hypocrisy, his hateful snobbery, his utter incomprehension.

'You'll soon forget him when you go to university.'

'I'm not going to university. I don't want to go to university. And you can't make me.' She headed for the door. She had to get out of this room, away from him, her father. Her heart was thumping loudly, stomach-ache crippling her, her eyes blinded by hot vicious tears.

'You'd be surprised what I can make you do, my girl.' Philip Brunswick watched his daughter leave the room, at last feeling strangely calm and composed. He would stop it. It must be stopped.

For some reason he thought of his mother. The memory she had left was a feminine impression only – he remembered tears on her face, a sad mouth with scarlet lipstick, and the scent of her perfume. He remembered too, that her hair had been soft, tickling his face when she bent to kiss him good night. She would have loved his daughter, Philip realised, if she had ever known her. She would have told him he was a bloody fool ever to come to Cornwall, a fool for not managing his own life.

And what would his father have said of the position that Philip now found himself in? He would say he'd been greedy, that's what. Wanting Folyforth House, and everything it represented, had made him careless, believing that one day he would make enough to gain entrance there. Despite his power, despite his money, he had failed to make contact with the Trelawney woman. Nobody denied her existence, but they all – including Lynette – clammed up at the very mention of her name. Folyforth House seemed as empty as it had always been – but if she wasn't there, then where the hell was she? Or maybe – just maybe – she didn't exist at all. Maybe it was all some sick Cornish joke at his expense.

Whatever the truth he had to let it go, had to accept that his offer had never been high enough. Or as Audrey had once said, *Not everyone has a price.* Folyforth House had become an obsession, that was the truth of it. And too many other aspects of his life had suffered because of that obsession – his marriage and his daughter: he had even neglected his mistress, for God's sake. Lost control of her because he was so determined to keep self-control at all costs.

And he was a man who had once held a tight rein. A man who

knew exactly where he was going, who made his choices using logic and reason, not feminine emotion. The kind of emotion his daughter was displaying now . . .

But she would come round. She would understand that this was impossible. He'd make her understand. But he couldn't tell her the truth, could he? He suspected that Audrey knew about Lynette – although how the hell she'd managed that, he had no idea. But he couldn't tell Rowan, could he? And he didn't dare say any more to Audrey. My God . . . He began to shake.

He poured himself another drink. He had made a bloody mess of things so far. But everything wasn't lost. He would come through – there was no other way.

Chapter 11

Rowan considered the next two months to be about the worst months of her life.

Of course she'd known her father would try and stop her from seeing Glyn, but she hadn't imagined how relentless he could be. That he'd always be *there* after school, after dinner, early in the morning, giving her lifts door to door, curtailing her freedom in every way he possibly could short of locking her in her bedroom and throwing away the key.

And he had all the power, didn't he? He had a car, money, time, opportunity, control. He could do as he pleased. By comparison, she had nothing.

Still, somehow, she managed to get away from time to time, running to the folly, staying there as long as she dared, waiting for Glyn, always waiting for Glyn. But her sixteenth birthday came and went and still she hadn't seen him. She couldn't believe what was happening. She imagined that her heart was breaking.

One hot day in August when her father had driven into town for more office supplies, she gave the slip to the cleaning lady with the eagle eye who her father had left on patrol, and headed for the village. The phone was no good. She must see him face to face. She must find Glyn. She wanted to see him so badly that it was like a pain, burning her up. Anything was better than not seeing him, not knowing. He wouldn't like it. But she could wait no longer.

Audrey Brunswick watched her go as she often watched her, through the wide windows of the green room that led on to the garden and the outside world. She watched her go, and she wished – how she wished – that she could help her.

How many times had she struggled to find the strength to fight him? And how many times had she failed? Failed Rowan, she supposed.

She picked up her bottle of tablets and studied the label. She had read somewhere that this stuff was addictive, but that didn't matter too much now. It helped her though her days, helped her forget. One day drifted into the next. Existence, not living.

Would Rowan be able to fight him? She hoped so.

Sometimes, as she watched her daughter through the window of the green room, she willed her to fight him, stared at Rowan as if she could transfer what little strength she had left. Sometimes she was so confused, that she saw herself in Rowan, even envied her the passion she herself had never experienced.

But more often she knew exactly what she was. A woman who had allowed herself to become pathetic. A woman little more than a shadow. A woman with a lump in her breast that might or might not be malignant – who cared? A woman dependent on pills, who had as good as forsaken her own daughter. Audrey rapped her knuckles sharply against the arm of the chair. She must stop all this self-pitying nonsense.

If her own mother hadn't died when Audrey was a child . . . Perhaps then it might have been different, perhaps *she* would have been different – not so desperate to escape from a home that might never have had bars at the windows to keep her inside. Perhaps she wouldn't have married a man who had turned out to be rather like her father after all. Who could tell?

She watched Rowan disappear from view. Would she leave home as soon as she had the means to do so? Of course she would. Rowan would leave as Audrey should have left – would have left if she hadn't been so damned scared. Would have left if she'd ever been a person, rather than just a daughter, a wife, a mother. Every rôle of someone else's making.

Audrey stared at her garden landscape, empty once more. Perhaps, after all, this family was breaking up – had never been enough of a family, maybe.

She'd lost Rowan. She wasn't sure when or how, but she knew it had happened. She had lost Zita too, and that had been her biggest mistake. She saw that now. Now there was no-one to help her, and even that didn't seem to matter. She opened the bottle and swallowed another pill. Self-pitying nonsense, all of it. But she couldn't bring herself to care enough for it to matter at all.

Rowan walked down the hill, eyes fixed straight ahead. She turned right when she got to the waterfront, and went up the pathway to the Penbrays' front door. Taking a deep breath, she knocked quickly and loudly, before she could change her mind and run away. Pray God he was in.

Harry Penbray opened the door. 'Well, I never . . .' He scratched his beard, regarding her thoughtfully.

'Is Glyn there?' She peered past him.

'Glyn?' A look of confusion hovered over his gentle blue eyes. 'Glyn, you say?'

She nodded, and he opened the door wider.

She watched understanding dawn. 'I reckon he's around. Come on in, love.'

She couldn't believe it had been so easy. Why hadn't she tried to come here before? But of course, she knew why. Because Glyn would have flipped his lid. Glyn had always been determined that their relationship be kept secret. But now, he had left her with no choice.

She followed Harry into the narrow hallway past a rucksack and holdall squatting at the bottom of the stairs. So this was her lover's home – a narrow hallway and faded wallpaper. A carpet that was well worn and frayed around the edges. She smiled uncertainly at Harry.

'Glyn!' He shouted up.

A noise from above her, and then he was there, looking as good as he had the last time she'd seen him on the station platform after their two days in Bodmin. He was standing at the top of the stairs, dressed in denim jeans and a black tee shirt, looking down at her. And immediately she knew.

'Rowan?' He stared, as if he couldn't believe it was her. Then he thundered down the narrow stairs two at a time. 'What are you doing here?'

'That's a nice greeting.' She was shy, almost afraid to look at him. They'd never met in the normal places before – each other's houses, pubs or cafés. They had only ever met out of doors, and it seemed strange to see him now, inside closed walls.

'I wasn't expecting you, was I?' He looked over his shoulder, obviously flustered and ill at ease, then glanced at his dad. 'Is Mum . . . ?'

'She's out. For an hour or two, I reckon.' Harry's eyes were curious, but he was smiling, at least. Wasn't that a good sign? 'Offer young Rowan some tea then.'

'Tea. Yeah. All right.' Glyn hardly glanced at her as he half-pulled her into the kitchen, shutting the door behind them so that they were alone.

Alone at last . . . 'Oh, Glyn . . .'

'What are you doing here?' he hissed again, interrupting her.

'Glyn, I've missed you so much!' She threw herself into his arms. 'I had to see you.'

'Not here. For God's sake, Rowan.'

She drew back from his tense body. He was scared stiff. But what could he be scared of, here in his own home? Was it so terrible of her to come here? She frowned. She was no longer under age. Surely his parents didn't object to her for the same reasons that her father objected to Glyn? Was there a class barrier this way around too? Not for his dad obviously – Harry had looked quite chuffed to see her.

'I haven't got long.' She grasped his arm. 'My father knows about us, Glyn.'

'You told him?' He stared at her, and she saw the reproach, and, yes, a kind of hardness that had never been there before.

She let go. 'I had to tell him. He made me. After we came back from Bodmin. My alibi wasn't much of an alibi after all – Tania's mother told him she'd never seen me in her life.'

'Jesus Christ.' He swept his fingers through his hair.

'You've had it cut.' She reached out, tentative as she'd never been tentative with Glyn, to touch the short dark curls.

'Yeah.' He seemed embarrassed.

A thought occurred to her. 'But you must have wondered where I've been? You have been going to the folly, Glyn?'

'Course I have.' He half-turned from her. 'Well, I went a few times, only . . .'

'Only?' A sudden fear gripped her stomach, gripped the sickness that never quite went away. 'I'm pregnant, Glyn.'

He stared at her. 'What did you say?'

It should never have been like this. She had wanted to share the news with him in the folly, the wood or the bay. In one of their special places, just after making love when the warm glow of him was still on her skin, his taste still on her tongue.

'I'm pregnant,' she repeated. Why didn't he hold her? Why hadn't he kissed her? Why was he looking at her this way?

'How?' He was stricken, completely stricken.

'The usual way,' she snapped, then instantly regretted it. You and me, side by side in Bodmin, that's what she wanted to say, that's how she wanted to remind him of what they'd had. Was it in the past already? Then what about . . . ? What about this? She clutched her stomach.

His eyes went blank. She sensed that he didn't know what to say, that he had no idea how to deal with this. That she might have become a woman, but he had remained a boy.

'Glyn . . .'

'What are you going to do?' Nervously he moistened his lips.

'Me?' That was hard to take. Yes, it had been a shock to her too, but through all the sickness and the depression and the loneliness it had always been *their* baby, never just hers.

'Well, you're the one . . .'

'It's *our* baby, Glyn.' She grabbed his hand, put it on her belly, but he pulled away as if she'd scorched him.

He put his hands on the kitchen table instead as if he needed to steady himself. 'How far gone are you?'

'Not far off two months, I suppose.' She eyed him warily. 'Since Bodmin.'

He blanched. She knew he was remembering. Remembering like she'd been remembering, replaying it in her head, that moment when he hadn't pulled back. She hadn't let him pull back, she reminded herself. But he had made no objections. He had wanted her to have all of him, just as she'd wanted all of him. Wanted too much of him.

'Have you seen a doctor?'

'No.'

'Told anyone?'

'No.' She watched him. Only you, she thought.

He looked nervously across at her, so vulnerable and weak that she felt the stronger, so much stronger, she realised, than he.

'You'll have to,' he said. 'Tell someone.'

'I just have.'

His eyes flickered. 'What can *I* do?'

Rowan reached out her hand to touch his face. How she loved the feel of his skin. She wanted to touch him more, but it wasn't possible now. An awful sadness edged into her. He had asked what he could do. The father of her baby and he'd had to ask . . . *You could hold me and love me and kiss me. You could tell me that everything will be all right. That you'll care for me and our child whatever they say.*

'I don't know.' All of a sudden her strength sagged, and she groped for a chair.

'Are you all right?' His eyes were worried now. Didn't want his pregnant girlfriend flaking out in his mother's kitchen, now did he? That would be embarrassing to someone who didn't like planning ahead. Or *was* she still his girlfriend . . . ?

'What do you care?' She took deep breaths. Was it the baby? Or was it just that he didn't want her any more?

He held her hand in both of his. 'Rowan, I do care.'

She looked into his eyes. So much love flooded her, it was frightening. 'Do you?'

'Of course.' He knelt at her feet. 'But we have to talk about what we're going to do.'

'Do?'

'Well . . .' He took a deep breath. 'We can't keep it, can we? You're only sixteen . . .'

She snatched her hand away. Him too. Only sixteen. 'People get married at sixteen,' she snapped.

'I can't marry you, Rowan.' He stood up, towering over her. 'I'm going away for a while. I'm leaving. It's all arranged. I can't marry you.'

'Away?' She remembered the bags in the hall. But how could he go away? 'Without telling me?' she whispered. If she hadn't come here today he would have left without seeing her. And here she was begging him to marry her. What a fool she'd been.

'I came to the folly.' His voice grew urgent. 'Several times I went there to see you. To tell you . . .'

She looked up at him.

'To tell you we should cool things down for a while.'

'Cool things down?' She got heavily to her feet. She was pregnant with his child and he wanted to cool things down? 'That's just great.'

'I thought we were getting too involved.' He sighed. 'I do love you. I'll probably always love you. But we're only sixteen . . .'

If he said that again, she would scream.

'I'm going.' She walked out of the kitchen door. 'Goodbye, Glyn.' She should never have come here. Maybe her father had been right all along.

'But I do love you.' He followed her to the front door, grabbed her arm. 'I do love you, Rowan. Please believe me.'

What did he want from her? For her to take his love and not him? Some sort of sacrifice?

She turned to look at him. His face was a boy's face, his eyes betraying for a moment their past passion, but also betraying his fear. And fear won the day. She waited, watching him, absorbing the look of him as if she must imprint it on her memory. The dark skin, the green eyes, the gypsy ear-ring, the slight cleft in his chin. And the black hair, so much shorter now. Things had changed.

'I love you, Rowan.'

She waited until he let go of her. It didn't take long. 'Not enough,' she whispered. 'Not nearly enough.'

Rowan was sweating and miserable by the time she got home, but sure of what she must do. She had money, saved from an allowance that had once been more generous than it was now, put safely away in a box under her bed.

She couldn't stay here – she had no reason to stay here now that Glyn was going, now that Glyn had let her down. She no longer had a mother she could turn to. She must run. And there was only one place, only one person she could run to.

In the pie and mash shop on Hammersmith Broadway, Zita was rubbing her back and staring out of the front window into a black night lit up by neon, by street lights and by the brightly lit gilt decorations of the pub opposite. It was a busy night, but they were easing off, ready to close, thank the Lord. And wasn't it about time – she considered for the umpteenth occasion – that they got in some help in the shop? She was just about to bend to clear another marble-topped table, when she saw a black cab pull up outside.

A girl clambered out, pulled a bag out after her, fumbled in her pocket for the fare.

'Rowan?' Zita wiped her hands on her gingham check overalls and was out of the door in a flash. 'Rowan?'

'Zita!' The girl practically fell into her arms. Her face was hot as if she had a fever, and even in the light from the shop, Zita could see that her eyes were wild, her pupils dilated, and her hair all mussed up.

'Why didn't you tell me you were coming?' Zita held on to her and supported her through the shop doorway. She must be ill.

Nell raised her eyebrows. 'What's this, then?'

'This is Rowan.' Silently she pleaded with Nell not to make a fuss.

Rowan held out her hand, smiled weakly. 'Pleased to meet you.'

'Looks like she'll go into a dead faint any second.' Nell took the hand offered to her and drew her into her arms. 'Come on, my love, it's upstairs with you. You need a good sit down and a nice cup of tea.'

Their eyes met over Rowan's dark head.

'Thanks, Nell,' Zita whispered.

'I couldn't stay there any longer,' Rowan muttered into the ample bosom. 'It was just . . .'

'Not now,' Nell soothed. 'All that's for later. First let's get some hot sweet tea down you. That's what you need.'

'You're very quiet,' Nell observed the next day as she and Zita were half-way through the lunchtime session.

'That's because I'm thinking.' And by God, didn't she have a lot to think about?

Nell took a container and filled it with mash and the luridly green liquor. Oh yes, there was still a demand. And why shouldn't there be? 'And where is she today?'

'I sent her down the road to buy herself a dress.' Zita was thoughtful.

'Needs a bigger size, does she?' Nell took the customer's money, and gave the change.

'How the heck did you know?' Zita stared at her. It hadn't taken her long last night to get Rowan's defences down low enough for the whole story to be poured out into Zita's sympathetic ear. Pregnancy. Wasn't that exactly what Zita had been most afraid of?

Nell fetched more pies for the warming cupboard. 'Didn't take a genius to work it out. All that crying. Stomach pains, love in her eyes, young girl runs away.'

'She hasn't exactly run away.'

'What would you call it?' Nell scooped up some mash for the next customer, putting the meat pie in a paper bag.

'I'd call it grabbing some thinking time.' Though Zita had been the one who'd thought and thought – all night – and not got very far. The girl had been a fool, there was no disputing that. But she'd learned her lesson good and proper. No disputing that either. She wasn't much more than two months gone. There was time. Either way, there was time.

'Does her father know?'

Zita glanced up as the door opened. She glanced up and felt a shudder of distaste run through her. 'Maybe you should ask him.'

'What?' Nell looked up.

'Is she here?' Philip Brunswick glared from one to the other. 'Is my daughter here?'

The door opened again. 'I'm here, Father.' Rowan's clear voice rang out.

Philip turned, blinking at her as if he no longer recognised her face. 'Is there somewhere we can talk?'

He seemed calm enough, but Zita couldn't help remembering the night before she had left Cornwall. He had seemed calm then too until he'd practically jumped on top of her. He could have protected her from Audrey's accusations, could have told the truth, admitted that he'd made a drunken pass at her that had gone wrong. Instead, he'd left Audrey believing that Zita had betrayed her. She didn't want this man here, she realised, calm or not.

'Upstairs,' Rowan said. 'Is that all right?' She turned to Nell. 'Is it all right for us to go upstairs to talk?'

169

Zita wanted to refuse, but it wasn't her flat. She wanted to put herself between Philip Brunswick and his daughter, but it wasn't her place, was it? Anyway, there were customers to serve.

'She can look after herself, that one,' Nell said, as father and daughter disappeared through the door marked *Private*. 'Don't you worry.'

But Zita did worry. She didn't like it. And she didn't trust Philip Brunswick one bit.

Half an hour later, when things slackened off, she ran upstairs to see what was happening. She could hear them going at it hammer and tongs in the back room, him yelling, her repeating the same words over and over:

'I told you. I'm *not* coming home. I'm *not* going to university.'

'Where will you go? You can't stay here. How can you stay here?' he bellowed.

Zita walked in the room. 'We'll look after her,' she said. 'She can stay here for as long as she wants.'

Rowan's face was ashen. She turned to Zita with grateful eyes. 'Thanks, Zita, I . . .'

'And what do you think you'll do here?' Philip's eyes were bulging. Rowan backed off.

'What do you think will become of you here – in this place?' His arm swept round to encompass more than the flat and the pie and mash shop. More like a way of life, Zita thought.

She stepped towards them a second too late. She stepped forwards, but already he had grabbed Rowan and was shaking her as if she were a bag of bones.

'I'll teach you . . .' he was saying.

'Let go of her,' Zita shrieked.

And he did so. But as he let go, Rowan clutched at her stomach, her face contorted with pain as she doubled over.

'Phone an ambulance. Quick!' Zita ran to her, helped her down until she was lying on the floor, fetched a cushion for her head.

'What's happened? What's wrong with her?' Philip Brunswick's face was almost as white as his daughter's.

'She's pregnant,' Zita told him. 'But that might be one thing less she's got to worry over, thanks to you. Now get that ambulance here. And fast.'

PART TWO

Chapter 12

Rowan Brunswick turned to wave goodbye to a couple of other students standing on the steps of the college, before making her way to the underground station to get back to Hammersmith.

It had been three years since the miscarriage – three whole years since she'd lost Glyn's baby – and she had seen neither of her parents in that time. She didn't want to see her father. Sometimes she thought of him, remembered days in her early childhood when he had given her time, before he started giving her only money. She remembered him as a figure who had wanted to control. And she remembered that afternoon in Nell and Zita's flat. She would never forget the cruel light in his eyes as he shook her, never forgive him for losing her the baby, losing her Glyn.

She had lied at the hospital – made up some story about falling down the stairs, to explain her miscarriage. But she hadn't done it to protect her father, she had done it to make him go away, to make him leave her alone now that he had destroyed all that was left of Glyn.

But she was conscious of very different emotions whenever she thought of her mother.

'Don't give up on her,' Zita urged.

And so she wrote to her often – long rambling letters, a diary of her new life, her days at college, evenings studying or helping out in the pie and mash shop which was still going strong; Nell and Zita had even employed a part-timer to give a hand during this past winter – which was their busiest time – and had decided to keep her on.

But she never received a word in reply. Perhaps her mother wasn't well enough to write. Maybe she didn't want to. Perhaps Rowan wasn't wanted back in Cornwall. Perhaps she had somehow been cast out by her behaviour, by her refusal to go home with her father, by the fact that she'd turned to Zita, her surrogate mother, in her time of trouble.

Rowan considered this as she went down the escalator staring at the posters and billboards without really seeing them, travelling as most people seemed to in London – wrapped in a veneer of privacy and silence.

Time moved on in London. People moved and time moved with them – unlike in Cornwall, where often time seemed to stand still.

Rowan had made the best of life without Cornwall. But it was hard to have left it at the time she was closest to belonging. And yes, she missed those small grey villages flanked by wide open spaces of sea, scarred moorland and dramatic crags of granite and slate. The narrow lanes, precipitous cliffs, the bays tucked inside the arms of the jagged coastline, the sand, the swimming, and the wild sea breezes, the screeching acrobatic sea birds and even the dour Cornish fishermen. She missed her own wild landscape, the seclusion of her special places – the wood, the mystery of Athwenna Trelawney and Folyforth House, the romance and chill of the folly. And most of all, she missed Glyn.

Feeling like just another robot she stepped through the sliding doors of the underground train, holding on to the hand rail, swaying slightly from side to side in rhythm with the speed and the rush, carefully not looking into people's faces. Very different from Cornwall indeed.

Three years ago she had thought that not a day would go by without her thinking of Glyn Penbray – he had seemed so impossible to forget, so stamped on to her life. But almost to her surprise, within a matter of weeks, whole days passed where she smiled more often than she thought of him.

But that didn't mean she was free of Glyn. So she wrote – care of his parents – once a month, without fail. She wrote to tell him what she was doing and where she was, but also to remind him of her existence, of their days in the folly, the wood, and the bay. Their days on Bodmin Moor when he had told her that he loved her.

She wanted to remind them both – although she didn't need reminding. It seemed as if those days were etched so deeply into her heart that she couldn't help but remember. Couldn't help but be scarred.

Because she still loved him.

Rowan got out at Hammersmith, took the steps two at a time and made her way out to The Broadway. She didn't blame Glyn for what had happened. Like he'd said, like they had all said – she and Glyn had been too young. Just a couple of kids.

But she was a fool for still loving Glyn Penbray, even if she could smile without him.

Zita was cleaning cupboards out when she got in. Rowan stepped round her and took off her jacket at the same time, flinging it on to the counter. 'Spring cleaning? Again?'

Zita laughed. 'It's therapeutic.'

'Says who?'

'Says whoever it was that gave me a brain that works best when my hands are busy.'

'You're priceless, you are.' Rowan kissed her cheek. 'I'll give you a hand.'

'Oh no, you won't.' Zita pushed a stray strand of auburn hair from her forehead and added a streak of cleaning fluid. 'How was college?'

'Great.' Rowan got up and stretched lazily. Ironically it was Zita who had been responsible for her going to catering college in the first place.

After her miscarriage, Rowan had looked around for a job, but found nothing she was as interested in as working in the pie and mash shop.

Nell and Zita teased her unmercifully, but also had to admit that she was good with the customers, prepared to work hard and a decent cook into the bargain. So they took her on.

'I think we should diversify,' she announced after her first week's work.

'Do what?' Zita and Nell stared at her.

'We don't do enough different kinds of food,' she explained. 'We could draw in more customers – especially young ones. How about chicken and ham pies? Some fried fish? We could even introduce some different sauces – lemon and thyme butter sauce . . . parsley potatoes maybe?'

'This is a pie and mash shop, not a chippie or one of your fancy restaurants,' Nell grumbled. 'And the sauce we do is just fine.' But she gave in over the chicken pie, and the customers loved it.

The following week Rowan announced that pie, mash and liquor wasn't very nutritious, and they should think about vegetables.

'Vegetables?' Nell echoed.

'Peas are traditional enough, aren't they? There's no novelty in peas.'

But the next week it was carrots and parsnips, '*maybe with a honey glaze?*' And the following week Zita caught her preparing huge bags of broccoli.

'They were on special offer down at the market,' she told them. 'I could stir fry them in sesame oil with courgettes, chicken and black bean sauce.'

Nell had been long-suffering up to this point, while some customers at least were coming back for more, but here she drew the line.

'This is supposed to be traditional English fare,' she told Rowan. 'We succeed by specialising. That's the name of the game. You want to cook different food – you do it in your own time and in your own place.'

Rowan was disappointed, but it made Zita thoughtful.

A couple of days later she dragged Rowan down to the library to look through some of the brochures on adult education.

Rowan groaned. 'I'm really not interested. I told you, Zita, just like I told Father before, I don't want to go to college or university. I'm happy doing what I'm doing.' She sighed melodramatically. 'And if you don't like it, you'd better tell me to go.'

Zita laughed. 'But how about catering college?'

Rowan stared at her. 'You mean . . . ?'

'It'll be hard work, mind,' she warned her. 'But you don't belong in the pie and mash shop. You're young. You've got too many new ideas. And good on you. Maybe in the end you'll get to be a chef, then you can run your own place, make all the decisions, do what the heck you like. How would that suit you, eh?'

Rowan laughed. 'Most chefs are men, aren't they?'

'You going to let a little thing like that stop you?' Zita tucked her arm into Rowan's. 'If you don't try, you'll never know.'

So Rowan had enrolled that September on a course that still gave her enough time to help out in the shop. She was now coming to the end of her second year, and although it was hard work, she loved it. She'd even been commissioned to do some dinner parties in her spare time, and her confidence had grown. When she was working with food she became more in control, she felt.

Zita agreed. 'You're scatty and you're wild,' she told her. 'But with a kitchen knife in your hand and an oven beside you . . .'

'I become tidy and organised?' Rowan suggested.

Zita shook her head. 'Never in a million years. But you create, my love. That's what you do.'

'I'm about finished now in any case.' Zita squeezed out the cloth. She was still an attractive woman, Rowan considered, but she'd lost a lot of her old fire. She wondered if Zita ever thought about Cornwall, ever pined for what she might have had with Harry Penbray. She'd never mentioned him, not once.

'And while I remember, Will Stafford was here earlier. He asked if you were free tonight.' Zita rolled her eyes suggestively.

'I've told you time and time again, Zita. He's just a friend.' Rowan tried to laugh. But she hadn't wanted a man since Glyn, hadn't really looked at one.

Zita shrugged. 'Maybe one day.'

'Maybe.' But maybe one day she'd go back to Cornwall, more like. Glyn Penbray had not yet entered the past for Rowan, and she wasn't quite sure how to put him there . . . or if she even wanted to.

'He's a nice lad.' Zita smiled, as if she were remembering something from her past. 'He deserves a nice girl. He deserves to be loved.'

'I'll tell him, I'm sure he'll appreciate it.'

'You may laugh . . .' she glanced at Rowan. 'But sooner or later he'll be somebody's lover and then . . .'

'And then?'

'Better move fast before you lose him – that's all I'm saying.'

'Zita, Will is just a friend. Now, are you going to tell me what else he said, or have you got any more words of wisdom for me first?' Rowan shook her head in despair. Zita was such a hopeless romantic at times.

But Zita only laughed. 'He said would you go down to Charlie's at around six for a quick drink. He wants you to meet someone.'

'Sounds intriguing.' It was her night off but she rarely went out, unless it was with Will or occasionally one of her college friends. But it was Will's employer, Charlie Walters, who had commissioned her first dinner parties. This could be work, and every job was good experience as well as providing some handy cash.

Rowan glanced at her watch and shrugged her jacket back on. 'I'd better get down there.'

Will Stafford was a cabinet maker, restorer of antique furniture, and student, in about equal parts. He had done his City and Guilds, so he informed Rowan the second time they met, but was still doing a more specialised course in furniture design and graphics part-time whilst working for Charlie Walters.

Charlie had been a cabinet maker too in his younger days, still ran a workshop from his home and maintained his contacts. He was a kind of sponsor for Will, she supposed, recommending his work and helping to involve Will in exhibitions and open days.

Like Zita and Nell, he was from Hammersmith originally, and he was also an occasional frequenter of the pie and mash shop, which was where Rowan had first met him.

'This may seem a tired old cliché,' he had said the first time she served him. 'But what's a girl like you doing in a place like this?'

'I enjoy working here.' Rowan bristled, not really approving of the man standing at the counter who was wearing a flashy suit, sporting a bright red tie, and wearing too much chunky gold jewellery for her taste. Or for a visit to a pie and mash shop, come to that.

He put up one hand and she got an even better view of some of that jewellery. 'Don't get me wrong, my dear,' he said. 'I'm not knocking it.' He grinned, displaying lots of teeth. 'It was always good enough for my old mum, God bless her, so it's good enough for me.'

'Was she from round here?' Despite her initial distaste, Rowan was interested in what he had to say. The man was a mixture of money and working class roots.

'Just down the road.' He pointed a fat finger. 'She had a little terrace, two up, two down.' He met her stare without flinching. 'And I haven't travelled so very far away, believe me.'

As the weeks went by, Rowan overcame her initial disapproval and slowly began to relax when Charlie Walters was around, eventually even confiding in him that she was studying at catering college.

And that's when he asked her to cook at one of his dinner parties.

'Oh, I couldn't possibly,' was her instinctive reaction.

'Fair enough.' He shrugged.

But when Rowan told Zita about it, she thought Zita would explode.

'You passed by an opportunity to do a private dinner party?'

'Yes, but . . .'

'Call yourself ambitious?'

'I am, Zita. But . . .'

'Pathetic, more like,' Zita snorted. 'You'll never get anywhere with that kind of attitude. A bit of backbone, a bit more in the way of balls, that's what you need.'

Rowan decided she had a point, so the next time he was in, she told Charlie she'd changed her mind. 'If the offer's still open, that is . . .'

His eyes barely flickered. 'The offer's still open. A woman's entitled to change her mind, my dear . . .'

Still, Rowan smiled as she remembered how nervous she'd been when she arrived at his elegant riverside house on the Mall. Would the rocket leaves wilt? Would the hollandaise sauce curdle? Would the lemon islands float – or sink without trace?

And just as she'd convinced herself it would be hopeless, that she may as well walk out, and throw ambition out of the nearest window, Will Stafford had poked his head round the kitchen door.

'Hi. You must be Rowan.' He watched her as she peered into a large saucepan. 'Are you managing okay, or are you miles out of your depth and drowning fast?'

'Drowning,' she confessed.

'Don't worry. I'm sure it will be wonderful.' He sniffed appreciatively. 'It smells wonderful.'

'I can't understand why I'm so terrified.' She was trying very hard not to panic, but for some reason she seemed to have forgotten how to cook.

'Charlie tells me it's your first time. I'd be terrified. But there's really no need.'

Carefully, Rowan eased the salmon out of the pan. 'Oh God, I'm sure I've overcooked it. Look.' She touched the fish with her fork and it flaked immediately.

He peered over her shoulder. 'Push it together and give it some swirls of sauce and garnish. Instant repair job.' He handed her the hollandaise and indicated the sorrel.

She did as he suggested and it looked wonderful.

'Better then superglue any day.' He raised his shaggy eyebrows.

She giggled. He was right too.

'I'll give you a hand to take them in.' He threw her an oven glove.

'Thanks.' Rowan smiled gratefully, looking at him properly for the first time. He was a big, gangly individual, a bit of a gentle giant, not fat but all arms, legs and hands – at a guess a few years older than she was – and with a shock of red hair, a sprinkling of freckles and very bright blue eyes.

'My pleasure.' He stuck out his hand. 'Will Stafford. We'll talk later. To tell you the truth, I'm only here because one of Charlie's guests is commissioning a piece of furniture from me and wants to discuss it over dinner. I don't really belong.' He grinned. 'Now I suppose we'd better get this fish in to the hungry diners.'

And sure enough they had talked later. They talked a lot over the next few months and became firm friends – in fact Rowan realised that Will was the first real friend she'd had of her own age. Apart from Glyn, some voice whispered to her. But he hadn't been a friend, had he? Glyn had been a lover.

She found Will and Charlie in the workshop behind Charlie's house.

'Sorry to disturb you . . .' Rowan hesitated, as always slightly self-conscious that her friendship with Will might lead Charlie to think that she tried to pick up men at his dinner parties.

'You're not.' Charlie strode towards her, his balding head gleaming. 'We're finished here. And congratulations are in order.'

'Oh?'

'That was some delicious feast you prepared for us last Saturday.'

Will glanced at her and pulled a sad face. 'Good one, was it? Why wasn't I invited?'

Charlie's gaze was ever so slightly patronising, she noted. 'This was strictly business. Property business,' he elaborated. His smile took in the pair of them. 'Nothing for you young things to be bothered about.'

He came closer. 'Thank you, my dear.' He pressed something into Rowan's hand, and left the workshop.

'*Nothing for you young things to be bothered about,*' Will mimicked. 'He can be such a condescending git at times.'

Rowan laughed, opening her palm to see a £50 note nestling there. It was much too much, he'd already paid her for the party.

Will looked over her shoulder. 'Your round, I think.' He whistled.

'Why did he . . . ?' She stared up at him. Will knew Charlie a lot better than she did.

His mouth twisted. 'Because he probably made thousands on some deal or other, thanks to your food.'

Rowan fingered the note. 'Property?'

'How do you think he made his money? He started in the days when you could make a fortune at it, and he hasn't lost out since then, believe me.'

He sounded bitter. 'Don't you like him, Will?' Rowan hadn't even made up her own mind about Charlie Walters yet. He seemed okay and he'd certainly helped her out. But there was something about him she didn't quite trust, something she wasn't quite sure of.

Will shook his head as he climbed out of his working overalls. 'Not always. He's all right most of the time, I suppose. And he's done a lot for me . . .' He glanced at her. 'But I don't want to think about him now.' He grinned. 'It's a lovely evening. Fancy a walk along the tow path? Then we'll have an excuse to get a drink in at the Old Ship.'

'I'm sure you can twist my arm.' One thing Rowan missed about Cornwall was the walking, and she knew that Will, Derbyshire born and bred, felt the same way about the Peak District countryside he'd been brought up in. She wasn't sure why he had left Derbyshire. Maybe, like her, he had just needed to escape.

The riverside between Hammersmith and Barnes Bridge wasn't exactly the country, and it was rarely deserted, but it was about as near as Hammersmith got to countryside. And it was certainly pleasant on an evening like this one. There was a splendid view of the moored boats and the terraces and riverside houses of Chiswick and Hammersmith, the sun painting the iron balconies of the upmarket Mall houses, and the willows and poplars rising and drooping as gracefully as dancers along the river.

'So who's this mystery person I'm supposed to be meeting?' Rowan asked him as they walked side by side along the tow path.

'A lady friend of mine.'

'Oh yeah?' Rowan wasn't sure whether she was relieved or not to hear this. Will deserved to be somebody's lover, Zita had said. But didn't everybody? And how would she herself feel about that? Glad for him, she hoped. Rowan had indeed been worrying lately that Will might be harbouring romantic intentions towards her. And that was the last thing she wanted. That, for sure, would mean the end of a beautiful friendship.

He laughed. 'My sister Diana, to be precise.'

She smiled up at him. Was she pleased, disappointed, or just indifferent? 'She's in London, then?'

Will had told her that his younger sister was coming to college here in September. She had stayed with him on several occasions and had fallen in love with the big city, as Will put it with a wry smile.

'For a week. I feel like a tour operator already.' He groaned, but Rowan wasn't fooled in the slightest. She knew how much Diana meant to Will, and she'd been looking forward to meeting her.

'Have you been showing her the sights today, then?'

He flicked a piece of sawdust from his red hair. 'No, I've been fighting woodworm today.'

'Nice,' she laughed.

'An inlaid walnut chest.' His big hands drew the shape of it in the air. Rowan was always surprised by the way in which such big, clumsy looking hands could create such intricate carving and bevelled forms.

'Did you win?'

'I will eventually.' He shook his head in despair. 'It was left to rot in a garage. I ask you – how could someone treat a piece of beautiful furniture that way?'

She smiled. 'But it will be beautiful again?' That's what she liked about his work. He could take a piece of furniture that had possessed some glory in the past, and make it worth something once more.

'Oh yes.' He stopped walking. 'It has these incredibly elegant brass and ebony handles. And the shape of the legs . . .' He drew a curve in the air. 'Almost as nice as yours.'

She laughed with some embarrassment. 'You're not selling it to me, you know, Will.'

'I won't need to sell it to anyone.' He opened the pub door so she could go in. 'It'll sell itself. Those kind of pieces always do.'

'So what's Diana been up to today then, while you've been waging war on woodworm?' she asked him when they were settled outside the pub with their drinks.

'Jed's taken her to Madame Tussaud's. I thought she'd be back by now.'

'Oh?' Idly, Rowan watched the boats on the river. She had heard Will mention his friend Jed Montague several times, and was quite surprised she'd never met him. It was almost as if Will were intentionally keeping them apart.

'And tonight he's having a party,' Will told her. He watched her appraisingly. 'How about it?'

'Am I invited?' Rowan sipped her lager to hide her surprise. She wasn't sure she fancied mingling with what she called the arty crowd that Will knew in London. She knew that he'd first met Jed Montague at Chelsea Art College. Surely she would feel out of place?

He laughed. 'No-one's *invited*. It isn't that sort of party. People just go.'

She glanced up at him. 'It's not really my kind of thing.'

'But Diana's itching to meet you. She'll make my life a misery if you don't come. It could be a laugh. And Jed . . .'

'Jed?' She couldn't make out his expression.

'Jed wants to meet you too.'

Rowan considered. She could stay home in the flat, have a bath, wash her hair, watch TV. She could crack open a bottle with Nell and Zita once the pie and mash shop had closed up for the night, listen to their familiar banter, read a book, or even do some studying. She grinned. Or she could live a little. 'In that case, how can I refuse?'

'You'll come?'

Rowan pretended not to see the eager light in his blue eyes. 'I'll come.'

'Right.' He jumped to his feet. 'I'd better go back and get into the shower before Diana hogs the bathroom then. I can see we're gonna be making a night of it.'

Chapter 13

Will and Diana picked her up at nine, and they took a cab to Chelsea, to a Victorian style pub with a burgundy and gilt theatrical façade, that was, Will informed her, just around the corner from Jed's flat.

Inside, the place was warm and welcoming. There were rich red brocade curtains at the windows, upholstered pews to sit on, polished mahogany tables, engraved mirrors of cut and bevelled glass and Victorian style arches separating the bars.

Will's sister Diana, who was wearing the smallest little black dress Rowan had ever seen, proved to be a tiny and vibrant version of Will. She had the same bright blue eyes and a mass of equally red hair, but her alabaster skin and delicate bone structure gave her a kind of brittle vulnerability that Will lacked. She too had a sense of fun, but whereas Will's was laid back and relaxed, hers bubbled freely.

'I can't wait to live in London,' she enthused, sipping her white wine. 'All these parties. It's exciting, isn't it, Rowan? Better than boring old Derbyshire any day.'

Rowan smiled. Although only two years her junior, Diana seemed so incredibly young. 'It depends on what you want.' She glanced at Will. He had told her that he'd grown up amongst fields, hills and valleys. Personally she'd rather have that any day.

'Isn't it what *you* want?' Diana's eyes were wide and ingenuous. 'To live in a city with a bit of life about it? To live in London?' She laughed.

Rowan shook her head. 'Not particularly. I miss living in the country.' For Rowan, London had simply been a way of escaping from her father and an unbearable situation. Of course she liked the friendly working-class atmosphere of the pie and mash shop in

Hammersmith, the easy companionship of Zita and Nell, and even the challenge of juggling college with work. But London without Zita would never have drawn her.

'I just don't get that. Everyone who's anyone lives here,' Diana assured them.

Will frowned. 'I'm overjoyed to hear it. But you'll be working while you're here, and don't you forget it.' There was a protective expression in Will's eyes as he looked at his sister. He was six years older than Diana, Rowan reminded herself; Diana was quite the little sister.

Diana pulled a face, 'Of course I'll *be working*. But not all the time. In fact, not most of the time if I have my way.' She grinned. 'And before you say a word, I should remind you that I'm a big girl now.'

'Not that big,' he growled.

Rowan couldn't help feeling envious of what Diana took for granted – the presence of an older brother to keep an eye out for her, to care about her, defend her if necessary. 'What will you be studying?' she asked her.

'History.' Diana wriggled with pleasure. 'Jed says he'll take me to the British Museum tomorrow if we've got time before I have to go back to boring old Derbyshire.'

'And if he hasn't got a hangover,' Will put in.

'He told me he never gets hangovers. Doesn't believe in them, he said.' Diana seemed proud of this.

'Very convenient,' Rowan murmured. She was beginning to wonder more and more about Jed Montague.

Will laughed. 'And very typical.'

'Really?'

'Don't you know Jed?' Diana asked her. 'Haven't you met him before?'

Rowan shook her head, noting Diana's sympathetic expression. 'I've never had the pleasure.' She met Will's eyes and they exchanged a glance of amusement.

'He's wonderful,' Diana enthused. 'His flat is great – there's so much space, it's a terrific place to have a party, simply wonderful. He's a photographer, you know. His work is . . .'

'Wonderful?' Will and Rowan spoke in unison.

Diana laughed. 'Well, it is.' She glanced impatiently at her watch. 'And shouldn't we be getting over there? We're missing the party. And you must be itching to meet Jed, Rowan.'

Was she? Rowan finished her drink and wondered if she'd made a big mistake in coming here. 'I just can't wait,' she told them.

The front door was half-open, with sounds of the party washing through, and Diana dashed on ahead. Rowan could hear an East 17 dance track combining with chatter and laughter, but she hung back.

'It'll be very casual. Don't worry about a thing.' Will put an arm around her shoulders. A few seconds and it would have been a friendly reassuring gesture, but he left his hand there too long and squeezed her upper arm. She glanced up at him in alarm, only to see a certain expression in his blue eyes.

'Rowan . . .' he began.

Deftly she slipped from his hold. She would not be introduced to his friend, to these people, as Will's girlfriend – no way. It wasn't true, and it *wouldn't* be true, she told herself. She stiffened with resentment. And if it had been part of the deal when he'd invited her here, then he shouldn't have kept it in the small print.

But before she could say more, the door opened wider, she turned, and found herself face to face with an extraordinary male individual just an inch or two taller than she was, with a shock of spiky blonde hair and the most beautiful hazel eyes she'd ever seen. The fact that Diana was clinging to one arm like a limpet gave confirmation of his identity.

'Well, hi.' He didn't take his eyes off Rowan as he beckoned them inside. 'I was beginning to think you wouldn't make it.'

'Rowan . . .' Will's voice sounded both strained and resigned against the backdrop of the disco beat and party conversation, 'meet Jed.' He folded his arms, leaned against the white wall of the hallway. 'Jed . . . this is Rowan.'

'Come on in. Please.' Right from the beginning, his closely focused attention was like a spotlight.

Rowan blinked, dazzled by the intensity of it. Whatever she had expected, it hadn't been this. There was something about him . . .

Rowan didn't believe in love at first sight, but she certainly believed in fascination. And this man was, she sensed it immediately, fascinating and therefore dangerous.

He was dressed in a baggy suit, floppy cravat kind of tie and, she noted, expensive Italian-looking shoes. This attire made him appear different – quite different – from the people milling around him. And he was perfectly sure of his own status, a true individual, standing out from the crowd. She was glad she'd decided on jeans that hugged her figure fairly satisfactorily and a plain white shirt. You could never go wrong with jeans. She might not stand out in the crowd, but she'd rather play safe for once.

With a sudden smile he took her arm and she almost snatched it back, scared of whatever it was that she was fascinated by.

But, 'Let me get you a drink,' was all he said.

As he moved away, she craned her neck to take in her surroundings properly. The flat was crammed full of people trying to look cool – girls in tiny skirts and tops, lean and hungry looking young men in shades. The air was full of smoke, music, laughter.

Absorbed, she took in the stylish contours and stark decoration of the flat which, as Diana had promised, was extremely spacious. In front of her was a glass and chrome staircase leading to another floor, and she could see through an open archway into both the kitchen area and what she supposed to be the sitting-room area, from where they stood in the high-ceilinged hallway. The colour scheme throughout was monochrome – black, white and grey.

Rowan turned back to Will – who seemed all of a sudden to represent some sort of precarious security. 'Some place,' she muttered under her breath. Some place, some man. She must be on her guard.

'It sure is.' Will stood, hands in the pockets of his jeans, watching her, as if assessing her reactions. The thought occurred to her again – had he intentionally kept her away?

'I thought you'd be impressed,' he said, as if partly answering her unspoken question.

'I am. It's amazing,' she breathed. This was quite outside her experience, a million miles from the understated conservatism of her parents' house in North Cornwall, even further from the comfortable but messy flat above the pie and mash shop in Hammersmith.

'His people are loaded,' Will muttered back, with what she took to be some sort of resentment. 'Look here, Rowan . . .'

Abruptly, Jed materialised in front of them again, and close by was Diana. 'Go and dance, there's a good girl,' he told her.

Rowan waited for a sharp reply and was surprised to see Diana obey. Some power he seemed to have too. She shivered. Power over people.

He handed Rowan a glass of wine and stared into her eyes as though she might possibly be the most interesting person in the world.

'Do you always tell people what to do?' she asked.

He smiled. 'Only when they want me to.' Very quick. Very smooth.

Around them people shuffled and shimmied past – a mass of bodies and glasses. Music by Blur was pounding from the CD player. Some girls were giggling, high and hysterical. Someone knocked into her and spilled their drink.

Jed took no notice of any of this. They might be alone. 'It's great to meet you at last. I've been nagging Will like crazy.'

'Have you?' She smiled cautiously.

He smiled back. 'Now I can see why he's kept you all to himself.' Once more his gaze never left her face, but his extravagant words made her feel uncomfortable rather than flattered. What on earth had Will been saying? And why hadn't he brought her to meet this man before? Just what was he so scared of?

She glanced at Will, still standing beside them, pretending nonchalance. But she thought she could read the answer to her questions in his eyes.

'Don't say it . . .' She laughed nervously. 'You've heard so much about me.'

'I certainly have.' Still, he didn't take his eyes off her.

'I hope it wasn't all bad.' Rowan wondered if that counted as flirting, she wasn't sure she'd ever learned how. She tried to smile, but her mouth felt tight and nervous.

'None of it was remotely bad.' Jed turned towards Will who was watching them, an inscrutable expression on his face. Jed clapped him on the back. 'And any friend of Will's . . .' He stopped. 'You haven't got a drink, mate. Help yourself from the kitchen, won't you?'

There was a pause before Will turned from them. 'Sure.' He glanced at Rowan. 'I'll be right back.'

'He adores you.' As Will left them, Jed leaned closer, holding her arm once more, seeming to whisper, although the noise around them was so loud, that it was hard to tell for sure. 'You know that, don't you? I don't want to tread on any toes.'

Decision time. The thought clattered into her brain, unwelcome, really, since it was far easier to drift and it had come very quickly. But she knew this was a turning point as clearly as she'd known those days in Bodmin were a turning point for her relationship with Glyn. It was as if someone had leaped out and stuck a signpost in front of her eyes.

'He's a friend.' She spoke firmly, thinking of the incident outside Jed's front door, which still rankled. 'Just a very good friend.'

Jed grinned. 'Then he won't mind if I monopolise you.'

Her eyes narrowed. 'I'm sure you've got lots of other people to . . .'

'I want to talk to *you*.' He led her with the faintest tug of the arm, into the main room of the flat. It was full of dancing bodies, and the music was even louder in here, the fug of smoke more oppressive. He drew her into a corner. 'Come on then. Talk to me.'

'We are talking.' She had to shout to make herself heard. Had to lean very close to him. How on earth could they hold a conversation in here? 'We *were* talking.'

He pulled an expressive face – irritation with the people at his own party, with the noise. 'Ah, but I wanted to get you alone. I want you to tell me about yourself.'

She must have let a flicker of fear into her eyes because his tone changed immediately.

'Don't worry. You're safe with me. I just want to talk.'

'Why?' She stared at him, flirting forgotten.

'Because I want to know who Rowan Brunswick really is. What she does with her time, what she thinks about when she's alone. If she has dreams.'

Rowan felt her throat constricting with panic. 'Everyone has dreams.' Anxiously, she peered over his shoulder. Diana had stopped dancing and was staring over at them, looking disappointed. She obviously had a massive crush on this man, and the last thing Rowan wanted was to antagonise the girl she'd only just met, whom she had hoped might become a friend.

'So tell me yours,' he persisted.

She ignored this. 'I thought the idea of throwing a party was so you could talk to lots of people, not just one.'

An old Rolling Stones track came on, *Brown Sugar*. Rowan smiled, remembering Zita dancing to this once in the kitchen back in Cornwall. 'Now this is what I call dance music,' she had said. More people began to dance, wiggling hips, thrusting their arms in the air, stamping their feet, shouting the chorus line.

Jed glanced behind him. 'I don't think their conversation would even begin to drag me away from you.' He turned back to her, laughing – at his own dialogue perhaps.

'You invited them here.' She was beginning to get desperate, half-wishing she'd stayed in the hallway and waited for Will, as surely she should have done.

'Okay. I give up.' He shrugged, took her hand, clasping it firmly in his. 'You won't let me monopolise you? Then I'll show you what this lot have got to say. Come and meet some of them.'

She had to laugh, had to go with him, and there followed a crazy half hour when Jed, refusing to release her hand, led her round the party, introducing her to people here, there and everywhere. 'Hiya, Jed . . . See ya, Jed . . . How are you doing, Jed? . . .' And through-out all this, Jed kept his body close to hers, only speaking and smiling at them, like an actor addressing a sea of faces in an auditorium. But she wasn't one of the audience, she realised with a shudder of pleasure. She was one of the main players.

'Another drink.' He handed it to her. 'Another conversation, or are you ready to be monopolised?'

Rowan laughed. She would have to fight for control of her own lines. He reminded her of a spider, and she was beginning to feel distinctly like a fly.

How much had she had to drink? She felt dizzy from the wine, but also from his company, from the heat that seemed to flow between them, and from the dancing, gyrating bodies. The pounding bass line of the music, the chatter and laughter were ringing in her ears, her throat was dry from the smoke, her mouth aching from smiling at Jed, at the growing reality of this unspoken bargain they seemed to have made. She was on a high, having a wonderful irresponsible time.

Then the music slowed, the sound of Whitney Houston's voice picked and threaded its way through the blanket noise, easing and tranquillizing, strong and sure. Voices were lowered, bodies relaxed, the movements became looser, more fluid. Jed let go of her hand and opened his arms. 'Dance with me?'

She nodded and in one movement he slipped off his jacket, threw it on a nearby chair, and drew her towards him.

It was a beautiful song. An evocative love song of loss and longing . . .

Rowan tried to relax against the warmth of his body, her hands around his back touching the black silk of his shirt. To her mortification, she had never danced with a man this way before. Glyn was the only man she might ever have danced with, but she and Glyn had never danced. Never held each other this close without making love – for she could feel the hardness of Jed's chest against her breasts, her lips were only an inch from his neck, their legs were brushing together with every movement, every beat. But it was easy. She wanted to grin. Because all you had to do was sway slowly with the rhythm, and she didn't even have to think about that. It just came naturally.

The richness of the song strung a tune over her senses, made her loose, yet alert, alert to every breath he took, the slightest sigh, the rise and fall of his chest as he breathed. And alert to his touch, his hands on her shoulder blades, the gentlest of pressures, and the scent of him – what aftershave could possibly make him smell so sexy?

Something, whether the music, the headiness of the scent, the proximity of him or his magnetism was slowly turning her limbs to liquid, as if at any second she might dissolve on to the carpet at his feet in a puddle of confusion, with Whitney Houston's voice plucking at her senses, sweeping her into a sensuality that she barely recognised as desire.

Dimly she was aware of the music ending, replaced by some reggae, people stomping and laughing.

Will stood in the corner, tall and fierce like some ancient druid warrior, watching them. 'Well, you've certainly met him now,' she thought she heard him say.

She tried to concentrate on Will, but couldn't focus – realising too late that she was looking through him as Jed had just been looking through the people at his party, as if Will were in the audience too. But this was Will. He mattered . . .

She'd drunk too much wine, she realised. It had never happened before, but she was drunk. Good God. She started to giggle.

'Let me show you round the rest of the flat,' he whispered hotly into her ear, and even as she saw Diana coming towards them, she followed him out and away from the music, through the sitting-room, into the hall, up the glass and chrome staircase.

He's going to seduce me, she thought. She giggled, unable to take the idea seriously.

Someone came out of a room at the top of the stairs.

'Can't you use the downstairs loo?' Jed complained, holding Rowan a little tighter.

'There's a queue,' the man grumbled.

'Come and see the bathroom.' Jed beckoned her inside.

She let out a low and very unfeminine whistle. It was furnished with mahogany panelling and deep sea-green tiles, the taps were Victorian-style and gold-plated, the bath sunk into a raised tiled platform. Behind the bath was a large lone palm.

He smiled, led her out and shut the door. 'And this is where I work.'

She heard the pride in his voice, followed him into a studio, that was again unlike anything she'd ever seen.

She wandered further into the large room, gazing around with wide and curious eyes. Diana had said he was a photographer, but this was one heck of a studio! The walls were matt black, and the high ceiling pure matt white.

'Why black and white?' She meant all over the two-storeyed flat but he answered for the studio alone.

'For better lighting control.'

'It's . . .' She was lost for words. It was certainly – like Jed himself – different, and proud of it. It was an uncluttered room, furnished only by a chesterfield, various lights, a tripod, a cupboard with photographic equipment bursting out of it, and various dish-shaped reflectors. 'It's amazing,' she said at last. 'You don't go in for much furniture in this flat of yours, do you?'

He grinned. 'Minimalism. That's what I like.'

'The bare bones?'

He nodded. 'Too much clutter and you can't see the wood for the trees, as they say.'

'Hmmm.' She went over to the corner, where a small dressing table was curtained off from the rest of the room. She drew the curtain back and glanced at him, a question in her eyes.

'Make up area.'

'And through here?' She pointed to a door.

'The dark room.'

He folded his arms, watching her.

'It's quite something . . .' Now that they were alone and away from the rest of the party, she felt self-conscious, no longer drunk or on a high. She didn't know quite what to say to him.

'*You're* quite something.' He took a step towards her.

She laughed, not sure what the next move would be. She had thought Diana such a child, but Rowan was an innocent herself, she realised. She may have fallen in love very young, she may have first made love with a boy at the tender age of fourteen. She may even have become pregnant and suffered a traumatic miscarriage at only sixteen. But there had only ever been one boy. Now she was nineteen and – true enough – an innocent in the city. There had never been another boy. She had never even dated a man – unless you counted her rendezvous with Glyn in the folly. She was an innocent compared to a man like this. A man like this . . .

'You're beautiful.' He was close to her now. He stood in front of her, filling her vision, tilted her chin until she was looking up at the pure white ceiling, ran his fingers along the lines of her cheekbone, and back down to her jaw. 'But not just beautiful.' He paused, still studying her. 'There's something else. Something special. A kind of presence . . .' He let his hand drop from her face. 'Would you let me do your portrait sometime?'

It wasn't what she'd been expecting at all.

His lips were very close but he made no move to kiss her. Once more her eyes were drawn towards his. Hazel with flecks of brown, green and grey.

'I couldn't afford your prices.' She spoke without thinking. Why

194

would she want a picture of herself, for heaven's sake? She had no-one left to give it to.

He laughed. 'Quite delicious. Quite delightful.'

'What is?'

'You are.'

'Why?' She glared at him. He was laughing at her.

'It would come free.' He spread his hands. 'No charge.'

Oh yeah? She felt his hand take hold of hers once more as he led her towards the chesterfield. There was always a charge, wasn't there? 'I don't know . . .' She hesitated, an image of Zita coming unbidden into her mind.

'Don't you want your picture taken?' He drew her down on to the chesterfield.

This was it, then. They were going to make love, right here in his studio. *Precautions*, she heard Zita's voice. But a man like this would know all about precautions, wouldn't he? He was experienced. A man of the world.

Do I want to? Another voice, her own.

He touched her hair, pushing it away from her face. 'You shouldn't hide behind all this,' he said.

A shudder of longing ran through her. It was like . . . It was like the sweet rush. Not the same, but it might be all she had left. *Yes*, she answered herself. Yes, she wanted to make love with this man. He had stolen into her senses, hadn't he? He felt right. And they had made an unspoken bargain. Why bother to wait until she knew him better? She knew him well enough now . . .

'All right, then,' she said, almost forgetting that she was talking about the photographs.

'Soft focus.' He leaned back, frowning slightly, still watching her. 'I have to study you . . .' A glimmer of a smile touched his mouth. 'I have to get it right. I think of photography as an art, you see. It's not just snapping pictures.'

'I'm sure it's not.' She wanted another drink, looked for her glass, but it was empty.

'I've got some champagne in here.' As if this were an everyday occurrence for him, Jed opened a fridge full of bottles and cans. He extracted a bottle and ripped off the foil.

'Lovely.' She tried to pretend this was normal for her too. But it wasn't normal, and she didn't want it to be. She wanted it to be different, magical, exciting. And it was.

He poured the streaming liquid full of bubbles into her glass and she sipped cautiously. It was delicious. And yet he still made no move to kiss her. Instead he took a pack of cigarettes from his pocket and lit one with a match, leaning into the flame, his hazel eyes turning amber in its glow.

'Can I see some of your work?' She wasn't sure why she said this, only that she wanted to prolong the moment, stretch the experience out for as long as possible.

'Sure you can.' He put the cigarette in an ash-tray by the side of the chesterfield, and grabbed a portfolio from a stack of them piled nearby. 'This is the portrait file. You'll want to know what you're letting yourself in for.'

She took the file from him, opened it on her lap, and slowly turned the pages, barely glancing at the faces smiling back at her, conscious throughout of his body heat, so close to hers, of the scent of his aftershave, the sound of his breathing.

'What do you think?' His voice sent shivers cascading down the back of her neck. He reached out his hand and let his fingers trail up her bare arm, touching her shoulder, caressing the small hollow under her collar bone. How long? she kept thinking as she turned more pages. How long before he kissed her?

His work was good, there was no disputing that. He captured looks, personality, mood and atmosphere. His portraits weren't of the conventional variety. They were parts of real people, moments captured as if they hadn't been posed at all, but as if the photographer had just happened on them by chance, grabbed the moment with his camera, rather as Rowan herself was grabbing this moment here and now.

It was funny, but you felt as if you knew them in some indefinable way, she thought, as she came to a beautiful blonde with an air of translucence to her eyes and skin. As if you'd met them before . . . Rowan frowned.

'She's a nice girl.' His tone changed, and Rowan knew immediately that he had slept with her, whoever she was. Had he seduced her here on this chesterfield? Had he made her feel important? Subjected her to the kind of focused spotlight he'd trained on Rowan all evening? Had he met her at a party, made his selection, and asked to do her portrait?

'She's very beautiful.' Rowan's throat constricted. She looked up from the portrait and found herself confronting the hazel eyes. 'A friend of yours?'

He laughed, clearly not embarrassed in the slightest. 'Superficially pretty,' he corrected. He held her gaze. 'Everything between us was like that – superficial.'

'I see.' This was what innocent girls in London could avoid. His fingers on her neck became more insistent. Was it too late to back out of the bargain?

'I only did her portrait a few weeks ago,' he went on. 'She wanted a picture of her and her boyfriend. Strange sort of guy . . .' He turned the page. 'This is him.'

Rowan stared. Glyn was looking back at her, unsmiling, almost accusing. Glyn with his dark hair curling around the collar of the open-necked shirt he wore. Glyn with his acid-green eyes, the slight cleft in his chin and gypsy ear ring.

'Glyn.' The sound was forced from deep in her throat, from some isolated, almost forgotten part of her. 'Glyn . . .'

Chapter 14

Glyn Penbray had never really settled to London.

Of course, he hadn't exactly wanted to come in the first place. It had been his mother's idea, planted like a seed in his brain. And it had seemed like a solution of sorts. Because he was running scared from the girl he loved, running scared from commitment and going public.

But he began to have second thoughts about going away when Rowan came to visit him. How could he leave her?

When Rowan came to the cottage . . . He was astounded at her nerve that day, he half-wanted to take her in his arms and kiss her, not chase her away. Only he hadn't had the guts.

It was true that he'd avoided the folly – unwilling to tell her he was leaving Cornwall, not knowing how she'd react, convinced she'd try to change his mind, and she just might succeed at that.

But coming to the cottage like she did . . . She scared the living daylights out of him. And pregnant! He didn't have the first idea how to deal with that. It was a blow to the gut all right, that was.

But after she left he thought and thought, and by the time his mother returned home he knew what he must do. He had to stand by Rowan. He couldn't leave her to cope entirely alone.

'I'm not going to London after all,' he told her. 'I don't reckon it's such a good idea.'

'Don't talk twaddle.' Lynette dished up his dinner and shoved it in front of him. He saw her look accusingly at the old man as if this change of heart were down to him.

'I mean it.' Glyn began tucking in to the fish pie.

'Harry?' Her hands were on her hips, blue eyes flashing daggers.

'It's nought to do with me.' His dad was perfectly calm. 'Let him have his say, will you?'

'Oh, I'll let him have his say, all right . . .'

Glyn fidgeted nervously. His mum didn't half worry him when she was in this mood.

'I'll let him have his say and then he'll feel the back of my hand, he will.'

'Mum . . .'

She pointed her knife at him. 'I've gone to a lot of trouble for you, my lad. Everything's arranged.'

Harry looked across at her. 'What's arranged?'

'Never you mind,' she snapped. Her tongue was like a whiplash, Glyn thought. Neither he nor his father seemed able to control it.

'Anything arranged can be un-arranged even sooner, I reckon.' Harry put some fish on his fork and lifted it to his mouth, staring at his wife the whole time.

She glared back at him, only wilting slightly. 'It's the best thing for Glyn,' she said in more reasonable tones.

'You think so?' Glyn could hardly believe his dad's nerve. Sometimes – the times that mattered – he just had this way with him.

'I know so.' She turned her attention to her son. 'And I might as well tell you that I know what you've been up to. Or should I say *who* you've been up to?'

Glyn felt himself turning crimson. He looked to his dad for support, but Harry Penbray was concentrating on his food. Clearly he'd passed the buck of defiance over to his son. 'So?' was about all Glyn could manage.

'So what do you think her father will do to you, then? When he finds out?'

'He knows already.' At last Glyn looked up at her.

Her eyes narrowed. 'And what makes you so sure about that?'

Glyn stared at the fish pie congealing on his plate. He shrugged miserably. 'I dunno.' He didn't have the guts to come right out and tell her that Rowan had been here. She'd flip her lid, wouldn't she?

But at least she didn't know Rowan was pregnant. Christ. What would she say if she knew that?

He shivered. But everyone would know sooner or later, wouldn't they? Rowan wouldn't be able to hide it for ever. She wouldn't *want* to hide it for ever. And what would Rowan's father do then? A bit more than keep her inside the house, no doubt of that.

Glyn began to shake. What if Philip Brunswick knew already? What if she'd run straight home and told him? What if he were on his way here right now? He looked at his mother, sure she could see right through him.

'Do you honestly think a man like that one would let the likes of you cavort with his daughter and get away with it?' Lynette was on her feet again now, slamming dishes and plates around. She whipped Glyn's dinner from under his nose and scraped the food noisily into the bin. 'They've got money, the Brunswicks have. They've got money and they've got class. Upper class. Do you know what I'm saying, lad? Do you know what the likes of them think of the likes of us?'

'That's not the way things work any more . . .' he began, remembering what Rowan had told him once. She had been so sure.

'Who do you think you're fooling?' his mother snapped. 'Open your eyes. Take a look at the real world for a change.'

Glyn hesitated. What about Rowan? Shouldn't he be helping her, protecting her? Guilt mixed with the fear, churning and curdling in his head, in his heart. And over and above the guilt and the fear was his mother's face, and her hand pressing down on to his.

'You go away from here, my lad,' she was saying. 'Just for a while, to keep me happy. Go to London and have a good time. Don't want to be in the firing line, now do you?'

Again, Glyn tried to catch his dad's eye but Harry wasn't having any part in it.

'Glyn?'

'All right.' He held his head in his hands. 'All right then, I'll go.'

Only then did his dad look up. And Glyn would never forget the expression in his eyes.

But Glyn's heart had never been in his London life.

Someone – he didn't know who – had organised a flat for him to share with two other lads, and the chance of an office job – an interview with a private utility company.

He went along, and much to his surprise he got the job. But it was dreary. They told him he'd have to start at the bottom, being only sixteen and with no qualifications, which meant making tea, sweeping up, and filing. Time dragged by in a way he'd never experienced before – even worse than waiting for the bell at the end of RE lessons.

London night life was all right though – there were plenty of pubs, bands and girls. Girls liked him, which was a bonus. Blokes from London laughed a bit at his accent, until he learned to take the piss out of himself before they did, but girls loved it. They treated him as a kind of little boy lost, and Glyn wasn't complaining. Little boys that were lost got given lots of goodies.

His flatmates were a bit on the un-cool side, but the place was comfortable and unbelievably cheap – which was a good thing because his wages were a pittance. So much for London rates.

When he told some girl how much he was paid, she laughed and accused him of having a sugar daddy. 'Or maybe in your case I should say sugar mummy . . .' And she'd shrieked with laughter and passed him a joint. Easy come, easy go.

That was another thing he liked about London life – anything you might want was easily obtainable if you knew the right places to go, the right people to talk to. He'd never tried most of this stuff before. Everything was here. A lot of it was crap – Glyn scorned the instant feel good of Ecstasy and the buzz of crack. But he liked a good smoke, and pretty soon he had a circle of mates, a string of available girls, a CD player, and a place to go every night of the week. It wasn't Cornwall, but life wasn't so bad.

He kept meaning to go back – but what was there to go back for? He couldn't face Rowan after what he'd done to her. And there was no work.

When, after a year of making tea and filing, he got the sack for coming in late so often after a heavy night out, he drifted into another job in another office, a tax office this time because a mate had told him you could come in late every day there and no-one would even notice. If you worked there two years you could get a short service gratuity – a one off lump sum payment – so you could use the money to go abroad and live a little.

'But don't stay there too long,' his mate warned him. 'After five years the SSG becomes a preserved pension. And you don't want to be thinking about junk like that at your age.'

It was a different office, sure, with different people and different colour files. But the funny thing was, it felt exactly the same.

Glyn knew that he'd lost something when he left Cornwall. He had lost Rowan Brunswick – and he often thought of her, even as his first year in London stretched into two and then three. But he had also lost his sense of self – his sense of self in the landscape, which he knew he'd never find here in this grey city. Too many buildings, not enough trees. Too many people, no space.

He was marking time, he supposed. That's what it felt like. He kept meaning to break out, to find something else, something new that had some meaning . . . But he wasn't sure how to start. And he'd never got round to it somehow.

He came across Melanie Fowler in a pub in Chelsea. She was pretty as ever. She had grown her hair and those come-to-bed blue eyes of hers held even more promise than they had in the old days at the back of the school playing field. She was surrounded by blokes but still seemed glad to see him, and before he knew what was happening they started getting it together.

He hadn't meant that to happen at all. It wasn't that he didn't find Melanie attractive – a guy would have to be half-blind not to find her attractive. But Glyn had reservations. Since Rowan, he had been strictly a one-night stand kind of a bloke, and he would have preferred it to be that way with Melanie too. It was safer and it was easier. But Melanie had this way of making that impossible. She had this way of making him continue to want her.

Melanie kept him interested. She would do outrageous things, just out of the blue. They could be sitting in a pub and she'd start undoing the buttons of her top, watching him.

He would try and stop her, more concerned with looking around to check no-one had noticed. 'Stop it, Melanie. What the hell d'you think you're doing?'

'I want you, Glyn,' she would whisper.

She'd be practically getting her tits out, then as his eyes bulged and he hissed, 'Not here, Melanie, for Christ's sake,' her hand would snake under the table they shared, find the zip of his jeans and . . .

Well, she was outrageous. Glyn would have to bundle her outside, hoping that no-one noticed his prominent erection, and back to his flat pronto. Sometimes they didn't make it to his bed, quite often they didn't want to. They had done it on the kitchen table, on the drainer, against the wall of the hallway by the front door, on the worn carpet in the sitting-room, in the bath and in countless positions in his bedroom. Melanie was insatiable, and Glyn found her very hard to resist.

But from Melanie he got something more precious than just good sex. He got a taste of Cornwall, a taste of his past. Melanie shared his roots – she was as much part of the Cornish landscape as he was – and that made it still harder to keep things casual between them. He could talk to her about Folyforth, the people there, his mum and dad. Of course he couldn't talk about Rowan . . . He had tried once, tried to discover if there had been any scandal attached to the family who lived up on the hill. But Melanie knew nothing.

'That girl left almost the same time as you did,' she said. 'For a bit we actually thought . . .'

'What?' He turned away from her, pretending indifference.

'Nothing.' She grinned. 'It was impossible, and you're not that crazy.'

But had it been as crazy as he'd always imagined? When he really thought about it, his time with Rowan seemed about the sanest of his life.

It was Melanie who had dragged Glyn along to this party tonight, in a posh flat belonging to some pseudo-cretin called Jed Montague. Glyn knew him vaguely – the guy was a photographer; he'd even taken Glyn's photograph a few weeks ago. Glyn hadn't wanted his picture taken at all – why the heck should he? – but Melanie had pleaded, fluttered her eyelashes and all the other parts of her anatomy that did strange things to his resolve.

'You know . . . *the* Montagues,' she had said as if that was supposed to mean something.

He was a good photographer – Glyn had to concede that much – but Glyn had taken an instant dislike to him. Jed Montague reminded him of the money people, the people who lived on the other side of some invisible barrier that couldn't be crossed. Like Rowan. But he also knew that Jed Montague was a good contact for Melanie who had ambitions to be a model and was still building up her contacts and her portfolio, probably in that order. So he had complied.

'Have you been to bed with him?' Glyn felt grumpy tonight, determined to find fault. Lately he had become more and more dissatisfied, with his work, his life, with himself. And besides, he didn't want to be here. He wanted to be . . . well, he wasn't sure exactly where he wanted to be, but these trendy types pissed him right off.

'Of course I have.'

That pissed him off too. 'Why, of course? You don't sleep with everybody, do you?' He looked her up and down. 'Or do you?'

He meant to hurt, but it seemed to wash right over her. 'If someone might be useful, and if he's the slightest bit attractive, then yes, I do,' she said. 'Don't worry – I'm not stupid. I take precautions. But how else would I get to know a bloke like him? How else have I got the slightest chance of succeeding in what I want to do?' She looked at Glyn as if he were being particularly dense. 'I happen to like sex, in case you hadn't noticed. And it's not a bad weapon to have. It's a tough world out there, Glyn. And the business I want to go into is the toughest of the lot.'

That sounded like a line from the movies, he thought. Perhaps he *was* being dense – he certainly didn't understand those kind of values.

'It didn't mean anything, if that's what you're on about,' she went on, taking his arm. 'It's only sex. It's no big deal. Everyone does it.'

'Yeah, sure. Everyone does it.' They were standing in the kitchen. Around them the party was really taking off, and most people had drifted to the sitting-room to dance. Someone had put on that Whitney Houston song, a real choker. Glyn felt the joint in his waistcoat pocket.

'I'm going to get some fresh air.' What he wanted was a quiet smoke, but Melanie seemed to have other ideas.

'Let's go up to the roof garden.' She led the way outside the back door, and up an iron spiral staircase.

He followed her. She seemed to know the place pretty well. Maybe she had come up here with Jed. Maybe this was where they had done it, between the window boxes of petunias and pansies. On top of the city, so to speak.

'So what are you getting in a stress about, then?' she asked him, as he lit up and sucked gratefully. 'I thought that was how you wanted it to be between us. Casual.'

Glyn waited for the hit to recede. 'I'm not the man for you, Melanie.'

She laughed, low and sexy. 'Oh, I know you think that. But *you* know that I've always been sweet on you.'

'Do I?' He watched her appraisingly.

'Course you do.' She moved closer. 'Back in Folyforth, yours was the name I scratched on my desk. Melanie loves Glyn. Wrapped in a heart.'

He smiled. Took another drag and passed the joint to her.

'That was a long time ago.'

'Not so long.' She watched him. 'My feelings haven't changed.'

'No?' It seemed like centuries ago to Glyn.

'Still, I always wondered . . .'

'What?' He glanced at her sharply as he moved to the iron railings of the small roof garden and looked out into the night. People. Buildings. Lights. A busy night was going on out there.

'I always wondered if there was someone else.' She took a deep drag and passed the joint back to him. 'Was there someone? Back in Cornwall?'

'No chance,' he replied quickly. No chance for him and Rowan Brunswick, that was for sure.

'And how about us? Is there any chance for us, even though you think you're not the man for me?' Melanie stretched, languorous as a cat, and pulled off her camisole top in one graceful movement.

He stared at her bare breasts, for she was wearing no bra, a fact that hadn't escaped his notice in the early part of the evening. 'Anyone could come up here.' His voice thickened slightly.

She giggled. 'I was rather hoping you might.'

Resolutely, he turned away from her. 'I told you, Melanie. You shouldn't waste your time on me.'

'It's my time.' Her voice was barely audible. 'I think we're doing okay.' She paused. 'And if it doesn't work out . . . well, as your dad would say, there's plenty more fish in the sea, I reckon.'

Glyn laughed, but even as he laughed a gut feeling of homesickness

washed over him. He gripped on to the railings. Thought of himself
with his dad out on the boat at night-time. Rolling on the waves. The
blue-black scroll of the sea, the inky curtain of the sky, the stars and
the moon that made your neck ache and your mind start to wander.
And then he remembered that night on Bodmin Moor. It had been a
clear sky then as well. When he'd told Rowan about the stars . . . He
sighed.

'What is it, Glyn?' She came closer, still half-naked in the balmy
night air, her breasts rubbing against his arm, her nipples hardening.
He ached to touch, to squeeze.

'I was thinking about the stars,' he told her. It sounded pretty daft.

She took his hands from the railings and cupped them around her
breasts. 'Tell me.'

With a start, Rowan realised that Jed was staring at her as if she'd
gone bonkers. Then his expression changed.

'A friend of yours? A lover?'

She nodded unhappily. 'Both.'

'You've gone so pale.' He touched her face, seeming to hesitate.
'He's here, you know.'

'Here?' Rowan clutched on to the edge of the chesterfield, trying
to control her shaking hands.

'At the party. I saw him earlier on.'

In an instant she was up and heading for the door.

'He'll probably be with . . .' Jed began, but she was already gone,
away from him, out of the studio, running down the chrome and
glass staircase.

Glyn, here at this party? How come she hadn't seen him? Surely
she couldn't have passed him by and just not seen him? Had she
been too drunk? Too absorbed in Jed Montague?

She raced around the hallway and sitting-room, horribly sober now,
scanning the kaleidoscope of faces. Nothing. Into the kitchen and
the same story. A few people drinking beer and wine, a floor with
cigarette packets practically afloat in spilled beer. Nothing.

She leaned against the kitchen door, glanced outside and spotted
the iron staircase. She slipped out, silent and wary.

Rowan wasn't sure where it led – maybe it was only a fire escape

– but some instinct forced her up the spiral, almost to the top. It led to a garden, she could see that now. And two figures stood, with their backs to her, leaning against the iron railings, looking out over the city. Two figures silhouetted in the clear moonlight.

'Castor and Pollux. The twins.' His voice was low and yet clear.

Rowan shuddered. She couldn't believe she was hearing this. But it was Glyn sure enough.

'What happened?' A breathy voice. A silhouette that, pieced together with the portrait in Jed's studio, became Melanie Fowler.

Rowan put her hand to her mouth.

'They became stars. They were put side by side in the heavens. Never to be parted.'

Rowan took a step backwards down the staircase.

'Oh, Glyn. That's a beautiful story.' They turned slightly, his hands on her breasts. Bare breasts.

'Maybe we should do it, here, under the stars,' she murmured.

'You're crazy . . .' But as she arched her back, he bent his head, down towards her breasts.

Rowan turned and ran, not caring how much noise she made, clattering down the staircase, thinking only of getting out of sight. For they would never know, must never know that she had been there.

The noise distracted him. 'Sounds like we just had a visitor . . .'

'Some bloody voyeur.' She frowned.

Glyn watched her. 'Who could blame anyone? You were born to seduce men, you were.' He released her, stared out over the railing at some wild figure running away from the house as if it were on fire. He smiled, remembering the folly and Rowan. Standing on the battlements watching her running into the wood. Rowan? He rubbed his eyes. He was dreaming, wasn't he?

'You're thinking about Cornwall again.' Melanie's voice was petulant. 'Every time we start getting it together you go mooning off into the past.'

He laughed, but she was adamant this time.

'Why don't you go back there if you're so in love with the boring old place?'

Glyn stared at her as she pulled on her camisole top, covering her nakedness. He'd thought it often enough. But she was right, and here on this roof-top garden, he couldn't think of one good reason why he shouldn't return. He didn't belong here, never had. He wanted Cornwall. It was in his blood.

'Maybe I will,' he said, taking her hand and pulling her down the steps. 'Maybe I will, at that.'

She couldn't bring herself to go back into the party, so Rowan ran towards the road, flinging her arms up, desperately hailing a taxi cab. At last one stopped and she climbed in wearily.

Glyn was in London. Not only in London, but even closer than that. Glyn had been at that party, at Jed's party. Near to her, yet still a million miles away.

She sighed, thinking of the scene she'd witnessed on the roof-top garden. Glyn and Melanie Fowler. He'd told her about the stars . . . How could he do that?

Whatever they'd had, it was over. It was time to put him out of her heart for good.

In the house only halfway up the hill above the village of Folyforth, Audrey Brunswick sat quietly in her high-backed chair listening to the sound of her husband fornicating upstairs. Lynette Penbray was loud. But then, tarts always were, weren't they?

And he didn't care either. The man that she'd married cared nothing for her humiliation. He no longer even bothered to pretend. He had brought her here, to their house, as if she could pretend she was Lady of the bloody Manor.

Yesterday, her husband had invaded Audrey's sanctuary for the first time since Zita had left them. He had walked right in without even knocking. As if she were nothing.

'I'm putting the house on the market.' He stared out of the window, stiff and upright, not even glancing her way.

'You're moving, then.' She tried to take this in. It meant of course that she would move too. But not with him, surely not with him.

He appeared not to notice her choice of words. 'I need to raise some capital.' She noticed his adam's apple working, a sure sign that he was perturbed. He would be hurt by losing this house, it would cause him pain.

'What's happened?'

He twisted round to face her. 'What do you care? When have you ever cared?'

She drew back, faintly alarmed by this attack. She had money of her own, money that she had never bothered to speak of. But she would not offer it now.

His mouth twisted, 'You've never had to work for it, have you? Everything you've ever wanted has just fallen into your lap, hasn't it? And that's all you do, just sit around on your arse and wait for someone else to do it all for you.'

She winced. Was that how it seemed?

'I suppose you've lost a lot of money,' she remarked conversationally. Clearly he was blaming her for something he'd done.

'Too much.' He tore his hand through his greying hair. 'Too bloody much.'

She laughed, very low. 'You won't be moving into Folyforth House, then?'

'Bitch.' He stepped forwards as if he might slap her, then apparently changed his mind and walked out of the door instead. 'Bitch,' he shouted as he slammed it.

Audrey sat for a long time without moving, until the noises from upstairs ceased. Slowly, she got to her feet. She had thought a lot about her husband in the hours since that conversation. A lot about Zita and Rowan and how she had come to be as she was now.

She pulled the small brown leather suitcase from the wardrobe. There wasn't much she wanted to take with her. A few clothes, a few books and personal belongings. Some letters and – she hesitated – her paints.

Moving over to the bamboo table she picked up the telephone receiver and called a cab. It would be an effort. She hadn't stepped outside this house for a long time, but she couldn't move to another one. Not with him.

She picked up the case, and went to the front door to wait. Maybe she would even begin to walk down the drive. Yes, it would be an effort but it was one that must be made if she wanted to survive for a little longer.

Audrey wasn't sure how long she had left. She felt the bottle of pills nestling in her pocket. They would help her. But she wouldn't see anyone about the lump in her breast, she was determined not to tell a soul. She would not allow herself to be mutilated or pitied, neither would she endure the treatment that would be prescribed. Her own mother had died of cancer and Audrey could still remember some of what she went through – how she had been destroyed even before death.

Audrey would retain some dignity, she was set on that. It was all she had left. And she would make her peace with those she had never stopped loving. For if she were going to sink any lower – any lower than listening to her own husband's sexual encounters – she had better do it with people who, at least once upon a time, had cared.

Chapter 15

The next morning brought a dozen roses delivered to Rowan.

'An admirer, I see.' Zita was preparing to open the shop as Rowan picked up the card that accompanied the deep red velvet blooms. 'I didn't think Will was the type.'

'They're not from Will.' Rowan felt a flush stealing to her cheeks. The message was short and to the point:

Dear Cinderella. I tortured your address out of our mutual friend. These are to replace the kiss I never gave you.

'Will's got a rival then, has he?' Zita laughed and Rowan poked her playfully in the ribs.

'No, he has not. I keep telling you, you old bat, but you never listen. Will Stafford is just a friend.' But Rowan frowned slightly. She hadn't seen Will since the party, and for once she wasn't exactly looking forward to doing so. Had she made a fool of herself last night?

Zita turned to face her, her eyes teasing. 'Then who's been sending you red roses?'

'Wouldn't you like to know?' Laughing, Rowan held them tightly to her breast, breathing in the faint perfume, dangling the card in the air above Zita's head.

She ran up the stairs to the flat. Jed. She felt bad about Jed, knowing full well that if she hadn't seen that photo of Glyn in his portfolio last night, she probably would have made love with him, let alone just kissed him. It had been a long time – over three years – since she'd last made love with a man, with Glyn. And last night Jed had woken her up from the slumber.

But she *had* seen the photo, hadn't she? The sight of Glyn's dark, loved face had delivered a blow straight to the solar plexus. She had behaved like a silly schoolgirl in front of Jed, had broken their unspoken bargain, and worse, had found Glyn well and truly in the arms of another woman. So much for true love. So much for all that claptrap about the heavens and the stars that he'd spouted to her on Bodmin Moor, that she'd believed in so passionately, that she'd kept in her heart for so long.

'Damn Glyn Penbray!' She slammed her fist into the solid wooden bannister. Damn him for imprisoning her and then not telling her she was free. And damn him for not answering her letters.

What had he done when they'd been forwarded to him? Laughed? Shown them to Melanie Fowler? Thrown them unopened into the bin?

Still more of a surprise was the unexpected visitor who arrived in the afternoon.

Rowan saw her first. She was doing the Saturday afternoon shift in the pie and mash shop with Zita. She looked up as the door opened, to see a pale, sad-faced woman standing uncertainly on the threshold of the shop.

'Mum?' She rushed over.

Zita's head shot up. She stared at the tall thin figure. 'Audrey?'

They sat her down at a table, brought her pie and mash, which in turn brought a smile to her lips, and stared at each other, all three of them, in shared disbelief.

'You've left him then?' Rowan asked her later, when they were up in the flat drinking tea.

Audrey nodded. 'He said he was moving house. I couldn't bear the thought of going with him. Of going anywhere with him,' she added sadly.

Zita snorted. 'Would have been better for all of us if he'd moved out a long time ago.'

Audrey turned to her. 'I'm so sorry, Zita.'

They hugged, whilst Nell shook her head in mock despair. 'You'll have to stay here, I suppose. Maybe I should thank my lucky stars the Brunswick family isn't any bigger.'

'Only till I get myself sorted out.' Rowan could see that her mother was relieved at the offer. She could only guess at the effort it had cost her to leave.

She sat at her mother's feet. 'What will you do?' She couldn't imagine her here, couldn't imagine her actually doing anything.

'I thought I had money.' Absent-mindedly, Audrey stroked her daughter's hair. 'But when I checked with my solicitor . . .'

'It's all gone?' Rowan's voice was bitter. 'I suppose he took it?'

Audrey let her hand drop to her side. 'I never bothered about the money. But it seems I signed it all over to your father. Can you believe that I'd forgotten?' She sighed. 'He invested it.'

'And?'

'And lost the lot.'

'Bastard,' Zita breathed.

'What about maintenance?' Rowan asked her. 'Shouldn't he at least pay you maintenance?' She looked up at her mother.

'I don't want maintenance.' Audrey sounded unusually vehement. 'And I doubt he's got it to give.'

Rowan stared at a new Audrey Brunswick, sitting on Nell's sofa bed. It seemed as if her decision to leave Rowan's father had at least given her a bit of life back.

'I want to cut all ties. I'll manage on my own.' She hesitated. 'For a while.'

Zita put a hand on Audrey's thin, pale one. 'Why now?'

Audrey hesitated. Should she tell them? Should she admit to this affair of Philip's that she'd found out about such a long time ago, that she'd assumed would simply go away as well as not matter any more? Should she admit to the humiliation of hearing him and Lynette Penbray having sex in what had once been the marital bed? She shook her head. 'I've had enough,' was all she said. 'I've come to the end of the line.' She wouldn't tell them about the lump either. Not until she had to.

'But what will you do?' Rowan said again.

She was so changed, her daughter. Audrey could hardly believe it. She seemed so composed and sure of herself. So confident, and – yes, so beautiful with her lovely grey eyes and long dark hair, hanging past her shoulders now. Audrey felt a stab of love, an urge to tell her daughter how much all those letters had meant to her, that they'd helped her through, that she had kept every one. And she would tell her soon. She had made a new life for herself, this daughter of hers. Thank goodness at least, for that. Ah, Rowan. Audrey might have forsaken her, but she had possessed the strength after all – the strength to find her own way.

'I'm not sure yet.' She glanced at the three kind faces. 'I'll work, of course.'

Zita and Rowan looked doubtful.

Audrey stiffened. They didn't think she was capable of it. She might not deserve this kind of a welcome. But she knew what she was capable of. 'Other people do,' she said crossly.

'But you're not other people, Mum,' Rowan laughed. 'You've never worked in your whole life.'

'It's never too late to start.' Audrey glanced across at Nell, sensing an accomplice, a woman who wouldn't treat her like a piece of delicate china. 'What do you think, Nell?'

The other woman smiled. 'What were you thinking of, love?'

'I don't know.' Audrey hadn't thought that far ahead. It had been effort enough just to leave.

But Zita moved towards her, took her hands. 'Maybe you could work in an art gallery? You know, like you wanted to before. You've got the skills. I know it would be hard work, but . . .'

For a moment tears blurred her vision, as Audrey remembered how much she had wanted to set up the art gallery in Padstow. The effort she had put into it. How Philip had done all he could to make it impossible. How she had let her ambitions fade into nothing . . . losing part of herself in the process.

'Zita . . .' Audrey got to her feet to embrace her. She had mistreated this woman, acted as her employer when she should have been her friend, under-estimated her badly, never appreciated her nor perceived her loyalty. Kicked her in the teeth instead of sticking up for her. Through pride. She had allowed Zita to do everything she could to help Audrey and her family, and then she had sent her away. 'Do you really think I could?'

'Why not?' Zita stood firm. 'You're as capable as the next person. And more qualified than most.' Her eyes narrowed. 'Maybe you'll even take up painting again.'

*   *   *

'It seems to be our week for unexpected arrivals,' Nell commented drily when a brown package arrived by parcel post a couple of days later. It was for Rowan.

She opened it when she got back from college, her mother, Nell and Zita clustered around like kids round a Christmas tree.

'For heaven's sake,' Rowan chided. 'Is there no privacy around here?'

'Not a lot,' Zita informed her. 'Or so I've always found.'

Rowan slid her fingers under the paper and opened the box. Inside was one white fluffy slipper.

'What the heck . . . ?' Zita began.

But Rowan burst out laughing, recognising Jed's scrawled handwriting on the accompanying card. 'Let's see . . .':

Dear Cinders. I couldn't find glass. Will this do? No doubt a visitor from the court will be around some day with an identical slipper.

'He sounds a bit odd, darling,' Audrey seemed worried. 'How well do you actually know him?'

Rowan grinned. 'Not half as well as I'm going to.'

'Atta-girl.' Nell slapped her on the back and she, Zita and Rowan all laughed.

Zita opened her arms to include Audrey in the small circle. Audrey was trying her best. 'You're doing great,' she whispered. It wouldn't be long before she would open up and tell Zita about whatever it was that was bothering her, Zita knew that. But she could also see that the banter that came so easily to the rest of them left Audrey feeling high, dry and excluded. 'Don't worry,' she murmured in Audrey's ear. 'That daughter of yours knows exactly what she's doing.'

Rowan squeezed her mother's arm. 'If it's good enough for Cinderella . . .'

The following Saturday, Jed Montague himself turned up in the pie and mash shop during Rowan's morning shift. She raised her eyebrows although she'd been half expecting him. 'Pie and mash, love?'

He grinned. 'It's a bit early in the day for me.'

Rowan absorbed the look of him, only half-relieved that he appeared just the same, that the fascination was still there. He was wearing jeans and a waistcoat today, more casual, but strangely, he didn't seem as out of place as she would have expected him to be.

'This is interesting . . .' She saw him looking around. He had a carrier bag from Harrods in his hand.

'A bit humble for your taste, isn't it?' she teased. Although the truth was, they got all sorts in here. She was glad that he'd come, that he could see where she lived, the place she thought of as home. He would have to take her as he found her. But would he take her?

He shrugged. 'Actually, I was thinking it would make a great backdrop for some shots. Those art-deco mirrors are amazing. And I love the tiles.'

She grinned. 'You photographers. You have such one-track minds.'

Meanwhile Zita was eyeing him with some interest. 'Prince Charming, I presume?'

He laughed. 'Not for me to say, madam.'

'Why don't you fetch him some coffee?' Zita suggested, wiping her hands on her gingham checked overall. 'And get some yourself while you're at it. Take a break.'

'It depends . . .' Rowan moved over to the coffee machine.

'On what?' They both watched her.

'On whether he's got the other slipper.'

In front of all the customers and Zita, Jed pulled a white fluffy slipper from the Harrod's carrier bag, and got down on one knee. 'Would you do me the honour?'

She put it on and a few of the customers cheered.

'Quite a showman,' Zita commented.

Laughing, Rowan took the coffee over to a corner table. She had never been treated like this, never had so much attention bestowed on her. And to her surprise, she loved it.

'Will you come out with me tonight?' he asked. 'To dinner?'

'After that performance, how could I refuse?' But a flutter of excitement did a swift somersault in her breast. This was it, then. She hadn't lost her only chance by behaving like an idiot. She would be seeing him again.

They talked for a few more minutes and then he gulped down his coffee and was gone with a grin, a wave and a kiss that he blew on his hand towards her.

Rowan took deep breaths, trying to recover. The man was like a whirlwind.

'Well, I never . . .' Zita was beside her. 'That's some Prince Charming. I half expected to see a white horse reined up outside.'

'Hmm.' Rowan rose from her seat, piling the thick china cups on to a brown tray. Where would he be taking her? What would she wear, for heaven's sake?

'But be careful, love,' Zita warned. There was a look in her eye that Rowan couldn't quite make out.

'What of?' Rowan flicked back her hair. She felt confident, strong and sure, in a way that she'd never felt confident with Glyn Penbray.

Zita bent to wipe a cloth over the already spotless marble-topped table. 'He's not Will Stafford, just you remember that.' She grinned, and the moment of seriousness passed. 'And you know what they say about those castles in the clouds . . .'

He didn't take her to some posh hotel as she had half-dreaded, but to an informal wine-bar near Chelsea where two musicians were playing the blues.

Jed ordered cucumber and dill salad, seafood spiced with cumin, and a bottle of Frascati, and proved to be good company. When the subject turned to photography his enthusiasm was noticeable. But he didn't hog the conversation. Pretty soon he asked her about catering college.

'One thing I'm curious about . . .' He took her hand, their first physical contact of the evening. Already they were drinking coffee, their meal finished.

'Why I'm working in a pie and mash shop? A place that was always so working class? So East End and so . . . old fashioned?' She had wondered how long it would take him to get round to it. 'A nicely spoken girl like me?'

He smiled. 'Don't get me wrong, Rowan. That place is great. It's a part of the past no-one would want to lose. And I don't think of myself as a snob.'

She eyed him carefully. 'No, I don't think you are. But there's a call for the old working-class traditions,' she smiled. 'Even in Hammersmith. You'd be amazed.'

'Not really. But I am curious. How did it come about?'

Haltingly, Rowan told him a little about her background, leaving huge gaps but describing the closeness she'd always felt for Zita, and Zita and Nell's determination to keep the pie and mash alive in west London. She also missed out the bit about her miscarriage. 'I had a row with my father,' she explained. 'And I had to get away. So I came here. To Zita's.'

'And worked for your keep?'

'Something like that.' She hesitated. 'Even my mother has come to live here now.'

'Your mother . . . ?'

'She left my father too.' For some reason, Rowan found herself giggling at her own statement. Too much wine perhaps. This was getting to be a habit when she was with Jed Montague.

'Whew.' He grinned. 'Your old man must be one hell of a guy.'

As they walked home, hand in hand, she waited for him to ask her about Glyn, but he never did, and she was grateful. Maybe . . . if things worked out between them, if she got to trust him, she would tell him. But until then, she would make do with a visit to his castle in the clouds. Rowan chuckled silently to herself. She reckoned she deserved a taste of paradise.

The flat seemed strangely hollow and bare now that it was empty of people. And yet its very emptiness emphasized the minimalist style.

Rowan looked around. There was no mess, that was what seemed so odd; the place could be unlived in. When she thought of the flat above the pie and mash shop in Hammersmith, she thought of the huge sofa bed that took up most of the space in the sitting room, the antique pine dining table that Will had restored for Zita, the assortment of chairs, cushions and plants. Things . . . There were things everywhere in Nell's flat but nothing matched – clocks, ornaments, china vases, photographs, boxes of tissues, bits of knitting, newspapers and magazines. Things that had to be moved every time you wanted to sit down.

'Just dump it on the floor,' was Nell's byword whenever they had visitors. 'Excuse the mess. Grab a seat. Just dump all that stuff on the floor.'

Rowan smiled. Here there were black leather chairs, smooth and cold looking as if they'd never welcomed anyone's backside in their life, a chrome and glass coffee table, and a black wood-stained bookcase, full, she noted as she wandered over to take a closer look, of books about photography.

He came up behind her, his breath warm on her neck. 'There's one place I didn't get round to showing you the other night . . .'

She stiffened. Not the roof garden. She didn't think she could face being taken up there.

'Not scared are you?' He took her arms, gently pivoting her around to face him. 'I'll only *show* you the room if that's all you want. I wouldn't force you into anything.'

'The room?'

'The bedroom.' His hazel eyes seemed to draw her into some kind of sweet conspiracy.

Because that wasn't all she wanted, was it? Just to be *shown* his bedroom. She wanted to stay there for at least a while. And he knew it.

He led the way up the now familiar chrome and glass staircase, and instead of heading for the studio, went through a different panelled door.

'My bedroom,' he announced, as if introducing her to a person.

She laughed with delight when she saw it, for all of Jed's personality, missing in the rest of the flat, seemed to have been crammed into this one room. It was decorated in blue and lemon, and it was cluttered – there was no other word for it – with an assortment of books, magazines, clothes, a couple of old coffee mugs and glasses, pencils, paper, cameras, a telephone, a portable TV, and a CD player. And in the centre of the room, littered with more paraphernalia as well as huge fluffy pillows and a lemon quilt, was the biggest brass bed that Rowan had ever seen. The kind of bed, she thought, that you could live in.

'Come into my parlour,' he whispered, shutting the door behind them.

'Said the spider to the fly,' she whispered back. But she didn't need inviting twice.

Jed turned out to be an expert lover. He removed her clothes with infinite tenderness, kissing every part of her body as he did so.

When she was naked, he sat her on the lemon quilt of the high brass bed and she watched as he took off his own clothes. Naked, he was surprisingly thin but wiry, his body quite pale and somehow vulnerable, like a child's.

He wasn't, she concluded, the kind of man with whom you could struggle and rip off each other's clothing with wild abandon. Jed's kind of loving wasn't about abandon. It was about controlled and exquisite pleasure.

'Let's get into bed,' he whispered.

And they both slid under the lemon quilt – which smelled fresh and newly washed, Rowan noted in some strangely objective part of her. He had known then, that she would come back here, that she would end up naked under the quilt of his brass bed.

He caressed her, slowly, a bit at a time, with gentle exploring fingers, and following his lead, she caressed him back, letting her fingers trail over his thin shoulders and down to his chest, as if they were playing a game of love, moving counters inch by inch, forward then back, but slowly and surely proceeding towards the finishing line.

His touch relaxed her, smoothed away her first-night nerves, her fear of being physically loved by anyone other than Glyn. Gradually it struck her that she was enjoying it. She was enjoying the sensation of love spread with luxury, of making slow sensuous love in a bed made for that purpose. It was so, so different from the way in which she'd mostly made love with Glyn – on the hard ground under the sky, with all the accompanying discomfort from nettles, insects, sand, and cold breezes that used to whip her into rapid and passionate orgasm.

With Jed, every motion, every stroke was both tender and carefully considered, as if this was the way to bring sensuality to its utmost peak, to squeeze every last ounce of pleasure from every touch, before graduating on to the next.

And each movement built her desire for him. Each touch was another foothold for him until he had reached her summit, the summit of her longing, and she cried out for him, wanting him, needing him inside her now. He reached for a packet from the bedside table, smoothly, swiftly, not breaking the spell.

222

'I never knew it could be like that,' she told him when it was over, as they lay side by side in the brass bed, holding hands, both staring at the ceiling.

'It should never be "wham bam thank you, Ma'am",' he said. 'That's not the way to get the best pleasure. Not the way to treat love, either. It's a travesty.'

He was right. And yet . . . It hadn't been wham bam thank you, Ma'am with Glyn, had it? It had been uncontrolled passion. And however much she had enjoyed making love with Jed – and it had been making love, there was no other adequate way to describe it – there had been no uncontrolled passion.

She sneaked a look at him. He looked satisfied and happy. Maybe it was her fault. Maybe she still couldn't let go. But then again, she felt good too. She stretched. Very, very good. So. Maybe this would be enough, after all.

Chapter 16

When a couple of weeks had passed by with Rowan hearing nothing from Will, she went round to his bed-sit. She would not allow this to come between them. Will's friendship was too important to her.

'Oh. Hi,' he said when he opened the door, his blank expression hardly encouraging.

'Hello, stranger.' He looked, she thought, as if he'd just got out of bed. It was mid-day and yet Will, a notoriously early riser even at the weekends, appeared bedraggled and weary. His shirt was half-undone, his eyes bloodshot and bleary, his red hair was a tangled mess, and his chin was unshaven. She, on the other hand, who *had* just got out of bed – her lover's bed – was confident that she looked pretty good.

'Growing a beard?' she asked him.

He touched the fierce red stubble. 'What's it to you?'

Rowan frowned. 'Only asking.' She hoped he wouldn't be cross. She had a whole glorious Saturday to herself, and she'd made excuses not to spend it with Jed, preferring instead the idea of a day spent pleasing herself – pampering herself in a hot bath perhaps, taking her mother or Zita out shopping, making it up with Will . . .

He continued to block the doorway.

'Aren't you going to ask me in?' She glared at him.

'It depends . . .'

'On what?'

He folded his arms. 'On what you want, of course.'

Rowan sighed. 'Will, what is this all about? Won't you tell me?' She knew though, didn't she? Her suspicions had been proved right. Will objected to her seeing someone else. It was obvious. He had hoped they could be more than friends.

'Nothing. I don't know what you're on about. There's nothing to tell.' His face was a mask of indifference, but still he stood there guarding the door like the great warrior from the past she'd first spotted at Jed's party.

'Oh, let me make us a cup of tea, for heaven's sake.' Exasperated, she pushed past him. This was no time for social niceties. If they were to remain friends, then they had to sort this out, find out where they stood with each other.

'Come in, Rowan,' he mocked. 'Make yourself at home, why don't you?'

Ignoring him, she grabbed the kettle. 'Is it because of Jed? Is that it? Do you mind my seeing him?' She asked this with her back to him, partly because she felt ridiculously self-conscious about the whole thing, partly to give him time to recover, or adjust the mask, or whatever he wanted to do. Anything so that Will the valued friend could come back to her. Perhaps it was selfish of her. Yes, it *was* selfish. But she needed his friendship; suddenly she couldn't bear the thought of losing him.

'Yes.' His voice, when it eventually came, sounded small and lost. And it surprised her; she hadn't expected such sad honesty.

'But you like Jed, don't you?' Rowan swung round to face him. 'Why do you mind my seeing him when he's supposed to be such a good mate?' She sighed, cross with herself, wanting to bite back the words. Of course it would make no difference that the two of them were friends, if anything it would make the whole thing worse. If he cared. There would be constant reminders.

'A good mate doesn't necessarily make a good partner for my best friend.' His blue eyes met her gaze without flinching.

Best friend? Rowan ploughed on regardless. 'You said he was a great laugh. You said people couldn't help liking him.' This was half-hearted. Rowan felt she had taken the wrong direction somewhere along the road of this conversation and she wasn't quite sure how she could back-track. So instead she plunged onwards into deeper water. 'You introduced us, for heaven's sake.'

'And maybe I shouldn't have. You don't know him like I do.'

As a matter of fact, Will Stafford was extremely angry with himself, not for introducing Rowan to Jed Montague – that was inevitable and he'd put it off for much too long – but for neglecting to warn her about him. She had a lot of common sense – it was one of the things he admired about her, that she wasn't silly or fluffy like a lot of girls he met – so if she'd had some warning, if he'd even given her a hint, he couldn't help but think that she would have seen through Jed.

'Don't I?' she demanded.

Will wasn't after a row. But she looked pretty angry now, those grey eyes of hers like turbulent waves. And he couldn't blame her. 'No, you don't.' He knew that he sounded bitter and childish. And worse, he couldn't tell her any of it now. What would have been a warning would come out as sour grapes. He bit his lip. But he wanted to let her know, he should let her know that Jed was renowned for his habit of claiming women's hearts.

He carried them round like a banner – and not necessarily one at a time – proclaiming his power loudly to anyone who'd listen. Then he broke them into tiny pieces and stamped all over them. Will had witnessed it so many times. Jed Montague – great fun to be with, amusing, generous and even loyal in his own way – was a rapacious womaniser.

Will had – a long time ago – made him promise not to break Diana's heart. And to give Jed his due, he treated Will's sister more like a kind uncle than a prospective lover – despite Diana's undeniable encouragement. But Will had instinctively sensed that Rowan Brunswick would unknowingly present a challenge that Jed would be eager to take up.

She would have been protected by being his own girlfriend – even Jed wouldn't have made a play for her then. But much to Will's bitter disappointment, it hadn't happened for him and Rowan. She treated him so obviously as a friend, and nothing else, that he'd found himself unable to make the right moment or move somehow. It didn't come easy to Will; unlike Jed he had never found relationships with the opposite sex either easy or satisfying. There always seemed to be too much missing. Until Rowan.

He had been stupid, he saw that now. He had foolishly hoped, prayed even, that Rowan would immediately see through Jed. That she was meant to be Will's girl, not Jed's. That she would laugh at Jed the way he did, the way that Jed laughed at himself when he described his sexual exploits to his mates in the pub. It had been funny in the past. But Will couldn't bear to think of Rowan being talked about that way.

'No, you don't know him at all,' he said sadly, aware that she would only hold this against him. Loyalty. He wasn't exactly making a good impression on that score.

'Some mate,' she muttered, confirming this.

Last Sunday he had gone round to Jed's flat in the middle of the afternoon to find him developing photographs of Rowan.

'You've seen her, then?' Moodily, he left the dark room, half hoping his sudden exit would ruin the negatives. But it was too late. Too late for the photographs and too late for Rowan. And he had, after all, known it was coming. He'd been waiting ever since Jed opened the door to them on the night of his party, and he'd seen the look in Rowan's eyes. Known it long before Jed came round to hassle him for her address. There hadn't seemed much point in refusing.

'I've done a lot more than see her.' Jed brought them out to show him, black and white prints of the most wonderful, the most sexy girl in the world.

'Spare me the details.' But Will had been unable to stop staring at her face.

Jed laughed.

Will couldn't bear the sound of his arrogant laughter. He glared at him. 'Don't hurt her, Jed.' Though if he did, wouldn't Will be there to comfort her?

'I wouldn't dream of it.' Carefully Jed put the photos away, all but one. He handed it to Will. 'Want a copy?'

Wordlessly, Will nodded, unable to refuse.

'I wouldn't dream of it,' Jed went on. 'Because this one is different.'

'Different?' Will's voice came out as a hoarse croak.

'Yeah.' He sounded thoughtful. 'Rowan Brunswick is very different, in case you hadn't already noticed . . .' He shot him a sharp glance that was more like a blow to Will's heart. 'I think I might be in serious danger. Of falling madly in love with her.'

Will's world plunged into a sudden and stumbling kind of semi-darkness. Because that was worse, wasn't it? Much worse than he had imagined.

Coming to his senses, Will swiftly pulled the curtain back round the bed. But he was too late. She'd seen it – the picture on the wall, done in soft focus.

Rowan stared at her own portrait, the head and shoulders shot that Jed had taken last Sunday morning. It was well-done, no denying that. But neither was there any doubt that she looked like a satisfied and sensual woman. A woman who had very recently been made love to.

She shot him a questioning glance. 'When did he give you this?'

'Does it matter?'

Rowan frowned. Maybe she should be asking why he'd given a copy to Will. Surely he hadn't been gloating over his success with her? She didn't want to think that might be true.

'Do you mind?' Will seemed embarrassed.

'Mind?'

'Me having your picture on the wall?' His eyes were very blue, and very angry. But it wasn't anger towards her, she realised.

She stepped towards him, put a tentative hand on his arm. No, she didn't mind him having her picture on the wall, but she wasn't sure she wanted him to have *that* picture. It seemed wrong somehow. She was struggling. Struggling to get them back on to their normal footing, but not sure how to achieve it. 'Will, I only mind us not being friends. Are we still?'

There was a long pause. 'Of course.' He looked down at her.

For a moment she was unmoving and silent, just wondering.

Then, 'I've missed you,' she said. It was true. She had been astonished at how much she hated the thought that he might be angry with her, that he might think her a fool, or even worse cheap and easy for sleeping with Jed.

'Have you?' He reached out his big hand as if to touch her face, and then let it drop to his side.

'My seeing Jed doesn't mean that we can't still be friends.' She looked into his eyes. 'Does it?'

It was strange, she reflected, that this was the first time they had been wholly serious with each other. As if they had become so used to joking, that this new seriousness was causing awkwardness, difficult rifts in their relationship.

It seemed like an eternity before he answered, and when he did so the seriousness had gone, although she didn't know whether to be relieved or not.

'Bugger the tea,' he said. 'Let's take a walk down by the river and get ourselves a beer.'

'I thought you'd never ask.' She picked up a comb and chucked it at him, glad that he'd broken the tension, that the awkwardness could be banished with a laugh and a joke.

'And Rowan . . .' At the door he stopped her, the seriousness returning, very briefly to his voice.

'Yes?' For no good reason her heart was hammering.

'I am your friend,' he said. 'Any time you need one.'

Glyn Penbray returned to North Cornwall at the end of that summer, having worked out his notice. He achieved the promise of a short service gratuity cheque in the post, by the skin of his teeth.

But he had been back in Folyforth for less than a fortnight when he came home one day to find his father packing a bag.

'Where you off to then, Dad?' Glyn was guiltily aware that since he'd been home he hadn't spent as much time with his father as perhaps he should have done. Mostly he had been wandering around all the old haunts, brooding, wondering where Rowan Brunswick had ended up, and wondering what he should do with himself next.

'I'm getting myself a new place.' Harry Penbray fixed him with a look of certainty. It was the look that his father had worn in the past, on the rare occasions he'd decided to put his foot down.

'A new place?' Glyn stared back at him. What did he need a new place for? Weren't his father and their cottage a fixture in Folyforth? His mind raced. What the hell had been happening with his parents while he'd been away? 'What do you mean a new place?'

'What I say.' With infinite patience, Harry zipped up the bag. 'I'm not taking much. If you need me, you can go along to the Post Office at Port Treworth. They'll know where to find me.'

'You mean you're leaving Folyforth?' Glyn's eyes were disbelieving. 'Leaving Mum?'

Since childhood Glyn had always been able to imagine his mother walking out on his father. It had often seemed likely. She got fed up with him, she nagged and complained, even threatened to go more than once. She'd always been pretty; he could even see how her easy sociability could have led to her eloping with some stranger, going off to the better life somewhere that she'd always maintained she was destined for. But she never did. And Dad . . . He'd never imagined his dad going anywhere, apart from out to sea.

'She'll manage just fine without me,' Harry said now. 'You know your mum, I reckon.'

Oh yeah, he knew his mum all right. 'She'll go crazy,' Glyn muttered. And who would be left to pick up the pieces? He would, that's who.

His father seemed to know what he was thinking. 'I've had enough, my lad,' he said. 'It's your turn now. You know all about the tides and the fishing. I've taught you everything I know – if you've kept any of it in your head.'

Dumbly, Glyn nodded. Fishing? His mum would freak out. She'd always been determined that he'd never take that road.

'Up to you of course. If there's something else . . .'

Glyn shook his head. He'd always loved being out at sea, that was the truth of it. He'd missed the sea in London.

'But I'm leaving all the nets, all the gear, the boat and that. So if you want it . . .'

Glyn nodded once more.

'Cat got your tongue?'

'I don't know what to say, Dad.' Glyn wanted to hug him close, that's what he wanted, but he and his dad had never had that kind of relationship, had they? And he didn't want him to think he wasn't up to the responsibility. He could handle it, couldn't he? He'd be the man of the house now.

Harry nodded. 'There's lots round here that'll not know what to say. They'll be surprised, shocked even.' He chuckled, as if this idea appealed to him. 'I promised myself I'd wait till you got back, give her something to hang on to . . .'

'How did you know I'd be coming back?' Glyn blurted.

'I knew.' Harry smiled his toothy grin. 'It's in your blood, I reckon.'

Something happened to Lynette Penbray when her husband left her. Everyone in the village agreed, but none felt it more keenly than Glyn.

It had been left to him to tell her that Harry was gone. He had accused him of cowardice, but knew before his father answered that there were other reasons.

'I don't reckon I owe her that much,' Harry said. 'And it seems to me she'll be expecting it.'

And sure enough, although Lynette had paled, grabbed his arm, and looked for a moment as though she might faint, Glyn was also sure that it hadn't come as a complete surprise.

'I should never have told him,' she kept repeating, over and over, her sharp eyes looking for once glazed and vague. 'I should never have told him. I only wanted to shake him up. I never thought he'd go.'

When he reluctantly confided that he would be going out to sea to try and make his living, she had only laughed without humour.

'That's right. You follow in his footsteps.'

'It's all I know,' he told her.

'You had your chances.' He thought for a moment that she was accusing him of something, but she wasn't even looking at him. She was staring out of the window, towards the waterfront. And as she stared she straightened her back.

'We'll be better off without the old bugger,' she said.

But she had changed. Instead of looking beaten, or even upset, she became even more vivacious than before. She dressed herself up more too, in skirts that were just that bit too short, and blouses just that bit too tight. Her make up became sloppy, her lipstick too red and her eyeliner too dark. And all the time, as the women of Folyforth muttered to themselves over garden fences, she wasn't getting any younger.

It was as if the woman who had always been a bit of a laugh, the barmaid with whom the male customers liked to flirt simply because they knew it was harmless – she was a good-looking woman but hardly a threat with old Harry Penbray waiting back at home – had become little more than a cheap tart.

Stories continued to fly around the village, of who she'd been seen cavorting with – now and in the past – and how she didn't have the least idea how to embrace middle-age gracefully.

And Glyn heard a lot of them. He heard and so he threw himself into his fishing as Harry Penbray had done before him, so that he didn't have to listen.

One story, however, was not so easy to ignore.

He heard it one evening when he was in the snug of the bar at the Bull and Packet, tucked away out of sight. It was a Friday night and Dewy and Tamsyn Jago from next door were in too, but it was early so the pub wasn't full. His mother was serving in the other bar, but he kept getting glimpses of her as she passed. A few strands of dark hair were escaping from her piled up chignon, her voice was getting louder, and he was pretty sure she was already knocking back the gin and tonics like there was no tomorrow. How would she last out the shift without getting paralytic and falling over somewhere? How long before they fired her? And what the hell would they all do then?

But what he heard in snatches from the couple at the bar made his blood run cold. Made him grip hold of his tankard of beer as though he might crush the metal with his bare hands. His mother? And Philip Brunswick? His mother and Rowan's father? No. He couldn't believe it. Wouldn't believe it. And there was more. Too much for him to take in right now. He couldn't think about it. Wildly, he ran from the pub.

The next day, Melanie Fowler came back to Folyforth.

Glyn hadn't expected to see her for a long time – they had parted on good terms, but her ambitions had kept her in London, and he was done with London for good.

'How long are you staying?' he asked her, when they met up on the waterfront. He was glad that she didn't laugh at him for turning to the sea for his living, like some had done. Some who were probably jealous that he'd got himself even a taste of city life.

She watched him re-arranging the nets, laying them out to dry. 'I'm back for good, I think.'

He straightened himself, stared at her, uncomprehending. 'What about the modelling?'

'I gave it a go, didn't I?' She shrugged. 'The simple fact is – I'm not good enough.'

He thought of her beautiful body. 'I wouldn't say that.'

She smiled gratefully. 'I told you it's a tough business. I wasn't up to it.'

'Oh?' He smiled at her. Had Melanie changed her ways, made adjustments to her values after all?

'I got told a few home truths,' she admitted. 'Let in on a few secrets of the trade, you could say.' She seemed close to tears.

'Both of us ending up back here – that's a turn up for the books.' But Glyn liked the thought. Melanie was a perfect comforter, and that's exactly what he could do with right now.

'Destiny, do you think?' She smiled uncertainly, as if unsure of her welcome.

Glyn thought of his mother. He thought of his mother, and he thought of Rowan. Then he took Melanie's hand, leaned forwards and kissed her. 'I'd say destiny, for sure.'

Chapter 17

'Sometimes I wonder why I let you drag me here week after week,' Rowan complained to Will. The year that was coming to an end was getting to be a cold one, and since it was half time and Chelsea hadn't even looked like scoring, Rowan was beginning to think longingly of log fires, hot soup and perhaps a glass of mulled wine.

'You love it,' Will informed her. 'In the last cup match you told me you couldn't understand why it had taken you so long to appreciate the game of football.'

Rowan stamped her feet to get her circulation going. 'That was on a warmer day.'

'True supporters . . .' he wrapped his blue and white scarf more firmly around his neck, 'come to Stamford Bridge, rain or shine, snow or . . .'

'When it's just freezing bloody cold.' She searched in her pocket for chocolate, and unwrapped it with some difficulty since she was wearing brown suede mittens.

Around them, the supporters were subdued, all of them wanting a lift, as if needing some kind of confirmation that they hadn't been mugs to pay out their hard-earned money at the turnstiles just to come and watch twenty-two grown men kick a football and each other around the pitch in about equal doses.

But Rowan had to admit that Will was right. At the end of the summer before last, at around the time that she had first started seeing Jed Montague, Will had invited her to a football match as a kind of peace offering. As if he was trying to say sorry for having a go at her, or sorry for caring maybe.

She had agreed in the same spirit, come along to Stamford Bridge half-dreading the prospect, and ended up having a brilliant time. Will had bought her crisps and coffee and explained the rules of the game in between yelling at the referee for faults ranging from bias to blindness, Chelsea had won 4–0, and she had gone home hoarse, happy, and filled with a kind of glow – the glow of winning.

Since then, she had accompanied him to most of the home games, much to Jed's bewilderment and scorn.

'What do you see in it?' he demanded. 'Cricket's one thing, and with a bit of luck you can even sit down in the sun to watch it, with a nice cold glass of lager in your hand. But football . . .' His lip curled. 'That's for brainless louts.'

'And that makes you narrow-minded. And a snob, into the bargain,' Rowan told him with a laugh. 'Football's exciting. I love it.'

He shook his head in despair, whilst Rowan continued to go, caught up in the exhilaration of the league competition, the cup run, in shouting matches with opposing fans – although sometimes Will had to grab her arm and whisk her away before she said too much – and in the heady atmosphere of Stamford Bridge. She even accompanied Will to some of the away fixtures – boozy affairs with beer on the train and before the match, where she had to be more restrained, and where – as away spectators – they were herded into a certain section of the ground. She was hooked. Match of the Day was no longer a cue for getting up to make coffee, but a highlight of her week-end.

Besides which, it was a rare chance to be on her own with Will, and she valued his friendship perhaps even more than she had done eighteen months ago. Since she'd been seeing Jed, and since a desire for independence combined with finishing at catering college and getting a job had persuaded her to move into her own flat, Jed had tried his hardest to monopolise her time.

He was often busy himself, with photo sessions and photo-shoots, but expected her to be always available whenever he was free. But she just couldn't do it. She was already juggling her new job with seeing the three women she thought of as family at the pie and mash shop, and Jed would have to accept that. And she still needed time to see Will and Diana.

Will returned from one of the refreshment stalls with coffee in fragile plastic cups. 'By the way, I've got a message from Charlie,' he told her.

'Oh?' She was immediately interested. Charlie Walters continued to offer her a dinner party to arrange once a month, and she did it whenever she could. Charlie was a generous employer, and it gave her the chance to be more adventurous. Rowan had come a long way in the confidence stakes since Charlie's first dinner party when Will had helped her mend the fish.

Not only that, but Charlie had also been instrumental in getting her the small flat in Hammersmith that she now occupied. He had been in the process of converting a run down house into two flats, one of which he now rented out to her. Rowan had shared initially with a flatmate from college, who stayed for almost a year before getting married, and since September with Will's sister Diana, who had wanted her second year at college to be outside hall after a year of living in. They were beginning to form a close unit, a kind of foursome – Jed, Will, Rowan and Diana.

'He wants me to bring you to dinner.' Will spoke with nonchalance.

'Do a dinner you mean.' Carefully, she held the steaming cup of coffee between her mittens and sipped, burning her tongue and the roof of her mouth. Why did the coffee from those blasted machines always have to be so damned hot?

'Nope.' Will grinned. *Bring* you to dinner.'

Rowan stared at him. 'What for?'

Will shrugged. 'A business proposition, he said. Who knows, with Charlie?'

'When?' She felt a flutter of exhilaration. It would be rather fun to be sitting at Charlie's beautifully polished mahogany table instead of serving. And she was extremely curious. She still wasn't one hundred per cent sure about Charlie Walters. In her dealings with him he had been all charm. He had also been good to Will – and maybe his fondness for his protégé had carried through to her, Will's friend. But – there was always a 'but' in her mind. Perhaps she was just being silly. Perhaps the cynicism that she seemed to have acquired since her experience with Glyn had left her too suspicious of people's motives.

'Next Saturday.' Will was warming his big hands around the plastic cup. 'Bloody awful coffee,' he said conversationally. 'Are you free next Saturday, or do you have to work?'

Rowan frowned. It was her night off from the restaurant in Chiswick where she worked, but Jed had suggested going out to eat. Just the two of us, he'd said, a pre-Christmas celebration. 'I'm not working,' she told Will. 'I'm supposed to be seeing Jed, but I'm sure he'll understand if I put it off. We can always make it some other night.' Who was she trying to kid? Jed would be more than a little peeved, she knew it.

Will raised his plastic cup. 'To new ventures.'

'Nothing ventured, nothing gained.' She lifted her cup in response to his toast, and took a wary sip. 'Yuk.'

'And how is Jed?' Rowan got the distinct feeling that Will had been leading up to this. Whenever he saw her alone, he nearly always asked, although in fact he probably saw Jed as much as she did.

'All right.' She thought of Jed, as ever, with some ambivalence.

'You don't sound very sure.'

'I'm not sure.' She sighed. 'I'm never sure.'

'But you're happy.' He was trying to sound casual, she knew that. But she wasn't fooled one bit. Although, in truth, she didn't even know how Will Stafford felt about her these days.

'I suppose.'

'And you love him?' Will had never asked her this before, and she was shocked. She stared at him in surprise.

He shrugged. 'I just wondered.'

'I'm not sure that I do love him.' She didn't know if this were true, but it seemed the only answer she could give Will. At least right now. And if she didn't *know,* if she didn't want to shout her love for Jed from the rooftops, then she supposed that her words must be true. She wasn't sure that she loved him at all.

She did know that he was fun, that he had shown her a different way of life, taught her a lot about making love that the girl who had only loved in the wilds of North Cornwall hadn't even dreamed of. She knew that it was difficult to maintain a distance from him, that her precious independence had to be fought for, that she had to claw it from his grasp before it was gone.

But she often asked herself what Jed wanted from her. He was attractive, intelligent, successful, sought after . . . And most women, including Diana, adored him.

She smiled. For a while it had come between her and Diana, when Will's sister had first moved to London. But the younger girl's life at college – which presumably included a medley of new and exciting men and social activities – had apparently rescued Diana from her obsession with Jed. She still adored him, and would admit it freely. But she no longer seemed to resent Rowan for getting what she couldn't have. And since she had moved in with her, they had become friends. Rowan was beginning to think of Diana as the younger sister she'd never had.

Still, she felt self-conscious when Jed occasionally stayed the night at the flat. She thought, once or twice, she caught a sadness in Diana's expression when they left the sitting-room hand in hand, and she found herself holding back when they made love, in case Diana was awake, listening, on the other side of the wall.

But when they were in Jed's Chelsea apartment, their sex life was good, although it had never reached the passion that Rowan had been half-waiting for. Perhaps what she'd had with Glyn Penbray was a one-off. Perhaps its intensity had been due to youth and inexperience. Perhaps it would never happen to her again – that sweet rush of passion that was only too easy to recall.

As for Jed, he didn't always seem satisfied . . .

'Why are you holding back?' He often asked her these kind of questions, usually during sex, as she lay half-dreaming, lost in the easy sensuality that he made such an integral part of their lovemaking.

'I'm not.' That was how she always replied.

'Yes, you are.' On this occasion he was more petulant than usual. He stopped caressing her shoulders and slumped to one side, staring into space.

Rowan sighed. 'I'm not, Jed.' She stroked his arm. 'Really, I'm not. I'm fine.'

'But you're not mine.' He lay on his back in the brass bed, isolating himself from her.

She felt the beginnings of fear. 'Is that what you want?' she asked him at last. They had never really talked about it – what they wanted from each other.

He was silent.

'For me to be yours? For me to *belong* to you?' She couldn't keep the distaste from her voice.

'No!' He raised himself up on one elbow, glared at her from those beautiful hazel eyes, swung his legs over the side of the bed and jumped out. 'Of course not.'

'What then?' She wasn't convinced.

He came over to her side of the bed. 'I want you to *feel*.'

'I do feel.' She felt angry too.

'I mean really feel.' He made a fist as though he wanted to strike her, then let it fall into the soft lemon quilt. 'I want you to love me.'

'Well, of course I do.' Of course, of course. Here, they were on difficult ground.

He had said it first, only a week after their first sexual encounter. 'How I love you, Rowan Brunswick. You're simply precious, you really are.'

And she had laughed, unsure how serious he was making this new relationship, deciding to play safe, to keep it a half-joke. 'Yeah. Of course you do.'

And maybe she loved him a little – because he was funny, because she was in his bed and he was loving her body with his. Further than that she refused to go.

'But I do,' he had insisted, refusing the playful definition. 'I do love you. I loved you the moment I saw you.'

'You don't know me,' she had teased, unwilling to play the game.

'But you're here aren't you?' His voice had been soft.

'I'm here.'

After a month or two she had given in at last. 'Of course I love you,' she started saying, as if he were mad to doubt it. 'I wouldn't be with you otherwise, would I?' And, 'You're just being silly . . . you don't need to ask . . . we don't need to keep *saying* it.' What surprised her the most was – wasn't it supposed to be women who worried like this, who were insecure, who needed emotional and verbal back-up to what they could see with their own eyes, feel with their own hearts? It wasn't supposed to be men like Jed – successful, confident men who related easily to the opposite sex, men who had it all – who needed such reassurance.

And why was it so infuriating? Instead of pity she felt irritation. She didn't want Jed to talk about it – she just wanted him to do it, to be there, to let whatever they had find its own way without worrying it into being something else all the time.

But perhaps he knew deep down – perhaps they all knew deep down, those who were insecure – what their partners wouldn't even admit to themselves. Because how could she admit love when she wasn't sure, how could she let love pour from her voice, her heart, when it wasn't flowing swift and unstoppable? Didn't the admission of love mean that she would be betraying someone else? Would part of her always be unavailable? Was that why part of her wouldn't let go? The part that still belonged to Glyn . . .

'Perhaps you should move in here. With me.' He didn't look at her as he made this suggestion. Instead he pulled a black silk robe around his body and concentrated on tying the sash.

She stared at him, willing him to look up. 'Is that what you want?' There were vast areas of Jed's life that she knew nothing about, that she wanted to know nothing about, because knowing would mean that she must give him access to more of *her* life, and there was very little left private as it was.

'Maybe.' He opened the door to the bedroom. 'If we're going anywhere, you and me.' Lazily, as if this question were unimportant he leaned on the door, watching her. 'Are we?'

Rowan realised that she must be honest. 'I don't know,' she admitted.

He nodded. 'That's what I thought.'

She watched him leave the room, and heard the door to the studio open and shut firmly behind him. This was the closest they had ever got to a row, and he'd done it before – left her stranded in the blasted brass bed like some rejected Pre-Raphaelite heroine, whilst he disappeared to the studio to work. And the studio was his territory. It was time that she returned to her own.

Meanwhile, half-time was almost over, and Will was still staring at her. 'You two haven't had a row, have you?' He cheered as the team came back on to the pitch ready for the second half.

'A row?' She returned the chocolate to her pocket, and scrunched the white plastic of her empty coffee container angrily in her fist. 'Come on, you blues!' she yelled.

'With Jed.' He glanced back at her rapidly, before returning his attention to the pitch.

'Of course not.' Rowan knew that when she saw Jed again he would behave as if nothing had been said, nothing had changed. Everything would be fine . . . until the next time.

Glyn turned his head to glance around, to see Melanie coming down the aisle towards him. She was swathed in white, wrapped and haloed in it, white with deep red roses. He wished – how he wished – that she had not chosen roses.

She reached him at last, turned for his smile of reassurance. She was such a pretty girl – and she needed him. She was safe and she was sexy. He knew exactly what he would get from Melanie and it was all he wanted, all he could have for his own.

He saw his mother from the corner of his eye, half-behind him, dressed in navy and white like a sailor. He saw his mother, thought of Rowan Brunswick, and listened very hard to the words that were being spoken.

Lynette Penbray knew that she would not cry. She hadn't wanted Glyn to go to any girl, but if it had to be anyone, then far better for it to be a girl like Melanie Fowler. Melanie was a type, very much a safe bet. Melanie might make him contented, but never would she make him happy. And since she didn't hold the key to his joy, she could never cause him pain.

Lynette sneaked a look at her husband seated in the pew beside her. She knew that he hadn't wanted to return to Folyforth, but she had sent Glyn over to Port Treworth on her behalf, to beg and beg if necessary. She needed him here beside her on this day, as she had never needed him before.

She wished – how she wished   that things could have been different. At the start she too had thought she could make her husband happy. Didn't they all think that, these girls who imagined sex as the be all and end all for any man? She sighed, and saw Glyn shift in front of her, aware of her every move. Yes, they all thought that, and maybe it was like that for some men. But not for men like Harry Penbray. And not for her Glyn.

She had thought she and Harry would be happy, but then she had sensed her own shortcomings, seen that there was something else he needed, an indefinable something else that he got closest to when he was out at sea, not in bed with her.

It had made her mad. It had made her so mad and made her so greedy. She had really come to believe that she was destined for more, that the material world could offer her what she deserved. And so she had ruined whatever she and Harry might have had left – not much, some would say. But maybe enough.

She watched the couple standing in the front of the church. Melanie would have a part of her son. But the rest of him would belong to Lynette now that he was married and safe from the clutches of another woman – a different kind of woman.

She smiled. That was how it should be. She was his mother. She had cried for him, borne him, raised him and loved him. He could be hers now, in a way that he had never been before.

At the reception Harry Penbray made his excuses and prepared to slope away as soon as he decently could. He didn't want another confrontation with Lynette – he had come here today for Glyn's sake, not hers. He wanted no reconciliation or even a promise of future friendship between them. He wanted to be up and out of it.

But at the station he bought a single ticket instead of using his return, and prepared himself for a long journey. Would she want to see him again after all this time? Was he being a fool for the second time in his life – chasing after what he could well do without?

And yet . . . Could he do without it? Should he do without her? Something drew him to Zita Porter. He had to find out how she was doing, what she was doing, and if she wanted what she had once seemed to want, back in Cornwall. She had cared then – enough to try so hard to say goodbye. Would she have tried so hard if goodbye was all she meant to say? Didn't he owe her at least a trip to London?

*   *   *

London, however, proved much larger, louder and busier than he had ever imagined. Harry was daunted. He had planned to find a place to stay the night – as much as he had planned at all – but the prices made him wince. He had precious little, and what he did have he wasn't about to throw down the drain. So he decided to make his way to this pie and mash shop place right there and then though it was after ten o'clock at night.

He saw her through the steamed-up glass – as if he could recognise not even the shape of her, but something much less easily defined. He waited a moment, summoning up his courage, then walked uncertainly in. It was crowded, and not at all like he'd expected. It was noisy, friendly, warm, and blowed if the other woman wasn't there too, standing next to Zita at the counter, the woman he'd helped back to the house that time. Audrey Brunswick. *His* wife – the man Lynette had been seeing for years. Lynette had told him in a fit of pique – as if expecting him to be impressed. He wasn't. He had always half-known there was someone. What difference did it make when there wasn't enough love in the first place?

Zita, this small but vital woman, had touched some special part of him. Someone pushed past as he stood there drinking in the look of her, but he hardly noticed. She looked exactly the same – a bit tired, but she was smiling, and he loved that smile. It gave him a lift in his heart, just seeing that smile.

Someone in front of him said, 'Pie, mash and liquor please, love.'

He watched her serving, amazed she hadn't sensed his presence. A few kind words, a laugh, and then it was his turn. She still didn't look up.

'Pie and mash please, love,' he repeated.

She stopped in mid flow, the potato scoop held in her hand, her eyes wide as she stared at him. 'Harry . . .' she breathed. 'Harry.'

He grinned. She was pleased to see him, that much was obvious. 'Hello, Zita.'

'Harry! Harry!' And then she was round the other side of the counter, giving him a more wonderful hug than he could ever have imagined. More than he deserved too.

'Zita.' He stroked her hair, knowing at last that he'd been right to come, right to follow his instincts. Silly fool – he should have come a long time ago. Not a lot seemed to matter, with this woman in his arms.

'How long can you stay?' They were upstairs in the kitchen of the flat, drinking hot chocolate, warming their hands, looking into each other's faces.

It was past midnight and the others had made a tactful withdrawal. But Zita couldn't think about going to bed, she could only think about sitting here with Harry, only feel that she had always been sitting here with Harry.

'Not long.' He shook his head. 'I can't miss too many tides.'

She tried to ignore the shaft of disappointment that made her cold again. 'You've got to get back to Folyforth, I suppose,' she said. 'Back to your wife . . .' Then why had he come?

He laid his hand on hers. 'I'm on my own now, Zita.'

'Oh?' Her heart did a somersault and backward kick.

'I've got a place further up the coast. Only a rented cottage, like. In Port Treworth. Another village, but the same country, the same sea.' He grinned. 'It's what I know. It's not much . . . but it's mine.'

She felt his hand, warm on hers. 'So it didn't work out, between you and Lynette?' she asked, almost scared to know the details.

He laughed. 'You knew that much before. It were more of a question of when I was going to leave, I reckon.'

'And when did you?'

'When the boy came back.'

'Glyn.' She remembered the boy at the window. She also knew now that Glyn Penbray had been Rowan's lover. Their paths all seemed to be destined to cross and intertwine. 'How is he?' She met his blue, honest eyes.

'Married.' Harry squeezed her hand. 'How's the girl?'

Zita stared at him. 'Did you know about the two of them?'

'Only later, after you left. She came round to the house.' He reached out, touched Zita's face. 'I could see it written all over her – that she loved him.'

'And him?' Zita was wondering how she could break this to Rowan. She appeared to have got over her experience with Glyn Penbray –

she spent much of her time with Jed Montague these days – but first love . . . it had been intense all right. Who knew how she would take it?

'He loved her in his way, I reckon.' Harry looked down, as if he didn't want to think too much about this. 'But I'm not so sure as he would have fought for her.'

'Against Philip Brunswick?' Zita was confused. She could understand parental opposition when they were so young. But now? If they had loved one another now . . . ?

'Against his mother, more like.' Harry's mouth was set, and Zita sensed that the subject was closed. She only hoped it was also closed for Rowan. She didn't want to see her hurt more than she was already.

'And how about you and me, Zita?' He watched her. 'I've spent some time on my own. I was wondering if you might be wanting to come over and visit, like. Maybe stay for a while . . .'

What was he asking her? She stared into his face, his lovely weather-beaten face.

'I haven't got much.' He took her other hand. 'But what I have got – well, it's yours, I reckon.'

'Dear Harry.' She got to her feet. 'Would you come into my bed tonight? Would you, please?'

She watched his eyes cloud with confusion. 'But . . .'

'But nothing. I want you Harry Penbray, and I want you now.'

In the morning, she lay awake with the man beside her who had held her all night long. But she couldn't allow the bud of happiness resting quiet inside her to explode and burst through as it wanted to. Last night they had laughed like children, made love like innocents thrown an unexpected gift. And now? She was tempted to grab this flush of happiness, this late, unexpected chance, this sensation of sudden and spilled emotions. She wanted to keep laughing.

But this morning the laughter had evaporated. Because today Harry would return to Port Treworth – he had commitments, he'd told her, a living to make. He still went out fishing and had made an agreement with a seafood restaurant that had opened on the quayside. He had laid out all the money he possessed for new nets and equipment – he must get back there.

And not only that, Zita knew that he'd want to get back. It was his life. He loved her, she knew that now – accepted his easy confidence as she hadn't accepted it in the past – but he could never make his life here in London, in a place that was so alien to him. He would never survive, and she would never ask it of him.

Yet how could she leave?

Wearily, she climbed out of bed, went to the kitchen to put the kettle on. But Audrey had beaten her to it. She was sitting at the old wooden table, her chin cupped in her hands, deep in thought.

'Penny for them?' Zita circled her warily. Audrey was part of the reason why she'd never be able to leave London. Audrey had arrived here ill and desperate, clutching at Zita as if she were a life raft that could save her. It had taken Zita a month to find out about Philip Brunswick's sordid little affair with some woman in the village – no surprises there. But it had taken a while longer before Audrey finally broke down and told her about the lump in her breast that she was sure was cancer. Out it all came at last – her mother's death, her own fears, her sense of inadequacy bred by her father and nurtured by her husband. Zita grimaced. Audrey's father had about as much to answer for as Philip Brunswick did, damn him.

Action was second nature to Zita, and within a week she had taken Audrey down to the doctor's, and booked her an appointment at the hospital.

'I don't think I want to know,' Audrey moaned, in the bus on the way there.

'You don't have to do anything about it,' Zita told her. 'But you do have to *know.*' She sighed. 'How can you go on – not knowing? It's not possible, love.'

Audrey had been almost taken aback to discover that the lump wasn't malignant after all. Almost disappointed, Zita would have said, as if she'd geared herself up for it.

But since then she had taken huge steps. She had come off the anti-depressants, and she had found herself a job in an art gallery off the Fulham Road. She was expected to do the lot – mounting, framing, hanging and selling, and it was hard physical labour. But it had given Audrey back her self-confidence. And even better, or so Zita thought, she had got out her paints again.

So how could she leave her now? Audrey had survived, had made her home here, had found something for herself here. And Zita was part of that something. Nell needed her, Audrey needed her, and the pie and mash shop needed her too. It was her living. She wouldn't be dependent again.

So that was it then. Neither she nor Harry could ever leave.

'I was thinking about you and Harry.' Audrey stared at her. Her eyes were red and raw as if she'd been up all night. 'What would have happened if I hadn't sent you packing when we were in Cornwall? You were in love with him, weren't you?'

'Was I?' Zita stared out of the window. She didn't want to think about it too hard.

'Of course you were.' Audrey scraped her chair back on the linoleum floor. 'Any fool could see it. I've never seen a woman so moony-eyed. You were all over the place.'

'Maybe.' Zita blinked.

'What would the two of you have done?'

Zita shrugged. 'Who knows? He was married, wasn't he? What could we have done with Lynette Penbray in the background?'

'Lynette Penbray . . . ?' She stared at Zita. 'You mean Harry is . . . Harry Penbray?'

'You've been working too hard, love.' Zita shook her head. 'Course he is, who did you think he was?'

'Harry Penbray . . .' Audrey repeated the name to herself. 'You never told me. And his wife is . . . ?'

Something in her expression told Zita what was going on. 'Not the woman who was having it off with Philip?' she whispered.

Audrey nodded. 'The very same.'

'By God . . .' Zita was lost for words. But it made no difference, did it? She still couldn't leave, could she? Even though she was sure that Philip Brunswick was firmly in Audrey's past and there to stay.

Audrey was frowning. 'What do you mean he *was* married? Are you saying that he isn't now?'

'He left her.' Zita made the tea. 'Maybe he would have left her before. I don't know. He lives alone now. I don't know about her and Philip . . .' What did it matter, she wanted to scream. What did it matter when she couldn't have Harry, when they were separated by geography and by people – the people they had committed themselves to before they even dreamed they would want to commit themselves to each other.

'Will you go and live with him?' Audrey's voice was only a whisper. A whisper that seemed to echo around the cold kitchen. The heating had only just come on, the room hadn't yet warmed up for the day.

'Of course not.' Zita slammed cups on to a tray. What was this – the bloody Spanish Inquisition? What did they all want from her?

'Why not?'

'Why do you bloody think?' Shaking, Zita poured out the tea, grabbed the tray and opened the door with a practised foot.

In her room, Harry was waking up. He looked at her with sad eyes. The laughter had gone from him too. He knew, didn't he? He knew what she had to do.

It was an hour before they emerged from her room.

'You could come and stay though,' he said. 'For a few weeks in the spring maybe.'

'Maybe.' But she didn't know if she could bear it, to be there with him and know she had to leave.

In the kitchen Audrey and Nell were waiting for them, standing like a delegation.

'What's all this?' Zita captured a stray strand of auburn hair and tucked it behind her ear. 'Going to tell me I'm not allowed male visitors in my room at night, or what?'

'We just wanted to let you know that you're not indispensable.' Nell grinned, a grin that stretched over her entire face.

'What?'

'You heard.'

Zita looked from one to the other of them, standing side by side as if they were ganging up against her.

'We want you to go,' Audrey said.

Zita stared at her. 'Thanks a bundle.'

'You know what I mean.' Audrey's voice softened. Her eyes were still red but they were also smiling. 'I mean that I want you to live your own life, go your own way. It's time I learnt to stand on my own two feet.'

Zita gripped Harry's arm. What was she saying? What were they telling her?

'About bloody time you thought of yourself for a change,' Nell muttered.

'You can always come back,' Audrey assured her. 'Any time. There'll always be a place for you.'

'Nice of you to say so.' Zita frowned. 'What will you do?'

'Same as before.' Nell spoke sharply. 'Nothing'll change. Doesn't have to, does it? Audrey will come to bingo with me, and I'll go along with her when she wants to go poncing around those art galleries of hers. We'll get someone else to help in the shop. I don't want to buy you out. I'll just send you a share of the profits every month.'

'But . . .'

Nell and Audrey linked arms. 'We'll manage just fine.'

'What makes you think I want to go anywhere?' Zita glared at them, because they both looked so certain. 'Well?' But inside she was singing. Singing like a blooming nightingale.

'Don't you?' They gazed around at each other, all four of them, and at last Zita looked at Harry and laughed.

She could let it spill over after all. She was flush with it. She would sing all right. Like a hundred blooming nightingales. She just didn't know if she'd be able to stop.

Chapter 18

———◆———

'So – have you been thinking about Charlie's proposition?' Will put this question to Rowan as the two of them trudged up Primrose Hill behind Jed and Diana who had raced on ahead.

'You could say that.' Since last night she'd thought of little else, and she was still thinking about it now, although she had expected these surroundings to distract her. She looked around her.

It was a beautiful winter's morning, the wind was slicing through her like a palette knife, but at the same time the sun warmed her fingers through the woollen gloves she wore, and out of the wind the thickness of her clothes made her hot.

The snow lay heavy on the ground, the clean bubbled surface broken only by the imprint of their footsteps – there had been a heavy fall last night and they were among the first here today. Around the ridge of the hill clumps of hawthorn, chestnuts and plane trees with branches drooping under their new white coats, screened the surrounding terraces and flats. They could have been out in the country – but this was London, and they were not. Every unpopulated patch was only round the corner from all the people and places.

'Come on, you two!' Diana was standing on the top of the ridge by a tall chestnut tree, waving. 'Get a move on!' She and Jed were laughing, stamping their feet with the cold, the toboggan leaning against the tree trunk beside them.

Rowan was quite surprised Jed had even bothered to come today after the fuss he'd made about her going round to Charlie Walter's for dinner last night.

'It's your free week-end,' he'd moaned. 'It was supposed to be special.'

But she had refused to put it off. 'We can go out any night,' she told him. 'But this might be a chance in a lifetime.'

'Oh yeah?'

She kissed his cross mouth. 'Oh yeah.'

He had, however, jumped at Diana's idea of getting up early to go tobogganing on Primrose Hill. Rowan had hoped to have a chance of a quick word with him – as yet he knew nothing of Charlie's proposal – but since they'd been here, Jed had hardly spoken to her. And she could see that Diana, pinpricks of bright pink in her cheeks from the cold wind, her red hair a madcap halo around her head, wasn't complaining one bit.

Rowan pulled her scarf more tightly around her neck. Maybe he had a right to be peeved with her. She knew she shouldn't have broken their date, but her career was at stake, and her career was important to her, if not to Jed. More important than he knew. She didn't want to be dependent on him, or anyone else for that matter.

And what a business proposition it had been.

'I just don't see how I can possibly refuse,' Rowan told Will.

It had been a faultless dinner – just the three of them – but no expense spared.

'Not up to your standard, my dear,' Charlie told her.

She flushed. 'You're just being kind.' But when he said – my dear – to her in that way, she couldn't help but recall her reservations. The man was smooth as glass, but a heck of a lot more difficult to see through. Sometimes Rowan couldn't even begin to guess what he was up to.

'I value you,' he told her. He reached out and patted her hand, as an affectionate uncle might, leaving his hand on top of hers for a few moments. 'And you should value yourself.'

'She does.' Will leaned forwards, an uncharacteristic vehemence in his voice that made Rowan look at him in surprise. 'We all do.' There was something in Will's eyes . . . some expression she couldn't catalogue, that rather worried her.

'Quite right. Of course. I'm sure you do.' Charlie removed his hand, and she was glad.

She wriggled her fingers. His restricting hand had been unpleasantly moist.

'I'm sure you do,' he repeated, straightening his tie. 'Absolutely. And that's where I might come in.'

'Oh?' Rowan sipped her coffee, waiting for him to go on.

'Might I ask if you're happy working where you are?'

Rowan exchanged a swift glance with Will. He knew her views on this subject only too well. She was always moaning about work to him, poor chap. 'Frankly, no.'

'And may I ask why?'

She laughed. 'How long have you got? The pay's lousy, the hours are long. I can't stand either of the chefs – as a matter of fact, they boss me around something rotten. And half the food is processed and cooked in the microwave. It's not exactly what I got qualified for.'

She hesitated. She had imagined after she finished at catering college, well qualified into the bargain, that it would be relatively easy to walk into a kitchen and just . . . start being creative. She had imagined – foolishly – that people would want her, quickly appreciate her talents, that she would actually be allowed to *cook*. Only it hadn't worked out quite like that. A good job in the restaurant business was apparently hard to find. Even with qualifications, no-one started anywhere near the top.

'Anything else?' He was smiling as he watched her, sipping his claret, slowly licking his lips. Not a remarkable looking man by any stretch of the imagination – a bit too short, a bit too solid – with watery eyes and a balding head he tried to disguise with those strands of hair he did still possess. But there was still something about him, a certain self-confidence, acquired, she supposed, through a string of successful undertakings. Who wouldn't be self-confident with a record like Charlie's behind them?

'It's very unimaginative and terribly boring,' she said.

He leaned closer and she caught a whiff of his aftershave. Something not altogether pleasant – too strong, too overpowering. 'And what would *you* do?'

'Do?' Her fingers played nervously around the stem of her wine glass.

'If you were running the show.' He sat back, still watching her.

'I'd have a really varied wine list for a start,' she began. 'So that

253

people coming in for just a glass or small carafe of wine could choose from a wide selection. It would be a speciality of the house. We'd get known for it. And we'd stock lots of different bottled beers and lagers.'

'Hmmm.' He stroked his chin thoughtfully. 'And the food?'

'The food would be bistro style . . .' She paused, thinking hard. 'But different too. People have got used to eating well in London. I'd have to strike a careful balance between originality and – well, being dependable. People aren't interested in nouvelle cuisine any more. They want their food to look good, yes, but presentation isn't everything. More important is a sense of . . .'

Charlie smiled encouragingly. 'Yes?'

'A sense of the natural. Herbs, spices . . . Returning to home cooking. But home cooking for the 90s, using fresh organic vegetables, cooking methods like steaming and stir fry that preserve natural vitamins and minerals.

'I'd steer away from processed food, from additives, from factory farming. From all inhuman treatment of our resources – animal and vegetable.' She paused for breath. 'Have you any idea how many more people have become vegetarian since the beef crisis?'

'You could have something there, my dear.' He watched her.

'We'd attract young people in the evenings – maybe with some music, but not just kids who only want to drink and not eat. And office staff at lunch.' Rowan was getting into her stride now, forgetting who she was talking to, thinking only of the wild mixture of ideas careering around her head.

She looked from one to the other of them, suddenly self-conscious. 'I'm sorry. I've been rambling.'

'Not at all. Can I offer you a liqueur?' With a thin smile, Charlie got to his feet.

Rowan wished she could bite back the words. More like a speech, really. It had been a casual question from Charlie and she'd shot off like an express train. He must think her a complete idiot.

'Sambucca?' he asked, indicating an elegant green bottle. 'I don't have you down as the cherry brandy type.'

'Mmm. Please.' With a slight, surprised raise of the eyebrows, she accepted the liqueur, watched as he carefully placed a coffee bean on top of the thick clear liquid in each of the three glasses. He had rather small, fat fingers but his nails were perfectly manicured, and there wasn't a splinter in sight. His cuffs were starched, his cuff links gold and too large. One would never guess, she thought, that he used to be a cabinet maker like Will.

With a flourish, Charlie extracted a gold lighter from his pocket and lit the vapours coming from the liqueur. He did the same to the other two drinks.

Rowan watched the blue flame burning as the scent of roasting coffee bean and rich liqueur filled the air. When would she learn to keep her mouth shut?

'You're a girl of ideas.' Lazily, Charlie leaned back and lit a cigar. 'I like that.'

'Too many ideas perhaps.' Following Will's lead, she blew out the flame. It dried her lips and she tasted the vapours on her tongue.

'Not at all.' He waved his cigar rather grandly in the air. 'Like I said, you should value yourself.' He grinned, looking, she thought too self-satisfied for words. Just how genuine was this man? Was he being kind, or did he have some ulterior motive?

'Should I?' she murmured.

He nodded. 'Of course. I value you, my dear. You see . . .' He flicked ash into a cut glass ash tray. 'I happen to be diversifying myself. A little place has come on to the market and I've just put in an offer.'

'A little place?' Will asked.

'A restaurant.'

Rowan held her breath. She didn't dare imagine what might be coming next.

'I like those ideas of yours,' Charlie told her. 'What would you say to working for me?'

'In what capacity?' Will asked quickly, but Rowan put a hand on his arm to stop him. This was her affair, she wanted to deal with it in her own way.

'Go on,' she said.

'As manager, chef, whatever you want your title to be.' He grinned once more. 'Words don't matter too much, in my opinion. The fact is, you'll run the show . . .' He leaned closer. 'With my approval, of course.'

She stared at him, hardly able to believe what she was hearing.

This was more than a lucky break. This was the kind of thing you heard about happening to other people. And you thought . . . why not me?

'Well?'

She took a deep breath. 'It sounds wonderful . . .'

'But?'

'But, why me?' He was taking one heck of a chance, wasn't he? Why should he do that?

Charlie got up to pour more coffee, every movement oozing self-assurance. 'You've proved yourself, my dear.'

'Only at dinner parties.' Suddenly Rowan felt extremely nervous. This was one hell of a responsibility for a girl only just out of catering college. Was she ready for this?

He shrugged. 'That's good enough for me. If you can cook, you can cook. If you have the right ideas, then you can put them into action . . . with the right kind of money and help behind you, of course.'

'But this is different. Very different from organising a dinner party.' Rowan was conscious that she was almost trying to dissuade him, or at least she was testing him, as if his confidence in her capabilities might rub off on her to increase her own belief in herself. And how she wanted to believe in herself . . . She sipped the liqueur, the liquid burning her tongue, snaking down her throat like a flame chasing air.

'I know it's different.' Charlie put out his cigar. 'I'm a business man and I'm well aware what I'm asking. I've given it a lot of thought.'

'And . . . ?'

'And I think you deserve the chance.' He folded his arms. 'Are you interested? Do you want to talk terms? Or . . .' He paused, watching her, a gleam in the pale eyes. 'Don't you think you're up to it?'

She smiled at him, instantly recognising the challenge. So he knew her at least well enough to realise that she would take up a challenge, that she couldn't resist it, wouldn't want to resist it. 'I'm interested,' she said. 'Let's talk terms.'

'I think,' Rowan said warily to Will, 'that this is the best opportunity I've ever had. And the best I'm likely to have. Don't you?'

'Ye..es.' She heard his reservations.

'But?'

He was silent, and she stopped walking, looked up at him. His eyes were bright, yet troubled. The beard that she had once accused him of growing, actually existed now – red, amber and brown – making him look like more of a gentle giant than ever in his tawny duffel coat as he hauled the toboggan behind him.

'What is it, Will?'

He stopped. 'Nothing. Charlie's okay. Or at least he's been okay to me . . .'

Why was it that he didn't sound sure? 'So you think I should accept his offer then?' Will's opinion was very important to her. She trusted his judgement.

He shrugged. 'I guess so.' Then he grabbed her hand and they carried on walking. 'But be careful, Rowan. Keep looking behind you.'

'I will.' She squeezed his hand. 'Don't you worry about me.' But she wanted him to, didn't she? She liked that feeling. She was glad that he cared.

'Come on, you slowcoaches!' Diana yelled as they reached the crest of the hill. 'What a couple of old fogies you two are.'

Rowan pulled a mock-disapproving face and jabbed her in the ribs. 'Be quiet, child. Have some respect for your elders.' She glanced at Jed, but he still wouldn't look at her.

'Come down with me, Jed.' Diana pulled at his arm.

He looked, Rowan thought, like a beautiful lounge lizard, leaning lazily against the tree trunk in his green trench coat with the collar up, his hair spiky and his hazel eyes glowing bright like a bird's. For the first time he glanced at her, and a grin twitched at his mouth.

'Do you mind, Rowan?' Already, Diana was climbing on the sledge.

'Nope.'

She stood with Will, taking his arm, and together they watched them careering down the hill, Diana shrieking, clutching on to Jed, her head thrown back with delight.

No, Rowan didn't mind, because as a foursome this was how they naturally gravitated. Diana and Jed like a couple of kids – him loving every second of her adoration, revelling in the spotlight of the attention that Rowan supposed she herself wasn't so willing to provide. And then she and Will, bringing up the rear, always talking, interested in the same subjects, more subdued perhaps, but providing each other with a mental stimulation that Rowan sometimes couldn't get from Jed, and certainly couldn't get from Diana.

But there were other things . . . Rowan told herself sternly. There was plenty that she got from Jed. In many ways he still fascinated her as much as the day they'd first met.

Afterwards they bought fish and chips and went to a movie. It was a Woody Allen comedy, but most of the jokes passed Rowan by, and she was only half-aware of the three people with her, just grateful for the darkness which gave her a chance to marshall her thoughts.

Could she really have been offered the opportunity to run her own restaurant? Not on her own, exactly, but as a kind of manager. And with good money, too, according to the contract that Charlie had offered.

'I'm not interested in my employees slaving their lives away for me,' he had told her after dinner. 'A good employer expects commitment, a hundred per cent commitment if you like, but not slave labour.'

The hours weren't bad. Of course they were long and antisocial, what else was there in the restaurant business? But there was a fair amount of time off . . . 'Provided you can find someone you trust to be left in charge,' he told her.

And she knew just the person – Julie Bateson, a girl from catering college who lacked Rowan's ambition, but who had a certain talent and wasn't afraid of hard work. They'd got on well, and she knew for a fact that Julie was out of work.

Now she just had to tell Jed of her decision.

Rowan sneaked a look at him. He was sitting next to her with Diana on his other side, both of them laughing their heads off, apparently without a worry in the world.

She would tell him when they went back to his flat tonight, after the others had left and before they made love in the big brass bed. She would make up with him, be nice to him. He was bound to be in a good mood, having been flattered by Diana all day.

How would he react? Rowan sensed that he wouldn't like it. She suspected that the more she was in charge, the more Jed felt threatened, and that the more successful she was, the more he wouldn't approve. She frowned. A couple of times he had even hinted to her that she didn't have to work, that he had more than enough to provide whatever she might want.

But that didn't suit Rowan. Not one bit. She would simply have to prove to him that he had nothing to fear, that her independence would enrich not damage their relationship. That they could grow as equals, as partners, loving but not dependent.

In the event it didn't work out quite as she had planned.

Will and Diana came back to the Chelsea flat with them for coffee, Diana followed Jed into the kitchen when he went to make it, whilst Will and Rowan sat on the floor and played backgammon.

Will had bought a bottle of wine back with him and he disappeared into the kitchen to find a corkscrew, returning with a face like thunder.

'What is it?' Rowan stared at him.

'Forget the bloody coffee, I'm off.' He pulled on his coat.

Rowan looked up to see Jed lounging in the doorway, a wide grin on his face. 'You'd better run along with big brother, Di.' He smacked her playfully.

'Oh, all right.' Diana looked cross. She turned to him and her face lit up once more. 'Thanks for a wonderful day though, Jed.' She reached up on tip-toe and kissed his cheek.

'That's all right, baby.'

She heard the front door slam, then Jed came over to her, bending to close the backgammon board. He ran his fingers lightly from her ankles up her legs to the tops of her thighs, and round to her hips,

'She's still in love with you,' Rowan told him.

'I know.' He laughed. 'And who could blame her?'

She shifted round to face him. 'You shouldn't encourage her. It's not fair, and Will doesn't like it.'

His face darkened. 'I'm a bit pissed off hearing about what Will likes and doesn't like these days.' He glared at her. 'Although you'd be an expert in that department, I suppose.'

So that was it, then. 'You shouldn't be jealous, it doesn't suit you.'

He pulled a face.

He was, she thought, like a child in so many ways. 'What did you say to Will?'

'To Will?' His eyes narrowed slightly in that way she recognised, his kind of prelude to passion. 'I don't know what you're on about.' His voice thickened as he pulled her to her feet.

'Oh yes, you do. He looked furious when he came back in here.' But she allowed Jed to lead her into the hall.

Slowly, his arm slung over her shoulders, they made their way up the chrome and glass staircase. She could feel the tension – his need – radiating through her. And she wondered, as she sometimes did, if this was all they had in common. Would they manufacture more, would they continue to develop and find their way? Or were they destined just to be part of a foursome – only a couple when they climbed into the big brass bed?

'I don't have to say *anything* to Will in order to annoy him.' His voice was petulant now, as he selected a CD and slotted it into the player. It was one of his late night saxophone compilations. One of his music-for-sex collections, she thought, rather unfairly.

'What do you mean?' She watched his face as he began undressing her, gentle and slow, taking up the rhythm of the music, as his body would soon also take up its rhythm. As if he and the music were part of an orchestra, working towards the climax of a bloody symphony, she thought.

'I don't have to say anything in order to annoy him, because he disapproves of just about everything I do,' Jed told her.

'That's not true. Ouch!' His teeth were unusually sharp on her shoulder. He wasn't relaxed as he usually was when they made love. Something, she knew, had happened between Jed and Will. Something that Jed was obviously not intending to tell her.

'Sorry, baby.' He slipped off her bra. 'Forget about Will Stafford and his blasted sister, will you? You and I have got much better things to think about.'

'Hmmm.' The touch of his fingers was pure sensuality. How could she worry that this was all they had in common, when this was such pure bliss?

His lips nuzzled into the soft hollow of her neck.

'Mmm.' She slipped her hands inside his shirt, pulling it from his shoulders. She couldn't think of them, could she, when his hands were all over her body, caressing, stroking, bringing a hungry desire to the surface – out from wherever she kept it so well hidden. She could forget, then, almost everything else, and enjoy.

Afterwards she lay back and wondered how to broach the subject of the job.

'Great sex.' Jed lit a cigarette, raised himself up on one elbow to stare at her. 'Great body.'

Rowan opened one eye. 'You sound as if you're going to give me marks out of ten.'

'Nine and three quarters.' He bent his head to lick her nipple, she watched his tongue dart out and his smile as he saw it harden for him.

'Is that all?' She smiled back at him. 'You're one hell of a mean marker.' But she could see that his mind was on other things.

'Let me get my camera, baby.'

She laughed. 'Don't be silly, Jed.'

'Yeah, but you look so bloody good lying there.' He kissed her lips and she tasted the smokiness of his lips and tongue. 'I want to capture that look.'

'You'll just have to hold it in your memory until next time, then.'

He jumped from the bed, and she spotted him reaching for his automatic camera.

'No!' She pulled the lemon quilt around her, ducked her head down. 'I said, no.' Her voice was muffled into the pillow

'Why not?' Putting the camera down he tugged the quilt away from her. 'Why not, baby?'

'Because this is private.' She was suddenly angry now, angry with Jed for not understanding, for not accepting no as no. Anger welled up inside her, hot and self-righteous. 'I want my privacy.'

'It would stay private.' He laughed. 'It would only be for you and me, baby. You know, it would be a turn on.'

'No.' Getting up, she began pulling on her clothes.

'What are you doing? What have I said?' He tried to stop her but she pushed him away. 'All right, forget it, no photos. Only get back in bed, will you?'

'No.' Her mind was made up. She knew that he hated the initiative being taken from him, but she wanted to leave and she wanted to leave now.

'Why?' He seemed so pathetic, standing there naked, that she almost relented. But why should she? Why should it always be on his terms?

'I just want to get home.' She didn't feel safe with him. There was a gleam in his eye that told her he might even go and get a camera when she was asleep, he so hated being thwarted.

She ran downstairs, called a taxi and stood shivering by the front door until it came.

'You're crazy, you are,' he called down from the top of the stairs. 'When will I see you?'

'Soon,' she shouted back. But she knew why she had minded so much. It was because she didn't trust him. And if she didn't trust him . . . then what was she doing here at all?

Chapter 19

Two months later, as winter was still refusing to budge an inch to make way for spring, Will finally put into words some of the sensations that Rowan herself had been experiencing.

'I'm feeling restless,' he said, shoving his big hands into the pockets of his coat.

'In what way?' She tried to sound casual.

'I'm not sure.' She felt the brief glance coming from under his shaggy eyebrows. 'I'm not getting anywhere. I'm not moving on. I'm stuck in a ditch and right now I can't even find the energy to climb out of it.'

'I think I know what you mean.' Rowan took his arm, not allowing herself to show how his words had affected her. He was her solid rock of dependency. She didn't want to think of him as unhappy, but neither could she bear to think of him moving on.

'*How* do you know?' He turned to face her.

She sighed as someone jostled into her, catching her off balance. They were on the riverside towpath above Hammersmith Bridge on the afternoon of the Boat Race, a traditional meeting-place for them and about five thousand others it seemed, although most of the onlookers were further upriver, nearer the finish at Chiswick Bridge. 'Because I've been feeling a bit like that myself,' she admitted.

She was still working at the restaurant in Chiswick. Charlie's purchase of the new restaurant, to be called Mercurys, had not gone through as quickly as either of them would have liked. It was now in the process of being decorated and furnished, and at long last Rowan was working out her notice, eager to get started on the new project. Perhaps her own restlessness would disappear when she was actually involved in Mercurys. She certainly hoped so.

'It's different for you, though.' Will's voice held a note of bitterness that she was quick to notice. 'You've got your new job round the corner.' He paused. 'And you've got Jed.'

'Have I?' She wasn't so sure about Jed. She and Jed went on as people do. He was ever attentive, always considerate in bed but still petulant from time to time. She could put up with that – it could easily be explained by a childhood of being spoiled by doting parents with more money than sense, not really his fault. But their relationship wasn't getting anywhere. It was, as Will had just described, static. They were stuck in a rut. And maybe she too lacked the energy to climb out of it. It just seemed easier to stay together, and something still held them there.

'I thought you two were okay.' Will was looking away from her, towards the river. The sounds of the Boat Race were drawing closer, the cheering of the onlookers as the boats approached, yells of encouragement from the supporters on the team boats behind them. Soon, they would come round the bend in the river and into view.

'We get on – most of the time.' But at other times Rowan found herself wishing that they could just air their resentments and have a flaming row like other couples seemed to do. Perhaps then they could make up or break up. Perhaps then their relationship would seem more real, she might believe in the two of them, more than she seemed to at the moment.

'Only most of the time?'

She laughed, easing the tension. 'Who has it good all the time?' Maybe Will was right, maybe the restlessness was in her imagination, maybe everything would fall into place once Mercurys was open. Even Jed.

'Where is he anyway?' Will looked around, his gaze scanning the crowd. 'I thought you said he was coming today.'

'He is.' She shrugged. 'He was.' There was no sign of him. But she couldn't admit to minding Jed's absence too much. There was still an awkward atmosphere between Will and Jed, and the foursomes of last autumn and early winter had faded until they'd become a rare occurrence. Diana too went her own way more and more these days; she and Rowan had never become as close as Rowan had once hoped they would. As for the two men, it had become easier to spend time with them separately, rather than together.

She sneaked a look at the big man beside her. 'Will you move away?' she whispered.

'Would it matter?' The blue eyes were immediately on hers, meeting her question with another, one she wouldn't consider.

'Of course it would.' How formal she sounded. She wasn't surprised to see him turn from her in disgust.

'Why, *of course*?'

She squeezed his arm. 'You know why. You're the best friend I ever had, Will. I'd be lost without you.' Lost and lonely. She couldn't stomach the thought of London without Will. He was part of it, part of her life here.

He put his hand over hers, only for a moment, but she could feel the tension in his fingers. Did Will Stafford still care, after all this time? Could it even be one of his reasons for leaving?

Against her better judgement, she found her thoughts drifting back to North Cornwall. To the folly and to Glyn Penbray. Time didn't always change things, did it? Sometimes it didn't heal, sometimes it only made the chains stronger. She still hadn't entirely laid Glyn to rest – the image of his dark lean face, the gypsy ear ring, the black curls, still had the power to move her, to make her a shuddering wreck – even in her dreams.

Rowan blinked, realising that Will was looking at her. There was, she thought, a kind of disappointment in his eyes.

'They're coming!' someone called, and the crowd heaved as the two boats appeared. Rowan hung on to Will. It was almost like a wave at a football match, and as always she was surprised at the strength of feeling – the Boat Race after all was a university affair. The coxes were screaming, and the people around her began cheering as their part of the river became the focus for the excitement, as the straining rowers skimmed their craft through the smooth water, keeping to a tight formation and even rhythm.

'They're neck and neck,' Will murmured. Then suddenly he bellowed, 'Come on Oxford! Come on, you blues!'

'They're both blue,' she reminded him.

'Yeah, well, come on you dark blues hasn't got the same ring to it, has it?'

They laughed.

In the wake of the Oxbridge rowers came the usual flotilla of vessels, consisting of TV crews, the safety boats and team boats, with lights flashing and people yelling and cheering. The noise gradually spread along the river, rising to a crescendo as the boats passed them, then eventually dwindled out of earshot, as the bend in the river took the rowers out of sight towards Chiswick Eyot, then on to the bridge and the finishing line.

'Cambridge have got it.' The prediction seemed to spread back down the river bank. 'Oxford will never catch them now. They're tiring. They're losing it.'

Will shrugged. 'At least I didn't put any money where my mouth was.'

By this time the crowd around them was beginning to thin, and the moment of seriousness between them had passed.

'I'm going to slope off now,' Will stuck his hands in the pockets of his coat once more. 'I've got to see Charlie.'

'Have you? Oh yeah, of course. Sure.' Rowan was at a loose end. She didn't want to go home, she would have liked to go somewhere with Will, to talk to him about this restlessness, to find out what he intended to do. But it wasn't fair, was it? She wasn't being fair. She was beginning to feel as if she were just using him – when Jed wasn't around.

It's not like that, she told herself crossly, watching his tall red-headed, slightly hunched figure disappear through the bystanders. Then how was it exactly?

She flicked back her hair. She would go to Jed's flat, talk to him, find out why he hadn't turned up at the Boat Race, maybe even find out what was going on between Will and Jed.

There was no answer at the flat in Chelsea, and after a brief hesitation, Rowan decided to use her key. She had never used it before – it had seemed more important for them both to preserve certain areas of their privacy even from each other. But she had come all the way over here, and she wanted to see him. Maybe she might make some coffee, wait for his return.

The kitchen was immaculate as always and cold. Instead of making the coffee in there, she ran up to his bedroom – the room that was more like a bed-sitting room, with its clutter of personal belongings, which she knew to include a small espresso maker, mugs, and milk in the fridge. She smiled as she looked around her. It was a mess, but at least this room was alive. The rest of the flat, despite its shrieking stylishness, was sterile and lifeless.

While she waited for the coffee to brew, Rowan flung herself down on the big brass bed on top of the lemon quilt, and thought about what Will had said.

He was restless – she could understand that. Will was talented, but he had always operated in Charlie Walters' shadow. Charlie arranged exhibitions of Will's work, found him his clients as often as not, and even arranged the printing of brochures and delivery of furniture. Will was protected by Charlie from some of the harsh realities of the real world. He never had to bother about mundane issues like when the rates might be due, or whether the bank would foreclose.

But in another way, she considered, Will had been a good bet for Charlie. He could bask in the reflected glory of Will's success – and he was a success, for she had never heard tell of a dissatisfied customer, and Will seemed to have more work than he could handle. Besides, she had seen his work, seen how he could transform an old battered chest of drawers back into a piece of beautiful furniture. And she had seen his own designs – moving from his head through his pencil, on to his sketch pad, on to the drawing board, and eventually coming alive – individual pieces with a certain originality that made her proud of him. Charlie Walters was very far from being stupid. He must be getting a cut. So these days, just who was helping who?

What would Will do? Where would he go? She turned herself over on to her stomach, and buried her face in the pillow, the scent of Jed's aftershave hot in her nostrils, in her head. If Will were to leave London, how would she manage without him? Who would she go walking with? Who would take her to football matches? Who would turn up after he'd finished working and drink endless cups of coffee with her? Who would she talk to? Who would understand?

Angry tears pricked at her eyes. Anger with herself, because she was being a selfish cow, she knew it. She had no claims on Will, none whatever. He was just a friend – that's all he'd ever been, a

JAN HENLEY

bloody good friend. Perhaps it was her own fault for not trying to find more of them.

The espresso machine hissed angrily, and Rowan jumped off the bed to pour out some coffee. As she cleared a space on the small table littered with papers and magazines, she knocked a manila envelope to the floor and its contents spilled out on the carpet.

'Shit.' She began collecting them up. Photographs . . . She stared at the first one. It was of Diana Stafford and she was completely naked.

'Oh, my God.' A sense of dread dipped through her.

Rapidly, she shuffled through the contents of the folder. There were about thirty photos, a whole reel of film, and Diana was more or less naked in all of them. He had taken a whole reel of film . . . And this was not just erotic, tasteful kind of naked either. These were pornographic pictures, she realised. Diana was pouting prettily, offering herself up to the camera – up to the camera man. There was desire in her eyes, desire for Jed, and he had used it. Used it to create a portrait of a woman wanting sex. The kind of woman that would turn other men on.

Rowan shook her head in despair. She felt sad, she felt shocked. And she felt sick, sick to the stomach.

And yet Diana didn't look like Diana. Appalled, Rowan sorted through them again. She was wearing make up – lots of it. In one shot, she was wearing only a black lacy bra, which was coyly covering only one breast. The other strap had slipped down her shoulders, and her breast was peeping out of the black lace, the nipple hard and erect. As if it had just been kissed . . .

'Oh, Diana,' Rowan whispered.

In another shot she was half-lying on Jed's blasted chesterfield, naked, her legs drawn up provocatively, leaving absolutely nothing to the imagination. In another she was kneeling, her small breasts pushed together to create more of a cleavage. In another she was standing, dressed only in stockings and suspenders, hands on hips, beckoning with her eyes . . .

How could he? She shoved the photos back in the envelope, not even wanting to touch them. She knew quite well that from time to time Jed handled what he called erotic photography. She knew, but it

268

wasn't something she had ever wanted to dwell on.

'It's like I'm a doctor,' he had told her. 'I'm dealing with the naked body, but only as a commodity. It's not a turn on. I stay objective, I always have. I stay behind the camera.'

She had tried to argue. 'But it isn't a commodity, is it? The naked body shouldn't be a commodity.'

'Not up to me, baby.' He shrugged. 'Market demands, you know.'

'But you're perpetuating it, Jed.' Why wouldn't he see? It wasn't pornography as such that she objected to, it was the ideas that clung to it. Ideas that usually came from men and were for men – to the detriment of women's self-esteem. 'It devalues women,' she said.

'Don't give me that feminist crap.' He began to look angry.

'But it's true . . .'

'Listen, baby.' He grabbed her shoulders, looked straight at her, and for the first time the hazel eyes seemed cold. 'If I don't do it, there's still gonna be hundreds more out there that do.'

'That doesn't make it okay.' She glared back at him. He didn't have to do it, did he? He didn't have a living to make, he was hardly a struggling photographer. 'If everyone thought like that, it would just go on and on and . . .'

'Hey . . .' At last he softened, pushed her hair gently from her eyes. 'If you don't like it, baby, then I won't do it. It's what you want that matters to me, not what the punters want.'

She had nodded, not able to explain to him. He didn't understand. He simply did not understand. He thought she was jealous, that she hated the thought of half-naked women cavorting around his studio. Well, yes, that was true, to an extent. But that wasn't half of what it was all about . . .

'Jed . . .' How could he have taken such advantage of the power he held over Diana? How could he have allowed her to do this? And . . . she put a hand to her mouth. What on earth would Will say? Should she even tell him . . . ? He was upset enough with Jed already. She couldn't begin to imagine how he would react to this.

She heard a key in the door, stuffed her fist in her mouth to stop herself from crying out. How could she confront him with this? He would think she'd been prying, and he'd be furious that she'd discovered how he'd been lying to her. And yet she had to confront him with it, didn't she? All she could think was, poor Diana, poor Diana.

Footsteps sounded coming up the stairs, a faint humming that sounded all wrong to Rowan, and then the door burst open.

'Bloody hell,' said Diana Stafford. 'What the hell are you doing here?'

Rowan stared at her. Having just seen so many pictures of her naked, it now seemed bizarre to see her clothed. 'I might ask you the same thing.'

Diana coloured. 'Jed gave me a key. He asked me to fetch something for him,' she began.

'Was it these?' Rowan handed her the envelope, watched her face.

She turned white, grabbed the folder but didn't open it. She must know what was inside. Jed must have shown her. They must have sat together, looking at them. 'I don't know what Jed will say . . .' She spoke with some difficulty. 'When he finds out you've been poking around in his room.'

'I don't give a damn what he says,' Rowan snapped. 'And I wasn't poking around, as you put it. I've got a key too. In case you happen to have forgotten, he's my boyfriend, and I might well ask you why he's been taking photos of you. Pictures of you naked, Diana.'

Diana was silent. She hung her head slightly, red hair cascading over her raincoat. The folder of photos dropped to the floor.

Rowan grabbed it back again, spread the photos out in her hand like a deal from an oversized pack of cards. 'Why did you do it, Diana?' God knows, she had never had the kind of friendship with Diana that had come so easily with her brother, but she had imagined them to be closer than this.

Diana glanced up. Her blue eyes held no hint of any such closeness. She was glaring at Rowan as if she hated her.

'It's no big deal.'

'No big deal?' Rowan stuck one of the photographs into her face. 'Look at it. It's pornography, that's what it is.'

'They're private.' Stiffly, Diana took the photos back, gathered them into a neat pile and replaced them in the folder. She put them back on the coffee table. 'You had no right to look at them.'

'You should tell him not to leave them hanging around then, if they're so private.' Rowan slumped back down on to the bed. What could Jed have been thinking of? She was just a kid.

Diana straightened her back and looked Rowan full in the face. 'They weren't just hanging around. This is his room. This is the . . .' She seemed as if she were about to go on, then suddenly stopped.

Rowan stared back at her. Remembered Jed's words. He had wanted to take photographs of *her* naked, hadn't he? After they had made love. *They'd be private, baby,* he had said. *Just for you and me. They might even be a turn on.*

She frowned, not liking the way her thoughts were leading. And why did Diana have a key to Jed's flat?

'Where is he?' she muttered. She wanted to have this out with Jed, not with Diana. She was right – these photos were none of Rowan's business. But Jed – *he* was still her business.

'I don't know.'

'Do you know why he did it?'

'Because I wanted him to.'

Rowan could have screamed. 'But why, Diana? Why did you want him to?'

'It's my body.' She flung herself on to the settee which was littered with Jed's clothes. She picked up a denim shirt and held it against her face for a moment. 'I can do whatever I want with my own body.'

Rowan shook her head. 'You're worth more than this, Diana.'

'Jed knows what I'm worth.' Her voice was low.

'Are you sleeping with him?' Rowan held her breath.

Diana laid the shirt tenderly on her lap, smoothing its creases. 'You had to find out sooner or later. I wanted to tell you before. I told him it wasn't fair, that you weren't stupid, that you'd put two and two together and make four. I thought it was obvious . . .'

'You wanted to tell me *before*?' Rowan stared at the hands holding Jed's shirt in such a proprietorial manner. Diana's fingernails were bitten down to the quick. 'How long has this been going on?'

'A couple of months.' She hesitated. 'We didn't want to hurt you.'

'Hurt me?' Rowan felt the anger rising. Anger, but not hurt. She pointed at the photos. 'Can't you see he's just using you, Diana?'

She shook her head. 'He loves me.'

'He loves himself, more like it.' Rowan felt tired, so tired of all this. Wearily, she picked up her bag, got up and moved towards the door. The decision had been made for her. This was the end for her and Jed. She was surprised at the relief she felt. But she was sorry that it had happened this way . . .

'You don't understand him.' Diana looked so unbearably vulnerable sitting there on Jed's settee. Damn Jed Montague.

'I understand him only too well.' Rowan opened the door. She wished she didn't, that was the truth.

'But you knew I'd always loved him,' Diana said mournfully.

Rowan looked back at her. 'So?'

'Did you think I could just stop?'

Rowan shook her head. What could she tell her? 'I didn't think it was that sort of love.'

She had dismissed it as infatuation, expected Diana to have grown out of it. And she had never imagined that Jed himself took it seriously, took Diana seriously. Yet why shouldn't he? Diana was a lovely girl and Jed was a man, a man whose ego needed massaging more than most.

And Rowan, of all people, should know about first love. She had been a fool.

'Rowan?' Diana looked up at her. 'Forgive me, Rowan?'

Slowly she nodded. There was no point in bitterness. Maybe she didn't care enough for that. But neither did she have energy left with which to comfort this girl.

'He's bad news, Diana,' she warned her.

'But I love him.' Diana smiled. 'And maybe I can give him what he wants.' She indicated the photos.

'I never could.' And Rowan was glad of that, if nothing else. She had always half-known that Jed required a woman to be one hundred per cent his. He didn't want a career girl, she wouldn't be surprised if he had turned to Diana from sheer petulance when Rowan had put her career in front of a date with him.

She walked down the stairs and out of the front door, took the key from her bag and stuck it back through the letter box. Let Diana explain to her lover what had happened, she had no desire to. She didn't want a row, didn't want recriminations and accusations of betrayal. She hadn't loved him enough. It was as simple as that. Only her pride was hurt, after all. And she knew, depressingly she knew so well, what Jed would say.

It was only a bit of fun, he would laugh. *It didn't mean a thing.*

But if that was sexual freedom then she didn't want it. It was too free, so free that it was meaningless. And neither did she want Jed. It was over.

Rowan was working in the restaurant in Chiswick that night, and it wasn't until eleven o'clock that she was able to take time out to sit down with Will at an empty table. She wanted to, and yet she was dreading to. Could she bring herself to tell him?

'How's tricks?' he asked her.

She stared at him. More than anything she didn't want to hurt this man. All evening she had been running it over in her head – but she knew she'd never be able to keep it from him. He would want to know it all – why she'd broken up with Jed, how Diana was involved, and then of course, Jed and Diana would be bound to come out into the open and he would know anyway. But what about the pictures? Should she tell him about those?

He took her hand. 'You look dreadful.'

'Thanks, Will.' She smiled ruefully.

'I mean dreadfully tired.' He leaned closer. 'What's up?'

'It's Diana . . .' She put her other hand over his. 'Diana and Jed.'

'Diana and Jed . . .' he repeated. There was a strange, almost glazed expression in his blue eyes, but he didn't look shocked. Neither did he ask her what she meant.

'You knew.' She snatched her hand away.

'No.' He took it back. 'I thought . . . I thought there might have been something going on.' He sighed. 'It was months ago – the day we went up Primrose Hill. But Diana swore it hadn't gone any further.'

'Any further . . . ?' She remembered. The bad feeling between Will and Jed had dated from that night. She and Will had been playing backgammon, he had gone into the kitchen to fetch a corkscrew . . . 'What happened?'

'I saw them.' Will seemed embarrassed. Avoiding her gaze, he ran his fingers fiercely through his hair. 'I'm sorry, Rowan. Maybe I should have told you. I saw them kissing in the kitchen.'

'Kissing in the kitchen?' She stared at him, feeling a fool for not realising herself. 'Yes, you should have bloody told me.' If she had known before . . .

'I tackled them about it.' He frowned. 'They both insisted it was nothing. I didn't want to hurt you, I didn't want you to think . . .'

'Yes?' She watched him.

'That I was trying to break the two of you up.'

She nodded. 'I see.' She couldn't blame him, could she? She had snapped his head off when he'd tried to warn her about Jed once before. And at least he had the grace not to say he'd told her so.

Will slammed his fist on the table. 'That blasted sister of mine. She promised me there was nothing in it. Wait till I get hold of her . . .'

'It's not Diana's fault.' Rowan thought of the photos 'Jed . . .'

'And that bastard as well.' Will seemed furious. 'He promised me he wouldn't lay a finger on Diana.'

Rowan stared at him. 'You really distrusted him that much?' And she had vainly supposed that Will was trying to put Rowan off Jed in the beginning simply because he had wanted her for himself. When in reality, he merely wanted to safeguard his friend as he had his own sister. She blushed.

'I've always liked him as a mate,' Will protested. 'There's only one thing about him I could never stand.'

'The way he is with women?' she guessed, feeling more than a little foolish.

He shrugged. 'But you . . . He told me you were different.'

'Not different enough apparently.' She spoke lightly but she was aware that she was deceiving him. For a start, she had determined to say nothing about those pictures. It was Diana's life, Diana's business. As Diana herself had said often enough, she was a big girl now. If she wanted to get involved with Jed on his terms, then it was up to her. Will couldn't run her life. He was her brother, not her keeper.

But Rowan was deceiving Will about something else too, wasn't she?

'What will you do?' he asked her.

'Finish it, of course.' No good pretending that it was easy. That it wasn't wiping out her energy along with her self-confidence. It certainly wasn't easy, even if her heart was far from broken. 'It wasn't

274

working anyway,' she whispered. 'You knew that.'

'Did I?' Their eyes met, met it seemed for a long time.

'I'm glad it's over,' she said softly. He had the right to know. She was relieved that he knew.

But Will only stared at her. Whatever she had expected it wasn't this. He stared at her with an inscrutable expression that made her want to hug him close to her, and after what seemed like an eternity, he got to his feet and strode out of the restaurant.

'Will . . . ?' she whispered.

The next day, after her lunchtime session, Rowan went over to Mercurys to see how the decorating was coming along.

She had persuaded Charlie to go for colours that exuded freshness – whites, linens, shades of raw silk and the palest calico and natural raffia. After some deliberation they had decided to use beech to enhance the look, and already Rowan could see how it would be.

The workmen had finished early, so she let herself in and found herself completely alone in the building for the very first time. It felt wonderful. Private, special and exciting.

Slowly she walked through the restaurant area itself, her footsteps padding across the bare floorboards that had already been stripped ready for varnishing, mentally charting where the tables would be, how the bar would look, which up-lighters and which plants she would put where. Charlie had more or less given her carte blanche to create the effect she was aiming for. And she couldn't wait to try it out . . .

She walked through the open archway that would be strung with variegated ivy, and into the kitchen. Not much as yet, but the new cookers, hobs, freezers and larder fridges were all on order.

Charlie had said they would be open in less than a month, although it was hard to visualize just now. She had already planned her first month's menu, and intended to keep it flexible – to be dictated by the weather, customer approval, and of course what top quality fresh produce was available at the best price.

Rowan hugged her arms close to her chest. She needed this place now, even more than she had before, needed this new project to take her mind off Jed and Diana, even to bury the ghost of Glyn Penbray. Mercurys, she decided, would root her to London, as the folly had rooted her to Cornwall. This place would satisfy her as no man seemed able to. This place would never leave her.

'Well, well, well. What do we have here?'

She spun round in alarm, but it was only Charlie Walters standing there in his dark suit. 'Oh, Charlie. I didn't hear you come in.'

He smiled. 'I thought we had burglars. I was going to creep up on them.'

She laughed. 'And then what would you have done?'

'Pounced.' He loosened his tie.

'Not that there's much to steal yet.' She sighed, looking around her. She was so impatient to begin.

He came closer and she could smell the cigar smoke clinging to his clothes, the brandy on his breath. Charlie had clearly enjoyed a good lunch. 'There will be,' he promised.

'Yes, there will be.' She looked straight at him. She had never really had an opportunity to thank him for what he had done for her. 'This means a lot to me, Charlie. This place, the chance you've given me.'

He looked her up and down and for a fleeting second she felt uncomfortable. 'You're worth it.' His voice was thick.

Some danger signal rang in her head. This was the first time she had ever been alone with him. Before, there had always been Will, or workmen, or guests at a dinner party. And he had never looked at her quite like this before.

'I've got a bottle somewhere.' He stepped over to the pantry and started rooting around. 'Here we are.' He produced a bottle of cognac.

'Not for me.' She shook her head.

'But you must.' His voice was insistent, his eyes, as they drilled into hers, would not take no for an answer. 'We have to toast this place. It's unlucky not to.'

She hesitated. 'Just a small one, then.' What harm could one drink do? After all, if she was going to do business with this man, if he was to be her employer, she must at least show some degree of trust. He was not about to abuse his position, now was he? He wouldn't jeopardise a promising business venture.

But from nowhere she recalled the doubt in Will's eyes. *Keep looking behind you,* he had said. Now what exactly had he meant by that?

In the meantime Charlie had found one cognac glass and one wine glass, rinsed them under the tap and now handed her the largest. 'Cheers.'

'Cheers.' She sipped warily. She had never been a brandy drinker, in fact the stuff made her feel slightly sick.

'To Mercurys.' He grinned. 'I think I'm going to enjoy being a restaurateur.'

'To Mercurys.' She knew she was being silly. What had happened with Jed had unnerved her, made her unreasonable, made her look for ulterior motives when there were none. This man was harmless. He was a bit of a lush and a bit of a smoothie, but she didn't have to love him to go into business with him. She could deal with him, no problem.

'And to us.' He took a step closer. 'To the two of us.'

Her hands were shaking. 'To our business venture,' she said pointedly. Strictly business, Charlie. Please, Charlie . . .

He moved quickly for such a solid man. Two steps and his hands were on her shoulders, his face close to hers, the alcohol on his breath repulsive to her, his thick lips wet with saliva, the smell of his sweat mingling somehow with that too powerful aftershave he wore. Mingling into a nausea that sank into her senses.

Almost simultaneously, but a second too late she ducked away from him, her hands moving swiftly up and out to push his arms away from her, to break his grip, while at the same time her weight shifted forwards against him. A simple move, a move that Glyn had shown her in the woods one day.

Her glass of brandy tipped and smashed on the stone kitchen floor. She stared at it for a moment, then at him. He mustn't speak. Whatever happened, he mustn't speak, he must be silent, be sorry, go away and never let this happen again.

'Come on, Rowan,' he said instead. 'What's the matter with you? Loosen up a bit, will you?'

She stood stiff and straight with fists clenched, weight balanced. 'Is it part of the deal?'

'What?'

'Is it part of the deal? Was there something I missed in the small print?'

'I don't know what you're on about, silly girl,' he muttered under his breath.

'Sexual harassment.' She watched him. 'Was it part of the deal?' She took a deep breath as her dreams disintegrated in front of her. But now she had to be brave, very brave. 'Because if so, the deal's off.'

'What?' He stared at her.

'You heard.' She had the power now. She could feel it coursing through to her fingertips. She could do and say whatever she liked.

'Cheeky cow.' He seemed to be pulling himself together. 'It was only a bit of harmless fun.'

'Harmless fun.' She nodded. That sounded familiar. Very familiar and very like Jed. It sounded like Diana too. But if it was so much fun then why the hell wasn't she laughing?

He took a step closer. 'A looker like you.' He reached out his hand towards her face, looked down at the short skirt and black tights she was wearing. 'You're asking for it, aren't you? I thought you'd see how it was. I do you a favour. You show me you're grateful. Good business, that is.'

Rowan couldn't believe what she was hearing. Okay, so the man was half-pissed. But he must have always assumed she'd come across for him, it must have been in his mind when he offered her the job, for heaven's sake. Was this the ulterior motive? Was this what he meant by a business proposition? Was it not just Rowan Brunswick, chef and woman of ideas that he wanted, but rather the entire package deal?

She shook her head. She was no package.

He mistook her silence for vulnerability. 'Come on, then.' He stepped closer, his hands moving towards her breasts. 'You and me would make a great partnership, I've always known it.'

'Get your hands off me, you bloody sex maniac.' She kicked him neatly in the crotch and watched in some satisfaction as he doubled up in pain.

He was panting, blowing, trying to get his breath back. 'Bitch! If you think you've still got a job here . . .'

She stood over him, in control, remembering a favourite phrase of Nell's. She'd heard Nell say it once to an extremely irate customer who had gone too far, and it seemed more or less in keeping now. 'You can stuff your bloody job, Charlie,' she told him. Clearly, so there was no mistake. 'You can stuff it right up your arse.' And she walked out of Mercurys wine bar, without once looking behind her.

Chapter 20

———◆———

Philip Brunswick did not walk as far as the disused tin mine. He stood in the lane outside Folyforth House and simply stared through the wrought iron gates at the house itself, not daring to take the path that would lead him closer. That would be too close for comfort.

He sighed. This was a big day for him. He was moving house. It was a time of change, of new beginnings and fresh possibilities. He should be full of hope.

But there was no disputing that he had failed.

He gazed at the square leaded windows, the old granite of the walls and the blue-black slate of the roof. He looked at the old oak front door with the bell-pull that he'd never pulled. He would never do it now, never walk through that front door. He would never live here, in this house, with its magnificent chimneys, and its bedrooms looking out over the valley and the smooth stretch of green down that led to the cliff and the sea. What a view, the best ever. But he would never own that view, never live here on the top of the hill, master of all he surveyed. He could never be in control here, he could never belong. Because he had failed. What would his father think of him now?

His shoulders slumped as he turned away from the high slate walls which surrounded a garden that must once have been beautifully landscaped, but was now an unkempt jungle. Wasted, all of it wasted. And Philip was convinced, utterly convinced, that if he had been able to buy this place when he had the means – when they had first come to Cornwall to live – then everything would have been different. He would not have lost his daughter, his wife, his money. It simply wouldn't have happened. He would have been protected somehow, by this place, by the status it bestowed.

Throughout his working life, Philip had doled out advice – financial advice. He had made money in the seventies when it was there for the taking, had made money for a lot of other people too. He had told clients how to compartmentalize their financial lives, had learned to listen to the early whispers, predict the way the wind would blow and recognise the signs before anyone else did. It was all a question of timing

But the recession of the eighties had hit him harder than he had realised back then. The market had never improved when he expected it to. The bad times had gone on for so much longer, until now, the situation was past recovery. Somewhere along the line, Philip had lost that sense of timing, misheard the whispers, predicted gale force winds when ultimately a breeze barely fluttered.

Before trudging back down the lane towards the house that was – just about – still his, he glanced quickly over his shoulder and paused. Surely there had been a movement behind that front window by the door of Folyforth House? He stopped, waiting. But there was nothing.

The place was empty. How could it not be? A woman called Athwenna Trelawney might pay the rates, might own the place, but what use was it, knowing that? As Audrey had once predicted, it was no use whatsoever if she wouldn't sell. The place was out of his reach, had always been out of his reach. Athwenna Trelawney – some nobody – had prevented him from belonging. Some faceless, anonymous old woman had done this – *dared* to do this – to *him*, Philip Brunswick.

He returned, slowly, to the house he *had* managed to buy all those years ago when they first came to Cornwall, the house that was in reality no longer his, since contracts had been signed. It had actually belonged to himself and Audrey, although he had arranged for the deeds to be transferred to his name only some time ago, when she had first started giving him trouble.

Trouble . . . He still wasn't sure what had happened to Audrey. She had seemed so sensible in the beginning, when they first met, when they were first married. No nonsense kind of sensible. The kind of woman a man could rely on, even though she might put him down in public occasionally

Frigid, yes, and not altogether the most understanding of women – she was never gentle, rarely thoughtful of his welfare. And she always seemed to be asking for something, but he was never quite sure what it was.

Philip was aware that he never really measured up, that he had failed her too in some way. And of course he'd never been able to control her as he would have liked – not in the beginning, perhaps not even in the end, since she had left him after all. But still, he had not expected her to flip like that either – to become practically a recluse in her own house. Her and those bloody tablets of hers. She wasn't just in the green room, she was on another planet most of the time.

Perhaps he shouldn't have allowed Lynette into their house, not when Audrey was there, no matter how incapacitated or withdrawn she was. He supposed he had been tempted by Lynette, and that was the story of his life really. Temptation . . .

And he'd been tempted too by the idea of going too far, of pushing Audrey until she truly was under his control. The final humiliation. Lynette had gone on and on about it – wanting to do it in his house, although he couldn't for the life of him work out why.

But in the event she was right – it had been a bit of a laugh having her there in his bed, available and sexy in a way his wife had never been, even in the beginning. Everything was to hand – her body, the whisky, champagne for Lynette, cheese, crackers and her favourite liqueur chocolates.

It was warm, it was cosy and, as he watched her wandering around the room dressed only in the briefest of silk underwear that he himself had bought for her, he could almost convince himself that this was how he wanted it to be. He could almost imagine her living here with him, as a permanent paramour, like a live-in prostitute you never had to pay, because you were master. Master and in control.

When she came over to the bed and squatted in front of him, her breasts still ripe and plump and hardly sagging although she was no longer the young girl she once was, he took her as if he too were a young man again, in his prime. Took her with aggression and carried on and on, until he thought he had lost it, but in fact, when it came it was an earthshaker of an orgasm. 'Bloody hell, sugar.'

She was moaning under him, moaning and shrieking, and for a moment he thought of Audrey downstairs, horribly alone in the green room. And then he didn't care; that became, as Lynette had promised, part of the thrill, part of his revenge. Lynette could make as much noise as she wanted. He even encouraged her to. She could come and come and come. He would make her. Audrey might even see what she'd been missing.

Lynette stayed all day – for the whole of one glorious day – it was after midnight when she put on her clothes to leave.

Philip didn't mind – he was glad to see her go by then. They had experienced a feast, but he was tired of eating, he was full. He wanted to sleep now. Tomorrow he would become Philip Brunswick, financial adviser, once more, and Lynette – however much she had satisfied him – had no part in that scenario.

It wasn't until the next day that he realised Audrey had actually left him – just upped and left him, showing a strength he had imagined to have been sapped out of her during the past years.

He was shocked, disappointed too. Life without Audrey was unthinkable – it felt as if someone had cut off a limb and then told him to carry on as before. She might not have been of much use to him, but she had always been there. Without her he felt suddenly unsure, as if she had been – without him realising it – part of his identity. As if this were not really his world, as if even – after all these years – he might not really belong.

He considered calling the police, reporting her missing, but couldn't bring himself to do such a thing. He knew, of course, what had driven her out. She might not have fallen for his threats about moving house, but certainly she had heard Lynette. She had heard, and she had left. He'd felt he'd been cheated. Because he would never know if he had hurt her.

Philip packed the last of his things and reflected on his time in this house since his wife had gone. He had managed to save the house, not once but twice. Twice he had hoped to salvage at least part of the fortune he had once possessed – amassed by a combination of financial know how, dubious dealings on the stock market, and his wife's considerable legacy from her well-heeled family. Why had he been so greedy? Why hadn't he stopped when he was ahead?

He didn't need to wonder where she had gone. He guessed she'd run back to London, following Rowan, and following that bloody woman. It all came down to that bloody woman – she had a lot to answer for, did Zita Porter. He was only surprised that Audrey had asked him for nothing. Pride, he supposed. She'd always had plenty of that, damn her.

He remembered her saying *not everything has a price*, and recalled how it had baffled him. He had thought she wasn't living in the real world, that she was a dreamer, a loser, head in the clouds. But sometimes he wondered – what was it like up there? Better than this, maybe?

He considered, several times, going to London, trying to see them, especially see Rowan. But he was scared that Audrey would recognise him as a failure, scared of what she might do to him if she had recovered that old strength of hers. He wanted to see Rowan, he longed to see his daughter, despite everything that had happened between them. If she understood . . . if only he could make her understand, then maybe she would see why he had acted as he did.

But in the end, after what he had done to her, he was scared of that too. She didn't know the half of it, did she? If Rowan wanted to see him, she knew where he was. She could come here, couldn't she? He had washed his hands of her once, but she'd know he would be only too glad to see her again – well, wouldn't she?

She had never come.

At last he was ready to leave. He checked the ticket in his wallet. He wasn't taking much with him to Spain. He had considered – only for one mad moment – taking Lynette. Her husband had left her, she'd wasted no time telling him that. But things had been strained between them ever since Audrey had gone. It had been a bad night indeed when Lynette discovered that Audrey had left him.

'You never told me! Why didn't you bloody tell me?' On and on she ranted and raved. On and on. As if it really mattered . . .

'I thought she was here, in the house. All the time we . . .' And then she broke down and cried, just cried in his arms.

He felt bloody awkward – didn't know where to put himself really, for she'd never cried before, there had only ever been sex or the promise of sex between them before.

'What about me?' she moaned. 'Will you marry me now?'

He looked at her. Her make up was smudged, and this time she didn't appear in the least attractive. Her face was lined in the harsh light, her eyes red and tired. 'I can't marry you,' he said.

'You could find her, get a divorce.' She chose to misunderstand him.

'I'm going to Spain,' he said, wanting her to leave.

Her face lit up. 'Take me with you. You've always promised to take me to Spain.'

He shook his head. How could he take her anywhere? A woman like her simply wasn't the thing. She would let him down, she would be a dead weight around his neck. And besides, she had changed. It wasn't just a question of age, although that was part of it – a certain type of woman had no chance of ageing well. But it was more than that. Lynette was a different woman these days.

Audrey would have understood, but how could he possibly explain it to Lynette?

When it came down to it she had no class. She was only good as a tart, and that was not what he needed right now. He had contacts, new contacts, and he must make the right impressions. This was a fresh start for Philip, and Lynette could not be part of it. She would have to try to understand. She was not indispensable. What she offered could be found on the market elsewhere, and sadly she was getting beyond her sell by date. It was time to say adieu.

Lynette Penbray could not believe the evidence of her own eyes when she opened her front door to see Rowan Brunswick standing there, bold as you like. It had been a long time, but she recognised her instantly.

'What the hell . . . ?' She pulled her dressing gown belt tighter around her. It was four in the afternoon, but it had been a bad night, the worst. She had let things slide. Now she had no job, no man. *If you were to get yourself in shape again, Lyn,* the manager of the Bull and Packet had told her. But she knew what he was on about, and she'd told him what he could do with his job. Didn't he know she was a woman destined for better things?

'I'm terribly sorry to disturb you.'

'Are you indeed?' So, the girl was polite. But why shouldn't she be, with the upbringing she'd had?

'Only I just wondered . . .'

'Yes?' Lynette stared at her, unblinking. What was she doing here, for Christ's sake? Lynette might be exhausted from a night of next to no sleep and a lot too much to drink, but if this girl imagined that she was about to make things easy for her, then she was sadly mistaken.

Rowan began again. 'You don't know me.'

Lynette folded her arms. The hell she didn't.

'But I'm a friend of your son Glyn's.' She hesitated. 'I *was* a friend of his, anyway, when I used to live here.'

'Really?' Friend – well, she supposed that was one way of putting it. His little whore would be closer to the mark in Lynette's view. What kind of a girl would let a boy take advantage – and at such a young age? To hell with a refined upbringing . . .

She watched as the girl shifted her weight on to her other foot. Lynette had to admit that she looked tired, she'd probably been travelling most of the day, and no doubt Lynette should ask her in, offer her tea or whatever. Wasn't that what people did? The right kind of people, the people with the right sort of upbringing? She tasted her own bitterness on her lips, but made no offer of welcome, only waited for the Brunswick girl to go on.

'I heard he came back to Cornwall.' She took a deep breath. 'Could I see him? If he's here, that is.'

Lynette's eyes barely flickered. 'He's married.' She took great satisfaction in saying that, in seeing the girl's shoulders slump as if she'd been whacked in the chest. So – she still held a candle for him, did she? More fool her. 'He doesn't live here any more. Like I said, he's a married man.' And you have no business with him, she added silently.

'I see.' Rowan's gaze dropped. She started to turn away.

'You see nothing.' She wasn't sure why she'd said that, why she chose to prolong what should have been very quickly over. But Lynette was conscious of her bitterness turning into anger. Hot sweet anger against this girl and her family.

Rowan looked up at her in surprise, and at the same time Lynette saw Tamsyn Jago at her front door, peering curiously over the low fence.

'Come inside.' She almost dragged the girl in.

By this time some of Rowan's colour had returned. 'Even if he's married, I still need to see him. Where is he living now? Will you at least tell me that?'

'Why do you want to know?' Lynette led the way into the kitchen, automatically reaching for the kettle to make tea. 'You can't see him, you know. I told you how it is – he's married now.' And out of your clutches, thank the Lord, she thought.

Rowan stared at her. 'Why does it matter to you so much? Why do you hate me?'

A sense of power ran through Lynette's senses. Suddenly she knew what she was going to do. And she savoured the knowledge, silently to herself. 'What makes you think that I do?' she asked in a conversational tone.

Rowan shrugged. And then as if the subject was too much for her in her current frame of mind, she said, 'My father was still living here when I left.'

'Was he now?' Lynette watched her sit down on one of the tatty plastic stools drawn up at the kitchen table – without being asked, she noted.

'I went up to the house, but he wasn't there. He must have moved away.' She looked very small and vulnerable now she was seated.

Lynette's mouth twisted into a smile. 'Wanted to see him then, did you?' Her hand made a fist almost without her realising it and she had to concentrate hard to uncurl her fingers.

'Not really.' Rowan glanced up at her. 'Not exactly.' How could she explain it all to this woman, Glyn's mother, who rather unnerved her, who seemed to dislike her although Rowan couldn't imagine why, and who seemed somehow familiar, as if she'd seen her somewhere else, a long time ago . . .

'You thought you could make up with your father,' Lynette sneered.

Why was she so angry? Rowan frowned. 'No . . .' She hadn't intended making up with him, there really had seemed so little to say to him. But he was her father, wasn't he? She had felt almost duty bound to go to him first, when she'd arrived in Folyforth, duty bound and – yes, compelled to go the house of her childhood, the house she knew so well. And she had been curious to find out how he was managing without them all, whether he even regretted the loss of herself, of her mother.

'Oh yes, you did.' Lynette fiddled with the tea and poured boiling water almost viciously into the teapot. 'You thought you could turn up out of the blue, make up with him and everything would be lovey-dovey again.'

Rowan stared at her. 'No, I didn't.' It was just that she had been so confused by everything that had happened in London. She supposed that she'd needed to run away for a bit, and Cornwall had seemed the obvious place.

'And he would have had you back, wouldn't he?' She laughed. 'He would have had you, he would even have had your mother back.'

'She wouldn't come back.' Rowan got to her feet and they stood glaring at each other, locked in conflict although Rowan didn't for the life of her know why. 'She would never go back to him.'

Lynette's hands were on her hips. 'No. And I don't blame her either.'

'Do *you* know where he is?'

'Why should I?'

They were both out of breath, both staring.

Had she seen this woman with Glyn – was that why Lynette Pembray seemed so familiar? And yet, Rowan had always thought she didn't know his mother. His father, yes, but she had never met his mother, surely she hadn't? Or was it Glyn she recognised in this woman – certainly they shared the same black curls, the same kind of dark passion.

Glyn. He was married, as she had feared. And although that was the worst scenario she'd pictured, although she perhaps should have been more devastated than she seemed to be by the news, still she knew she needed to see him. Perhaps this woman was right. Perhaps she shouldn't have come here, perhaps this was the last place she should have run to. But where else could she have gone?

What had happened in London – first with Jed, and then Charlie – had become conflated in her brain until her senses were reeling with it all. She had lost her new job, her promise of a new start. And without that new start it had seemed vital to come here, to lay the past to rest, as if without that final chapter she'd never be able to start again, never be able to face the future in the way she wanted to face it. She had to free herself from the chains of the past, the chains that still held her to Glyn.

She had come here to see Glyn. Make or break. She needed to see him. She needed to *know*.

'It isn't my father I've come back to see.' She spoke slowly. 'I want to see Glyn. I just want to talk to him.' But the expression on the other woman's face told her she was wasting her time.

'What's the point?' Lynette demanded. 'He's got somebody else now. He's got a wife. What are you after?'

'Nothing.' Her voice rose. 'So will you tell me where he is?'

Lynette shook her dark head.

'Or do I have to knock on the door of every house in the village?' Rowan paused. 'I would, you know.'

A smile twitched at Lynette's lips. 'You've got guts, I'll say that for you.' The smile faded. 'But I'll not have Melanie upset.'

'Melanie . . .' So he had loved her after all. He had loved her and married her, the girl from his home town. The girl who had become his wife. She felt a burst of anger. It should have been Rowan.

'Not when she's expecting,' Lynette added, her gaze riveted to Rowan's face.

'She's pregnant?' Rowan's stomach turned in protest. That was worse, much worse. For Melanie to be expecting Glyn's child.

Lynette nodded. 'So, now do you see there's no point? Now do you see why I won't tell you where he is?'

But Rowan was stubborn. She had to do this for herself. She didn't want to upset anyone, and she had no intention of trying to break them up. But still she needed to talk to him. 'I'm not a threat,' she whispered.

'What makes you think that, you silly young fool?' Lynette flung this out at her, every word steeped in resentment. 'What do you know?' She took a step closer. 'You know nothing, that's what you know.'

'What is it? What don't I know?' There was a certain look in Lynette's eyes, a look that she thought she had seen in Glyn's eyes once when they were making love on Bodmin Moor under the stars. It was the kind of look that passed right through you, a kind of glazed expression that reminded her of something, of someone else . . .

Slowly memory returned, one that she had put away, packed around with other unpleasant memories, like her first day at school and the day her pet rabbit had died. And as she remembered, she saw this woman again in her mind's eye. Much younger then, of course. In her parents' bedroom, her dark limbs wrapped around her father's pale ones, her head thrown back in abandonment and passion. Glyn's mother.

'You . . .' she said.

'Yes, me.' At last Lynette turned away from her to pour the tea.

Rowan watched, fascinated and appalled, as the dark liquid poured from the spout, poured on and on until the cup overflowed and the tea flooded the formica work surface. 'Stop . . .' She grabbed her hand. 'You'll burn yourself.'

Lynette shook her head like a sleepwalker half-waking. 'It doesn't matter.'

Rowan still held her wrist, needing confirmation. 'You and my father?'

She nodded.

The information slotted into place. This woman, Glyn's mother, and her father. 'Glyn . . .' His name slipped from her lips, a moan of dismay.

Lynette stared back at her. 'He's your father's child.'

Rowan froze. 'No.' She groped for the chair, sinking on to it gratefully. She saw the cruelty in Lynette's eyes, the desire for revenge, and she shuddered with revulsion. Glyn . . . ?

'My Harry could never have children.' As if unaware of Rowan's pain, Lynette brought the tea over and put it on the table, sat down herself, resting her chin in her hands. 'We tried and tried. It was hopeless. In the end we went to the hospital. Had tests. But Harry had a low sperm count, you see. They reckoned if I conceived it would be a miracle.'

'No.' Desperately, Rowan fought to adjust. Glyn Penbray. Not lover but brother. She heard laughter and realised it was in her head, her own hysteria.

'Oh yes.' Lynette looked past her as if not seeing her at all.

Rowan thought of Harry. 'He knew . . . about Glyn?'

'Didn't know whose he was.' Lynette sipped her tea. 'I wasn't that cruel. We didn't talk about it too much. He treated him like he was his own. But I reckon he guessed Glyn couldn't be a son of his right from the start – Harry wasn't stupid and he never did believe in miracles.'

Rowan thought of Harry and Zita. 'But he left you. Was it because . . . ?'

'Everything comes out sooner or later.' Lynette pursed her lips together. 'I told him about Philip one night. Taunted him with it, if you like. I'd had a hard session down at the pub and more gin than was good for me.' She glanced at Rowan. 'But maybe he would have left me anyway.'

Rowan shook her head. It was impossible to take this in. To digest the fact that the boy she had loved, the inseparable companion of her teenage years, was not a boy she should ever have loved in that way. She thought of their closeness, the almost telepathic bond between them. Twin stars, side by side. She thought of it all and she wanted to cry, to weep and weep until there was nothing left.

But in the meantime this woman was still talking and Rowan recognised that she was letting it all out, probably for the first time. She knew without being told that her father had treated this woman badly. She almost felt sorry for her.

'I met him in London,' Lynette said. 'My sister Esme was his secretary. He was already married, but I liked him from the first.'

Rowan stared down at the table, unable to speak, not wanting to imagine how it had been.

'He liked me too. We got on. I'd never intended to take a lover. But there was a spark between us. Sexual chemistry, I suppose they'd call it these days.'

'You must have known he'd never leave Mum,' Rowan cut in.

'Oh yes. I knew that.'

'Then why?' Why had she got involved with him if she knew it would never have a future? Why had she got involved with him when she already had Harry?

Lynette's eyes were dreamy with the memory. 'Women like sex too, don't they?'

Rowan was silent.

'Well, don't they?' she demanded.

'Yes, but . . .'

'I wasn't what my Harry wanted.' Her expression changed. 'He wasn't interested in . . .' Abruptly she stopped, seeming to recall who she was speaking to. 'Well, never mind about all that, that's done with.'

'And my father?' Rowan wanted to know all the details, now this had been started. She needed at least a point from which to begin.

'It was a physical relationship.' Lynette laughed. 'And one hell of a good one.'

Rowan shot her a look of distaste.

'Don't knock it,' Lynette advised. 'There's nothing wrong with slap and tickle. If it hadn't been me, it would have been someone else. He needed somebody . . .'

Rowan looked away. *He had my mother*, she wanted to say. But her mother had not been enough for him, had she? She had not wanted to give him the kind of love he needed.

'I was special to him, he always wanted me. And . . .' She leaned closer. 'I could have made him happy.' She sighed. 'He thought he knew me, your father did. But I could have made him happy. Even after *she* left, I could have done that.'

'Did Father know – about Glyn being his son?' Rowan asked her with some difficulty. If he had known, and surely he must have, then no wonder he'd gone crazy when he found out his daughter was seeing his son. No wonder he had tried to imprison her in the house, no wonder he hadn't objected to her going to London. At least she'd be out of Glyn's way, or so he must have thought. No wonder he had looked so horrified when he'd found out she was pregnant. How had he lived with himself – knowing that he might have been responsible for her losing the baby, just as he'd been responsible for its father and its mother coming into the world in the first place? My God, what a horribly tangled mess it all was.

'Of course he knew. I told him.' Lynette sounded proud.

'And then?' She thought of Glyn. 'Wasn't he prepared to stand by you? When you were carrying his child?'

Lynette stared at her. If looks could kill, that was it, she'd be well and truly out of it. 'Your mother got pregnant before he even had the chance to think about it. With you.'

'I see.' Now Rowan understood why this woman hated her so much.

'He gave me more presents, more money,' Lynette went on. 'Sometimes I had to hide the presents.' She sighed. 'But I always preferred them to the money.'

'And how did he feel about Glyn?' Rowan whispered.

Lynette's expression was bleak. 'He turned a blind eye. He pretended. Best way all round, he said.'

'I see.' But she didn't. She didn't see and she couldn't imagine how it had been, how her father could have done that.

'He helped out when Glyn went to London,' Lynette told her, almost proudly. 'Found him his first job. Paid part of the rent on the lad's flat.'

'Where is my father now?' Rowan asked dully. Maybe Lynette was right, maybe she would have made her father happy, and maybe it would have been better for all of them if she and Philip had simply left their respective partners and got on with a life together. But as she looked at Glyn's mother, she knew he would never have done it. He was too class-conscious, and Lynette Penbray would never have measured up, not in a million years.

'He pissed off to Spain.' She got up from the table with some difficulty, fetched a bottle of gin from the cupboard and took a deep unashamed swig.

No surprise that she was bitter. Philip Brunswick had ground her into insignificance, simply by acknowledging her worthlessness to him.

'Want some?' She held up the bottle of spirits.

Rowan shook her head. It might ease the pain temporarily, but she'd rather get it over with, she didn't want to be anaesthetized against all this. 'Does Glyn know?' It was a dull certainty within her. Glyn. Never supposed to be her lover. Somebody else's lover. Her father's child. Her half-brother.

Lynette nodded. 'He heard. When he came back from London. This is a small village. People talk.'

Rowan flinched at the thought. How had he taken it?

'Go home. It's over. Go back to London where you lot have always belonged. Just leave us be.'

* * *

294

After she'd watched Rowan Brunswick leave, a saddened solitary figure walking down towards the waterfront, Lynette Pembray began the business of getting dressed for the day.

She wouldn't think about that girl and her Glyn, it was her worst nightmare. And she wouldn't think of Philip Brunswick either – he had let her down too badly for her to spare him so much as a thought. Although, truthfully, it had been her own doing. She might not have given Harry all he wanted from a woman, but equally one man hadn't been enough for her. She'd been greedy – wanted too much that her Harry couldn't provide, and in wanting a bit of both of them, she'd lost it all. So she wouldn't think of it. Not now.

It took her an hour, and by then she was ready for the evening session at the Bull and Packet. Not to work, but to sit on the bar stool and talk to the customers. They couldn't deny her that.

The first person she saw was Dewy Jago, lounging by the bar drinking a pint.

'Dewy!' She sidled up to him. 'How are you doing? Going to put your hand in your pocket to buy me a drink?' She laughed. 'Or is it already there, just waiting for me?'

Dewy got to his feet, hardly glancing at her. 'Evening, Lyn. I'm just off actually. Tamsyn'll have me dinner ready. Another time, maybe.'

She watched him leave the pub. She wasn't fooled. He was avoiding her these days, and he wasn't alone.

In the mirror behind the bar she caught sight of her reflection. She'd put on too much lipstick tonight. It didn't make her look cheap, did it? It was supposed to be a classy colour. And as for her low-cut blouse – there were still men around who appreciated the sight of a decent cleavage as they supped their beer. Well, weren't there?

One quick gin and she'd be off. She wanted to talk, but the gin was cheaper at home. She had to drink a lot of it before it had any effect, but even then it wasn't too good at doing what it was supposed to do. It didn't help her to forget.

Chapter 21

—•◆•—

Rowan was breathing heavily by the time she reached the green glade. She stepped out of the wood, seeing it almost as she had seen it that first time, half-buried in the dip by rock, undergrowth and ivy, rising up and out of the wood, a ghostly grey ruin of a building. The folly.

Although she did not run from the sight of it as she had done that first time, still her initial steps towards it were tentative ones. Anyone could be here . . .

But it looked just the same – the round tower still pasted with moss, bound with ivy, the castle battlements, the rusty octagonal clock with only an hour hand. And the weeds still grew around the granite walls, bindweed, dandelions and thistles, though not as thick now as they would be in the summer when some of them would reach almost to the arrow slit window itself.

She reached out to touch the speckled stone as she had done so many times before, finding it as cold and unyielding as ever. She went round to the small doorway, took a deep breath, and pushed and pushed, until at last it gave way, with a creak and a moan of the hinges as if no-one had opened it in years. Rowan frowned. Surely Glyn would still come here? Surely marriage and prospective fatherhood – here she gulped, the thought was still hard to allow, brother or no brother – wouldn't have stopped him visiting the secret places that were once so important to him?

She walked slowly up the stone spiral staircase and through the gap that led to the battlements. The granite hollow that she used to rest against was dirty, unused, dark with moss and damp, silent as a grave. She rooted around and pulled out one of the cushions that they'd brought here for the sake of comfort, she and Glyn; it was rotting now, barely recognisable. No-one was here. And it seemed as if no-one had been here either, since she'd left Cornwall. Was that possible?

Rowan squatted cautiously against that old hollow of stone, closed her eyes and warily let them all swim into the surface of her mind – Glyn, Jed, Charlie, her father, Glyn's mother . . .

A noise on the stone steps made her snap open her eyes and jump to her feet.

'Glyn . . .' Was it really him? She waited for her heart to lurch inside her as it always had before.

'Hello, Rowan.' He took a step closer towards her and she instinctively took a step away.

Glyn, after all this time. Glyn, who now seemed as utterly familiar as always, a little older than the boy who had stood in Jed's roof garden silhouetted in the moonlight, and much older than the boy who had been her first lover. But still the person who was closeted in her heart, bonded to her.

Rowan shivered. She had convinced herself that Glyn Penbray no longer visited the folly. And what of Athwenna Trelawney – how had she taken their desertion? 'Did your mother tell you I was here?' she whispered. It seemed unlikely – Lynette Penbray had been adamant on that score.

'I saw you leaving the cottage.' He leaned against the battlements. As ever he was dressed in jeans with a thick ribbed jumper and no coat. He was still wiry but not as lean in build as before. Glyn had put on some weight. Married life must agree with him, she thought bitterly.

'And you followed me.' Still, even knowing what she did, she felt drawn to him, pulled by the past they shared.

He nodded. 'I knew you'd come here.'

'*You* never come,' she blurted. 'I can tell. The place hasn't been touched.'

Glyn didn't bother to deny it. Instead he walked over to the edge of the battlements, looking down over the wood. 'No, I don't.'

'Why not?'

'Too many painful memories.' He turned to face her.

She held his gaze for as long as she could. Painful memories, she knew all about those. But did he imagine they were exclusive to Glyn Penbray? She took a deep breath, knowing they were treading on dangerous ground. 'So why did you follow me here? What do you want?'

He thrust his fingers through his hair, raking the short dark curls back in a gesture she remembered only too well. 'I wanted to see you.' He took a step closer and this time she didn't back away. 'Didn't you want to see me? Isn't that why you came? Isn't that why you were at my mother's house?'

Dumbly, she nodded, and twisted away from his gaze. How could she explain to him that she had wanted to put him to rest? That he was haunting her, and she wanted to be free?

He was silent for a few moments, just watching her. At last he spoke. 'She's told you, hasn't she?'

Rowan nodded.

'About me being married?'

Still, he kept up the pretence. She sighed. 'Glyn, she's told me everything. Don't you understand? I know everything.' And would to God she had known of this years ago. Her father might have kept silent once upon a time in order to save his marriage – perhaps that was understandable – but he should have told her eventually. It was his responsibility. He owed her at least that much.

'She's told you about your old man? About their affair?' He tried to laugh. 'Who would have thought it, eh? While you and me were . . .'

She nodded. 'And she told me about us. Who we are.'

He was silent. After a few moments he slumped against the battlements. 'I couldn't believe it. I still can't believe it.' Slowly, he turned to face her. 'I bloody hate them for that.'

'I know.' Rowan understood, because she had felt the same.

'So she told you the whole thing?' Glyn whistled, low and long. 'She never bloody told me. She let me find it out for myself. I had to overhear village tittle-tattle to find out, I did.'

Rowan appreciated his resentment. It must be even worse for Glyn. His mother had let him believe that he was the son of Harry Penbray. Glyn must have had an awful lot to come to terms with. More than she had ever imagined. 'I still can't take it in,' she admitted to him.

'Me neither.' He moved towards her again, and all at once she was in his arms and he was holding her close. She had often imagined this, but never dared to dream it would happen.

She buried her head in his shoulder, needing comfort. And yet this – the reality – was nothing like it had been in imagination. Glyn was nothing like she had imagined him to be, nothing like she remembered. He looked familiar, he even felt familiar. He still smelled of the woods and the sea. But his touch lacked the urgency that had pulled her into passion. Her heart was not lurching in the slightest. And what they had shared seemed too far away now, it almost didn't seem real at all.

'That's why . . .' he was muttering into her ear. 'That's why me and Melanie . . .'

She drew back from his embrace, staring. 'But I heard you, Glyn. In London. I heard you talking to her about the stars, about love.'

'What?' His eyes were confused. He was still holding her by the shoulders.

'At Jed Montague's party,' she told him. She really didn't want to remember that time. Up until then she had believed in a future with Glyn. Unlikely perhaps, but still there in her heart. 'I saw you and Melanie, up in the roof garden . . .'

She saw the moment when he remembered. His expression changed, the pressure grew on her shoulders. 'And you ran. I saw you. You were there.' His mouth twisted. 'Why didn't I believe it was possible? Why didn't I run after you?' His voice broke and he pulled her closer, this time not into a comforting embrace but into a kiss.

For a second – a split second – she followed his lead, out of habit, she supposed. Then she realised what they were doing, and she broke abruptly away from him. 'No, Glyn.' He was her half-brother. It should never have been, and it would certainly never be again.

'I hadn't forgotten you.' His voice was low. That voice had thrilled her once. 'Even that night, I was thinking of you. I was thinking of us on Bodmin Moor and . . .'

'You're my brother.' She had to stop this.

He touched her hair, a last gesture. 'Who knows for sure?'

'I know.' And she did, it was true. She understood why she had always felt so close to him. There was a bond between them, had always been a bond between them. But it was not the bond she had imagined it to be. There had been passion – oh yes, she couldn't deny it. But the passion of a young teenager didn't hold her now. That feeling, that excitement he had always aroused in her, had long gone. It belonged to her past, to a kind of childhood – even to a kind of dream – not to the woman she had become.

'Why did you come back here?' he asked her. 'To Cornwall?'

'I was running away.' Rowan trailed her fingers along the dusty stone. That was how it had been. She hadn't even considered her actions, she had told no-one. She had packed a bag and caught the train. Simple, uncomplicated.

'You never did that before.' His laughter was soft, behind her. 'You were always brave. I was the coward. I was the one who ran away.' His voice broke. 'I should have stood by you, Rowan.'

'You know I had a miscarriage?' She held his hand tightly.

'A miscarriage?' He stared at her. 'But I assumed there was no baby. Mum said . . .' He hung his head. 'Christ, Rowan, I had no idea.'

'But I wrote and told you.' Rowan frowned. So many letters . . . 'You never answered any of my letters.' And she was almost embarrassed to remember them now, letters she had gone on writing regularly right up to the time when she had seen Glyn with Melanie on the roof garden.

'Letters?'

'I sent them to Cornwall. To the cottage . . .' Her voice tailed off. Of course. Lynette Penbray had done a very good job of keeping them apart. She had bargained on them never coming across one another in a big city, in London, thought it less of a risk than having Glyn here, always available, should Rowan Brunswick ever take a trip home. And she had backed her options by ensuring Glyn believed there had never been a baby, and that he never received one of Rowan's letters. He must have assumed, as she did, that his lover had forgotten him. It was almost funny, when she thought about how long he had stayed in her heart and mind.

'Just wait till I get my hands on her.' Glyn's mind had clearly followed the same direction; his eyes were angry, his mouth set.

Rowan laid a hand on his arm. 'No, Glyn. Your mother would have stopped us somehow.' She sighed. 'She would have told you the truth much sooner, done anything to keep us apart . . .' She met his gaze. But Glyn was right. He had been scared and he had been weak, she had always known it, always hoped she had courage enough for the both of them.

'You don't know what she's like . . .' he began, as if wanting to justify that weakness.

'No.' Her voice was firm. 'It's too late now. She did what she had to. You and I would never have been together.'

'I never told anyone about this place,' he whispered.

'Not even Melanie?'

'Of course not Melanie.' His laughter when it came was bitter. He didn't love his wife, Rowan realised now. Poor Melanie. It would be hard for her.

'But I hate it.' Glyn slammed a fist against the granite. 'It's bloody spooked, this place is.'

'You don't mean that. You've always belonged here. I never did.' She watched him. He had never really told her much about the folly and its history – how it was linked to Athwenna Trelawney.

'You belong well enough to go to Folyforth House,' he said dully. 'Athwenna'll tell you whatever there is to know about the folly.'

'I'd like to . . .' Rowan thought of the times she had seen Athwenna, the times she had lacked the courage to speak to her, sure that she didn't belong, that she would never be told the old stories about the folly, about this part of Cornwall that had become such a precious part of her growing up. She moved towards the spiral staircase. She would talk to Athwenna, and then she wanted to be gone. She shot one last glance at Glyn, a moment's regret for what might have been.

'Will you go back to London?' His hands were gripping to the stone castellation, his face set.

'I don't know.' London as a place held no appeal. She wanted another place. But there was someone she had to see in London – if she could find the courage, if she thought there was any point . . . 'Be happy, Glyn.'

'I'll try.' Glyn turned and stared out at the wet wood. 'But you've spoiled me, you have. I don't reckon I'll ever be happy without you.'

Rowan could feel his eyes burning into her back as she ran from the folly, through the glade and into the wood, stumbling down the path that led through the trees towards the fence, the wheal and Folyforth House.

Once there she stood outside the wrought iron gates, staring towards the square leaded windows, squinting to see if the shadowy figure was watching her. She took a step closer, thought she saw her, old Athwenna Trelawney, at the window. Slowly she pushed the gates open, went in, walked to the old oak door, and pulled the rusty bell pull.

The small, bent figure of Athwenna opened the door. 'So you've come.'

It sounded as if she had been expected. 'Yes.' Rowan stepped cautiously into the dingy hallway.

It was dark and slightly scary. The place smelled musty, unlived in. Dimly as her eyes grew accustomed to the half-light – for heavy curtains were drawn together at the windows – she could make out tapestries adorning the walls and a dusty chandelier hanging from the ceiling. In front of her a staircase led towards a gallery landing. Furniture was shrouded with white dust sheets and cobwebs hung from the chandelier.

'I've come.' She peered at the wizened old woman beside her, her skin faded and withered but the eyes still bright. 'Glyn thought you wouldn't mind. That you might tell me about the folly.'

Athwenna nodded. 'You found the folly. It may be you deserve to know.'

Rowan thought of the atmosphere of romance she'd always felt there, and thought of herself and Glyn. 'Was it a lovers' meeting-place?'

To her surprise, the old woman laughed a wheezing laugh. 'For you two it was, for sure.'

'But before . . . ?' Rowan frowned.

The old woman's glance as she moved into the shaft of wintery sunlight thrown through the leaded window of the front door was a shrewd one. 'Yes, there were others. There'll always be lovers, especially first lovers. But that wasn't why it was built. And what's more, the folly was never a folly, not in the true meaning of the word.'

'Because it had a purpose?' Rowan murmured. She had always

known it. A folly was a whim, a meaningless gesture of a rich eccentric perhaps, a bizarre monument to a mood. The whole reason for a folly was that it had no purpose – it could be a castle frontage with no castle behind it, a kind of practical joke, or it could be merely a celebration of a creative spirit.

But the folly in the wood wasn't like that. She had always felt it had a purpose, maybe even a slightly sinister one. She had always been conscious – even in the good times – of a frisson of fear inside the place, an atmosphere of dread that often used to make her shiver even on a hot summer's day.

Athwenna nodded. 'It was built for the smuggling trade. Way back – back in the eighteenth century, so the story goes.'

'Smuggling . . .' Rowan breathed. That explained a lot. It explained the folly's proximity to the sea, and the path that led up from the bay. It explained the fact that it was hidden in a wood and that the look-out would tell you who was coming from that wood. It even explained the deep stone cellars. 'But – why a mock castle? Why not just a . . .' she hesitated 'just a shed or something? Why go to all that trouble?'

Athwenna laughed her wheezing laugh that caught in her chest and became a cough. 'The land was owned by the Maddoxes back then, my dear. Old Maddox had a lot of money and a lot of power too. He and John Carter were like that . . .' She crossed her fingers.

'John Carter?'

'Oh aye. One of the ancestors of Davy Carter, he was. And he had nothing in his mind but contraband by all accounts.'

'Davy Carter . . .' Rowan tried to get it straight in her mind. 'So why did Maddox build a castle in his grounds?'

The old woman shrugged her thin shoulders. 'Who knows? It were the time when it was a sign of status to have the wherewithal to afford a folly. Maybe it appealed to his sense of humour. Who knows? To have a folly built on his estate that was actually the most profitable thing he ever did, I reckon.' Her laughter returned, and this time she began to wheeze painfully.

'Come and sit down.' Rowan led her to a chair. 'So it was a store house? Nothing more, nothing less?'

Athwenna smoothed the dust sheet and sat down. 'I reckon that was the original idea. Old Maddox had everyone in his pocket. The stuff could stay there as long as he liked, there was no chance of him getting done for it. Then when the coast was clear it could be taken out and sent to London or wherever.'

'I see. But you mentioned Davy Carter? Who was he?'

'Nothing but a poor fisherman.' Athwenna drew her shawl closer around her. 'It was a long time since John Carter had made a fortune out of contraband. He never got his due from old Maddox and the Carter family stayed poor. Any profits they did get, John Carter poured down his throat.'

'And Davy found the folly?' Rowan prompted.

'Davy fell in love with a girl he couldn't have.' Athwenna's faded eyes looked closely into Rowan's face. 'Like someone else we know, eh?'

Rowan looked down.

'He fell in love with the daughter of a Customs officer, of all things. The fellow who was responsible for putting together a squadron of anti-smuggling ships. She was called Elizabeth Parham.'

Rowan knelt on the dusty carpet at her feet. 'Go on.'

Athwenna's breathing was quick and shallow. 'The Parham family moved to Cornwall. Elizabeth was a wild thing at times by all accounts. She used to escape from her governess and go off exploring all round the old Maddox estate.'

'She found the folly,' Rowan breathed.

Athwenna nodded. 'Still being used for smuggling.'

'And that's where she met Davy Carter.' Rowan clapped her hands. She had always known that the folly was for lovers.

'They fell in love.' Athwenna's eyes became glazed and distant. 'But they knew they could never marry. They were on different sides. They were worlds apart.' She got to her feet with some difficulty and pulled the dusty curtains. The unexpected light filtered through the hallway and lit up the worn red carpet, the faded gold tapestries. 'Even love can't help you when you live in different worlds.'

'What happened to them both?' Rowan asked.

Athwenna smiled. 'Well, Elizabeth was a brave little thing. She was all for eloping. But Davy . . .'

She clutched Rowan's wrist with her thin claw of a hand. 'He's not a bad lad, you know. He never meant to hurt you.'

Rowan frowned in confusion. Was the old lady's mind wandering? But she realised what she meant. 'I know that.' She spoke softly.

'She was young, headstrong,' Athwenna said. 'She thought he had let her down.' Athwenna loosened her hold. 'But he'd only let himself down, that was all. He married a local girl. He wasn't happy, he always regretted not following his heart. You'll know all about that sort of thing, I reckon.'

'And her? What about Elizabeth?' What had happened to the rich girl who was wild and impetuous? Who, when she loved, threw herself into it heart and soul?

'She married too.' Athwenna smiled, reached out to touch Rowan's hair.

'And was she happy?' For some reason, Rowan needed to know this.

'I reckon she was.' Athwenna Trelawney sounded tired. 'I reckon she found someone from the shadows she'd hardly seen before. I reckon she had it in her to love in the kind of way that makes a soul happy. Don't you, my dear?' Slowly she rose to her feet and opened the front door. Her face was lined and yet peaceful.

'But how do you know all this?' Rowan was reluctant to break the spell, unwilling to step out into the sunshine, as if sensing that this legend, this woman, and everything the folly represented, would be lost to her if she did.

'Davy Carter married a local girl called Lowenna.' Athwenna nodded as if to herself. 'They had a girl, Jennifer. She was my great-grandmother.'

Rowan stared at her.

'The women of the family have always known the story. And young Glyn, he always seemed a lot like Davy Carter to me.' Rowan smiled. She too had seen the romantic, almost piratical side of Glyn from the first. She too could imagine him as a smuggler from way back. 'And what do the women do with the story?' she asked.

'They use it as a way of telling their daughters to follow their hearts.' She glanced at Rowan. 'I don't have a daughter, my dear.'

Rowan touched her hand, unutterably moved. It seemed that she belonged after all. 'And this place?'

'This was the Maddoxes' old house. It was left to the Carters a long time since. I reckon some of them Maddoxes knew what they owed to the Carters.'

Rowan thought of her father. 'What will you do with Folyforth House?'

Athwenna laughed. 'I think I'll be giving it back to Cornwall, my dear. Cornwall deserves to belong to the Cornish, don't you reckon?'

Rowan nodded. She stepped out into the winter sunshine at last. 'Maybe, but . . .'

She turned but Athwenna Trelawney had gone before she could even thank her, and the door had shut noiselessly behind her. 'But maybe the rest of us can come back to visit sometime,' Rowan whispered. 'I'd like that.' She would keep coming back here. Because in a way, it still felt like home.

Rowan Brunswick stood in the living-room of the cottage Zita shared with Harry Penbray in Port Treworth, and looked out to sea. It was cold, grey and unwelcoming. The same sea that she had known at Folyforth, for they were only twenty miles down the coast, and even the same sea that had given the Carters and others like them their living.

Zita had gone into the village, a different Zita with flushed rosy cheeks and a haze of happiness around her that had never been there before in all the time Rowan had known her.

Rowan had left Folyforth and come here the day after she'd seen Lynette, Glyn, and then Athwenna Trelawney. She hadn't told Zita and Harry the story of the folly – she would only tell her daughter – or one like her. But Zita and Harry were aware that she'd seen Glyn and that whatever had existed between them, it was now over.

'Maybe you'd like to settle here,' Harry told her. 'It's not a bad place, and we'd love to have you.'

'You're very kind.' She squeezed his arm, thanked him, but she didn't belong here, she didn't even think she belonged in Cornwall any more – she had moved on. Besides, this was their place, Zita and Harry's, and she knew they were happier alone.

'But come here whenever you like.' Zita grinned that old grin. 'Think of it as your country retreat. We may not have a spare bedroom – but the floor's yours whenever you feel the urge.'

Rowan smiled to herself. Good old Zita, she was a treasure and a half.

Hearing a tap at the door she went to open it, expecting to see Zita laden with shopping, for she was cooking a special meal for the three of them tonight.

She was, but there was something else, some glint of mischief in her eyes. 'We've got an unexpected visitor,' she said. 'Lucky I got in lots of food. Surprise!'

Rowan half-frowned. The last thing she wanted was to have to make polite conversation with some stranger.

But then a familiar face appeared behind Zita, and swam into her vision. 'Will?'

'It was your mother who told me where you'd be.'

It was later, much later and Will was stretched out on Harry's old settee with his feet up drinking his fourth cup of coffee.

Rowan was sitting on the floor, leaning back against the settee and from time to time Will was playing with strands of her long dark hair as if it were the most natural thing in the world to do.

It had been a wonderful meal – full of laughter and blasts from the past, as Zita called those stories from the old days. But now Zita and Harry had gone to bed, and Will and Rowan could sit and talk as they had sat and talked so often, for what seemed like years.

'I've never been so glad to see anyone in my whole life,' Rowan confessed, laughing up at him. His red hair was longer and more untidy than ever, his eyes the same intense blue. His beard was tangled salt and pepper with bits of auburn thrown in for good measure.

'Really?' His tone changed.

'Really.' She felt confident and she felt sure, perhaps for the first time. A new chapter was beginning. She had laid her past to rest.

'Rowan . . .' He swung his legs to the floor and leaned towards her. 'I've decided to branch out on my own. I want to cut myself off from Charlie Walters.' He pulled a face. 'And everything he stands for.'

'Because of me?' She searched his expression. She didn't want to be responsible for a downhill slide in Will's career – although she wasn't at all sure that was the way he'd be travelling. It could be the best thing he'd ever done.

He shook his head. 'It's been coming for a while. I should have done it ages ago.' He hesitated. 'I might as well tell you I've had it with London. I've decided to move back to Derbyshire.'

'Oh.' She felt her spirits dip into despair, remembered how he'd walked out of the restaurant in Chiswick that night. So she would lose Will after all. Lose his friendship and . . .

'What does "oh" mean?' His eyes were questioning. 'You need to give me some clue, Rowan. I don't know what you're telling me. I don't want to make the same mistake I made once before.' He put his arm around her and it felt so good, so right that she couldn't for the life of her remember why she had resented it so much that first time.

She only knew that this had crept up on her, that it had always been here, just waiting in those shadows that Athwenna Trelawney had talked of, for the right time. And now the right time had arrived. She trusted this man, cared for him and missed him when he wasn't around. She wanted to turn to him in her troubles, she wanted to help him through his. Rowan wasn't afraid to love him – and she knew that Will could be as brave as she might ever need him to be.

'How much of a clue do you want?' She looked towards him, and as he smiled she reached up her hands, took hold of his face, and kissed him full on the mouth. His eyes widened, his lips responded, and after that she didn't know what he did because she was giving herself up to something she thought she'd never feel again – an amazingly deep rush of pure passion.

It seemed a long time before they drew apart, both staring at each other for confirmation.

'That was some clue,' he murmured.

'It was intended to be.'

At last he grinned. 'I was thinking . . .'

'Yes?'

'There's lots of openings for a clever young chef in Derbyshire.'

'There are?' She felt an irresistible tugging at the corners of her mouth. 'As it happens I've always wanted to visit that part of the country.'

'You have?'

'Hmmm. They say the Peak District is beautiful at this time of year.'

'I can vouch for that.'

She could tell by his face that any second he would begin kissing her again.

'You're mad,' he whispered, moving closer. 'And I think that's what I love the most about you.'

Rowan felt mad all right. But she had another feeling too – that this was right, this was good, and that this could well be the most sensible thing she had ever done.

'*He deserves to be loved*,' Zita had said once before. '*Better move fast before you lose him. He'll be somebody's lover soon.*'

Zita had always given her good advice. And Rowan felt her smile get wider still. Somebody's lover, Zita had said. And Rowan knew exactly who that somebody would be.